le
temps
des
cerises

for Benji

le temps des cerises

Zillah Bethell

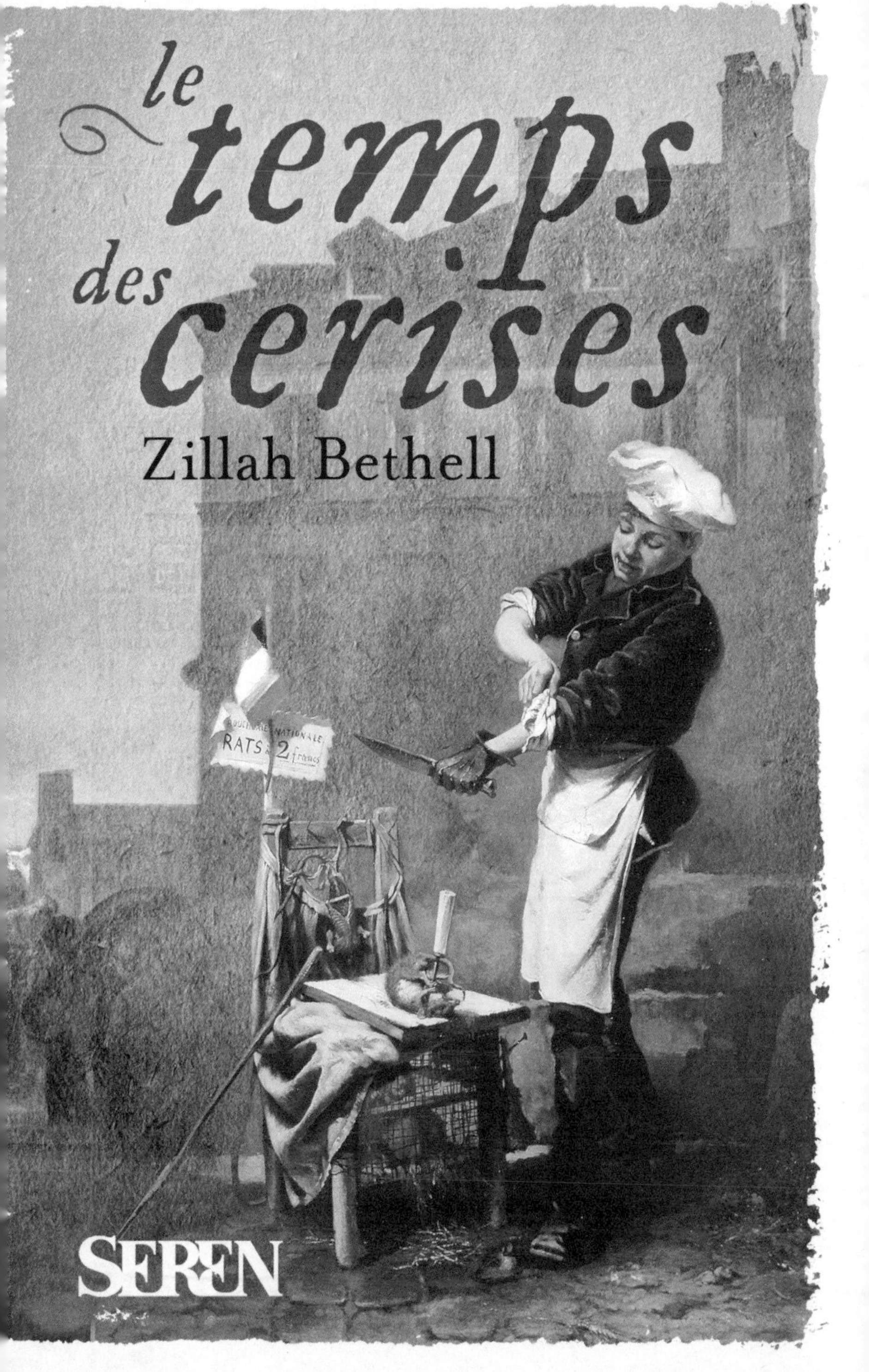

SEREN

Seren is the book imprint of
Poetry Wales Press Ltd
57 Nolton Street, Bridgend, Wales, CF31 3AE
www.serenbooks.com

ISBN 978-1-85411-522-5

A CIP record for this title is available from the British Library.

Cover design by Mark-Cavanagh.co.uk
from the painting 'Le dépeceur de rats' by Narcisse Chaillou
(Saint-Denis – musée d'art et d'histoire, cliché: Irène Andréani)

Inner design and typesetting by www.eifionjenkins.co.uk

Printed by Bell and Bain, Glasgow

The publisher works with the financial assistance of
the Welsh Books Council.

The author wishes to acknowledge the award of a Writer's Bursary from
Academi for the purpose of completing this book.

Mixed Sources

Product group from well-managed
forests and other controlled sources
www.fsc.org Cert no. TT-COC-002769
© 1996 Forest Stewardship Council

FSC

'The early heat from which we are suffering may be attributed to the presence of a comet not yet perfectly visible. It is common knowledge that in all epochs the appearance of a comet has preceded a great event. I am waiting for one particular great event in the world...'

Henri Rochefort (1868)

'Paris amuses itself on foot, on horseback, in a carriage; Paris amuses itself by day, by night; in the morning, in the evening; Paris amuses itself doing good, doing wrong; cheating and being cheated; laughing, weeping; hanging about, working hard; bankrupting, burning, killing itself.'

Pierre Véron (1862)

Part One: Waiting to Live, Waiting to Die

Chapter one

It was here, here she always felt most at ease, protected once by the city walls, twice by the grey stone slate of the convent and thrice, of course, by the hands of the Lord. Even now, in bleak midwinter, the garden shone in her mind's eye, overflowing in rhythm and colour, the plants breathing in and out their souls... only here could she praise the Lord. She whispered an *Ave Maris Stella* for the soldiers fighting at the ramparts, the French and Prussian high commands, the starving inhabitants of the city, the Sisters of St Joseph's and last but not least her dear friend Aggie who sat beside her on the bench of sweet woodruff, moaning softly and sweating profusely.

'Roast chicken,' she groaned now, holding her sides. 'It gives me stomach ache just thinking about it.'

'Ssh dear,' Bernadine chided her gently. 'We must keep our minds off it. How many have you done now?'

'One hundred and one,' Aggie declared proudly, indicating the horsehair basket on her lap all swollen up with red crêpe bandages.

'Well done!' Bernadine took a gold from her sliding box of coloured cotton and, holding a needle up to the sun, threaded it expertly. 'Only another fifty to go!'

Aggie sighed. 'If only I could live on grass and twigs I'd munch my way through every window box on the Rue de Rivoli as well as the Bois de Boulogne. Or a glow-worm living off dewdrops. Or a big fat spider catching flies! If you were a blancmange I'd eat you up!' She giggled at Bernadine's wry expression then wrinkled up her nose. 'The smell of gunpowder makes me feel even sicker. I wish I could sleep underground with the squirrels and wake up to springtime and peace... I'll never refuse one of Brother Michael's vermicelli soups ever again!' she added vehemently.

Bernadine smiled a little at that for she'd never known Sister Agnes refuse anything; and it was a source of wonder to the whole convent how she remained so plump on such meagre rations. Her own dress had been taken in twice already and it still hung about her like an altar cloth whereas Aggie looked fit to burst her buttons.

'He says the Emperor[1] spent a hundred thousand francs a year,' she went on with a gloomy air, 'on sugar plums! Imagine that!'

'I shouldn't believe everything Brother Michael tells you.'

'Oh yes indeed, it was in the papers. One hundred thousand francs a year on sugar plums. Pocket money for him. And the feasts they had at the Tuileries you wouldn't believe. Peaches in syrup was a great favourite. Brother Michael said the footmen scampered about like mice in white slippers, bringing him morsels of cheese. And walnut.'

'Goodness!' was all Bernadine could think to say, staring at Aggie whose face at that moment looked like a great sweating cheese itself.

'What would *you* have, Sister Bernadine? You can have anything you like. Anything at all.'

'Oh, Agnes.'

'Go on,' implored Aggie. 'Anything at all. A great banquet in your honour...'

'Oh alright.' Bernadine put down the bit of gold braid she was stitching and appeared to give the matter great thought. 'I'd have a savoury to start with of course... oyster soup I think.'

'Good choice. With new bread and butter?'

'Yes, with new bread and butter. Then I think I should like shrimps and watercresses... or maybe mussels with parsley sauce. I don't know; I'm torn between the two.'

'Both. Have both of them.'

'Alright,' Bernadine smiled. 'Both. The main course would have to be a delicious beef stew full of onions and carrots and potatoes and dumplings.'

'Dumplings!' echoed Aggie looking as if she were in heaven. 'I dream of dumplings.'

'For pudding I don't know – let me think...'

'Floating islands?' her friend suggested.

'Oh, yes.' Bernadine felt herself giving in at last. 'And gingerbread. How I love gingerbread.'

'Cherry nougat?'

'Chocolate mousse!'

'Rum baba!'

'Caramel cigars!'

'Peppermint creams!'

'Toffee terrine!'

'Raspberry sorbet!'

'Lemon meringue pie!'

They egged each other on, on and on and on until no more puddings could be dreamed up, not in a month of Sundays; and Sister Bernadine, wiping away a tear of laughter, said she hadn't eaten so well in ages and a few Hail Marys were in order after that little lot.

They worked on in silence then for a while on the little sweet-woodruff bench, Bernadine stitching gold braid onto cuffs and collars and wondering as she often did how such beautiful clothes could be made for such a terrible occupation. The brass buttons glinted in the sunlight, reflecting Aggie's plump white fingers rolling her little crêpe bandages. Now and then the sound of guns boomed in the distance like far-off thunder or St Peter snoring up above, but the air in the garden was soft and full of peace. A robin pecked at the sunken vegetable patch, peering from one bright eye and then the other as if he didn't know which to believe and Bernadine wondered idly if next year she wouldn't get honeysuckle and lemon verbena for the bees.

'Narbonne honey,' Aggie remarked upon hearing the suggestion, 'is the best in France. You can taste the wild flowers in it.'

Maybe some pale pink roses or buttercup yellow... to remind us of the original source of all light... and to make a splash between the old and forlorn-looking flower clock and convent wall. (It had been her idea – the flower clock – oh so many years ago... 'A marriage of nature and progress,' she had announced proudly to the visiting dignitaries... 'tribute to the great clockmaker himself and to symbolise the difference between earthly time run by hours, days, minutes of prayer and the timelessness, infinitude of heaven.' Quite the theologian, he had said and she had blushed... oh she had blushed...) Deep crimson perhaps to remind us of... the blood of our Saviour...

'Sister Bernadine?'

'Oh, yes Agnes?' She took up her needle quite purposefully.

'I... I...'

Bernadine knew Aggie well enough to know that she wanted to confess and she concentrated hard on an epaulette in an effort to encourage her.

'I… oh… do you remember last year when we went to the Madeleine flower market and came back with bunches of azaleas and wallflowers – Brother Michael said it would have been quicker to grow them.'

'Oh yes. What fun we had that day!'

'I wish we could have flowers all year round. It's so desolate here somehow.'

Bernadine laughed. 'You would not care for them half so much if that were the case. It is in the nature of a flower to be a surprise, an event. It would be like having Christmas every day of the week. How sick we would become of it.'

Aggie looked as if she didn't think Christmas every day of the week would be too much of a penance after all; but she lapsed into silence and closed her eyes.

Bernadine wondered if she shouldn't press her further on the matter, but she had always held firm to the belief that a confession was best delivered of its own accord prompted by the voice of God or the inner workings of the conscience; and besides it was too beautiful a day and the girl in no fit state, and so she let the matter drop along with her needle and fell back to basking in the warm winter sun and gazing upon her beloved little garden.

Desolate, yes, and sweet! A place to forget, to confess, to dream, to repent. How many hours had she spent inside these walls protected once by the city ramparts, twice by the grey stone slate of the convent and thrice, of course, by the hands of the Lord. Only here could she praise Him! Amidst the stained-glass panes of crocus and marigold, incense of lavender, spearmint and thyme and the hymns of ancient insects and orange-bellied singing toads which each struck a different note at sunset. As if God stood on the threshold of spring, took up his baton and said to the world, 'Let Earth's song begin. Let Earth's song begin…'

'Sister Bernadine?'

'I… oh… yes Agnes?' Bernadine took up her needle again with lightning speed.

'I have a secret,' Aggie panted painfully, her round face pallid and damp with sweat.

'The Lord knows all our secrets, Agnes,' Bernadine murmured automatically.

'It's not the Lord I'm worried about,' responded Aggie with a fearful glance at the low arched window of the convent where the Reverend Mother sat beneath her shelves of confiscated property, drawing up lists and timetables for the novices.

Bernadine decided to put the poor girl out of her misery. 'I know about the sweets you stole from...' she almost choked over his name, '... Monsieur Lafayette's. I do not believe it to be a thing of great weight. We are all so very hungry.'

'Oh, it's not that, it's much worse than that!' Aggie went on in a low panting murmur, her whole body trembling with emotion. 'I should have told you long ago but I felt so ashamed... and... it's obvious to me now that you would have understood... only person who could possibly help in my predicament. And yet...'

Bernadine's eyes opened wide in surprise. 'For goodness sake, what is it my child? What on earth's the matter?'

But before Aggie could open her mouth again to reveal her terrible secret her body was overtaken by a violent paroxysm and she suddenly toppled off the little sweet-woodruff bench and onto the ground with an almighty crash, sending the horsehair basket flying and the rolled-up bandages unrolling with gentle abandon past pyramid fruit trees, the greengage cage and the sunken vegetable patch.

Brother Michael was down in the cellar investigating what he privately termed the 'miraculous' ingredient of the convent wines – an allusion to the water he'd accused the steward of adding to the bottles of La Tour Blanche – when he heard a muffled scream; but thinking it was simply some nun in the act of self-mortification, he shrugged his shoulders and got on with his job.

'Oh, very Christian,' he muttered angrily, taking a drop of '68. 'Here's a little miracle for you!' Out of the fifteen bottles he'd investigated, sixteen of them at the very least, he'd noted down, contained the special ingredient and he was most aggrieved. Turning water into wine, he felt, was quite in keeping with a holy life but to turn wine into water was undoubtedly the action of an unsound mind, a mind not altogether in its rightful place. He corked up the bottle of '68 and moved a little unsteadily to a crate of '69, craving heaven as he did so for the remission of sins, the grace to live a holy life and to deserve some eternal rest.

'BROTHER MICHAEL? ARE YOU DOWN THERE?'

He came to an abrupt halt. He knew that voice. It was Sister Bernadine – Shady Lady as he privately termed her. Woman Rumoured to have a Past. One of the handsomest nuns in the convent with a lonely faded beauty reminiscent, he had decided in a poetic moment, of a wild flower pressed between the pages of a book. Still capable of giving off glows and hints, he reminded himself. Still capable of leading even a man like him astray. He trembled slightly, wondering if he oughtn't to hide behind the crate of '69 and hold his breath until she went away but a shadow over the open cellar hatch persuaded him to own up to his existence.

'Just checking the cellar for damp,' he called out in a surprisingly business-like tone. And wiping his fingers on his blue twill apron he started climbing the cellar stairs one step at a time, as St Bonaventure and Thomas Aquinas recommended.

'Oh thank goodness,' Bernadine exclaimed, all red in the face and breathless, giving off glows and hints no doubt to poor Brother Michael. 'Sister Agnes is in trouble. I believe she's suffered some kind of stroke. We must get her inside immediately.'

'A… Agnes,' faltered Brother Michael, blinking rapidly. The Prettiest Perfectest Peach in Paradise as he privately termed her. But Aggie was literally bursting with health. There could never be anything the matter with Aggie…

'Do you understand, Brother Michael: we must get her inside immediately!'

'Yes.' He suddenly flew into action, tearing past Bernadine as if he had wings, out of the kitchen and up the garden path at an astonishing speed to where Aggie sat propped by the little sweet-woodruff bench, moaning loudly and sweating profusely. 'There there,' he shouted, patting her on the head. 'Brother Michael's here now!'

Events took on the quality of a dream after that. It seemed to him that he gauged the situation at a glance. No detail escaped him of the red strewn bandages, scattered uniforms and coloured thread, Bernadine's distress, Aggie's howls. Nothing was lost on him – not the bright sun, nor the blue sky, nor the nuns gathering one by one, pale and peering their long, thin faces at him like a bunch of silly sheep.

'…bran poultice,' one of them bleated. He distinctly heard her bleat.

'Smelling salts!'

'Only yesterday…'

'Enema by the look of her!'

'Pale as a drink of water!'

He issued orders with remarkable fluency (though others might tell a different tale). He remained Calm amidst Chaos; took charge, took command, took off his girdle and tied it round Aggie's right leg, wrapped a bandage round her head; did all manner of useful and necessary tasks. He measured the distance by eye from where they sat to the convent wall, took pains to test the strength of his girdle by pulling on Aggie's left leg, calculated the position of the sun on her hair and the time it would take to reach her foot, meticulously planned each step of the route until in the end he came to the decisive conclusion (though with the feeling he'd spent a lifetime preparing for it) that Aggie must be got inside. And with that they half dragged, half pushed, half carried a shrieking Agnes through the greengage cage, past the pyramid fruit trees and over the sunken vegetable bed to the rooms where the Mother Superior sat, grim and foreboding, behind her desk.

'I am to blame,' Bernadine babbled as everyone shuffled in. 'All the talk of food brought on some sort of malady. She has the most terrible stomach cramps.'

'Gumdrops!' whispered the Mother Superior with a shake of her head.

'Oh no, it's not a mere case of indigestion,' Bernadine insisted, 'I am sure of it. She's in the most frightful pain. We must fetch a doctor at once.'

'War! More needy!' whispered the Mother Superior with another shake of the head. 'No doctors for gumdrops.'

Brother Michael stared at the Gentle Terror as he privately termed the Mother Superior. 'This is not the work of gumdrops,' he said in a tone of utter seriousness, pointing at Aggie who was writhing in agony on the floor. 'I could never believe this to be the work of gumdrops, Reverend Mother.'

And indeed it was not. A few minutes later, beneath the shelves of confiscated novels, facepaint, jujubes and lace knickers; the benevolent eye of a plaster Mary and infant Jesus and signs which read: *Here Silence is Always Kept* and *Insubordination is Everywhere*, Sister Agnes' confession was delivered of its own accord in the shape of a tiny blue baby girl, amidst much shouting and hysteria on the part of everyone concerned except for the Mother Superior who whispered for all she was worth and Brother Michael who stood open mouthed and tugging at his blue twill apron as if he were tolling the angelus.

Chapter two

Dearest Maman,
            Here I am in the thick of it still, as you see – though thank
God I sleep on my own bed tonight instead of this wretched straw pallet. The
mud is almost up to our knees after the sudden thaw but it is still bitterly cold.
Those socks you sent to me via Monsieur K. are a godsend, Maman. A real
godsend. It is the coldest winter ever they say. Of course it would be!

I have still not a scratch upon me, having seen no real action. Alphonse
has his chest wound from Le Bourget which aches a little more, he says, when
a pretty girl goes past! I envy him sometimes: his spontaneity, his ready
engagement with life, the ability to slough off an identity yet still be the same,
to wake up bright and breezy day after day. Constancy above all in all things.
I am weak willed as a woman. I wish that something would happen – anything
– if only to see if I could bear it. All this waiting around will be the death of me.
We while away the time somehow with cards and dominoes – wine is plentiful!
We have a few tables and chairs dotted about – a little sitting room at the
ramparts! All I need to feel at home is a roaring fire, some toasted muffins, you
knitting quietly in your armchair and Molly thumping away on the piano! Tell
her I expect a perfect rendition of the Moonlight Sonata when I next see her!

You would not recognise the city if you came to visit. It is quite simply a
fortress: the Louvre an armament shop, the Bon Marché a hospital (all your
favourite calicoes and linens being used to mop up the wounded!), the squares
nothing more than parade grounds. Not a single stump is left in the Bois de
Boulogne and the lime trees you loved so on the Boulevard Haussmann have
all gone for firewood. We have no lighting after dark (Paris, city of light,

extinguished!), the Prussians having cut off our coal supply from Belgium; and few carriages are to be seen because (don't read this bit out to Molly) the horses have all been eaten (Paris, city of the gourmet, famished!). Nobody knows how to make it palatable. Copies of The Practical Cuisine *are selling like hotcakes apparently as uppercrust housekeepers search for tips on 'how to dress exotic meats'! The rest of Paris searches for tips on how to dress thin air. I dream of a cheese green as an emerald and...*

Laurie broke off from his letter to blow on his numbed fingers, stamp his feet and take a sip of the watery coffee commonly referred to as mouth warmer – because the only thing it was good for was warming one's mouth. He rolled it around his tongue like a wine then spat it out again. What didn't he dream of here in this ruined landscape, acres of dreary white before him, the city like a crouching beast behind him. What didn't they all dream of but to win the war, get out of this stupid futile mess and go back home for good instead of this endless to-ing and fro-ing; though in fairness, he had to admit, some wanted it, to some it was an adventure, like Alphonse maybe, or the little gunner who rubbed his cannon down as if it were a horse or a woman and made snowmen on sentry duty just for the hell of it. Laurie crunched on the stale biscuit he'd been saving in his mess tin and reread the page he'd just written, wondering if its tone was sufficiently buoyant. He spent a long time over his letters, believing them to be a filial and fraternal duty, digging up curious and unusual anecdotes to entertain his mother and sister who sat in Toulouse in blissful ignorance. At least he hoped they sat in blissful ignorance. Sometimes he underplayed or over dramatised the situation a little, depending on his mood or what he thought might best amuse, generally writing behind a persona and keeping the full colour of emotion, whole complexity of truth for his poems and dreams. And if he ever did write straight from the heart, more often than not he crumpled up the page and left it unsent. Today he felt he'd been a little too honest and he finished up the sentence with a mildly facetious '*one of your baked eggs, Maman*' then sat back to rack his brains a little more and listen half-heartedly to the rest of the men who were drinking gin and playing pontoon.

'I've never seen so much make-up on a man,' Old Joubet was saying, picking his teeth and staring at his hand in disbelief. He always stared at his cards in disbelief – whether to bluff his opponents or because he really couldn't comprehend the blows Fate kept dealing him was hard to tell. 'He was wearing so much make-up at the Battle of Sedan he looked like a fucking *cocodette*[2]. What the hell's wrong with him anyway?'

'Kidney stones!'

'Syphilis!'

'His days are numbered in that area. The only thing that pops out nowadays is his tongue. His servant takes sugar tongs along when they go to the opera to stick the Emperor's tongue back in if he's been drooling too long at the ladies!' Little Coupeau, a dyer from Montmartre, was known for his salacious take on the world and everyone laughed including Laurie.

'No wonder his missus went round like a thunderclap.'

'That's why she kept sending him back to the front, hoping desperately he'd get himself killed!'

'He bloody nearly did,' Old Joubet resumed, still staring. 'God knows how the enemy missed him – you could see his fucking cheeks a mile off! Twenty-one,' he added, putting down an ace and king in spectacular fashion and collecting up his chips, still with a look of disbelief.

Everybody sighed and the gin bottle was passed round; somebody muttered something about foul play and was immediately shouted down by Bidulph, a good friend of Joubet's. Then the talk turned to the evening's entertainment – they were looking forward to the few nights off – some were going to the meeting at St Nicolas, others to Mabille's for the women. The name of a particular dancer cropped up in conversation and two young men at the end of the table almost came to blows over it; would have done so, in Laurie's opinion, if Tessier hadn't stepped in.

'Oh Tessier,' one of them drawled angrily, 'keep your club foot out of it, will you.'

There was a strained silence at that – all eyes on Tessier as he limped back painfully to his seat; and then someone shouted out 'on with the game' and he smiled good-naturedly because they all loved to watch him shuffle, his hands flew so gracefully over the cards. He put on an extra show this time with feints, slidebacks and sleight of hand stunts; and Old Joubet told him he should take a stall at the Gingerbread Fair while Coupeau said that the Queen of Diamonds coming out of his ear was the biggest thrill he'd had in years! Tessier got quite carried away and the whole thing might have got a little tedious if someone hadn't shouted out 'on with the game, on with the game'; but at least he was back to his old self again and sufficiently put to rights to call out to Laurie a moment later in a blustering tone: 'Hey Laurel leaves – how's it going? Tell your ma if she wants to know what her boy gets up to, to look up Léon Tessier, bookkeeper,12 Rue du Faubourg… he'll put her in the picture!'

Laurie smiled. 'Thanks very much, Léon! I'll be sure to do just that!'

He was fond of Léon – beneath the blustering was a good heart and a kind soul and he reckoned that out of all the members of 7th Company (apart from Alphonse of course) Tessier was the one he'd trust his life to despite the bad feet and poor eyes which to his utmost shame had kept him out of the regular army.

The card game went on as the afternoon sun drifted down over the camp. Two idiots were trying to light a fire with green sticks and brambles, smoking out the whole provisions tent; and an officer stood polishing his boots and roaring at a corporal to put the pegs in straighter because a gale was forecast that night and he didn't fancy ending up over the ramparts. Laurie felt quite unnerved by the pointless activity, the squabbles between the men, the endless hustle and bustle of squads changing shifts, the dirt and mess of it all – and it was times like this he craved the solitude of his own little room where at the very least he could be bored to death in peace. Here there was nothing but mud and white, swathes and swathes of mud and white that enveloped you like a cloak as you walked through the night and into the early hours, clasping your dew-laden rifle in your hand and listening to the sound of hooting bats, grunting owls and, hardly knowing which was which, fleeting snores of men for company. If he'd been an artist he'd have sketched a sentryman as a wingless owl or a bodyless head, képi perched at a jaunty angle, bayonet in the air, eyes fixed expectantly on a middle distance as though awaiting some out-of-doors theatrical production. Sometimes when he stared into the darkness a vision of the city would appear before his eyes: the grand old towers of Notre Dame and the elegant spire of the Sainte Chapelle swaying in the breeze above the drear white acres, like the lofty rigging of some ancient ship. And sometimes, in the solitude of his own little room, the view beyond the ramparts would rise above the bed sheets in ghostly immanence – all mud and white – an endless succession of days and nights…

Chapter three

Bernadine slipped through the convent gates – a shadowy figure in her black cloak and boots, black horsehair basket and inevitable black umbrella to fend off wind, rain and unwanted attention. She didn't have the time today to touch tubercular fingers, run her hands through lice-infested hair or give reassurance that the Lord was biding His time where the Prussians were concerned. How on earth did she know what the Lord had planned? He moved about in mysterious ways like a spy in the midst of them. Seemingly friendly at first, a good sort, the kind of man you could bare all for, lay your heart on your sleeve for and then, lo and behold, He was trotting off to the enemy camp with your secrets and your heart on His sleeve all bayoneted and blown to pieces. Leaving you bereft, apparently glad to be cleansed of all sin, all passion, all animated life. A chosen vessel. A vessel fit for the Holy Ghost to pour his goodly vapours into.

She stopped to blow her nose in the frosting air and scan the street. It was quite deserted and she smiled at all her unnecessary caution; few people would be travelling this path on such a grim winter's day – it was too far away from the bright lights and boulevards, too close to the lairs of waifs and strays, outlaws and strangely loitering men. 'We are close to the lion's den,' the Mother Superior would sometimes whisper to the trembling novices, 'and we must tread very carefully.' Strange how the convent had been built in such a sinister part of the city and yet, of course, not strange at all for its very motto was 'To bring Light into Darkness'. The railway was overgrown and rusted with disuse, barely visible beneath the melting snow and thick brambles and she felt a pang of regret that she might never again hear the merry whistle from inside those convent walls and stop to imagine the people going off for a day in the country, to visit a sick relative or simply for the thrill of racing into blackness and out the other side again. Beyond the railway line lay open country carpeted in a gently greying snow and criss-crossed with hedges, ditches and the silhouettes of stunted trees. It was quite deserted – not an animal or even an animal's tracks to be seen; and she smiled at all her unnecessary caution.

All roads from here in led to Monsieur Lafayette's or back to the convent and she hesitated a moment, umbrella poised between heaven and earth to stave off wind, rain and unwanted attention; but then the thought of Aggie's ashen face and the tiny blue baby's cries pushed her on again. The Lord was a supreme idiot sometimes, the way He let things happen. If Aggie died she would not forgive Him. If the child died she would not forgive Him. It was best to rely on yourself, take the lead and let Him follow, meek and mild as a lamb. She stumbled on down the track to Monsieur Lafayette's, railing at her God because there was no one else to rail against; and to drown out the voice which shouted in her head that she was the supreme idiot, that she had neglected her friend, her vows, her vocation again and again, that life on this earth was not so easily redeemable and that if Aggie died or the child died it was she who would remain unforgiven.

The green-painted shop sat squat in the road like a very determined and overgrown cabbage, and Bernadine almost held her nose at the sight of it. The faded lettering of 'LAFAYETTE: HERBALIST' and in lower case: 'Confectioner' could still be seen if you squeezed your eyes hard enough; and the windows that had once been gilded to protect the delicate essences of the interior now let in the full spectrum of elements. Snails hung frozen to the outside walls, sticking tight to their dream that this was indeed a live green cabbage and toadstools seamed the edge of the yard which was overrun in the main by nettles cultivated, the way the Romans did it, for teas, potions and the unaccountable delight of dashing one's hands against the malevolent leaves. Occasionally a daring daffodil or crocus tried to eke out a living in the four square feet of weediness but it was soon throttled to death for its presumption. Bernadine braced herself and entered the shop, blinking in the rapidly deteriorating light.

'Better to lose her to me than to the truth,' Monsieur Lafayette was saying to Mistigris, the stonecutter and notorious drunkard. (Bernadine was a little distressed to see the stonecutter there for she didn't want the subject of the statue coming up, not now. Mistigris had once made a statue for the convent and had never been paid for it because the Mother Superior had dubbed it appallingly inferior handiwork.) Both men were dressed in token gesture of the National Guard uniform with a red stripe down the side of their trousers and both were smoking cigars, their heads almost lost in a halo of smoke. Upon seeing Bernadine, Monsieur Lafayette coughed and changed the subject with a flourish: 'We await the Prussians as the Romans awaited the Carthaginians in their curule chairs. Do we not, sir?'

'Quite,' tottered old Mistigris, swaying a little at the hips. 'In our curules, sir.'

The shop looked quite different – emptier, of course, with a sad, neglected air. The cabinets still displayed their monstrous instruments, enemas, lozenges and syrups, tinctures of mallow, comfrey and myrrh; valerian root for the toothache, false unicorn powder for the gout; a variety of miscellaneous dried herbs; but the sweet boxes and jars that had contained pounds and pounds of shrimp sugar, jujubes, almond paste and peppermints were practically empty and all that remained on the counter was an old wig box and almanac. Bernadine tried to appear unfazed in the presence of the two men by pulling down the hood of her cloak, placing her basket on the ground and smoothing her hair straight, though her right hand clutched at the rosary beads sewn into the lining of her pocket.

'And you, my dear,' Monsieur Lafayette leered, his bald head and red lips shining through the cloud of smoke. 'We don't often have the pleasure. How long has it been? Sixteen or seventeen years, surely?'

'Not quite. I came in a couple of years ago if you remember rightly for the Reverend Mother's toothache.'

'Ah yes. And how is that… dear soul?'

'Very well.'

'Then it must be some commission from the Cannibal's Delight, I suppose. Tell her we are quite out of caramel cigars. She finished off the last box two days ago.'

Bernadine ignored the reference to Agnes – too aware of the terrible irony of the situation – and replied that she hadn't come in for sweets.

'Grease a few onions that one would,' he went on in a jocular fashion. 'Put her in a stew and she'd do the business of the butter and the goose fat put together!'

Mistigris laughed delightedly at that, though with no idea presumably who Monsieur Lafayette was alluding to, then staggered off into the back of the shop. Bernadine watched uncomfortably as he sat himself down beside the blue and white curtain that sectioned off the deeper recesses of the room. It was rumoured that behind the blue and white curtain lay a dirty mattress and stool, the purpose of which nobody knew but many speculated…

'You, on the other hand, my dear,' he chuckled, 'are a touch narrow around the shoulders for my liking. The Lord's been wearing you a little thin, methinks.'

'Not the Lord,' she murmured. 'Rest assured, monsieur, I should not have come if the business wasn't quite urgent.'

'How very mysterious and exciting. But what can poor old Modeste give you that your little garden cannot? I was under the impression it provided you with everything: love, succour, consolation, green beans…'

'Not this year, I'm afraid. In truth, Agg… one of the nuns is very sick and I need some healing herbs.'

'If you buy any two, I'll throw in a bottle of iron water.' He indicated the nails steeping in a carafe on the windowsill, the water already a clouded yellow; and Bernadine nodded.

'That would be very kind,' she smiled, mentally ticking off the herbs she needed as he brought out the silver spoon and little brass scales for the weighing. 'Yarrow, shepherd's purse, lady's mantle if you have it, raspberry leaf, camomile, nettle of course, and certainly a bottle of iron water. Please.' The cat was out of the bag now – she knew that – for the herbs she'd named were those commonly used by women after childbirth: to stem the flow of blood, lessen a fever, encourage milk production, strengthen the spirit and replenish iron reserves. She waited for Monsieur Lafayette to start poking fun; but for a while he did not. He simply set to work with an air of great diligence, weighing out the herbs on the little brass scales and into three-gram brown paper packets, fishing out the bad bits with his blunt, stained fingers, tutting when a golden camomile head fell to the floor and straining the iron water from the carafe into an old quart glass jar. Each time a gentle snore arose from the moth-eaten chair by the curtain he would raise a conspiratorial eyebrow as if the two of them were colluding in something while the poor old stonecutter slumbered; but it was only when the packets were lined up on the counter that he allowed himself to speak.

'Another one of you been viewing the moon then?' he said in his syrupy voice. 'No wonder St Joseph's receives such handsome donations.'

Bernadine caught sight of herself in the fly-spotted mirror behind the counter – a thin, ashen-grey face with two flaming points of colour on either cheekbone.

'Who can it be, I wonder. Surely not the Cannibal's Delight? It would account for her being the size of a balloon! Maybe we should have sent Gambetta off in her instead of the Armand-Barbès[3]!'

Bernadine lowered her eyes in case they betrayed her and busily crammed the packets into her basket, her mind racing. Well, one thing was for certain at least, a thing that had bothered her a little: Monsieur Lafayette could not be the father, he had seemed quite genuinely surprised in his own strange way and, loathsome as the man might be, she did not believe he would have taken Aggie by force.

Mistigris, by this time, had woken up with all the commotion and was veering towards the counter like the archetypal avenging angel. 'I've got a bone to pick with you lot,' he cried, pointing at Bernadine. 'You're a scurvy bunch and no mistake!'

Bernadine, almost reeling from the smoke and alcoholic fumes, valiantly stood her ground. 'Monsieur Renan,' she began sincerely, looking him square in the face, 'I'm truly sorry that you were never paid for the statue. It was quite wrong – you should have been – and I have always felt badly about it. Perhaps when everything returns to normal the Reverend Mother will see fit to do the right thing by you.'

Mistigris looked quite taken aback and he stuck his thumbs in his waistcoat pockets and gazed at her appraisingly. 'That's alright,' he mumbled at last. 'It was the stone's destiny to be a Virgin, in any case. I don't need paying for it.'

It was Bernadine's turn to look surprised and she gazed back at the white hair and creased face, wondering what sort of man he had been before the drink had claimed him. 'That's very generous of you, monsieur. Nevertheless the materials alone must have cost you a pretty penny. I shall try to put in a good word for you when any new commissions are required. Only the other day, the Reverend Mother was talking about having a calvary made.'

Bernadine pulled up her hood, hooked her umbrella to the horsehair basket and made ready to leave but before she could reach the door, Monsieur Lafayette had crept up and positioned himself in front of it.

'If anyone should require the services of old Lafayette,' he wheedled, 'they only have to ask.' He pressed her arm. 'Nicely. He can be very delicate when he wants to, old Modeste, and discreet. Delicate and discreet, isn't that so, Sister Bernadine?'

She looked at the pin black eyes and fat red lips with a feeling close to hatred. 'Goodnight monsieur,' she said with as much dignity as she could muster and, motioning him aside, stepped into the yard, her right hand still clutching the rosary beads in the lining of her pocket.

'Well, well, well,' said Monsieur Lafayette, shutting the door and smiling at Mistigris who had slumped down beside the counter in a crumpled little heap. 'Well, well, well! The Cannibal's Delight up the duff? That's quite cheered me up! I'd like to meet the man up to that job. It must be like scaling Mount Olympus!' And with that, he hopped over the crumpled heap of the old stonecutter and began tidying up behind the counter. When everything was set to rights, he peered over the counter to check that Mistigris was still out of the picture and then, with a guilty movement, pulled the lid off the wig box and brought out a small shining key. Slipping it into his pocket, he walked nonchalantly to the back of the shop and pushed aside the blue and white curtain. Behind the curtain lay the fabled mattress and stool as well as a box of hook-like metal instruments, a roll of bandages, a barometer, some worm-eaten chairs and a row of pictures against the far wall. Feeling his way around the varied obstacles for the light was growing dim even for him, Monsieur Lafayette padded softly over to a lewder version of Manet's 'Déjeuner sur l'herbe', brought the little key out of his pocket and stuck it between the naked lady's lissom white legs. The picture split in two, the cupboard doors swung open and a delightful aroma suddenly filled the air. A mixture of scents all jam-packed together of spices and sweets, candlesticks and tea biscuits, sugar loaves and licorice, pickled eggs and beetroot, boiled hams and cheeses, silver polish and peppermints. Monsieur Lafayette sniffed appreciatively, rummaging through his secret store cupboard over tins of Victoria sponges and earthenware pots and pots of Brittany butter until he unearthed what he knew to be a box of sardines. He brought it out, blew the dust off it then locked the cupboard up again, the picture magically re-composing itself. Then he got up and walked back into the front of the shop, slipped the key into the old wig box on the counter, smoothed his moustache in the fly-spotted mirror and knelt down beside the old stonecutter.

'I believe I have an invitation to dine chez Renan?' he bellowed into the poor man's ear.

'Quite,' cried Mistigris, leaping up with surprising agility and throwing his arms out to the counter for support. 'In our curules, sir. In our curules!'

Chapter four

Eveline Renan stood in the middle of her kitchen, staring in dismay at the contents of the saucepan. There was barely enough to go round, even with the few potatoes she'd found on the stall in the Rue Marcadet. It had boiled away to nothing beneath her very eyes like spinach always did, however much you thought you had at the start.

Well to hell with it, she suddenly decided, stirring vigorously with a wooden spoon, keeping it warm at any rate. She did her best and if anyone dared complain she'd throw the saucepan over their head! It was good to vent her feelings like that. She often did in the cramped little kitchen, waiting for her father and Jacques to return, bashing the saucepans, chipping the plates, yanking the door off the larder cupboard which was quite bare save for two carrots and a tin of pears she was keeping for Christmas. The longer she had to wait, it seemed, the more she fell to thinking about all the things that were wrong with her life. 'Stuck away in crumbling stucco,' she would moan a little dramatically over the chopping board. 'Barely a woman but with the hands and back of a fifty-year-old hag!' None of this was entirely true, of course, for the house (though made of yellowing stucco as all the houses were in that district) was hardly crumbling; her hands (though no stranger to laborious work) were soft and white as a lily and her back (though admittedly often bent over drudgery) remained straight and supple as a beech tree. But it did her good somehow to work herself up into a frenzy of misunderstood martyrdom. A frenzy which always ended in a list of grievances as long as her arm of things that needed to be done around the house such as the chimney that had to be re-pointed, the leak in the roof that had to be mended and, a particular bugbear of hers, the vine on the south wall that had to be cut back because the grapes had shrivelled to raisins and the wine they produced was sour as a lemon rind. Even her father couldn't drink it! Occasionally she tortured herself by imagining what it would be like to be a shop girl on the Rue Ornano, skimming through a life of bows and silks, sales and crinolines; or la Païva the great courtesan who lived on the Champs Élysées behind a fountain of eau de cologne and a flower-gemmed terrace. Even the life of a lowly dancer seemed preferable to her own, though her father had warned her it was all bunions and besides. Eveline thought that when you were short of the necessaries, a few besides would come in mighty handy.

She lit the lamp with trembling fingers. She always put off lighting the lamp for as long as possible to save on the oil and it was only when the statues in the corner started reminding her of bodies in the morgue that she succumbed to the need for light. The blue flame sputtered and smoked for a moment, throwing ghastly shadows about the room of Mary Magdalenes on top of each other, headless Baptists with begging hands and Jesuses grinning from ear to ear. Once upon a time her father could have made anything he wanted to out of clay, wood or stone but now his forms were a little distorted – the robes too long, mouths stretched too wide, the eyes a little too sly – as if his fuzzy brain and fumbling fingers lingered too long or cut too abruptly. They reminded her of the gargoyles in the Place Vendôme and they piled up in the corner like bones in a charnel house because nobody wanted to buy them. She sighed and set the table, bringing out the old, stained, but clean linen cloth and placing a spoon beside each bowl. One good thing about having nothing to eat was that there was little to lay, little to wash, little to prepare. It was an advantage certainly. If you wanted to look on the bright side then that was it. She smiled at the thought of making a case for lack of food and sending it round to all the cooks, bottle-washers and housewives in the area, distracting herself from the waiting.

She always seemed to be waiting for something: in queues for food, for her father to come home, to stop drinking, for Jacques to grow up, the war to be over, for Laurie to whisk her away to the Place de l'Etoile. Maybe everyone was waiting for something, even the shop girls and la Païva, though they seemed to have everything. Laurie was waiting for his poems to be published so he could afford to whisk her off to the Place de l'Etoile – or so he said. She didn't think anyone would want to buy his poems any more than they wanted to buy her father's statues, not when they couldn't even find potatoes, but when she so much as hinted at such a thing Laurie gave her a look which meant she didn't understand because she was a woman and only read newspapers and recipe books. It was Laurie who didn't understand, she fumed now, deciding then and there that he'd have to beg and plead till his knees were sore if he ever wanted her to go and live with him in the Place de l'Etoile. You couldn't fry poems. You couldn't eat words. And however much a rhythm might nourish your soul it didn't put flesh on your bones.

There was a commotion at the door and Eveline got up to let the two men in, her father staggering under the arm of his sturdy old friend.

'Two old sodjers back from a campaign. The bullets whizzed! I nearly lost my scalp to a Fritz. What's on the menu, then? Chopped Prussians?' Monsieur Lafayette smacked his great red lips at her – lips which looked, Eveline always thought, as if they'd sucked on too many caramel pipes or been stung by a bee.

'Sorrel stew,' came her rather sardonic reply.

'Sard*ine* and sorrel stew,' Monsieur Lafayette corrected, bringing out a small box from somewhere about his person.

Eveline tried to appear disgusted but only succeeded in looking pathetically grateful. She took the box and proceeded to empty its contents very carefully into the saucepan, resisting the urge to scoff the lot then and there with her fingers and be damned to the rest of them. Monsieur Lafayette always brought a morsel with him – she wouldn't have let him come otherwise – something strange and exotic, something she hadn't tasted for months or years, and something you couldn't find on the stalls in the Rue Marcadet or even on the black markets beyond the fortifications. He was a little tiresome and a bore but she put up with him for her father's sake, for Jacques' sake and for her own shrunken stomach's sake.

The fish swam in the juices of the pan, glistening with oil; and she added a few salt flakes, her mouth watering. 'We won't wait for Jacques,' she announced decisively. 'Please be so good as to sit yourself down, Monsieur Lafayette, and make sure Papa has his napkin on.' It was like dealing with a child, dealing with her father but it was no longer embarrassing for either of them because she was quite used to it and her father, more often than not, was drunk as a lord. She ladled out the stew, took off her apron and said grace all in a matter of seconds.

'Maythelordmakeustrulythankfulamen.'

She always said grace because, strangely enough, however drunk her father might be he never touched a particle of food until he'd heard it spoken once at least.

'Amen,' intoned Monsieur Lafayette while Mistigris sat staring absent-mindedly at the statues in the corner.

'Forwhatweareabouttoreceivemaythelordmakeustrulythankfulamen.'

'Amen,' Monsieur Lafayette intoned again with a wink while her father still sat staring at his statues.

'Please, Papa.' Eveline spoke gently now, picking up her father's spoon and placing it between his finger and thumb. 'You can eat now. I've said grace. Monsieur Lafayette has brought some wonderful fish!'

'Fish?' echoed Mistigris doubtfully, dabbling his spoon in the stew as if he were dipping his toes in a cold tub. 'Who is responsible for the fish?'

Monsieur Lafayette inclined his head. 'Your servant, sir.'

'She must have seen fish like these,' Mistigris went on dejectedly, 'between the reeds and the water lilies.'

Eveline sent a beseeching look to Monsieur Lafayette who smiled an acknowledgement and put down his spoon.

'Sea dwellers, my good man, not fresh water. Pike perhaps, rainbow trout indeed but not a sardine, dear fellow, never a sardine.'

'Green! Green, she was, and bloated when they fished her out of the Seine.'

'Yes, Papa.'

It was going to be a long night. A long self-pitying night if her father didn't fall asleep first. Thank goodness she had an escape route planned in the shape of a meeting at St Nicolas.

'You are a tragedy king tonight!' Monsieur Lafayette tried to jolly along the old stonecutter. 'You make the Emperor look positively cheery and he's been exiled to England. Look at what you have here: a daughter dancing attendance upon you, your best friend at your side, a splendid stew to get your teeth into...'

At that moment – as if on cue – Jacques burst through the door, catapulted out of the cold night air and into his chair to make the additional point, so it seemed, that Mistigris also had a son to be thankful for: a sturdy-limbed little urchin of thirteen or thereabouts with carrot-coloured hair, a freckled nose, a forcible chin for one so young and horridly dirty hands. After scolding him roundly for his tardiness, his hands, the state of his shoes and the unpalatable objects she'd found underneath his bed that morning, as well as anything else that came to mind, Eveline served him up his helping of stew and turned to her father.

'I wish you would support me, Papa. Dinner, what we have of it, is at six o'clock sharp. One day you will both come home and there will be nothing to eat because I will have eaten it.'

Mistigris looked a little ashamed and Jacques hung his head, mumbled an apology and then began spooning the food into his mouth as if he feared she would prove true to her word. By this time a tortoiseshell cat had streaked out of nowhere onto his lap and was purring for all she was worth and poking her nose up over the table to see what her young master had been given for his supper. Jacques tried to work out what proportion of his stew he should be saving for her by applying the weight/balance principle he'd been learning in balloon training. Figuring that Fifi could not possibly be more than half his weight, he concluded (to his great satisfaction) that three fish tails would suffice; and he deftly cut them off with the edge of his spoon and fed them to her under the table when nobody else was looking.

'There's a butcher on the Boulevard Poissonnière who's feeding up a cat like that for Christmas,' teased Monsieur Lafayette. 'He's going to present it as a turkey stuffed with mice and onion stuffing!'

Eveline shot him a venomous glance while Jacques cried out in alarm: 'You must never let her out, Sis. You must never let her out! And if you do,' he conceded, 'you must watch her!'

'I can't watch her all the time, Jacques. Honestly, everyone in this family seems to think it's my life's duty just to do their bidding.'

'There are cat snatchers on the loose looking for prime meat like that one,' Monsieur Lafayette went on unrelentingly. 'How old is she now, boy?'

'S... seven,' stammered Jacques warily, clutching Fifi to his chest.

'Ah, mature but still tender,' Monsieur Lafayette leered at Eveline. 'Just the way I like it. Clear eyes, wet nose... a butcher would give you seventy francs for such a juicy little bit.'

'How much?' Mistigris leaned forward over the table.

'*Papa!*'

'*Papa!*'

'It comes to us all in the end, my boy,' said Mistigris with a philosophical air. 'The Lord giveth and the Lord taketh away! He took your mother a little early of course, but then again she went to meet him bless her soul the bloody whore!'

'Papa!'

'I might just follow her one fine day into the deep dark waters of the Seine. The waves tight about me. Green...'

'Have a heart, old man.' Monsieur Lafayette slapped his friend on the back. 'You're giving me an indigestion nearly as bad as the one I got up at the ramparts when Colonel L. treated us to a slice of his Arab mare. There's patriotism for you. Ultimate sacrifice for France and his men. He'd reared her from a foal apparently. A little fiery for my taste...'

'...and bloated,' Mistigris finished mournfully. 'Terribly, terribly bloated.'

Eveline stared at him, white faced. 'You have a vivid imagination. Papa,' she muttered angrily. 'If you remember rightly it was I who visited her in the morgue and she wasn't green and bloated at all. In fact she was rather pale and peaceful looking.'

'Ah.' Mistigris sat back, grateful tears springing to his eyes. 'A wonderful woman your mother, Jacques. A street whore and a harlot but a wonderful woman all the same!'

The rain pattered down outside and they were all quite warm and sleepy after the meal. Jacques told them about his exploits at the balloon factory: how he had fed Old Neptune, one of the homing pigeons, who could carry thirty thousand messages on his own because they were typed in columns like a newspaper. Eveline listened half-heartedly, hoping the rain would have stopped by the time she had to go out because she didn't have any sugar water to straighten her curls with. She decided to wear her blue merino dress with the pink corsage and coloured stockings for the evening. She wanted to look smart but appropriate, the sort of girl you might expect to be living in a bright new house on the Place de l'Etoile, with a husband in the literary world. She wished she had some of the latest cosmetics that had been all the rage before the war broke out – the Queen Bee milk and honey preparations (by appointment to the Empress herself no less) but she reasoned that even if she had been able to afford them, she would have eaten them up by now, they smelled so nice and tasted so good. Youth and beauty will have to do, she told herself wryly.

Jacques was telling Monsieur Lafayette that when he grew up he wanted more than anything to be a famous balloonist like the great Nadar, and voyage over plains and ice caps, deserts and seas to the lands of the fearsome dragons and insects.

'You don't have to go up in a balloon to meet a dragon,' chuckled Monsieur Lafayette, taking out a cigar and a strip of matches. 'They're all over the place. I was married to one for a time. Until she ran off with a wolf!'

'One to the wolf and one to the water,' Mistigris started up; and Eveline glowered at Monsieur Lafayette in exasperation. 'See what you've done?' she demanded, stacking up the plates and crashing into the kitchen with them. The girls on the Rue Ornano wouldn't have to put up with all this. Theirs was a life of bows and silks, sales and crinolines. La Païva had an onyx staircase and a golden bathroom and what did she, Eveline have? A leaking roof, an overgrown vine...

'Sis, sis,' called Jacques, breaking into her thoughts. 'Can I borrow some stockings to practise my knots with?'

'No,' she shouted and then a little more gently, 'Well, perhaps an old pair... but not the coloured ones.' She watched him scramble down, the cat at his heels and streak out of the room.

'A little mother to us all!' Monsieur Lafayette remarked sententiously; and she glowered at him again. It was the last thing she wanted to be. At her age. He may have brought sardines but the man was a menace all the same. If he wasn't scaring Jacques half to death, he was upsetting her father, reminding him of things he didn't need reminding of.

'Dear heart, dear heart!' the menace declared now, puffing on his cigar like a fish on the bank, his legs stretched underneath the table. 'Does my heart good just to look at her. Upon my soul, it does my heart good to look at her. No gold dust needed on those fair curls. No gowns from couturiers. Dress her in a sack cloth and she'd outshine the lot of 'em. There are millions of girls in Paris, some virgins and innocents, some fast and loose, some fancy free; but there is only one, could only ever be one... Eveline.' Perhaps it was out of respect that he spoke in such a roundabout way, or even shyness for it was only now, upon pronouncing her name, that he turned to look at her.

There was a long silence punctuated by the snores of old Mistigris and the sound of Jacques clattering into the room.

'Monsieur Lafayette,' Eveline began at last, colouring a little though she could hardly take him seriously with his bald head and piggy little eyes.

'Modeste, please.'

'Monsieur Modeste Lafayette! You are old enough to be my grandfather!'

'Father surely!'

'Grandfather,' she assured him. 'And as I have pointed out many times I would not marry you if you were the last man standing.'

'Well, well,' said Monsieur Lafayette, blowing smoke rings over the stonecutter's head. 'The way this war is going I might well be just that.' And he coughed three times as if to emphasise the point or to sound a valediction for the soon to be departed.

Eveline pursed her lips and looked at Jacques who was fumbling about on the floor beside the laundry basket. He must have felt her eyes upon him for he stood up, beaming, and held out the stockings she had set her heart on wearing that evening. 'That's a slip in that leg and a quick release in the other,' he announced proudly; and then, as if the matter had engaged his brain for a while: 'What's a harlot, Sis?'

She stared at him blankly, not knowing whether to laugh or cry at the question or the little urchin who held her stockings all twisted up in his hands.

Monsieur Lafayette came to the rescue. 'An extra-ordinary mother, my lad,' he smiled. 'An extra-ordinary mother!'

Chapter five

I would fain have news of anywhere but here, Laurie wrote feverishly, taking up the letter from where he left off, *trapped as we are in our little ice palace! Do you have any Tales from Toulouse to tell me? Is the Pope still in place? Is Mr Gladstone still Prime Minister of England? Is the Princess Louise married, Eveline would like to know.*

And is it true that the Prussians skate on Lake Enghein and stare round-eyed at Versailles? Our papers tell of regular parcels of bierwurst, smoked cheese and macaroni being sent to the troops and we gnash our teeth in envy!

I am sure I have heard them playing their accordions and singing – it is like singing in the wilderness – in their harsh guttural voices. Alphonse tells me I am dreaming but Tessier assures me they are waltzing away to Eleven Thousand Maidens of Cologne! I wish I could believe him but he is a terrible prankster and in truth, if his command of German were as good as all that, he would have been taken for a spy by now! There is a veritable spy mania in Paris at the moment. Everyone is convinced their neighbour harbours some terrible secret. Only the other day a young widow (careful Maman!) was arrested because her neighbour reported her macaw doing semaphore out of the window; and some poor chap stuck his head out of a manhole only to get it blown off for his efforts! (No doubt building a magic tunnel to the Prussian camp.) Foreign visitors are so paranoid they're taking out adverts in the press such as: Mr Crumblehome/Castiglione/Cooper is not a Prussian, having been born in Chelsea/Venice/New York. Delete as appropriate!

I think we are all quite crazy with lack of food and being kept so long on tender hooks as Molly would put it! Not so very tender in truth.

I wish you both a Merry Christmas in the hope this letter reaches you 'par ballon' before the 25th. Think of me please as you scoff your roast turkey. I shall be in my rooms on the Rue d'Enfer or maybe with ~~Eveline~~ *the Renans.*

In hope of peace,
Your son,

'Hey, Laurie! Haven't you finished that letter yet?'

'Alphonse!' Laurie grinned in delight, letter forgotten, and stood to greet his friend who had appeared as always from nowhere – large as life, eyes twinkling, his strong graceful fingers wrapped round the neck of a hessian sack. 'What the hell have you got in there? Bismarck?'

'Yeah, and his balls. Let's just say it's a delicacy...'

'It's a lark!' someone shouted.

'Crow!'

'Your mother's nose!'

'Arse!'

'...for the bastards who dine at Brébant's while the rest of Paris starves,' Alphonse finished with a grin when he could get a word in edgeways. He took a swig of mouth warmer then spat it out with a grimace. 'That stuff gets worse!'

Laurie nodded. For as long as he could remember Alphonse had worked at Brébant's, in between his job as a waker-upper[4] and his political ambitions. He had said that to infiltrate the toffee-nosed and the upper crust you might as well serve 'em up their toffees and crusts – a little burnt and stale perhaps, just for the fun of it.

'It's Trochu's plan[5],' Tessier said suddenly, pointing at the sack. 'That's where it's been hiding. Alphonse Duchamp, master magician, delivers from his bag – Trochu's plan. Where did he find it ladies and gentlemen? The Hôtel de Ville? A government journal? The Ministry of War? No! The elusive article was found in a turnip field! Trochu's plan came from a turnip field!'

'Oh, you're good, Tessier,' Alphonse smiled kindly, running his fingers through his dark curly hair. 'I wouldn't want you on the other team.'

Tessier looked as pleased as punch and he poured Alphonse a drop of gin then shuffled the pack again, this time with his eyes closed. Bidulph muttered that he didn't want that bloody palaver all over again and the mood looked ugly again for a while until Alphonse said he'd go a round with the best of 'em; and then they all hoorayed English style and budged up a seat for him.

Laurie watched his friend slip back into the game as if he'd never been away from it and smiled ruefully. Trust Alphonse to lift the mood of the men with a merest flick of his fingers, a glance, a smile. If he so much as sneezed the whole world came running out with 'God bless you's' and handkerchiefs, hot gins and flu potions. It would have been sickening if he hadn't been his friend and even now he felt a slight stab of envy as he saw the men falling over themselves for a word of praise or pat on the head. Alphonse sat, so it seemed, quite oblivious to it all, earnestly studying his cards; and Laurie shrugged off the feeling as completely unworthy. He got up and went over to straighten the tent for the new squad, busying himself with shaping the straw pallets, re-directing the rusty saucepan under the leak and packing up their kit bags with identical mess tin, drinking cup, leather cartridge supply bag and first-aid box. By this time he could hear the customary howls of derision that 7th Company used to greet the new squad, the back slapping, friendly bickering, cries of 'Merry Christmas, you poor suckers' and Coupeau's voice above the rest, bragging about the bet he'd laid with Joubet to muff ten women by Christmas Eve and even that would be a breeze. Laurie lengthened his rifle strap to fit more comfortably around his bulky greatcoat and packed the letter away carefully in a side pocket. He was just taking a last look round the tent when Alphonse poked his head through the flap.

'What are you doing hiding away in here?' he demanded which Laurie knew was his friend's way of thanking him for packing away. 'You haven't forgotten the meeting tonight have you?'

'Of course not!' cried Laurie, unable to stop the note of pride creeping into his voice. 'Eveline will be there.'

'Ah yes.' Alphonse looked at Laurie's face with interest. 'The beautiful Eveline.'

And, shouldering their kit bags, they crawled out of the tent side by side into the twilight.

Chapter six

The meeting was in full swing by the time Eveline arrived, bare legged, drenched and unkempt, wishing she'd wrung that little urchin's neck. She had to stop for a moment as she entered the church because the heat and hubbub hit her like a train after the cold air and pelting rain. She still found it strange to see the church at night, so different, so unrecognisable – no flowers or prayer books, no bent heads, pious eyes, no priests in flowing garments, no body or blood of Christ. Instead, an altar table piled high with dirty plates, sticky glasses and dead-necked wine bottles; the *Marseillaise* instead of the *Magnificat*; and a congregation so different from the day it was scarcely believable. Hardened revolutionaries with zealous eyes and red kerchiefs; National Guardsmen roaring drunk and off duty; dilettantes seeking amusement; fat women and thin women both looking for food; refugees from the long cold winter nights and ragamuffins who sidled into the lonely back pews and fell asleep, only to be kicked out in the morning by an angry curate. The clubs were only granted access in the evenings and even that was grudgingly given; but Eveline reckoned that any priest would give his eye teeth and chalice away for a congregation this big, this enthusiastic...

She scanned the crowd, hoping to catch sight of Laurie and Alphonse with the other National Guardsmen in the choristers' stalls; but they were not amongst them. The candlelight played over a multitude of faces, some animated, some thoughtful, some cheerful, some emaciated; and the stained-glass windows glowed vividly above the stinking mass of warm, wet flesh. If God were a Belleville revolutionary, Eveline decided, what a following He would have! She spotted Laurie and Alphonse next to Tessier the bookkeeper who always kept the minutes in his small, neat handwriting. A table had been brought out of the chancel for him to make his job a little easier; and Laurie and Alphonse were crouched down beside him, presumably keeping his spirits up. Eveline felt her heart beat a little faster and, adjusting her blue merino dress, she cut across an empty pew and approached them via the chancel itself.

'You look like a drowned rat!' Laurie teased kindly, his eyes sparkling at the sight of her.

'Thank you very much!' she replied, slipping her hand into his and nodding at Alphonse who raised an eyebrow and enquired if it was raining outside. She was trying to think of a sharp retort when a woman behind told them all to shut up because Citizen Roly was about to take the floor.

'There have been two denunciations already,' Laurie whispered in her ear, his fair hair tickling her neck. 'A woman on the Rue Belhomme has been feeding bread to her four dogs. Four, mind! And General Thomas has been accused of playing billiards all day in his luxury apartments on the Champs Élysées.'

Citizen Roly took to the floor, a dapper little man in a black suit with a képi perched on his head. He took out a handkerchief, mopped his brow and began.

'We are in the 94th day of the siege!'

'*Hurrah!*'

'And I would like to make it clear first of all that I do not believe the government to be composed entirely of evil-minded untrustworthy criminals. I believe it to be entirely composed of a bunch of incompetent imbeciles!'

There were titters at that and Tessier scribbled furiously, beads of sweat breaking out on his brow. He had developed his own peculiar form of shorthand – the system Léon as he called it – which replaced words with symbols of his own choosing. For example, enemy was a cross, friend was an upturned smile, hurrahs were upturned pointing arrows, boos were downward, hello was a pair of eyes and the government a question mark. Unfortunately, because he had never produced a comprehensive guide to the system Léon (and in any case was adding to it day by day) his shorthand was completely indecipherable to anyone but himself

'We've been hearing about Trochu's plan for the last three months,' Citizen Roly went on. 'Well, where is it? What has happened to it? Has it flown off in a balloon?'

'*Ha Ha!*'

'Being a Roman Catholic, does General Trochu think he ought to run it past God before he puts it into action?'

There was general hilarity at that and the woman behind Laurie and Eveline slapped her thighs. 'Run it past God,' she guffawed. 'Did you hear that!'

Laurie squeezed Eveline's hand and she managed to keep a straight face by concentrating hard on Citizen Roly.

'Let us hope a pigeon brings it home before a Saxon eagle swoops,' he concluded sombrely.

'*Hear Hear*!'

'And what of the armies that were supposed to come to Paris' rescue? Have they all flown off in a balloon? Presumably they haven't starved to death like the 15,000 inhabitants of the city have done in the last three months!'

Shocked exclamations. Tuts. A barrage of boos.

'We were told yesterday that operations were suspended because of the ice. Ice, ladies and gentlemen! We are not trains running on timetables! We do not need to suspend operations because of the ice. Our forefathers fought at Sébastopol. I think we can suffer a few chilblains and chapped lips for the sake of our nation, for the sake of liberty!'

'*Hurrah! Hear Hear*!'

The organist struck up a few bars of the *Marseillaise* and Citizen Roly climbed down to great applause. Laurie took the opportunity to whisper in Eveline's ear that he'd missed her terribly and wanted her to come to his rooms after the meeting; she coloured up and nodded in agreement. Then he went off to get her a drink and maybe a bite to eat if there was anything remaining on the altar table other than crumbs. She felt quite lost without him, standing in between Alphonse and Tessier. Tessier was huffing and puffing over his minutes and Alphonse was looking very earnest and attentive though at one point she could have sworn he was staring at her legs. They felt very hot and pink in the warmth of the candlelight and she wished for the second time that night she'd wrung the little urchin's neck.

Next up was a very serious and sober-looking gentleman who worked at the Cail engineering plant, so he said, and was a father of four. He thought that the problem was not (as Citizen X had claimed the other week) a lack of weaponry or even an old and dilapidated arsenal. After all, statistics showed – if the audience would just bear with him he had the statistics at his disposal though he could not quite say where they came from – Ah yes: 300,000 cartridges were being produced every day; 300 cannon had already been manufactured in Paris which worked out at about 21 a week; and a large number of *mitrailleuse*[6] – he could not say quite how many but it was a great many and they must take his word for it. And if you did not believe the statistics which were ahem perhaps a little inconclusive… well… everyone knew that the bells of St Denis cathedral had been melted down for cannon and you only had to walk down the Rue de Rivoli and hear the hammering from the basement windows to know that work was afoot. No, it was not, he felt, the weapons so much as the training that was the problem. After all, they were a nation of shopkeepers, artisans, factory workers, artists… they had not been taught how to fight. With the best will in the world they were not trained soldiers. A small point, he knew – coughing and aheming – but worth making all the same.

'That was short and sweet,' muttered Laurie as the man climbed down, inclining his head to the muted applause.

'He's a good sort,' the woman behind remarked knowledgeably. 'You can tell by the state of his breeches.'

'I've got a statistic for him,' an old man growled under his breath. '10,000 Remingtons imported from America each week that were used in their civil war. If that's not old and dilapidated I don't know what is. I bet the only weapon he's fired is his own ruddy pencil. Training? He wants potty training!'

'Why didn't you say something,' demanded the woman behind. 'It's no good blathering about back here. No one can hear you!'

Eveline took a gulp of the fiery liquid Laurie had brought in a dirty wine glass and watched Alphonse take the floor. The church quietened down at the sight of him for he was well known and well liked and many believed he had a glittering political career before him.

'I agree with all the points that have been made so far this evening,' he began softly, his hands resting on the lectern, his strong face calm and composed. 'It is true that this government is at best incompetent; that our generals issue orders and counter orders and in their arrogance carry maps of Germany in their pockets when they couldn't even find their way around the Place Vendôme. I imagine Bismarck is laughing his head off.'

'*Hear Hear!*'

'We wait for Trochu's plan, for the government to act, to be attacked. We stand at our fortifications, look through our telescopes and wait.'

Eveline wanted to shout out that it was the women who queued for hours and hours in the snow, the rain, the mud, for a measly ration of soup; that it was the women who waited always, always waited for the men… and her eyes blazed with the fiery liquid and the thoughts his words provoked in her.

'This government would wait till doomsday and then say the course of events had been inevitable. The course of events is NOT inevitable. The course of events is NEVER inevitable. We are masters of our own destinies.'

Thunderous applause. Bravos. Hear Hears.

Alphonse held up his hand. 'We have come so far. We have a Republic, it is true.'

Cries of *vive la République.*

'The monarchy has gone. The Tuileries is now the Property of the People. We have come so far. We have rid this country of a noxious weed, a regime based on corruption and greed. Luxury built on rottenness.'

'The Duc de Morny's hair all fell out!' an old gentleman in a waistcoat shouted out. 'That's a sure sign of the pox!'

There was wild cheering at that though nobody quite knew what they were cheering for.

'Indeed it is,' smiled Alphonse. 'A sure sign of the profligacy of the rich who take their pleasures with YOUR gold. A sure sign of the oppression of the poor. A luxury built on YOUR sweat, YOUR toil, YOUR blood. Do you want to have a decent share in your own wages?'

'*YES.*'

'Then you must stop waiting and start acting. This government – this government would make a deal with the Prussians and restore the monarchy. WHY? Because most of its members served under it. Nepotism, sinecures, flatterers down to the lowliest most obsequious boot licker. And that is why the members of this government are pussyfooting round Prussia like a bunch of cats who've grown fat in their mistresses' laps!'

'Mistresses,' shouted the old gentleman in the waistcoat again. 'I've counted them up. He's had more than has ever been recorded in the annals of history ever. Sixty-six to be precise and those are the ones accounted for. Who knows what goes on in his *loge intime.* A few one-night wonders I shouldn't wonder!'

'We are no longer talking about the Emperor,' the old woman behind remarked a little tartly. 'We are on to the Republic now.'

'Republic, yes,' agreed Alphonse. 'But we might as well call it the Emperor for all the difference it makes. We've come so far but we must take the next step. Do you want to be masters of your own fate?'

'*Yes!*'

'Then wake up! It's a new day! Wake up!'

Laurie smiled to hear their old wake-up call. The one they had used to wake the factory workers and fruiterers, market traders and fancy hat-box makers in the early hours of the morning.

'We must stop waiting and start acting. This day. This moment. It is time to take the next step. We must form an assembly and elect an executive body…'

'*Hear Hear.*' A burst of feeble applause.

Alphonse stopped, as if he felt he'd gone too far and his voice changed, becoming softer, more compassionate, on intimate terms with his listeners. 'We live in changing times. Strange and puzzling times. But that does not mean that we need to be afraid. It is only when we wait that we are afraid. It is only when we let others take charge of our own destinies that we need to be afraid.'

The audience was hushed, hanging on to his every word. Even the drunk and disorderly Guardsmen were standing to attention in the choristers' stalls and the ragamuffins in the lonely back pews were swaying but still awake.

Alphonse's voice changed again. 'Alright. Enough,' he almost barked as if he had grown tired of his own high-flown words. 'While the government sings the praises of Trochu's plan yet never puts it into action; while the men in white coats at the academy work on smallpox germs to send to the Prussians; and while the great minds of the university debate the provisioning of besieged towns in antiquity… we had better get on with starvation and reality as best we can!'

The relief was palpable. Nerves strung up like violins were let down and subsided into laughter. The *Marseillaise* struck up again and everyone broke into song.

'Well done!' Laurie congratulated his friend, his eyes full of admiration. 'That was grand, really grand. You had them in the palm of your hand.'

Alphonse shrugged. 'Could have been better – but I got a little distracted by one or two members of the audience!' He patted Tessier on the back and grinned at Eveline. 'Don't have apoplexy over it old man. It doesn't really matter.'

Eveline stood weak kneed with the fiery drink and the thoughts his words provoked in her; and she watched him disappear into an admiring throng.

The mood in the church seemed quite changed after that. What had started off as a sombre, almost pessimistic little affair had turned into a festival, a free for all. Képis were flung in the air, eloquent gestures bandied about. A group of National Guardsmen made a ridiculous spectacle of themselves by doing the can-can down the nave and around the altar table though nobody seemed to care. Friends swore loyalty through thick and thin; enemies shed tears, embraced, broke up again all in a matter of minutes while sweethearts promised love and favours for an eternity. After the fiery drink and fiery words, any obstacle seemed surmountable. In the warmth of the candlelight, every battle won.

Laurie and Eveline decided to make their escape before the mob turned into a frenzy and before they could be roped into helping to clear away; and they bolted up the aisle like a runaway bride and groom.

Chapter seven

They raced past the concierge who was always asleep and up to Laurie's rooms. How she loved Laurie's rooms – so quiet, so peaceful. She liked to poke her nose through the small round window and gaze down on the higgledy-piggledy back streets behind the Rue d'Enfer with their overgrown gardens, crazy washing lines and filthy latrines. She tried to imagine the lives that went on behind the finger-smudged panes and patched-up curtains, developing all sorts of strange theories and complex interrelationships between the houses that fell within the parameters of Laurie's window.

'Mr 50 is in love with Miss 49,' she would announce solemnly after a few moments' speculation. 'They are going to elope. Mr 43 beats his wife!' These deductions were based on such trivial points as the fact that Mr 43 possessed a walking stick and Mr 50 had once hung his hand mirror out of the window at the same time that Miss 49 put her petticoat out to air. Singularly strange coincidences according to Eveline. She would have been most disappointed to discover that Mr 43 was a widower and had no wife to beat though he did have a carpet; that Miss 49 took in ironing and hung her petticoat out to signal her availability as a washerwoman, not as an ahoy to Mr 50 who, poor man, was up to his ears in debt and no more dreamed of eloping with Miss 49 than with the taxman.

'Up to your old tricks again?' Laurie demanded, taking her arm and pulling her gently away from the window.

'I am not up to my old tricks as you put it,' Eveline replied, flopping down on the cane chair beside the bed and grinning wickedly. 'I am simply an observer of humanity.' It was one of Laurie's own phrases and she brought it out deliberately to show him that she did listen to him. Sometimes.

Laurie smiled. 'And what did you observe tonight? That everyone was fast asleep in their own beds, even Mr 50 and Miss 49, and that nobody, not even a mouse, was stirring.'

Eveline pouted. 'One day you will see that a woman's instincts are a great deal sharper than a man's... a man's... silliness,' she finished at last, feeling quite aggrieved that she had indeed seen no sign of life, only blackness and stars and in the distance the square-topped belfry of St Jacques.

'I can offer you a coffee of a sort. A species without milk or sugar, an evolved coffee, Darwin might say. A coffee that has adapted to the environment.'

She nodded and agreed – so long as it wasn't made in the vermicelli saucepan. It was a long-standing joke between them. Laurie kept a vermicelli-spattered saucepan on the spirit stove after the fashion of Victor Hugo – though Eveline thought he did it to annoy her and whenever he offered her a drink or a bite to eat she always told him it had better not be in the vermicelli saucepan. She watched him bustle about, his fair hair gleaming in the lamplight and listened to him going on about the war, his nights at the ramparts and the poem he'd just finished which contained the line: *Only in the contemplation of flowers and moonlight may all men be equal.* She had thought it very fine and told him so. It could only be a matter of time, they both agreed, before his remarkable talent was spotted.

'And you,' he enquired gently, bringing over his new species in a cup. 'How are you? Your legs must be freezing to death!'

Eveline didn't want to tell him that her only clean pair of stockings were tied up in knots. 'Everything goes on much the same,' she replied. 'Jacques is Jacques and father is... well, father.' She turned a little red. 'I should christen this the Victor Hugo cup for it tastes of vermicelli to me!'

Laurie smiled. 'Did you know that when he was writing *Leaves of Autumn* he walked up to the top of Notre Dame every evening to watch the sunset.'

'Why ever did he do that?' cried Eveline. 'Does it look different from there than it does from the ground?'

'I imagine so. Else why would he have done it?'

'Perhaps because he is a madman who keeps pots of vermicelli on his stove!'

Laurie laughed outright. 'You caught me that time!'

They chattered on then for a while about everything and nothing, Eveline settling back with her cup of Victor Hugo. Laurie wanted to know all the details – nothing was too trivial for him – of what she had eaten, where she had been, how she had felt since they last met and she struggled to remember the spaces and moments of her days, the dull and necessary in betweens, the routines and the rubbish. It seemed to her that she simply waited, waited for him to come home and spell out the meaning of her existence, see the poetry beneath the squalor of her life. She didn't always believe there was any poetry, and it made her fearful sometimes that he was deceived in her. It was then she pretended to be even more what she knew he wanted her to be, taking an interest in his books, his ideas on Darwin and evolution, bending herself to an understanding and appreciation of the planes of reality he lingered on, delved into. At other times, a demon got into her and she wanted to upset the peace and quiet of the little room with its shelves of ordered books and sheaves of white paper by bringing out a string of coarse words or bursting into a bawdy song she'd heard her father sing: *like teeth behind lips, the strawberry spreads its sweet breath…*

'Are you well, Evie?' Laurie's voice was all concern. 'You seem a little… strange this evening.'

'Oh fine,' she assured him. 'It's just that sometimes, I don't know, I wish that I could do something.'

'What do you mean, do something?'

'I don't know. I just feel so helpless sometimes, sitting around doing nothing.'

'But you do so much. You look after your father and Jacques.'

'Oh yes, I do that alright. And I am sick of it. I'm sick of sitting at home and looking after them. Getting no thanks for it. I wish I could go out like you do and fight.'

'Fight?' Laurie stared at her incredulously. 'What do you mean, fight?'

'There are women battalions,' Eveline replied a little defensively. 'I heard a girl talking about one the other day in the queue at Potin's. They have their own uniforms and guns. They train just as the men do, fight just like the men do.'

'But it is a ridiculous notion,' Laurie smiled. 'You cannot possibly fight!'

'Why ever not?' Eveline demanded with a flash of anger. 'You're always saying I'm strong as a horse and fearless as a lion.'

'Yes, well.' Laurie looked a little taken aback and could only think to repeat: 'But you do so much already. You have even tended to the wounded in the Palais de L'Industrie.'

'I do not want to simper at the bedside of a gangrenous soldier,' she replied dismissively. 'I leave that to the society women and the *cocodettes*.' In truth, she could not bear to see the dead stacked up like biscuits in the green and foetid death shed – it filled her with an impotent disgust.

Laurie smiled distractedly. 'I hope you would simper at my bedside…
but what about your father and Jacques?' he repeated.

'What about them? It is always about them. It is never about me.'

Laurie said in a gentler tone: 'That is because they rely on you.
Without you they would,' he wanted to say 'starve to death' which was
probably true, but instead he said, 'they could not manage. They could not
manage without you, Evie. You know they could not manage.' He saw the
stubborn set of her mouth and went on: 'There is precious little glory in
war, Evie.'

Her eyes travelled to the uniform hung up behind the back of the
door and the chassepot rifle propped against the wall; and she shook her
head, angry at his not understanding. 'It is not about the glory,' she
muttered. 'You of all people should know that it is not about the glory.'

He did know. She was too modest and lacking in vanity for it ever to
be anything to do with glory. He knew, too, that in a world grown topsy-
turvy the only thing that kept him sane was the thought of her back home
where she belonged with her father and Jacques, doing the most simple,
harmless things: making soup, cleaning the floor, worrying about the
overgrown vine and searching for food. He wanted to keep her there on
a pin in a corner of his mind, simply for his own comfort; though one day
she might wriggle out of his grasp and fly away in all her beauty.

'I just don't want you to get hurt,' he said at last, looking terribly upset
and she smiled back at him.

'How could I ever get hurt?' She leapt up from the cane chair,
galloped over to the little round window and peered out of it. It was still
all stars and blackness and in the distance the square-topped belfry of St
Jacques. Nobody, not even a mouse, was stirring. There was no need to be
afraid. It is only when we wait, Alphonse had said, that we need to be
afraid. She turned suddenly and cried out impulsively: 'Kiss me, Laurie,
kiss me. Right here. Right now! Let me stay with you.'

Laurie stared at her in astonishment, wondering if the drink at St
Nicolas had been too much for her. Her cheeks were flushed and her eyes
glittered like a maenad's. He did not think he had ever seen her look so
beautiful, framed as she was before the porthole window, her chestnut
hair aglow, her wide red mouth trembling with emotion, her luminous
skin… He got up quickly and took her in his arms so that she did not
catch sight of the perturbation in his face. He wanted the first time to be
perfect, when they were married, when they had their own establishment,
when he had published a volume of poetry… not now. Not on the eve of
an enemy attack. Not after some wine and a slight disagreement, in a

moment of hot-headed foolishness. Love in the middle of war? What could be worse?

'Not like this,' he murmured into her soft, silken hair.

'What do you mean?' She pulled away from him, her eyes glaring.

He kissed her gently but firmly on the forehead. 'You would regret it, my love, and so would I.'

'Oh *well*.' She tore out of his grasp and made a great show of finding her coat, not even smiling (as she always did) when the cuckoo clock on the wall sprang into action for the eleven o' clock, its yellow beak popping in and out. 'I should like to go home now,' she announced coldly, fighting the tears of humiliation that prickled at the back of her eyes. 'As you say, Papa and Jacques rely on me.'

He walked her home, or rather, lagged a step behind as she marched silently through the cold empty streets, an occasional lamp throwing down a circle of light like a pool of moon glow or scrap of gold dust. He chattered on about this and that, knowing it would make no difference now. He asked himself if he could have behaved any differently but his principles and character told him he could not. Still he cursed himself for being so clumsy, so obtuse, for brushing her off like an insect, for not understanding. It was as if he got the impression of things rather than the things themselves. There they were walking along the Rue du Faubourg and yet he felt one step removed as if he were watching the process from afar. Sometimes he even composed a sentence about himself in the third person and the past tense – *He walked down the Rue du Faubourg with a heavy heart* – as if his real self had been and gone already and he was simply observing the clues left in his own wake. He was the Detective Claude[7] on the trail of his own self, so to speak. It worried him sometimes and he shook off the feeling of guilty indolence that often came with it and took her hand.

'I can never get used to the smell,' he remarked as they stepped into a pool of moon glow. 'And petrol is so different from the blue tone of gas.'

'Yes,' she replied, tight lipped and embarrassed, thinking that reality rarely matched her dreams. When he was away at the ramparts she imagined him almost a god and now here he was trotting along at her side like a lapdog, so eager to please, filling her with a sense of disdain.

'Do you miss your work?' he asked quite out of the blue as they stepped onto the Ramponneau. It had suddenly struck him that this could be the culprit, this could be the cause of her ennui, her moods, her excitability.

'Not really,' she sighed. Why ever should he think she missed greasing the heavy metal bread moulds, the flour stuck under her nails, the sickly sweet odour of yeast at the crack of dawn. 'No, not really. I'd like some bread but I don't miss the work.'

'You know I just want it to be perfect.' He stopped, forcing her to look at him. 'I just want it to be perfect, Evie.'

'Really?' Her lip curled in scorn.

'Yes, really. Believe it, Evie. Believe it. When we are married…'

'You assume too much,' she answered stiffly, wrapping her coat about her and moving on.

He knew that voice and face and shut up until they reached her door where he bade her a tense 'sleep well' and left.

She stared angrily after him into the darkness then went inside.

Chapter eight

Aggie lay huge and suffering on the small white bed beneath the large wooden crucifix; and the baby lay swaddled in the bottom drawer of the antique tallboy which had on the front a carmine engraving of the immaculate conception. Aggie had succumbed to a fever, a fever that raged around her body like a caged animal, drumming at her temples and stampeding up and down her veins, and Bernadine had brought her into her own room the easier to attend her. She watched them both without reprieve, jumping up at the least little sign to wipe a cooling flannel over Aggie's brow, spoon a few mouthfuls of the broth Brother Michael had made between her dry, parched lips, soothe the tiny blue baby's cries. She barely heard the angelus though it must have sounded for dawn, midday and dusk. Night and day had become indistinguishable to her as she watched and waited. There was nothing to be done but wait and pray, wait and see. Sometimes she clasped the Holy Book to her knee, feeling the gilt-cut edges with her fingers, and stammered out a few verses in a high contralto as if it might do some good. *My beloved is mine and I am his. He feedeth among the lilies until the day breathes and the shadows flee away.*

She'd rigged up a hammock for the baby, too, with blankets and hemp and on the table beside the bed stood the iron water as well as the medicinal herbs now decocted and tinctured into pots, a bar of soap, a candlestick and taper and a bowl of cooling water sprinkled with dry geraniums. She allowed no visitors apart from Brother Michael who brought his nourishing stews and broths, diced mutton and haricot, boiled beef, a wing of chicken and a slice of cake to tempt the invalid back to health. He must have searched heaven and hell for the food though Bernadine never asked him. She simply accepted the bounty brought out of the folds of his cassock and blue twill apron, thanking God for His grace and mercy. Once he brought an orange and she had shut her mind to the thought that he must have stolen it from some hot house in the Tuileries. Aggie had gasped in delight at the sight of it and Brother Michael had turned the colour of an orange himself, hanging about at the edge of the bed and wringing his hands, glad to be of use to the Prettiest Peach, yet saddened to see her so done in and done out as he put it. Occasionally he crouched down beside the bottom drawer of the tallboy and laid a thick and stubbly finger on the child's forehead, making the sign of the cross. Then he would sink back on the horsehair chair in the corner and hold his breath until Bernadine almost forgot he was there. He had a knack of fading into the background like a chameleon or a white cat in the snow, and once he stayed several hours before Bernadine, on the point of rendering some intimate service for her friend, had remembered he was there and shooed him away as if he were a small boy.

It must have been very late or very early, for the light that came through the narrow slit of window was too soft, too gentle. It bathed Aggie's face in a milky glow, a delicate muslin, then hit the wooden crucifix with the sweetness of a blade. The baby slept peacefully in the bottom drawer of the walnut tallboy – Aggie had managed to feed her before sinking back into a sleep of exhaustion. Bernadine watched them both, her own eyes drooping with fatigue. Up until now she hadn't been aware of her bodily functions, had felt no hunger, no thirst, no sore, aching muscles; but now an immense desire for sleep overwhelmed her and she must have dozed off for a while because suddenly she was in her beloved little garden, walking through snowdrops and shy peeping bluebells, her feet and habit wet with dew. The sun had the face of an angel, the sky new washed, new created. She smelled the smell of the earth, the grass, the sticky green sap of the trees, felt the silken downy buds of leaves. Gilded insects murmured in their flight and the chortling of toads trickled through the wall with the *kyrie eleisons* of a service. Disembodied voices of nuns and toads… She woke up suddenly in alarm and ran over to Aggie who still slumbered fitfully, her breath shallow and ragged. She dipped the flannel in the geranium-scented water and dabbed at Aggie's temples then went to check on the baby. The gentle rise and fall of the tiny chest calmed her a little and she sat back down on her chair, deciding to bring out her box of coloured thread. She would make some pretties for the baby. She must keep her hands and mind busy at all costs. When she started thinking too much about Aggie and the baby, let alone the father, an abyss opened up at her feet, too wide to contemplate.

Lighting another candle on her small workbench, Bernadine brought out the wicker basket which contained her coloured threads, scraps of satin and velvet, a wooden darning egg, nippers, a goffering cushion, pins, needles, a bobbin, leaves of green and brown paper and a pastepot. She would make a bunch of violets to welcome the baby into the world. It was a commitment to life, to the future. If she finished a bunch before the night was out then Aggie and the baby would live. She set to work with great diligence, rolling out paper stalks, sewing her satin petals, her fingers lost in the glitter and fragility of the work. It brought back memories of sewing orange blossom wreaths for the first vows, when the white veil was exchanged for the black; when there was no grey, no clouded judgement, just self-abnegation, penitence, a desire for perfection. When time was run by the hours of the convent, the singing of devotions, Prime, Tierce, Sext, None… and the anthem before bedtime, *O dulcis Virgo Maria*… How they had giggled when their shorn locks littered the Sister barber's floor – chestnut, gold, black, brunette…

'All for Jesus,' they had smiled at each other, almost hysterical. 'All for Jesus!'

And the coif that framed the head and made you look like a tortoise poking your face out of a starchy carapace. What a lot of ebullience she'd had to subdue! The little conscience notebook and flail with its ring and five chains to overcome pride and carnal desire, the leather belt of rosaries, the wooden robe worn beneath the scapular to symbolise the yoke of Christ and the bronze crucifix above the heart. A life against nature, her father had said and it was true. But in those days it truly had been all for Jesus. In those days. Before she met him.

The shy knock broke into her thoughts and she looked up to see Brother Michael creeping into the cell as if he were a fugitive.

'Brother Michael,' she smiled. 'What have you brought this time?'

'Sister Bernadine,' he replied, walking over to the workbench after a quick glance at Aggie. 'I have brought eggs!' And taking a red knotted handkerchief out of his pocket, he placed it on the workbench and slowly unwrapped it amidst the paraphernalia of bobbin, silk and pastepot. Four plump eggs sat gleaming in the candlelight, boiled and peeled and sprinkled with what looked like a dash of cayenne pepper.

Bernadine felt a jolt of saliva come into her mouth and she stared in astonishment.

'Well, what do you think? Will they do? Will they tempt the invalid back to health?'

'How on earth…?' Sister Bernadine began, shaking her head in wonderment.

Brother Michael grinned in delight, tapping the side of his little snub nose, a nose which turned quite violently heavenward. 'Easy for them what knows!' And he proceeded to tell her the tale of how he had travelled far and wide, evidenced by the state of his torn and muddy cassock, the scent of outdoors and smoke about him; his vigil by the chicken coop in the moonlight, holding his breath and fearful of farmers, foxes and pecks from cocks… his hands slithering through the straw until, with a shiver of delight, they came upon the warm, round eggs… the retreat, a flurry of feathers, a dog barking, a farmer brandishing sticks and the perilous journey home, stumbling about through the undergrowth, holding his apron out in front and then just a few moments ago, boiling them hard in the saucepan before the steward was up and nosing about.

'And how are your struggles with the steward?' Bernadine asked politely after congratulating him on his great adventure.

Brother Michael snorted. 'The steward talks very finely about *carpe diem* but he won't share his spice rack for love nor money.' He took an egg and popped it whole into his mouth so that it stuck out of his cheek like a sugar plum. 'One for each of us,' he indicated.

Bernadine smiled at his naivety and told him gently that it might be a while before the baby had any teeth to sink into a boiled egg. She didn't voice her concerns about milk or lack of it and the fact that there were no milch cows left in the Bois de Boulogne which meant that if Aggie died…

'Oh well,' Brother Michael joked. 'More for me!'

Bernadine helped herself, biting a small chunk from the top and chewing slowly then finishing the rest gratefully and greedily. 'That was delicious,' she smiled, wiping her mouth.

Brother Michael licked his fingers and stared at her seriously. 'You know the Mother Superior is on the warpath.'

'It had occurred to me that she might be.'

'She feels that the baby is, well, not best placed here.'

'That is for Aggie to decide… when she is well.'

Brother Michael stared at her in surprise. She looked frail as a May butterfly at her workbench but her voice was hard, almost defiant. He wanted to say more but one look at the Shady Lady's face told her he had better not. He decided to entertain her instead with stories and gossip from inside the convent. One young novice had been upbraided for wearing her hair curled up *à la mode* because she thought it looked very saintish.

'Saintish? Saintish?' the Reverend Mother had apparently whispered, white as a sheet. 'Devilish!'

And another poor girl who'd hung a black apron behind a pane of glass to cast a dark reflection was to be punished by begging for soup for a week in the refectory.

'I *have* missed a lot,' murmured Bernadine, going back to her bunch of violets.

'What is that you are making? Brother Michael asked curiously.

'Oh, something for the baby.'

Brother Michael turned a little red and he said suddenly in a loud, almost nervous voice: 'Our physical lives are ours to expend, indeed we are expendable but our spiritual lives are not ours to do what we want with. I shall eat the rest of the eggs, Sister Bernadine, if you do not put your face in at Lauds.' And he made as if to swoop on the handkerchief.

'I shall attend Lauds,' she promised, half-smiling, half-sighing. 'I shall attend Lauds.'

The bell for Lauds had spoken and the nuns flitted one by one from their honeycombed cells, flat as shadows or worn-out crows. Bernadine felt as if she were sleepwalking as she crept down the nave past the fourteen stations of the cross, and the yellow, red and blue of the Passion burst upon her like a dream. She thought she could hear birds chirupping from beyond the stained-glass panes and the sunlight straggled through in flames and rays, illuminating motes of dust like messages from heaven. Messages from heaven. She knelt behind a row of ancient backs, some crippled with arthritis and rheumatism yet still proud and straight for as long they needed to be; and she felt a wave of shame wash over her. The altar cloths were white and gold for Christmas and heart necklets decorated the altar of the Virgin. She avoided looking at the one where masses for the dead were held and fought to gain an interior silence. Beside her a nun threw coarse salt on the ground to torture her knees even further and Bernadine recognised her as the old abbess who'd been brought to the convent for shelter. They'd found her in the library, cutting up rare and illuminated manuscripts because the glowing gold of the parchment had seemed to her like a sin against poverty. Now she had the air of a small child, laughing and singing with her coarse salt and calloused knees. She might have been building sandcastles or watching a Punch and Judy show.

The words of the psalm were quite lost to Bernadine, she couldn't sing the devotions or pray – her conscience troubled her too much – and when she closed her eyes the only face she saw was Aggie's, pale and wet, and the tiny blue baby's beseeching eyes. She struggled to remember her favourite psalm from Tierce. *I lift up my eyes to the mountains… He shall not let thy foot slip. The sun shall not burn thee by day nor the moon by night. The Lord shall keep thee from all evil.*

She was out of step with the others, quite out of step and she thought they must be aware of it. Once, just once she felt the eyes of the old abbess upon her, eerily calm and smiling as if she knew everything, understood everything, and then they turned away. The Lord lets happen what has to happen, they seemed to say, at least they did in Bernadine's imagination. Her imagination attributed the words to the nun who'd gone mad in the library, cutting up her rare and illuminated manuscripts into inch-thick pieces. The Lord lets happen what has to happen. In the old days she would have believed it but not now. Now her mind spoke the words but her heart did not, they had an empty, hollow ring to them. Her lack of faith dawned on her with the clarity of daylight; and as the Sisters lifted their hearts all together for the *Deo Gratias*, she sat a sinner amidst a sea of worthy souls, a wolf in sheep's clothing, a hypocrite. The confessional stood in the shadows like the outlines of a sentry box, beside the bell rope, knotted and black from greasy hands. How many times had Father Stephen sat in there nibbling on a tablet of chocolate to keep his strength up for the inevitable list of petty slips, vanities and misdemeanours that waged war in the souls of the perfect nuns. How many times had real secrets of the soul passed from lip to ear, been understood, forgiven? She wondered how she could have gone on so long believing herself to be forgiven, believing she was living in accordance with the Holy Rule when all the time her body and soul raged against it.

She bowed her head and cried out from the *De Profundis. Out of the depths I cry to thee, O Lord. Do not forsake me now.* The words echoed in her head but there came no reply. No reply but the murmur of nuns like a drone of bees and the boom of guns in the distance like an Almighty reprimand. They filed out, one by one, flat as shadows or blackened ghosts and Bernadine noticed that the shoes of the old abbess were torn and misshapen at the toe from the press of praying. Her heart cried out within her. Humility was endless here. Humility was endless. She crept past the Passion with the self effacement of a gnat, catching sight of the Mother Superior who wafted towards her like a zephyr breeze and whispered softly in her ear, so softly Bernadine thought she might have been dreaming.

'No keeping! No redeeming. No keeping! No redeeming.'

And the boom of guns again in the distance, an Almighty reprimand.

Chapter nine

The queue for Potin's was swelling by the moment despite the hour, the drizzle and the drear, half-leaden light of the morning. Smiles were wan but resolute, umbrellas up – a sea of stripes in the sombre light – and metal soup tins glimmered in straw baskets, over arms and in red, frozen hands. Here and there a bayonet stuck up in the air, jagged and fearsome in between the umbrellas, indicating the presence of a National Guardsman bundled up and on duty to ensure fair play, an equal distribution of rations and to quell the fights that commonly broke out between the women. Fights that could turn uncommonly vicious, for the women used anything that came to hand: nails, teeth, handkerchiefs, even the spokes of their umbrellas. It was a standing joke amongst the Guardsmen that you had a better chance in arm-to-arm combat with a Prussian than with a woman in the queue for Potin's. Some had been there since midnight, taking it in turns with friends and relations who brought hip flasks, cocoa, mufflers and foot warmers. It was a dirty trick, a ruse, and a source of great aggravation to the women who had no hip flasks or cocoa, no chairs or foot warmers and no friends or relations to relieve them.

Eveline slipped into line behind a woman in a shawl and a servant's cap, with a little straw basket at her feet. She'd been standing there less than a minute when a smartly dressed woman came up behind in a muffler, *bottines* and wearing an amethyst necklace which reminded Eveline temptingly of a string of candied violets. She wondered why such a smartly dressed woman would be waiting in line and stared hard at the necklace. Perhaps it was paste. People did all sorts to gain respect and curry favour from the men who doled out the rations. It was not uncommon for women to offer themselves up for a scrag end of meat and bushel of potatoes. No subterfuge was too small. Everybody's need was greater than the next: an invalid back home, an ailing mother in law, a tiny baby, a delicate heart. There were those who trickled up and down the line, trying to jostle in higher up, preying on the weak willed, the gullible, the foolish and the holy. The nuns (or the holy crows) came off the worst, too saintly to push themselves forward, too trusting not to trust; and they ended up at the back, a little dark cloud, waiting to snatch up the leftover crumbs. Eveline felt a little sorry for them, they looked so thin and miserable, halfway to heaven already.

The woman in front stood dogged and immobile as a rock. Eveline tapped her on the shoulder.

'Any word yet?' she whispered.

'Just soup.' The woman peeked a currant-bun face out of her cap.

Soup, yes. There was always soup. They'd had soup up to the gills. Watery nonsense with something inedible floating around on the top.

'Nothing else?'

'Not yet,' the woman replied curtly as if she didn't want to be distracted from her mission.

Eveline stamped her feet and blew on her hands, wishing she'd brought an umbrella. The rut she was standing in was deepening by the second as drizzle dotted holes in the dirty old snow. Never mind, the shutters would be coming off soon and the line would get going. She stood on tiptoe, craning to see above the brightly coloured umbrellas and the hooded heads of Guardsmen. Suddenly, without warning, the queue surged forward and she almost lost her footing as the smartly dressed woman behind stepped on her heels in her high-heeled boots. A sea of umbrellas sheered off to the left like a serpentine wave or herd of sheep as a dozen or so women broke line and stampeded down the pavement in the direction of the Luxembourg. A rumour had started. Now and then a rumour started like a Chinese whisper and the women got wind of it, got the scent in their nostrils of something edible going cheap somewhere in the city. A boulangerie in the Salpêtrière selling croissants and buns for a franc a piece. Roos on Haussmann letting go fresh crabs and chitterlings for the price of old socks. She waited to see what it was this time and pretty soon word came down the line: smoked herrings from a grocer in the Madeleine. Two National Guardsmen had paraded a couple on the ends of their bayonets so it must be true. You could hear brains ticking out loud as women weighed up the risk of heading off for a chance of smoked herring – smoked herring for Christmas. What a feat! – with the safe bet of the queue. Those new to the job, more daring or simply gullible broke the line and ran off after the others while the old hands and those too tired or worn out to move, stayed put. At first, Eveline had dashed off at the slightest cry or excited murmur, but more often than not it ended in a goose chase; even if there had been any truth to the rumour in the first place, by the time you arrived all that was left was a greasy wishbone. She had learnt to stand her ground, firm and resolute amidst the hysteria and commotion. Herrings were tempting, but not tempting enough to get her to budge.

The desertion had caused quite a stir in the ranks: voices were raised, umbrellas flapped, soup tins rattled and banged like a collection of tambourines. What was the hold up? Why weren't the shutters off? The sun must be halfway up the yard by now. Squabbles broke out up and down the line as women accused each other of taking the opportunity to get ahead of them in the queue.

'And you're no better than you should be!' Eveline heard a shrill voice cry out, presumably at the nun who was wandering up and down the line with a vacant air, begging for milk.

'Any milk, madame? I have spices to exchange: cayenne pepper and black, turmeric and cinnamon.'

Most people looked straight ahead, pretending deaf and dumbness but it was so rare to see a nun walking up the line that Eveline met her eyes when she passed. She recognised her as a Sister from St Joseph's. She looked like a statue of the Madonna with her chestnut curls escaping her veil, her huge brown eyes black ringed, soft white skin stretched tight about the bones of her face. Bernadine, for her part, had recognised Eveline Renan, the stonecutter's daughter, and wondered as she always did how such a man could have fathered such a beautiful, fresh-faced girl then said a few Aves in repentance.

'Any milk, mademoiselle?' the nun asked gently. 'I have spices to exchange.'

Eveline shook her head. 'I have no milk, I'm afraid, but I will exchange if there is some today.'

'Thank you,' smiled the nun and carried on up the line. Eveline stared after her, wondering why a nun should need milk so badly.

At last the shutters were off and a shout went down the line.

Peas!

Carrots!

Spuds!

The words flew down the line like golden juggling balls or a magical incantation.

Peas!

Carrots!

Spuds!

And then to top it all, the word beef. Some yelled it, some whispered it in awe or disbelief.

BEEF!

BEEF?

Beef!

Beef?

A frisson of excitement went through the women. Everybody's thoughts were on beef: gravy, stews, broiled, roasted, jellies, sauces, horseradish cream, beef tea, beef suet… What a Christmas they would have! Those idiots who rushed off for a measly herring! And then, just as quickly, following the frisson of excitement came a frisson of fear. Would there be any beef left by the time *they* got there? And then the jostling began in earnest, the prodding, jabbing, poking… as women parried for position like jockeys. The high-heeled boots were doing some real damage to Eveline's ankles and she wanted to turn round and smack the smartly dressed woman but she kept her patience. The one in front was solid as a rock, dogged and determined, not giving an inch but not taking an inch either. And then just as quickly the word came down the line.

No beef. Beetroot!

The woman in front turned her currant-bun face to Eveline. 'No beef?' she said incredulously. 'But they said beef.'

'They lied,' someone cackled drily.

'But they said beef. How can they be so wicked?' asked the woman, looking quite disheartened.

'Yes,' Eveline said gently. 'I think there was a misunderstanding. They meant beetroot.'

'Beetroot?' repeated the woman, nonplussed. 'But they said beef.' Her face crumpled up and she wept. 'Auguste loves his beef so. It would have done his heart good.' And she picked up her little straw basket and stumped off out of the queue, her cap wobbling in disbelief.

'Wait,' cried Eveline. 'There's still soup… and carrots… and potatoes.' But the woman didn't turn back, she who had seemed as resolute as a rock had been knocked for six by an empty promise of beef.

By the time Eveline got to the front, there wasn't even beetroot left, just soup – watery nonsense with something inedible floating around on the top – and a potato. She watched the brawny arms spoon it into her tin from the great tureens, glad to be getting that at least. As she turned away, a young woman standing by the hatch handed her a card and she took it automatically before realising it was the girl who'd spoken the other day about the women's battalions.

'White railings. End of terrace. Next Tuesday,' the girl whispered after her. 'We'll show the men how it's done!'

Eveline glanced at the card in surprise. It was thick and black rimmed and printed on the front in delicate calligraphy it said: *Elizabeth T, Paradis, 2 Rue de Turbigo.*

And on the back the words: *Malheureuse la femme qui fonde sur les hommes son appui*[8]. It was a quotation of a sort. Eveline recognised it dimly but was unable to place it. Laurie would know of course but she wouldn't ask him. She slipped the card into her pocket, feeling proud and a little guilty. It was like being invited to join a secret society. The girls on the Rue Ornano and la Païva must get invitations like this all the time: cards for balls, luncheons, dinner parties and dances where the women whispered behind their fans, the men got drunk on champagne, where there were chandeliers and crystal vases, caviar and waltzes…

She swept down towards the Seine, swinging her tin and feeling quite happy: glad she had held out for the soup at least. She loved the river. It exerted a fascination over her as presumably it had for her mother, though Eveline had no intention of drowning herself in it. She loved the way it shone like a pewter mirror when the sun hit it. She even loved the fog that came off it: warm and enveloping like a great yellow overcoat, making you feel that you were strangely invisible. In the old days when she had time to spare, she had browsed among the stalls in the parapets that sold bird seed and liquorice water, parasols and shoelaces. Or sat beneath the rusty old arches of the Pont Royal, playing ducks and drakes in the greasy dark water and listening to the rumble of the omnibuses and wagonettes above her. There was always something to see on the water: flotillas of skiffs and dinghies, laundry boats with their great tall chimneys, barges laden with coal and bright golden apples. Now they were laden with cannon, and the little 'flies' and 'swallows' that had steamed up and down on jaunty trips with the visitors and tourists now steamed up and down with the wounded.

Or she used to go licking windows as Laurie put it, staring at the 'confections pour les dames' – the silk, satin and taffettas in the big department stores and despising herself a little for doing it. Now she was licking windows for real, sniffing out titbits and morsels to eat in the most unlikely of places. One woman had found a dozen eggs in a jeweller's shop displayed like a necklace of great white pearls. Another had found a bit of leathery pork in the back of a shoe shop! You just had to keep your eyes peeled and your nose to the wind. Her favourite hunting ground was the back of a good restaurant which was why she was heading in the direction of Brébant's. It occurred to her that Alphonse might be there but she didn't follow that line of thought too closely. She simply concentrated her mind on the rich pickings that were to be found in the bins amongst the old corks and parings – a bunch of radishes perhaps, some fried potatoes, a bit of black sausage in silver paper.

The sun was coming up now, trickling through the clouds and drizzle. Soon it would set the whole city alight, scooting over rooftops, down chimneys, through cracks and crannies until even the panes of Notre Dame caught flame and the carved suns on the Tuileries burnt red hot. Newspaper sellers were setting up their stalls along the bank, crying out the day's news in their husky early morning voices.

'*Eugene! Ses amants! Ses orgies!* Read all about it!'

'Our boys take the Rhine!'

Eveline smiled grimly to herself, not believing a word of it. There was always some tittle tattle about the old Empress – she'd had more lovers than la Païva by the sounds of it; and 'our boys' had taken the Rhine three times already that week. She wondered sometimes who wrote the nonsense in the papers and for what purpose, for it rarely seemed to have any bearing on reality; though perhaps it was better to read fiction than to read nothing at all.

Even before she turned the corner of the Poisonnière the odour of wine hit her nostrils and puffs of music twisted through the air. The revellers were still at it, stuffing their faces on hot, rich food, guzzling their vintage wines by the casket. Alphonse had told her it was the upper echelons that frequented Brébant's: the aristocrats and bankers, politicians and generals – the generals being apparently the most decadent of the bunch. She should have gone straight round to the back but she couldn't resist taking a look at the Christmas menu. She crept up to the front door which was decorated on either side with a dusty oleander in a majolica pot and scanned the menu.

Truffles à la Gazelle
Skate in black butter
Sardines with lemon
Tenderloin of turnip
Corned beef with tomatoes and cranberries

Preserved green corn
Roast chicken and peas
Salad

Peaches in syrup
Pumpkin pie
Macaroons
Nougat cherries
Chocolate plums
Café noir

Below the menu, a yellowing cutting from a newspaper recommended Brébant's as a first-class restaurant offering great wines, prime meat, early vegetables and delicate fish. And a satisfied customer had written: 'I defy any customer to try the "purée Brébant" without thinking they've died and gone to heaven.'

She was just wondering if the corned beef and pumpkin pie were destined for the American contingent of the city when she heard the proprietor's voice close at hand.

'What the hell was it? The Marquis can crack a peach stone with those teeth of his but that rubbish you brought yesterday was even too tough for him.'

'Can he now?' came Alphonse's dry response.

Eveline's heart jumped.

'Well, what was it for God's sake?'

'Dog.'

'Dog?'

'Yes dog. A big, fat mongrel to be precise.'

She didn't wait to hear any more. She slipped down the steps and through the cobbled arch and into the yard where the carriages were kept. A group of children like a bunch of noisy pilfering sparrows were hanging about by the bins, chuckling over one or two nuggets they'd discovered. They were dressed in rags, little more than skin and bone and her heart went out to them. She stepped back, letting them take their share. One bent a curious watchful eye on her then, deciding she was friendly, went back to its bin picking. A moment later Alphonse came round the corner with a pan of scraps – scraps left, no doubt, on the plates of the upper echelons. At the sight of him the sparrows rushed over, whooping and crying out in delight; and he placed the huge pan on the ground for them, laughing as their hands, faces and then practically their bodies disappeared into it.

'They know you,' Eveline said by way of greeting, stepping out of the shadows of the yard.

'Mouse!' smiled Alphonse looking quite unsurprised to see her there. 'How are you today?'

She suddenly felt close to bursting into tears, seeing him there in front of her; and she thought the argument with Laurie must have upset her more than she had realised.

'You look quite white.'

'I'm alright,' she stammered and then by way of distraction, before she could stop herself, she brought out the card and held it up to him. 'I'm thinking of joining a women's battalion.'

'Why ever not?' he responded after looking at it thoughtfully. 'Eveline brave and beautiful, a modern day Joan of Arc. We should all admire you. You would be decorated no doubt. Laurie would write a sonnet for you!'

'Oh Laurie!' She coloured furiously. 'He's against it. My role is to look after Papa and Jacques apparently. For the rest of my life.'

'Your father!' exclaimed Alphonse. 'That drunken sot! He's old and ugly enough to look after himself. As for Jacques, the more scrapes the merrier at his age. You're a slave in that place. Break free while you've got the chance. Else you'll be a little mouse forever,' he teased, his eyes twinkling.

Eveline stamped her foot and her hair fell out of her blue chenille all over her shoulders. 'I hate it! D'you know what I saw Papa doing the other day,' she confided suddenly, pink with embarrassment. 'He was going up and down the Rue de Rivoli begging for money with a bandage around his head and a pair of ears in a jar of wine. He kept saying the "barbarous Prussians" had sliced them off. It's shameful!'

'No it's not,' Alphonse grinned. 'It's ingenious! It's good to see he's still got a spark in that befuddled head of his!'

She smiled weakly up at him. His face was in shadow but she thought that he was staring at her, as she in fact was staring at him. Staring at him and wishing (as she realised with a jolt she often wished) that she could take Laurie's heart and soul and place them inside Alphonse's muscular torso.

'Does he still write you those poems?' he asked a little gruffly then, meaning Laurie.

'Sometimes. Why?'

'I'd give you more than poems,' he replied, bending down and kissing her on the cheek, then standing back and laughing as if he'd gone too far.

Eveline laughed too, and blushed, not knowing if he was joking because he was a friend of Laurie's and besides which, you just couldn't tell with Alphonse. Eveybody loved him but nobody knew him. Not really. That was half the attraction she supposed. Everybody wanted to know him.

'Will you come to watch Jacques?' she cried impulsively, deciding then and there that she didn't want to be alone with Laurie that day. 'We're going to see him balloon training!'

Alphonse nodded. 'Of course. I had better see him once more before we lose him to the moon!' He turned to go and then stopped as if a thought had suddenly occurred to him. 'By the way, where did he get the ears? They're not his own I take it?'

Eveline giggled. 'Oh no, his own are still on his head!'

And they burst out laughing together in the sunlight of the dirty back yard for the sheer joy of laughing, the noisy sparrows still pilfering at their feet.

Chapter ten

'Passengers for the two-fifteen to Moon City,' sang a dapper little man in a station master's cap, a whistle round his neck and ticket-collecting bag on his arm. 'The two-fifteen to Moon City departing from Platform Six and calling at Cloud Nine, Freeze Your Toes Off, Heaven's Gate and Rainbow's End!'

Laurie looked at Eveline who looked at Alphonse who laughed. Was the man an escaped lunatic? No trains ran any more from the Gare du Nord. The city was sealed off so even if they *had* left the station they'd have just gone chugging around in circles. Besides which, the rails were rusted over, with grass and weeds growing merrily in between.

'He obviously has too much time on his hands!' smiled Alphonse as they stepped into the waiting room then almost stepped out again in astonishment. Had they got the wrong place? This wasn't a waiting room. It looked more like a shipbuilding yard with a horde of brawny sailors heave-ho'ing over nets and ropes, sandbags and calicoes, their bulging forearms glistening with tattoos and sweat. It was very hot and full of a hammering din and the stink of varnish. The little café where passengers had once sat idly drinking tea and tasting dainties had been converted into a paint shop with pots and pots of glues and varnishes lined up on the shelves where the pastries had lived. A woman still sat behind the counter however, pencil and paper in her hand as if waiting to take an order for a pot of mocha and toasted scone. A group of sailors on the floor in front of her were in the middle of constructing a wicker basket like a giant picnic hamper and she stared at them sullenly now and then as if she held them personally responsible for the dreadful transformation.

It was all so extraordinary that Eveline found herself wanting to giggle and she turned away from Alphonse and Laurie lest they see her. It was a serious matter after all – the balloon factory – yet how could you not see the funny side. Outside was a man selling tickets for the moon, inside a group of sailors in a picnic basket and a woman in a café of glue! No wonder Jacques loved it. It was just like one of those fairy tales she'd read to him when he was younger with their giants and spells, witches and magic potions. She half expected him to appear in a puff of smoke and he obliged her suddenly, on cue as usual, though without the puff of smoke.

'Hi, you three,' he grinned, his red hair standing up from his impish face. 'Ready for the big tour?'

Alphonse patted him on the head, Laurie said 'lead on' and Eveline took his hand a little protectively. She couldn't believe he didn't get lost in such a place though he'd been coming here for as long as she could remember (when the Gare du Nord really was the Gare du Nord), obsessed with trains, wheels and anything that went fast, now obsessed with anything that flew. He stood there grinning, pleased as punch to have the adults under his command so to speak, especially Alphonse, and began in a grown-up, almost earnest little voice.

'I see you have met Mathilde.' He indicated the woman behind the counter. 'She takes the orders for the pots of glues and paints that are used to repair and varnish the balloons. She is very metikluss about the orders; and she knows how much each balloon soaks up – some are tougher skinned than others she says.'

They all looked at the woman who stared back at them sullenly.

'And you must have met the flight master at the front.'

So that was the little man who sang about the moon.

'He produces the flight timetables and checks the meter-logical readings every week… sailors are often used,' he whispered as they went past a bunch of sea-creased faces bent over a net big enough to catch a whale, 'because they don't suffer from air sickness and the high attitudes! Hi Pipington,' he called out to one of the sailors who was tying a bit of rope to the net.

'Hi Renan!' The grey-haired old man winked at him. 'How are your air legs coming along?'

'Not too bad,' Jacques replied with an air of importance. 'Not too bad at all.'

Eveline caught Laurie's eye, trying not to giggle but Alphonse frowned at them both and remarked that it was all very interesting, very interesting indeed.

They followed Jacques into the ticket office which was now a temporary post office. Laurie took an especial interest in this for it was here that the letters to his mother began their strange and perilous journey. Women in blue uniforms were charging about with stacks and stacks of letters and postcards, parcels and packages: sorting, stamping, filing, coding... they all seemed to know Jacques, greeting him with pats, nods, pinches and smiles, treating him like a little pet dog. One of them even offered him a cookie which, to Eveline's surprise, he declined with a solemn shake of the head. He was full of facts and figures about the whole process.

'One balloon can carry four people and twelve hundred pounds of mail,' he told them, 'which is equivalent to one hundred thousand letters.'

Eveline wondered if he were making the figures up as he made up excuses to evade the washing up or making his bed and she stared at him suspiciously, on the look out for the telltale twitch of the left eye; but he seemed innocent enough, his pupils bright and steady.

'The guvverment pays four thousand francs to the factory for every delivery and three hundred of that goes to the pilot of the balloon.'

'Blimey!' cried Alphonse, scratching his head and ignoring the interested glances of the more youthful postmistresses. 'I'm in the wrong job!'

Jacques grinned and suddenly put a finger to his lips. 'Can you hear that?' he demanded, pointing to the small blue door at the back of the room.

What? They all strained their ears but nobody could hear anything except the hustle and bustle of the women.

Jacques gestured for them to come closer and they followed him to the door and pressed their ears against it. 'Can you hear it?'

What?

'That!'

Then they heard it – a soft gentle cooing sound like the babbling of brooks or faraway lullabies.

'Those are the pigeons that will go tonight,' he explained in an excited murmur. 'They come from the Jardin des Plantes and wait here for the midnight flight. I will ask Monsieur Pagini if we may see them. He doesn't usually like them to be disturbed before an important mission.' He knocked softly on the little blue door then disappeared inside. They heard muffled voices for a moment and then he came out again. 'You may come in but you must take your shoes off.'

It was like entering an Indian temple where the laws and customs were very different from their own. What would Monsieur Pagini have them do next? They slipped off their boots and shoes, Eveline hoping desperately there weren't any visible holes in her stockings; and crept in through the small blue door. It took a while for their eyes to get accustomed to the light because the manager's office (for that was what it was) had been blackened out with crêpe paper and only a tiny portion of light trickled through a gap in the window. It was warm and stuffy with a faint musty odour; but quiet and strangely peaceful as the birds cooed and rustled in their straw-filled boxes. The figure of a man could just be seen perched on a stool in front of the window.

'Monsieur Pagini,' Jacques began, 'these are my friends Alphonse and Laurie and my sister, Eveline.'

'Good day.' Monsieur Pagini greeted them in a low, gravelly voice. 'May I ask first of all if any one of you has a cat, mouse, lettuce leaf or bar of chocolate upon you. Any or all of these will send Alice into a flap.'

No one wanted Alice (whoever she was) to go into a flap and they all vehemently denied having any such thing in their pocket; though Alphonse joked he'd give anything to have a bar of chocolate in his. A burst of nervous laughter greeted this, followed by a slightly embarrassed silence.

Jacques proceeded to tell them about the pigeons. They went out as cargo with the balloons and flew back with letters and messages from the rest of the world. These messages were reduced in size so that each bird could carry up to thirty thousand of them tied to his tail feathers.

'Old Neptune,' Monsieur Pagini interrupted proudly, 'brought back the news that Gambetta had arrived safely. It was his first successful flight. He is a bird of noble lineage. That night I got him his favourite dish of worms and honey.'

Everyone aahed and uummed with interest at this. The bird in question was pointed out, made much of and seemed to puff up a bit on all the attention. Like a *cocodette's* bosom, Alphonse remarked amusedly – an observation which didn't go down too well with Monsieur Pagini who huffed and ruffled up angrily on his stool.

'It is a very inervative proceedure,' Jacques went on quickly, with great diplomacy. 'These reduced messages are then taken to the Rue de Grenelle and read by magic lantern.'

Eveline listened in growing astonishment. It really was like stepping into a fairytale. Letters taken out by balloon, brought back by pigeon then read by magic lantern.

'The pigeon is a sacred bird,' Monsieur Pagini announced solemnly then. 'If I catch anyone dreaming of pigeon pie they'll feel the back of my hand.' And even in the darkness he could be seen to be looking in the direction of Alphonse.

'Do many of them make a successful return journey, sir?' Laurie asked then, sensibly and suitably deferential.

'That depends,' Monsieur Pagini replied thoughtfully. 'Peter, for example,' he pointed to a box next to Neptune, 'is easily waylaid. He is an idler, a flâneur if you like. He would go into every shop if you let him. Alice on the other hand,' he pointed to another box in the corner, 'is a gourmande. She knows the only place she will get a cabbage leaf and a bar of chocolate is back home and she flies direct, in time for supper. Poor little Squeak, however, is nervy and picky as a woman with child. He needs a great deal of encouragement but he shows promise. I tell them all to beware of anything with a Saxon plumage.'

'The Prussians train hawks to kill them,' Jacques explained.

'How beastly,' cried Eveline.

'Yes, it is war,' Monsieur Pagini replied calmly. 'There is always war especially in the human kingdom.' And he told them a little of his life history: how he had always felt more akin to birds than boys; how he had run away from home to sleep in the treetops; how there was nothing like the feeling of seeing a bird return.

'I can imagine,' said Laurie. 'You give them their freedom and then they come back to you.'

Monsieur Pagini nodded sadly. 'Yes, though some never return. That is their choice. You only ever see them again in your dreams.'

Jacques had so much to show them and wanted to get on before the practice flight to Moon City at two-fifteen. He led them down the corridor to Platform One and it was strange to see the dusty cushions from the trains piled high in corners with nobody to sit on them; and torn old posters on the walls advertising day trips to Champigny, Passy, Compiègne. How long had it been since anyone had been on a day trip to Compiègne?

A sober mood fell on the group as they descended to the rails, the din getting louder as they approached. Two men walked by deep in conversation, and Jacques pulled up, trembling with excitement though he refused to say anything until they were out of earshot.

'That,' he cried when they had turned the corner, a gleam of adulation in his eye, 'was Etienne and La Montain!' He stopped, as if they should know what he was talking about.

'Go on!'

'Etienne and La Montain! Etienne fell out of the *Celestial* and landed in a swamp just outside Paris. He lay there for hours with bullets skimming over his head then managed to escape over enemy lines by disguising himself as a cowherd. La Montain took a consignment of dynamite to Bourbaki's army[9] and got paid a thousand franc bonus for doing it.'

'Blimey,' said Alphonse. 'I really am in the wrong job!'

Jacques' eyes glimmered darkly. 'Yes you are,' he said in a strange determined little voice which caused Eveline to look at him sharply. 'Anyone who is not a balloonist is in the wrong job.'

Platform One was a spectacle. Trestle tables ran up and down the length of it, covered in bolts and bolts of cloth that were being stitched together by a score of women, some with machines, some by hand. The work produced a steady hum like the spinning of old spinning wheels or a hive of industrious bees stitching a magnificent trousseau for their queen. Orange-shaped segments of cloth were hanging from the iron-columned aisles and swayed in the breeze like banners in a cathedral.

'Is it true,' Eveline whispered to Jacques, 'that society women have given up their silk and taffetta dresses for the enterprise?' She rather liked the idea of a bunch of society women's dresses flying through the air like witches on broomsticks.

'No,' Jacques replied. 'That is a myth. They are made with cotton then varnished.'

Partially inflated balloons lay stretched out on the rusted rails between the platforms, tethered to old gas lamps. Everyone gasped at the sight of them, peering over the platform edge. Eveline thought they looked like a bunch of giant mushrooms; Alphonse said no, more like a row of whales and Laurie was moved to declaim a verse from Victor Hugo:

Human audacity…
To tame the wind, tornado, sea-foam, avalanche?
In the sky a canvas, and over the sea a shelf!

'Each balloon has a capacity of seventy-thousand cubic feet,' Jacques informed them sternly. 'And consumes the equivalent of seven tons of gas.'

'No wonder we don't have any street lighting left!' grinned Alphonse.

Jacques hustled them on; though they were held up on the way out by a commotion going on in what appeared to be a broom cupboard.

'The Professor is writing in the air again,' shouted a sailor, carrying a sandbag of ballast.

'The Professor is trying to design a steerable balloon,' Jacques explained. 'It causes him great aggravation.'

They joined the crowd, eager to catch a glimpse of the Professor. They saw a large man in an ill-fitting frock coat, surrounded by boxes and a hat-like contraption on his head. He was writing in the air with a stub of pencil.

'Oh dear,' sighed Jacques. 'He writes in the air when he is angry or out of paper.'

'They say he has a great mind yet he lives in a ménage à trois,' a seamstress chipped in with an edge of malevolence.

'He has been to Zanzibar,' another piped up.

'I don't know about all that but he is exceedingly tiresome,' said another.

Oh?

'He is English.'

Ah! They needed no other explanation. They beat a silent and hasty retreat but not silent or hasty enough for the Professor suddenly burst out of his broom cupboard.

'Balloons!' he thundered after them. 'Just like women. Fickle and full of gas. They soar above you all high and mighty, radiant with beauty but when you climb aboard and they've got you in their clutches that's a different story. You see their true colours then alright. They burp and fart just like the rest of us. Not to mention temperament! Up and down, up and down, round and round till you're giddy as a ruddy kipper. Design a decent woman and in my opinion you've got yourself a decent balloon!'

'I'm inclined to agree,' laughed Alphonse as they staggered down the corridor. 'Fickle and full of gas!' He eyed Eveline wickedly and she smiled back gratefully. Thank goodness he'd come along. It would have been unbearable without him. She and Laurie had hardly exchanged a word all afternoon; he'd just sent her the occasional sidelong glance full of self-pity and despair. Sometimes she wanted to shake him and she enquired now in a challenging voice: 'What do *you* think Laurie? Are we all fickle?'

He coloured up to the roots of his fair hair. 'I suppose I must defend womanhood from the professors and the... politicians. If they are fickle it is because we make them so.'

'Defend away! Defend away!' cried Alphonse. 'But it won't alter the facts!'

'The Professor is not that bad,' Jacques said then in a just tone. 'Sometimes he tells me about his ménagerie à trois and how it upsets him.'

The three adults stared at the boy. He was teaching them a lesson today and no mistake!

Next up was Platform Six: the two-fifteen practice flight to Moon

City. The Conductor stood brass-buttoned and uniformed, issuing orders and shepherding sailors to their positions. Two baskets hung from the girders, suspended on a pulley system that was being operated by a group of men hanging about on Platform Seven. One or two onlookers cheered and catcalled, geeing on the practice pilots but the Conductor scowled and bade them be quiet or be off. Eveline expressed alarm as she watched Jacques line up behind a brawny sailor.

'I thought you just watched the practice flights,' she cried, tugging at his arm.

'Oh no, Sis,' the imp beamed back at her. 'If there's a man down I step in for the day.'

'Two at a time,' called the Conductor, going up and down the line, checking the baskets as the men on Platform Seven brought them level with Platform Six. They were kitted out with grapnel rope, anchor, sandbags of ballast, all the equipment needed to replicate a real balloon – though there was no envelope above the basket, of course, and no valve lines. The Conductor brought out a little green flag.

'Everybody ready?'

The men on Platform Seven responded with another little green flag.

Eveline watched nervously as the sailor stepped into the basket followed closely by Jacques. The car spun sickeningly for a minute, then settled. The sailor had crouched down immediately, too perilously tall for the basket whereas Jacques could stand quite happily upright, his shoulders just reaching the edges. He waved and beamed at them, thumbing his nose at Alphonse then turning serious as the Conductor approached.

'Mathers and Renan, we are about to ascend. What do we do, Mathers?'

The sailor rubbed his nose thoughtfully. 'Throw out the anchor,' he suggested.

'Throw out the anchor!' cried the Conductor. 'Alright then, try it.'

Poor old Mathers heaved the anchor out of a large canvas bag and lowered it – all fifty feet of it – over the side of the car until it clanged on the rails. At a sign from the Conductor the men on Platform Seven let out the rope and the basket descended with a bump to the ground.

'Oh dear, oh dear!' The Conductor peered down at them. 'Is that what you did on board ship, Mathers? Drop the anchor and ascend among the coral reefs?'

'No sir.'

'Renan, what do we do to ascend?'

'Throw out Mathers,' Jacques replied cheekily, 'I mean ballast.'

'Right then, off you go.'

Jacques threw out a sandbag and the balloon gently ascended until it was halfway up between the platform and the girders. It spun a little as they all looked up at it.

'You've gone a little too high, Mathers. What would you do to correct it?'

'Sit still and don't move!' the sailor replied nervously, his nose just visible over the basket.

The Conductor sighed and gestured to the men on Platform Seven. The basket spun and jerked from side to side until Mathers' nose looked decidedly green.

'Renan?'

Jacques pulled an imaginary valve line. 'Lose a little gas, sir.'

'Correct.' The balloon dipped slightly. 'You are above the clouds, Renan, please describe what you see.'

Jacques called out over the basket in a clear confident voice. 'I am at about ten thousand feet. If it is daylight I shall see the shadow of the balloon against the clouds. If it is night I shall see only blackness. The barrow-meter will have lowered because the tempitcha of the air will have grown cooler. I must not remain in cloud too long for fear of vapours adding weight to the balloon.'

'How does he know all this?' Laurie asked in a whisper and Eveline shrugged her shoulders. Could this be Jacques whom the Brothers despaired of ever teaching the catechism? Jacques who made excuses to evade the washing up and making his bed? Jacques who carved his autograph on the legs of the school desk and stowed half-eaten apples in the spine of his spelling book? She felt proud yet a little guilty: she hadn't ever really listened to him when he warbled on about the balloons, too busy with her own cares and concerns.

'He's a natural,' said Alphonse, thumbing his nose at the little urchin in the air.

The Conductor fixed his eye on Mathers. 'You've had to land in a violent storm. How do you deflate the balloon all at once to stop it dragging you away to certain death?'

'Throw out the grapnel rope, sir,' said Mathers with utmost confidence. 'Throw out the grapnel.'

From the look on the Conductor's face it was obviously the wrong answer. Laurie felt a little sorry for the man crouched up there in his basket. It must be very confusing being spun and pulled in all directions. He knew for a fact he wouldn't want to do it.

'What was your rank in the navy, Mathers?' the Conductor asked in a wondering voice.

'Cook, sir. Head cook and bottle washer.'

'Ah... what on earth made you want to volunteer for this then?'

'It crossed my mind that on the long flights the men might get a bit peckish, sir.'

'And what would you propose doing about it? Start a cooking fire up there with a couple of sticks?'

'I hope I'd have the foresight to take matches, sir.'

'D'you know what inflammable means, Mathers?' The Conductor asked, his face quite purple.

'Yessir. It means it can float, sir!'

'Oh, so the boats you sailed in were all inflammable, were they?'

'I should hope so, sir. Else I wouldn't be here to tell the tale, would I sir?'

It was the final straw. The Conductor gestured to the men on Platform Seven and the basket suddenly started spinning, revolving like a te-to-tum, a monster peg top. Even the onlookers went dizzy just looking at it; though Jacques' beaming face went round and round, riding his airborne merry-go-round.

'Feeling peckish now, Mathers?' the Conductor shouted up a little unkindly.

'No sir,' came a sheepish reply from up above though nothing could be seen of the sailor – he was presumably lying prone and green at the bottom of the basket. After a few more moments spinning, the Conductor took pity on them and had them brought back to earth. Jacques gave the sailor a helping hand out of the basket and he swayed off down the platform, harried on by a jeering crowd.

'Get a good co-pilot,' advised the Conductor, patting Jacques on the back, 'and you'll do just fine.' And he went off to train the other balloonists while Jacques pretended a nonchalance under the downpour of praise and hearty thumps, though his eyes gleamed bright with triumph.

The three of them left the Gare du Nord not knowing what to say. They were silent with awe and respect, a new found respect for the extraordinary balloons and the people who worked with them: the industrious women who stitched, the varnishers and sailors, pigeons and professors; for the pilots who braved the enemy and the elements and last but not least for Jacques who had changed before their eyes from a boy into a man. Eveline was especially thoughtful, and slightly abashed that even her brother was doing something interesting and exciting. It was she who still lived in a fairytale, not him.

'You've done a wonderful job with Jacques, Evie,' Laurie said kindly as though he could read her thoughts; but it wasn't what she wanted to hear and she couldn't even bring herself to acknowledge what he said or smile back at him.

Chapter eleven

Monsieur Lafayette was first to arrive with a potted geranium, a crate of cherry brandy and a tin of 'surprises'. He was dressed up in a blue waistcoat and an absurdly high, ruffled collar which made him look like an ancient schoolboy. Eveline exclaimed over the geranium and placed it centre stage of the table – it gave the whole room a festive air. She was pleased with the results of her efforts. Everything sparkled. Everything shone. And the gold braid she'd stitched to the bottom of the tablecloth worked a treat.

'You look beautiful, Eveline,' Monsieur Lafayette said admiringly.

'Thank you,' she replied graciously. 'Is father not with you?'

'Er... no, he wanted to stop and take the wafer at St Etienne.'

'Oh, tell the truth, Monsieur Lafayette. I won't hold it against you.'

'Very well then. He went for a glass at the Cascades more than an hour ago... you really are a sight for sore eyes.'

'Thank you,' replied Eveline, giggling to herself. The man was mad. She was red as a Bengal lantern what with cooking, cleaning and dashing back and forth to the window to see if the sun had come out. They didn't need any Christmas decorations with her on the scene, glowing from tip to toe: red hair, red dress, red brooch, red stockings... Still, it was kind of him. He was a good sort really. She took the tin of surprises, childishly wanting to look, and put it in the kitchen. Monsieur Lafayette stood awkward and formal by the table, waiting for the others and making polite remarks about the weather and the mournful state of the city while she kept an eye on the first course.

'At least they can't stop us enjoying ourselves,' he remarked, meaning the Prussians. 'If we let them do that, they really have beaten us. Dear me, yes, that's when they've won.'

Laughter and knocking heralded the arrival of Laurie and Alphonse and they came in with a bottle of wine between them and a miniature rose tree. The latter caused a stir of consternation on the part of Eveline for she couldn't fit it on the table next to the geranium and she didn't want to show any favours. In the end she placed it on the windowsill much to everyone's approval. It fairly lit up the room and the smell was delicious. She wanted to know where they'd found such an exotic but they wouldn't tell. They looked very handsome in their uniforms, one dark, one golden, and Monsieur Lafayette eyed them suspiciously, surprisingly awkward in his ruffled-up collar.

'More rivals for the hand of dear Eveline,' he remarked upon introduction; and Laurie shot her an appalled look.

He joined her a few moments later in the kitchen. 'Who's that character?' he demanded.

'I've mentioned him several times,' she replied defensively. 'He's an old friend of Papa's.'

'Yes, but… I didn't think… he looks like a rogue, Evie.'

She felt suddenly hot and suffocating in the kitchen and she bade him go and open a window. Who was he to tell her who was a rogue and who wasn't? Who was he to tell her anything?

'You shouldn't be so hasty to judge,' she advised him when he returned. They were off on the wrong foot already, of course, as they always seemed to be these days. She just couldn't help herself. Something about him recently made her want to punch the air.

'How pretty you look!' he observed then. 'Is that your mother's ruby brooch?'

'Mmm.' He knew very well it was. It was the only piece of jewellery she owned. The only thing of her mother's she owned. It came out on special occasions like a star at night though generally she kept it in the toe of a shoe lest her father find it and pawn it for drink. She heard the door slam and her father's voice.

'Up with the good Lord! Down with the Bishop!'

He was obviously trying to convince everyone he'd had a fair sprinkling of religion that morning. Wiping her hands on her apron, she went out to seat everybody formally. Jacques was in tow behind her father, bedraggled and dirty in his sailor's suit though he'd promised to keep clean and out of mischief. But she didn't have the heart to be angry with him today.

'Papa, next to Laurie please – you can tell him all about the sermon. Monsieur Lafayette next to Alphonse and Jacques beside *me*,' she said a little pointedly to show him that the dirty suit had gone without reprimand but not unnoticed.

'You're the daughter of a Bishop, my girl!' Mistigris wagged his finger at her. 'And he's a very bad man!'

Eveline sighed. 'Yes, father, I know that. I'm only too well aware of it!'

It was best to get some food into him, she decided. She took off her apron and dished up the first course of bacon and peas. Everyone cheered up at the sight of it. Somebody said it smelled too good for horsemeat which led to a number of jokes.

'What did the bouillon say to the casserole?' Alphonse teased Jacques.

'I don't know,' giggled Jacques, his little wrists poking out of his dirty suit.

'Try catch me, you're from a racecourse!'

Everyone had a joke to tell then and another thimbleful of wine did the rounds while Mistigris went off to sharpen his carving knife, declaring that the beast was too much for him. He ground away on a statue of Mary Magdalene until everybody's nerves became quite frayed.

'Papa,' cried Eveline. 'The food is going cold. Will you come and carve up now.'

He gave them a lesson then on carving. It was an art apparently, both meditative and daring. It was not unlike carving a statue. You had to let the knife do the work. Everyone was sick to death of it by the time he carved his last painstaking slice. Even Fifi had jumped up on Jacques' lap and was peering over the table with impatience. Monsieur Lafayette said that he wouldn't mind getting a feel of her embonpoint though all the time he was looking at Eveline in her tightly laced bodice. Laurie went quite white and took another thimbleful of wine while Alphonse sat back in his chair, watching the proceedings with amusement.

They were just settling down to their food when a shadow darted across the window. Laurie who sat opposite was first to notice.

'What on earth was that?' he cried. 'Over there behind the rose.'

Everyone looked. The figure darted by again, almost bird-like in motion.

'It's Madame Larousse,' said Eveline putting down her napkin. 'The coal dealer's wife.'

'I thought she was dead!' muttered Mistigris.

'Hush Papa. She quite obviously isn't.'

And she wasn't. She was large as life, twice as natural, her nose pressed to the pane, her eyes big as saucers.

Eveline got up and went over to the window. 'Madame Larousse?'

'Yes dear.'

'Are you… alright?'

'Yes dear. I just wanted to wish you all a Merry Christmas.'

'Thank you. Merry Christmas to you.' Eveline was about to shut the window but something about the little woman's pinched-up cheeks stopped her. 'Are you quite well, Madame Larousse?'

Oh yes, Madame Larousse said. She was quite well. She had just been wondering if Eveline might be so good as to lift the lid on that delicious – bacon stew was it – so that she might get a whiff of it through the open window. It would do her a power of good. It would quite rejuvenate her! Nothing would give her more pleasure (she went on) than to be able to stand by the window, sniff the air, and watch them eating that delicious bacon stew, bushel of peas and – was it onion gravy she could smell?

Of course nobody wanted her out there sniffing the air while they gorged themselves and it was agreed that she had better come in. If you couldn't do someone a good turn at Christmas when could you? Madame Larousse shuffled in saying she didn't want to impose, plonked herself down beside Monsieur Lafayette and unlaced her corset in preparation for the feast.

'Whoa there, my good woman,' smiled the confectioner. 'I may have fought at Solferino but my heart's not up to that kind of excitement!'

Everyone remarked on the bacon. It was done to a turn – crispy with just the right amount of crackling. Peas – tender and sweet and the gravy, well, it was like the unction that flowed down Aaron's beard, said Mistigris. He was playing hard in the religious stakes today. Madame Larousse was visibly impressed by the biblical allusion and she said a little grace herself before tucking into her plate. For a while nothing could be heard but the sound of jaws working. Another thimbleful did the rounds and the mood became quite merry. Everyone was determined to enjoy themselves.

'Is it Larousse after the encyclopaedia?' Laurie asked with interest.

'Yes, dear,' muttered Madame Laroussse, chewing hard on a bit of crackling. 'I always said that if poor old Monsieur Larousse had had more of a brain he'd have set up a shop of encyclopaedias.'

'Dear me, yes,' agreed Monsieur Lafayette. 'There's nothing like an encyclopaedia for dipping into. Too heavy for general use but good for dipping into.'

'My, my,' cried Madame Laroussse, wiping her fingers on her napkin. 'You know where to come if you want an insult.'

Everyone stared at her in surprise.

'I simply said a Larousse was good for dipping into!' Monsieur Lafayette explained in an aggrieved tone.

'I know what you said!' replied Madame Larousse, throwing down her napkin. 'And I know what you meant! Filthy beast!'

Eveline tried to pacify the old woman by offering her another plate of bacon and peas but she wasn't having any of it. She insisted on swapping places so that she didn't have to sit next to the 'disgusting little man'.

Things got a little heated after that. Eveline was starting to regret her generosity and she brought the main course in with a flaming face. Mistigris gave another carving lesson for the benefit of Madame Larousse who simpered and sighed at his side.

Jacques remarked tactlessly that Fifi didn't like rabbit and nor did he – they preferred chicken; and Eveline, losing her temper, said if he wasn't careful she'd box his ears and he'd get what he was given.

They ate in a sullen greedy silence. Nobody commented on the rabbit except for Alphonse who said it was very good indeed and much better than the stuff they'd be getting at Brébant's. He chuckled to himself as though at a private joke and Monsieur Lafayette wagged a finger at him. 'You're a fox, young man. You may have a magnificent brush but you're a fox all the same.'

'To foxes!' cried Mistigris then who was drunk as a lord and toasting everything and anything he could think of. 'To foxes, rabbits, chickens and porks! Up with the butchers! Down with the good Lord!'

Everyone laughed except for Eveline who seethed at the thought of the time she had spent finding the rabbit, preparing it, cooking it… the ungrateful bunch! It was the last time she'd dish them up a Christmas lunch! In the end she had to go into the kitchen to regain her composure, Laurie following quickly after.

'It's a sign of a good party,' he consoled her. 'Uproar!'

She listened to the hubbub of voices and smiled weakly. 'See what I have to put up with?'

'I think Madame Larousse has taken a shine to your father.'

Eveline rolled her eyes. 'I was starting to regret my hospitality.'

'You couldn't just leave her out there sniffing the air!'

'No.' She giggled.

Laurie held out his hand. 'Friends?'

'Friends,' she agreed, taking it. When she'd mopped herself up a bit they re-joined the table. Jacques was fast asleep with Fifi in his lap; Monsieur Lafayette was saying to Alphonse that the trouble with the working man was that when he didn't get what he wanted he went to extremes and just started killing people – like Troppman[10]; and Mistigris was regaling Madame Larousse with the method and madness of his Art.

'The stone is just waiting to be born, waiting to be set free. And it will be what it will be. Sometimes I wish,' he went on mournfully, 'someone would take a chisel to old Mistigris, knock him out of his surroundings, smooth his rough edges, set the old fellow free again.'

'Ooh, would you now!' Madame Larousse flushed up. 'Dear me! What a degenerate!'

Laurie, fearing another bout of musical chairs, enquired quickly of Mistigris: 'Do you know what has happened to the Venus de Milo?'

'No. What?'

'She was packed up in a crate and taken from the Louvre in case it was bombed. It was a real cloak and dagger operation.'

'In the dead of night, I suppose,' said Mistigris for whom anything of import always happened in the dead of night.

'As a matter of fact I think it was. It was all top secret. Nobody knows where she is hidden.'

Mistigris let out a forlorn cry. 'Green! Green she was and bloated when they fished her out of the Seine.'

'Not today, Papa,' Eveline said firmly and he stared back at her piteous and obedient as a child.

Monsieur Lafayette did the honours for afters with his crate of cherry brandy and tin of surprises. The tin of surprises was a great success – it contained a real sponge cake and a packet of chocolate Bavarian helmets. No one had seen cake or chocolate for months; and the Bavarian helmets especially caused a stir of excitement. Madame Larousse quite lost her head over them, dipping them into her glass of cherry brandy and talking to them as if they were real.

'You little horrors!' She squinted at one. 'When are you going to start shelling us then?'

'When it is the right psychological moment[11] apparently,' Alphonse said wittily which set off a stream of jokes about the right psychological moment.

'Is it the right psychological moment for you to have a drink,' asked Eveline, getting into the spirit of things, 'do you think, father?'

'It is always the right psychological moment for that!' Mistigris winked.

Things got a little silly then; though Madame Larousse, unlacing her corset even further, remarked that it was good for the young to let their hair down when they had the chance. You never knew when your time was up. Look at poor old Monsieur Larousse in his coal shed now for good. Eat, drink and be merry, that was her motto.

'I should like to be buried in a barrel of rum,' said Mistigris, his thoughts still on a morbid track.

Under a sundial à la Romans, was Monsieur Lafayette's choice.

'By the cherry trees of St Denis,' said Madame Larousse mistily. 'How I love a ripe cherry.'

'Strawberries are more my poison.' The confectioner grinned obscenely at Eveline. Suddenly he got to his feet and started singing, his ruffled up collar halfway up his chin.

Red on the outside,
Hard on the inside.
Like teeth behind lips,
The strawberry spreads its sweet breath.

Not to be outdone, Mistigris staggered up and gave his version of 'Rose Blossom In Her Hair' in a cracked but surprising baritone.

When I first met her
She had peach blossom in her hair.
And it was true love,
My dear.

Madame Larousse stopped him going any further by bursting into a storm of weeping. Nobody could console her. It was thought she'd been moved to tears by Mistigris' rendition of 'Rose Blossom' but in the end it came to light that she wanted to sing her own little song – in gratitude for the meal. She'd been a soprano in her youth, had trod many a dance hall and though she said it herself had even been compared to the great Blanche Patois. If they didn't mind, of course. She didn't want to impose.

Eveline said that of course they didn't mind, they would be quite delighted and Mistigris led the cheering. 'Take to the floor, dear lady. Take to the floor!'

Madame Larousse stood up, arranged her violet skirts and struck a pose.

'Little Je… sus! Little Je… sus! ,' she burst out in shrill reedy voice. 'Little Jesus La La La.'

Everyone waited expectantly for the verse but she simply kept singing: 'Little Je… sus! Little Je… sus!'

'And the rest,' thundered Monsieur Lafayette.

'Little Jesus La La La.'

'Marvellous,' shouted Alphonse in an attempt to stop her; but the woman was indefatigable.

Jacques, having been woken up by all the noise, shouted out: 'Encore' before racing out of the room, giggling his head off, Fifi at his heels.

'Has he been drinking wine?' Eveline asked, concerned.

'No,' winked Alphonse.

Mistigris stared suspiciously after his son as though he thought the boy had engineered the whole pantomime; then apprehensively back at Madame Larousse grinning fearfully beneath her mop cap.

'Little Jesus!' The dreadful apparition swayed in the dull ashy light. 'La La La.'

In the end Monsieur Lafayette had to thump on the table to get her to stop. 'Enough madame, enough. I can see why that went down such a storm in the dancehalls. The memory of it will live with us forever.'

Madame Larousse flounced back to her seat and promptly burst into tears again. Everybody by this time was entirely fed up with her, though Mistigris, taking pity, patted her on the arm and she gave him a sidelong little glance.

As the ashy light grew darker, Eveline lit the lamp; and the statues jumped out at them like spectres waiting to join the feast.

'Happy Christmas everybody,' she smiled, playing the hostess and almost falling into Alphonse's lap. 'Happy Christmas everybody!'

Chapter twelve

By the time Christ had been born again in hearts, minds and imaginations, Aggie was dead for real. She lay huge and no longer suffering on the small white bed beneath the large wooden crucifix, a pectoral cross on her breast. Two candles lit her way to the Reconciliation, to that gentle eternal embrace; while a bowl of Holy water sat at her feet to cleanse her of all earthly defilement. The nuns had sung a Requiem in her honour; had tolled through the Cherubim and the Seraphim, Patriarchs and Prophets; had been to pay their last respects, one by one or in nervous giggling pairs. Some had given her a good drenching with the Holy water in the pious belief that she needed all the help she could get while others had sprinkled and flicked with an averted eye as if fearing to catch a contagion from that impure vessel. Still more had come to gloat and peep at the 'fruits of sin' swaddled up in the bottom drawer of the antique tallboy. Three stalwarts remained on the hard cane chairs beside the bed, their heads bent in the profound silence of prayer.

Bernadine stared in disgust at the bunch of violets she'd made, wondering why she'd put her faith in such superstitious nonsense. Aggie was dead. The child had lived, yes, but Aggie had died. Perhaps if she'd made a second bunch, one for each life... she shook her head in bewilderment. How ridiculous to bargain over death with a bunch of fake violets. Death came and went as he pleased, making no promises, breaking no hearts. It was God and men who made promises, broke hearts... The starlight crept in through the window, filling the room with silvery, fluctuating shadow, reminding Bernadine of a chapter from Prime: *Who is she that cometh forth as the morning rising?* Is this what it all boiled down to in the end? A cold white lump in a barren little cell? The fruits of sin slept peacefully, oblivious to it all, dreaming no doubt of fairies, food, love, Prince Charming...

Brother Michael had shuffled in and was kneeling at the edge of the bed wringing his hands. The girdle he wore to symbolise the bonds of our Saviour during the Passion seemed tighter than ever, almost lacerating his cassock; and the tonsure on his head had grown from the size of a Communion wafer to the size of a shining soup plate. He dipped his fingers in the Holy water, made the sign of the cross on the white marble forehead then sank back to his knees. His dry sobs filled the air, causing the stalwarts to stir restlessly in their devotions.

It seemed to Bernadine that time stood still, hanging suspended in the space between two chimes, two moments, two heartbeats. Is this what it all boiled down to in the end? A barren little cell filled with silvery shadows like memories of a past that wasn't over yet, a future that had been and gone already. On their way out the nuns would sing the *Te Deum* to thank God for accepting Aggie's nothingness. Nothingness. No light, no spark, no voice of God, no feeling of His presence. Nothing but nothingness from here to eternity. Just a barren little cell filled with silvery shadows where time hung suspended in a space between two moments, two heartbeats; two shakes of the thurible.

At length the silence was broken – Sister Frances, one of the eldest and wisest in the convent, sat up suddenly with a beatific smile and exclaimed: 'Dear child! Even in death she has a good colour.'

'Praise be!' said the second, rosy-cheeked little nun while the third stared lugubriously about her as if having woken from a dream, her eyes feasting on everything, her lips chewing mercilessly on nothing.

'She was a white lily snowed from heaven!' cried Brother Michael loudly, beating his breast, apparently glad to be able to vent his pent-up emotions.

Sister Frances frowned at him a little testily, as if to say that his place was in the kitchen, and he had no business in the cell of any nun – dead or alive – but she turned the frown into a smile and spoke with charitable kindness: 'Indeed, yes, Brother Michael. Indeed yes. A loving and generous spirit.'

'Oh, that doesn't do her justice,' shouted the monk, clearly quite beside himself – for he would never have dared speak in such a way to the Old Walnut as he privately termed Sister Frances. 'Not by a long shot. She was generous to a fault.'

'She always shared her peppermint creams with me,' the rosy-cheeked one admitted.

It wasn't quite what Sister Frances meant but she let it pass. 'Yes, indeed, Sister Luke. A most generous and loving spirit.'

'I remember the time,' Brother Michael gabbled on, seriously shaken up, 'when the Mother Superior hauled her up on account of her chicken legs.'

Sister Frances looked at him askance. 'Chicken legs? Whose chicken legs?'

'Aggie's. She smuggled them in last year during Lent and hid them under the mattress. I was going to...'

'Dear child!' Sister Frances interrupted hastily, trying not to look too shocked. She didn't want to hear any more about the escapades and misdemeanours of the dear departed – there was sufficient evidence in the bottom drawer of the tallboy! 'Such joie de vivre! Nowadays it is all joie de vivre. Perhaps a little too much joie de vivre,' she added as the fruits of sin let out a piteous little grunt.

The lugubrious one nodded in full agreement and turned her face to the child, a tut escaping her lips like a delicate puff of incense.

The baby's face was quite cool and Bernadine wrapped her up in another warm blanket. Soon she would have to get milk. The thought had crossed and re-crossed her mind without cessation. Milk. Was there any milk left in the city? She would have to journey far beyond the convent to find it, venture deep into the heart of Paris. The thought made her shiver and she stared at the tiny creature in alarm, wondering how something could be so vulnerable and yet so powerful at the same time.

'Sister Bernadine, am I right in thinking that Sister Agnes was posted to Rhône at one time for teaching duties?' Sister Frances, having observed the niceties, was now inclined to chat, and keen to include Bernadine. Being one of the 'living rules' of the convent her only vice was to occasionally bend them a little; and she did not think the Lord would turn His nose up at her for that.

Bernadine nodded. 'Yes. I believe she hated every minute of it.'

'Ah.' The wizened one nodded wisely. 'It was quite different in my day of course. We were to practise a Holy indifference to wherever we were posted. A Holy indifference.' She smiled with the quiet constancy of a martyr. 'Whatever we met with. Whatever they saw fit to throw at us. Often we didn't even have the bare necessities but in compensation we earned our spiritual fortune in no time flat, let me tell you, no time flat.'

'Alleluia!' murmured the rosy-cheeked one.

'Of course, there were the horror stories…'

The lugubrious one sat up in her chair. 'Horror stories?' she cried eagerly. 'What horror stories?'

'Well…' Sister Frances settled herself down nicely, crossing her legs by lifting one arthritic old knee over the other with a pair of equally arthritic old hands. 'You've heard of Sister Isidore?'

The nuns gasped. Sister Isidore was a legend. And not a good one.

'Oh, she started off well enough – a pleasing temperament, a soul bound to virtue, sound of wind and limb... when she was posted to Tassin they offered her all sorts, a classroom with a coal stove and bell, sunny and spacious accommodation... She thought she would be received like a countess... But in the end, oh me oh my, she was housed in a ruined abbey where rats and elderly monks attacked her bed.'

All heads swivelled to Brother Michael who was prostrate beside the bed, kissing the floor.

'Goodness!' gasped Sister Luke. 'It fair gives you the palpitations.'

'Doesn't it just. Her downfall in the end of course, was novels.' She shook her head. 'How many young girls have been lost through the reading of novels.'

'Praise be!' The rosy-cheeked one said a little wistfully while the lugubrious one coughed and turned a distinct shade of red.

It was hard not to stare at the body – it drew your eyes back again and again like a statue or a painting or a model reclining on a chaise longue awaiting the first brushstroke. How quickly she had gone cold. Bernadine had been astonished at how quickly she had gone cold. From life to death in a matter of seconds. As if the artist had changed his palette mid-air in temperamental fashion, turning the veins from wine red to silver, silver as the starshine that crept through the window, filling the room with fluctuating shadows. The corpse had emptied itself several times already with a gentle trickling, scaring some, provoking hilarity in others; but now it made no sound at all though Bernadine could hear Aggie's voice plainly in her ear, laughing, singing, rejoicing.

What would you have Sister Bernadine? A great banquet in your honour. Sugared almonds and pineapples are my favourite.

She would not abandon this child. Not this one. She made a silent vow to the corpse of her friend that she would not abandon this child. Never again.

'It's all fashion and futility these days!' declared the Old Walnut. 'Spiritual fortune is squandered, frittered away on novels, jujubes, facepaint, fancy note paper. The Mother Superior's shelves are bursting.'

Sister Luke muttered a discreet 'Alleluia' while the lugubrious one stared morbidly at Brother Michael who lay fast asleep at the bottom of the bed like a dog at the feet of his master.

'Not that I am all for self-abnegation,' Sister Frances went on tolerantly. 'I have always believed the laborious work of teaching to be sufficient exercise in the practice of mortification.' She chuckled. 'We used to say that the rule of silence was invoked simply to save one's voice for the classroom!'

Bernadine smiled politely and Sister Frances chattered on good naturedly. 'It is hard to live in a community. So little privacy. So many… sacrifices. But I like to think of our Saviour Jesus of Nazareth and the first community, if you will. Just imagine if he could not abide the smell of fish! Or the presence of some of his more dull-witted disciples.'

'Praise be!' said the cheery-faced one a little vacantly; and Sister Frances' face took on a long-suffering look.

'But we must persevere. Trust in the Lord. Keep our minds on each sunrise and each sunset. We need do no more.'

The words flitted round Bernadine's head like battered moths. Trust the Lord. Sunrise and Sunset. Sunrise and Sunset from here to eternity. For what purpose? To what end? Soon the sun would rise and the nuns drift away to mass and to make the necessary arrangements, leaving her alone in a barren little cell with the corpse of her friend and a blue baby girl. Her nerve failed her for a moment. *She* had sinned as badly as her friend. For what purpose did *she* remain living?

My beloved is mine and I am his,
He feedeth among the lilies
Until the day breathes and the shadows flee away

Who is that looks forth like the dawn
Fair as the moon, bright as the sun
Terrible as an army with banners?

Part Two: Living, Dying

Chapter thirteen

'What a send off!' murmured Alphonse as 7th Company made its way as best it could through the packed streets and crowded boulevards. Thirty-five National Guard battalions were setting off that day – a cold, muddy morning in the middle of January – to fight the enemy. It was to be a mass attack in retaliation for the bombardment the city had suffered in the last few weeks at the hands of the Prussians – General Trochu's plan come to fruition. Some said it was a mass suicide and that the beautiful men of Paris were going to their graves; but the people were out in their thousands, in any case, to cheer them on – waving flags, singing military airs and patriotic songs. It was like a public holiday: shops were shut up, wine poured, emotions soared – all for the glory of the Republic of course. More and more people came out of their homes to see what all the fuss was about, join in the fun, watch the procession of polished bayonets, boots and buttons pass by, some of the men looking gay and light-hearted, some looking grim and determined. Mothers wept; lovers sang and sighed at the same time; old men cursed, wishing they were younger while young boys ran alongside the troops, wishing they were older. An old gent sitting on the shoulders of his equally ancient wife shouted out in a trembling voice: 'Kick their arses back to Berlin, boys! Kick their arses back to Berlin!' He took off his hat and appeared to be weeping. 'Remember Austerlitz, Wagram, Borodino, Sébastopol!'

'Keep your hair on, Granddad!' cried Tessier, grinning from ear to ear. 'We'll shove 'em back across the Rhine, never fear. They won't get past Léon Tessier in a hurry.' And he promised the old man he'd bring back a bit of Bismarck's goose nicely cooked for him.

Laurie scanned the crowd, looking for Eveline, though she had said she wouldn't come and he looked in vain. He thought he caught a glimpse of her once behind a fountain on the Rue de Rivoli but it was nothing but a cascade of sparkling water. A woman dressed in a tricolour flag was trying to distract him, doing the rounds of the men, offering brandy and a kiss on the cheek for France and for victory. Coupeau was taking full advantage of the situation, gaining victory after victory after victory; he even broke the line and darted in and out of the crowd – a strange little figure almost dwarfed by his kit bag – getting as many smackers as he could from women who didn't dare refuse him for fear he was one of the poor men on their way to meet their maker. The rest of 7th Company however, Laurie noticed, looked as if they had the weight of the world on their shoulders; and he smiled a secret smile of delight: this was it! At last a taste of some real action!

Suddenly he spotted her as they turned onto the Champs Élysées. She was wearing a sky-blue dress and holding Jacques tightly by the hand at the edge of the crowd. His heart missed a beat. She had come! She had changed her mind and come! He didn't know whether to stare straight ahead as Alphonse was doing or turn and feast his eyes on her. In the end he turned and she caught his eye. The next moment she was trotting alongside, flushed and breathless, almost tripping over her skirts. Even in the early hours of a dull winter morning she was radiant and he wanted to take her in his arms then and there in the middle of the Champs Élysées – though of course he never would have. She kept opening her mouth to speak but the noise and commotion were too great and in the end she simply pressed something into his hand – it was a bunch of dried violets – her eyes huge and shining with tears. To hide his own emotion he buried his face in them and their sickly sweet odour filled his nostrils, making him feel quite light-headed. He was dimly aware that she lingered by Alphonse and handed him something too – he thought he caught a flash of dazzling red – but then they were turning sharply right and her face fell away with the bands and roaring streets and he was left with nothing but the odour of violets. He tried to imprint an image of her in his mind so that later on he could draw on each and every detail, wondering a little dramatically if he would ever see her again.

The march began in earnest then, through the south-west part of the city. Huddles of onlookers still watched and waited to cheer them on and a ragtag of children kept pace for a while. Jacques was amongst them, thumbing his nose at them both and Alphonse took a moment to thumb back and wave. A little girl in a yellow dress threw a posy which Tessier caught and slipped over the end of his rifle.

'Thank you, mademoiselle,' he said graciously, stopping to execute an elaborate bow as if they'd just taken a dance together. 'Thank you, mademoiselle.' And he threw a playing card over to her that landed at her feet and she knelt to retrieve it then ran off, giggling and blushing to the roots of her hair.

Joubet made some remark about clowns wanting their heads blown off but nobody paid him any heed; and they marched on in good cheer. Women still stopped and stared as they passed and Coupeau preened and chuckled in delight though most of the women, Laurie thought, were staring at Alphonse. He looked like a Greek god with his tall frame and sculpted features and Laurie wondered suddenly what Eveline had given him. It had looked like the ruby brooch she wore on special occasions yet he did not think that could be right; and he didn't dare ask his friend for fear of having his suspicions confirmed. Whatever it was, Alphonse had slipped it into his pocket and wasn't saying – he simply looked straight ahead, intent on where he was going, his strong face calm and composed, ignoring the calls and waves from girls who wanted him to notice *her*, smile at *her*. Had Laurie known it, he himself was the object of several shy glances and fervent prayers but he was too busy thinking about Alphonse… In the end he turned his thoughts to the battle ahead. To launch an attack from Mont Valérian and Buzenval[12] was a daring, surprising manoeuvre. The full spate of men bearing down on the fortresses, moats and barricades surrounding Versailles. He hoped that his nerve would not fail him. That he would pass the test. And he hoped that if he were to die it would be an honourable death.

He fought valiantly for his country
Fearless to the end…
A true soldier… and a true friend…

Each one was silent, lost in his own thoughts, kindled by the cheers of the crowd, replaying scenes of farewell with loved ones. They didn't mind the rain coming down at a fair lick now, creeping under their clothes, gently soaking them to the skin and turning the road to slush. They had the people behind them and God on their side – what couldn't they achieve? To an objective eye they were a motley crew, emaciated, thin as rakes with haunted eyes; but in their own minds they were indestructible. Ill trained and ill equipped they might be. Famished and bombarded to within an inch of their lives they may have been. But it made them even more determined to beat the Prussians black and blue. They would return dead or victorious, General Ducrot had said. Dead or victorious. Defeat would mean ruin and shame and it didn't enter into their vocabulary. Any doubts had been dashed by the warmth of the crowd and the men were glad and full of hope. The Battle of Buzenval would go down in history along with Austerlitz, Wagram, Borodino, Sébastopol… Tessier said as much as they left the Seine far behind and entered into open country.

Now and then they had to stop for other battalions to pass or because the battalion in front had come to a standstill. Thirty-five battalions was a good deal of men and led to a good many foul-ups. Laurie wondered why they hadn't set off in relay but then again it wouldn't have been such a spectacle for the crowd. Soon, of course, they would split off in different directions – some going to Mont Valérian, others to Buzenval. Still more had camped out the night before and were in position, waiting for back-up. Nevertheless, the hold-ups were exasperating and led to friction between the battalions – the men too full of themselves not to pick a fight with something. Some of the battalions were made up of *mobiles* – rurals recruited from the rest of France and regular fighting men. The National Guard battalions dubbed them 'yokels' and were in turn dubbed 'part-timers' by the *mobiles*.

'Butchers, bakers and candlestick makers!' sneered a muscled-up *mobile*, looking down his nose as he passed 7th Company.

Joubet, always quick to anger, threatened to punch the man's eyes out if he didn't shut up and Bidulph had to prevent him from actually doing it.

'Silence in the ranks,' shouted the Captain. 'Let them pass, please.'

'Keep it calm, sir,' grinned Tessier. 'Don't let your head swell so, sir.'

The Captain had an unfortunately large and bulbous head and was the butt of many jokes. He frowned at the stifled chuckles that greeted Tessier's remarks, oblivious to the comedy going on at his expense.

Sometimes they even had to stop for a dispatch rider galloping up with some telegram or other. It irked the men not to know what was going on and Bidulph, who had good ears, was always sent forward to try and make out what the rider was saying. Coupeau, on the other hand, ducked at the sound of galloping hooves, much to the delight and amusement of the others.

'Place your bets for the two-fifteen!' they teased him. 'This isn't Longchamps[13] you idiot. You won't get stampeded.'

But poor little Coupeau wouldn't be consoled until the sounds of rattling bit, creaking saddle and 'hefty hoss's breath' as he put it were far far away. Only then did he return to his former cocksure self.

The rain was coming down now in sheets – they were getting a real lashing from a cloudburst – and a thick fog was blanketing the country roundabout. Visibility became so poor as they progressed that Laurie could barely see the battalion in front and the path behind was practically obliterated. Shapes jumped out at him suddenly like an enemy ambush and he was forever tightening his fingers about his rifle in preparation for an attack. He hoped the weather wasn't an omen for the day's events. He was particularly susceptible to omens, good or bad, though he realised the thought processes involved were not entirely rational. It was just one of the little demons that skulked about his head and which he tried to stiffen his soul against. This little demon wasn't giving up that easily. The weather, he kept muttering, was a very bad sign indeed.

'Gawd Almighty!' grinned Tessier, splashing through a puddle in his clod-hopping boots. 'I'll need an umbrella with me at this rate!'

Laurie laughed, glad of the distraction – it was just some god-awful weather after all – and said he'd like to see Bismarck's face at a bunch of umbrellas descending on Versailles.

'Imagine,' giggled Coupeau, having gotten over his close encounter with the hefty hoss, 'battalions dressed up as cocodettes with bottines[14] and parasols. We bat our eyelids, flap our...' he wiggled his meagre little chest, '...attributes. Inveigle our way past buttresses, barrages...until lo and behold we are in the headquarters. We bring our weapons out of our bosoms,' the salacious little sod made a saucy gesture with his chassepot[15], 'and blow them all to kingdom come!'

The men laughed at the pantomime got up for their amusement and began to sing obscene songs about the enemy to keep their spirits up.

Bismarck the fat oaf
With a greasy moustache
Pleasured himself with a tart
And fell on his arse

'Bismarck the fat oaf
Pleasured himself with a loaf,'

someone added and everyone laughed. It was hard not to think of the Iron Chancellor sticking a baguette up his backside without smiling, even though most of them were hungry enough to have eaten it afterwards.

They were nonsense made-up little rhymes, usually on the spur of the moment but their message was clear. To hell with a bit of rain and fog.

They could launch an attack blindfold if they had to. And Laurie sang along as heartily as the rest of them.

After what seemed an eternity of marching they were given the order to halt. There had been no let up in the rain and everyone was secretly relieved to be able to take a breather, blow the drips of water from their noses. Their waterlogged packs weighed a ton, they chafed around the privates and their hands were almost blue hanging on to their rifles. They had to grumble a bit though to save face. Bidulph said he'd just reached his optimum rhythm and was going like the latest vélocipede; Joubet said if he waited too long his feet would swell up. Laurie nodded sympathetically – his left heel was killing him, rubbed raw by an ill-fitting boot and he wished he could stand barefoot in the virgin snow on the wayside; but no order had come to stand easy and they huddled together like sheep, backs against the wind. Only Alphonse stood apart, the rain running off him like water off a duck's back. He was staring at the sky as if trying to get his bearings and Laurie wondered if they were lost. The Captain had been laden down with staff maps and reconnoitring glass but he hadn't appeared to use any of them. He probably didn't know how to. A demon of doubt and creeping anxiety skipped into Laurie's head and he hunched his shoulders with the rest of the men, wishing he had a cigar.

'Silence in the ranks!' shouted the Captain a touch unfairly because nobody at that moment was saying a thing.

'Too much manure,' winked Tessier. 'With all this rain it'll grow to the size of a watermelon.'

After another hour of waiting with no order to stand easy the mood became sullen, almost angry. Joubet suddenly blew his top and threw his kit bag down on the ground, many of the younger members of the battalion following suit. He hadn't come all this way, he said, to stand in a puddle. What sort of a roundabout route was this? Trochu's plan, eh? What a surprise! What a strategy! The only surprise was that they'd got this far already. Lambs to the slaughter that's what they were. He read the papers. He knew what was what. A sop to public opinion, that's what this was. And where was the precious public? Back home with its feet up swilling wine like pigs!

'You haven't even clapped eyes on a Prussian yet,' Alphonse said sternly, looking him straight in the face, 'and you're already defeated.'

Joubet said nothing and Laurie felt a little ashamed. He too had been wondering what on earth they were doing, wishing fervently he were back in his rooms, reading a volume of Victor Hugo with Eveline staring out at Miss 49 and Mr 50. He tried to rally himself but the weight of his pack, the rain and the endless waiting oppressed him. He just wished that they would get going.

'Still,' said Bidulph gloomily, taking up the cudgels on behalf of his friend and peering from under his thick matted hair like a baleful sheep, 'I have read that Prussia is a grand empire in formation. That her system of compulsory military service has produced a marvellously efficient fighting force; and that, combined with the nationalist movement that has swept the country since Sadowa, has put her at the head of all the German states…'

'Shut up, Bidulph,' said Alphonse curtly and Bidulph was so surprised that he did.

Laurie tried to distract himself from the waiting by studying the men's physiognomies. It was strange, he felt, how occupations were reflected in the face and body. Coupeau, the dyer, with his red neck and ears as if a runlet of pink had seeped upwards from his shoulders; Tessier, the bookkeeper, with his small eyes and ink-stained fingers; Joubet with the ragged hard features of a street fighter; Bidulph the sallow-faced doleful intellectual. He wondered if he himself had a perpetually half-asleep look about him, being a waker-upper. He knew he possessed the soft soul of a poet but he didn't think that was visible to the naked eye. Alphonse, no doubt about it, had the look of a heartbreaker… Laurie wondered for the second time what Eveline had given his friend. It struck him suddenly that her farewell to himself had been more sisterly than anything; and he glanced suspiciously at Alphonse who was still staring at the sky as if he could read some secret up there.

All of a sudden there was a commotion at the front – a rider had galloped up from the opposite direction. Everyone clamoured about, eager to hear the news and Bidulph was pushed forward with his good ears. He came back a moment later to spread the word. *Buzenval broken through! Bellemare's lot advancing on St Cloud. Versailles to be taken by nightfall! Hurrah!*

What a cheer went up. This was more like it. The Prussians taking a peppering? Of course they were! Tessier gazed about him triumphantly and even Joubet picked up his kit bag with a perky air. The bugler let out a little burst to pep up the men and then they were off, the rain and the wait forgotten. 'Onward march! Onward march!' sang the Captain, his large face beaming like a beacon in the mist.

The going was tough – the rain had turned the snow into a glutinous mud and the men were practically wading through it, their faces bespattered, the red stripe on their brown trousers almost invisible. Strange shapes and sounds came out of the whiteness: an old farmhouse, a rotten apple orchard, the yapping of a dog, mournful cry of a bird. And in the far distance the recognisable whir and spin of the *mitrailleuse*.

'Time to join the party,' said Tessier merrily, taking great snorts and gulps of air. 'Sniff the air, folks. I smell the blood of a Prussian man.'

Nobody bothered to reply – most of them were bent double against the wind. More like a bunch of old crones, Laurie whispered to Alphonse, not *cocodettes*. He smiled grimly to himself. He was limping as badly as Tessier with his inflamed heel but at least he was upright.

'A crone with a parasol,' Alphonse gave a wry smile, 'can be lethal!'

Laurie grinned and jammed his képi down hard on his head. It had blown off twice already, involving mad dashes behind thickets and brambles and he wondered if he oughtn't just dispense with it altogether as many of the men had done, leaving a trail of hats cross country like a macabre little treasure hunt. He wished he could dispense with the weight of his kit bag. It bumped about on his back as if he were giving a tubby little child a piggyback. And he wouldn't mind getting rid of his rifle either – he kept swapping it from one hand to the other, trying to give each arm a small respite. But at least they were moving. He comforted himself with the fact that he was upright and moving.

No sooner had he thought such a thing than to his utter disbelief they were given the order to halt once again. A rider galloped out of the mist, spattering them with mud and shouting madly. Poor little Coupeau cowered behind Tessier but this time nobody teased him. They were almost too stupefied to think straight. Bidulph didn't even have the energy to go up and see what was happening; but word came down only too quickly.

General Ducrot had given orders to retreat. They couldn't get the guns up because of the weather!

The men stood open mouthed and aghast, half blinded by the rain and squinting at each other in astonishment. *What d'you mean, couldn't get the guns up? What d'you mean, General Ducrot had given orders for retreat? General Ducrot who'd headed the battalions on his splendid white charger? General Ducrot who had said they would return dead or victorious? Where was Trochu in all this? What about the plan? There must be some mix up. There must be some mistake.*

Joubet lost his temper for real. He was sick of being led by a bunch of imbeciles, he was sick of playing games and he wanted to know what the fuck was going on. This time he wasn't listening to Bidulph or Alphonse or the Captain. He walked off into the fog, firing his gun in protest. A little old fellow at the back, believing some skirmish with the enemy to be afoot, panicked at the sound and started jumping up and down in excitement and shooting into thin air, narrowly missing another member of the battalion.

'I'll blast 'em,' he shouted, jigging up and down. 'I'll blast 'em. See if I don't blast 'em!'

Alphonse, white with fury, marched up to the Captain. They exchanged a few angry words and moments later the order came to advance again.

'What the hell did you say to him?' asked Laurie as Alphonse slipped back into line.

'That I'd put a sugar plum in his head if he didn't get the men moving. Demoralisation will kill us before the enemy does. We'll have a riot on our hands if we're not careful.'

'What d'you think has happened to Joubet?' Laurie asked then, more than a little edgy at the strange turn of events.

'Don't worry,' grinned Bidulph. 'He'll be back.'

But Joubet didn't come back; or at least if he did nobody noticed for a moment later they were being fired upon. Bullets screamed out at them like sirens. Some, too surprised to move, were hit smack in the face, including the Captain. Others scattered into the undergrowth or, losing their nerve completely, fled the scene. Men trying to advance were hampered by men in retreat. It was mayhem. A tangle of arms, legs, kit bags and bayonets.

'Hold the line,' croaked the Captain, spreadeagled in the mud as fleeing feet leapt or trampled over him. 'Hold the line!'

But Alphonse had taken over immediately. 'Take cover!' he roared, brandishing his bayonet. 'Let the enemy show its face, don't fire blind.'

For once Laurie didn't agree with his friend. Presumably the enemy were firing blind so why shouldn't they? Take a few pot shots and hope to get lucky. He dropped to his knees and aimed into the fog but his hands were shaking so violently and his eyes smarting so badly that he couldn't do anything but kneel with a trembling gun in his hands. The air was filled with a shrill whimpering and he didn't know if it was the guns, his own voice or even a little demon carrying on in his head. To his astonishment a man dropped dead at his feet. He'd never seen a man drop dead before and he was surprised at how elegant, casual and discreet an affair it was.

He simply fell into the soft dark snow without a sound or a murmur. He made it look easy the way he did it.

Others weren't quite so lucky or so discreet. Someone ran by, squealing like a pig, his eyes rolling around in his head. Another toppled beside Laurie, gasping for breath and clutching at his neck. He didn't look much older than Jacques and his teeth chattered like castanets as he pressed his fingers to his throat. Laurie dug out a bandage from his kit bag and wrapped it around the wound but the blood still poured out in strange arterial pulses. He tried to tourniquet the bandage with the sheath of his bayonet but the sheath broke. He wanted to shout for help, for Alphonse, for anybody, but nobody could hear or was listening. He didn't know what else to do for the boy; he dragged him to a nearby hedge and sat beside him as the life blood leaked through the little white bandage. He wondered if he oughtn't to say a prayer but all he could think of was a line from Victor Hugo and he didn't think that was entirely appropriate. So he sat as if in a dream as the boy's breath grew more ragged and shallow. After a while it petered out and he knew that the boy was dead though he still felt quite unable to move. A riderless horse galloped by, its empty stirrups clinking eerily and he wondered if Coupeau was ducking somewhere out of sight. Men were still charging past with smoking guns and streaming eyes, but he didn't know any of them; and he hadn't seen hide nor hair of a Prussian. They'd shot from the mist like invisible men. Is that what God did? Shoot from the clouds like an invisible man? Bayonet with a ray of sunshine? Stop a heart with a turning world?

He didn't know how long he'd been sitting there when he felt a touch on his arm.

'Laurie!' It was – Good God Tessier old chap! Tessier the dear old game-legged bugger – crouching down and whispering at him urgently. 'Come on, mate. That poor sod's snuffed it. We've got to get going.'

Laurie shook his head stubbornly. He was quite happy here thank you under his hedge. It was quite comfortable, afforded great protection and if Tessier had any sense he'd have a sit down too. Wait for the whole thing to pass over. Nothing but a rainstorm. They could share a bottle of mouth warmer and he could recite a little bit of Victor Hugo to while away the time as he'd done for the young chap here who'd appreciated it greatly as far as he could tell. If the enemy came, well, too bad. He'd duck like little Coupeau or blast them away to kingdom come like the little jiggy man.

Tessier was staring at him in dismay. 'Come on, mate. Alphonse has taken the men back. You can't stay here.'

'Oh, alright.' Laurie agreed grudgingly in the end, mainly to humour his friend. He allowed himself to be dragged to his feet and led off back down the way they had come, the muddy track now strewn with debris, flags, kit bags and lukewarm corpses. They were heading for a wood at the top of the next field, Tessier said. It was safe and a good place to defend from – he was an old stoat for knowing that sort of thing; at least Laurie thought he said old stoat though it seemed a very odd word to use. Old stoat, old stoat, he giggled to himself, wondering if he'd lost his head at last. The copse seemed miles away to him but Tessier told him it was a trick of the light; and led him gently along the edge of the field, sticking closely to the hedge so as not to be detected by the enemy. The invisible enemy. They passed no one and no one passed them. The sun came out as they scuttled – like little field mice, Laurie decided, not stoats, they would look like field mice from the air – dancing over snow peaks and skating over iced-up puddles.

It was warm and dry in the wood and it looked to Laurie like an ideal place to sleep. He sank back against the trunk of an old tree and put his head in his hands. His fingers felt a wet sticky patch and he almost cried out in alarm. He'd been shot! No wonder he felt so light headed. As if he'd drunk a pint of wine. He thought he heard a bang like a firecracker going off but decided it must be a squirrel throwing nuts. That was the sort of thing that happened in woods – squirrels threw nuts at each other, old stoats knew where to look. His head was spinning and everything seemed to be dancing before his eyes. He could swear that was an old oak tree waltzing away to the rhythm of The Blue Danube in his head as badly out of time as his little sister Molly thumping away on the piano. Even Tessier was dancing, pirouetting and swaying on his game leg. He could spin with the best of them! The old bugger was wasted off a dance floor!

'Stop fooling, Léon,' he giggled as the bookkeeper's arms flung out from side to side.

But Tessier didn't stop fooling. If anything he began to dance more fiendishly than ever, his arms and head seemed to go one way, his legs another as if he'd split himself in half. Laurie rubbed his eyes. It was probably one of Léon's illusions like his sleight-of-hand card trick stunts.

'Hey Léon, stop fooling. This isn't the Gingerbread fair!'

But Tessier didn't stop fooling – he was playing dead on the ground; and to Laurie's surprise a French officer suddenly stepped out from behind a tree, picked up Tessier's gun which was lying beside the bookkeeper's clubfooted boot and silently walked off with it. He didn't say a thing. Not a word. Not a peep. Just marched off with Tessier's gun.

Laurie stared after him in astonishment. 'Hey you, what the hell d'you think you're doing? Yes, I mean you. Come back here you scoundrel.' But the figure didn't turn back and as it disappeared from view a sudden fury bit into Laurie. He stood up, leaning against the old trunk, and fired into the trees. He kept re-loading and firing until his fury was spent and he had no cartridges left. Then he toppled forward into snow and mouldy leaves, the smell of old and decaying things filling his nostrils, mixing with the sickly sweet odour of violets. His last conscious thought before everything went black was that the old stoat's remains would be as indecipherable as his minutes.

Chapter fourteen

Eveline gave the lion's-head door knocker a nervous tap. 'Mouse,' she thought she heard Alphonse teasing in her head and, laughing at herself, she knocked a little harder then stepped back to wait.

The girl from Potin's had been right in so far as 21 Rue de Turbigo had once been an end-of-terrace house. Now it stood alone beside a pile of rubble like a flower still standing in an expanding wasteland. The house opposite had taken a pounding too, leaving its occupants with a roof of stars; and a row of rusty saucepans sat outside as if to catch any drops of leaking moonlight.

She heard the sound of laughter like the clear tinkling of a bell and a raven-haired woman suddenly opened the door. 'Yes?' she said curtly, looking at her suspiciously.

Eveline brought the little card from her pocket purse and the woman's face relaxed into a smile. She waved her in, apologising for her 'rudity'. 'Men have been playing hoaxes,' she explained in a high, accented voice. 'We cannot be too careful.'

'Oh.' Eveline wanted to know what sort of hoaxes but she felt it a little impolite to ask. She was led down a corridor to a lamplit room and she stood on the threshold and gasped. It was like nothing she'd ever seen before. It made Laurie's room look like a monk's cell. Books lined the walls from top to toe and on the floor in place of tables and chairs were hundreds of rainbow-striped scatter cushions against which women of all shapes and ages lolled, leant, smoked and slept. The room was very warm and yet, Eveline noted, there was no crackling fire in the grate. Perhaps it was the rugs that glimmered softly from the ceiling, wrapping the room in a cocoon of warmth and colour, colour chosen and woven by ancient

Eastern eyes that looked out on silvery deserts and golden glowing sunsets.

Eveline hid a secret little smile of satisfaction. Outside was a house with a roof of stars and here was a house with a roof of rugs! It was like another of the fairytales she'd read to Jacques but this, at last, was her own adventure.

The raven-haired woman was taking names, ages and occupations and writing them down in a little black book. Eveline wanted to say, when it came to her turn, that she was an actress, a singer, a dancer... but in the end honesty led her by the nose as her father would have said.

'I work in a bakery,' she mumbled, hardly daring to meet the strange, green catlike eyes that were looking at her so appraisingly. 'I'm eighteen, I mean seventeen and three quarters. My name's Eveline Renan.'

'I'm Elizabeth.' The raven-haired woman broke into a smile as her eyes slanted up above her cheekbones more bewitchingly than ever. She smelt of roses, wore trousers and her hair grew down to her waist. Eveline envied her immediately. The effect of Elizabeth, she decided then and there, was the opposite of smelling salts! She made you want to swoon. No wonder half the women were lolling against their cushions. They'd gotten into Paradis and gotten too close to Elizabeth T.

The girl from Potin's was handing out fried snacks, cinnamon biscuits and what looked like a plate of Turkish Delight. Eveline took a bowl of biscuits and sat down on a cushion beside a gap-toothed old woman who introduced herself as Queenie.

'After the Queen of England,' she giggled. 'My husband said I had so many airs I should have been the Queen of England.'

'Surely not,' Eveline murmured politely, not knowing quite what else to say.

'Of course not! The little whelp was a drunken bastard. If anyone wanted to be the Queen of England it was him! Here,' she offered, taking a swig of wine and passing the bottle to Eveline. 'Put some colour in your cheeks. You look half dead to me.'

Eveline, not wanting to be seen to be 'putting on airs' accepted gingerly.

'Down the hatch! Down the hatch,' gurgled Queenie as Eveline tipped the bottle very gently to her lips. 'That stuff'll warm your guts. Put a bit of fire in your belly.'

It certainly did put fire in your belly! Eveline felt as if she were breathing out flames – it wasn't like any wine she'd ever tasted. She coughed and gulped, her face turning as red as her curls.

'Sshh,' whispered Queenie, putting a finger to her lips. 'We're about to begin. Maria has just arrived.'

'Who's Maria?' asked Eveline when she'd got over her fit of coughing. Queenie's face took on a reverential look. 'Maria is Elizabeth's...'

But Eveline didn't hear what she said because a great hulking figure marched through the door and the women started clapping and shouting 'Maria'. Maria was wearing trousers and a little waistcoat, a red scarf wrapped around her neck, her hair was cropped close to her head and she didn't smile at all. She simply took her place beside Elizabeth in front of the empty grate and stared around the room, her thumbs hooked nonchalantly under the broad belt of her trousers. When the whispers and shouts of 'Maria' died down Elizabeth began in her strange, passionate, exotic little voice.

'Many of you are here because you are dissatisfied with men. You are sick and tired of their drinking, their fornicating, their cowardice. We are in the grip of war, famine, disease and despair and most of them are drinking themselves out of their minds in bars or visiting our sisters in the Rue de la Vieille Lanterne[16].'

Eveline crunched a little nervously on a biscuit and got a dig in the ribs from Queenie for doing so.

'Some of you have come on a hunch, perhaps, an intuition. All the better for it. Intuition is women's greatest gift and better than anything man has yet to bestow upon the world.'

There were vigorous nods at this and Elizabeth smiled grimly. 'They say we are on the brink of revolution,' she went on, her vowels becoming more elongated than ever. 'I say it will be a revolution of women, women rising up to demand their rights, take their place on an equal footing with men. We will no longer be the slaves, whores, mistresses, handmaidens to the useless sex. We will no longer fill their fantasies, their dreams, warm their beds, cook, sew and clean for them. We will be their nightmares, their doppelgängers, their better halves in the truest sense. It will no longer be "Sauvez la France" but "Sauvez la Femme"! That will be our standard.'

'Sauvez la Femme,' the women repeated, nodding seriously. One young girl cried out: 'If men had to endure childbirth the human race would be extinct!'

'I'm afraid it would,' Elizabeth smiled. 'They are weak, spineless, insensitive – those are the good ones. The bad ones...' a steely look entered her eyes and she almost appeared to be shaking. Maria put a protective hand on her arm '...Well, let us just say they go by the name of Satan.'

'She was married to a Russian Count,' Queenie gurgled in Eveline's ear which Eveline thought was incredibly rude seeing how Elizabeth was still speaking, much ruder than crunching on a cinnamon biscuit. 'He subjected her to every *volupté* known to mankind. She was in bed for a month. Then she ran off with Maria and the Count's jewels and heirlooms. That's why she can afford all this.'

'We have guns and uniforms.' Maria spoke then in a deep, authoritative voice, stepping forward, fingers still hooked beneath her broad black belt. 'The only thing we ask is that you live your life as independent human beings and that you fight for the women of Paris – the mothers, grandmothers, sisters and daughters. Follow me.'

They followed obediently out of the warm soft cocoon down a small corridor and some hard cold steps to a mouldy, suppurating basement – Eveline, all the while, staring at Elizabeth's slender back and pondering what 'every *volupté* known to mankind' consisted of. The room was lit by candles and Aladdin lamps and flickering rays illuminated yellow patches and growing fungi on the walls. Two tables stood in the near corner, one piled high with guns, the other piled high with National Guard uniforms. Oak barrels were stacked against the far wall, chalk-decorated in men's names, smirking faces and phallic doodles.

'See a cock you dislike,' Queenie gurgled in Eveline's ear and she felt a fleck of spit dribble down her neck, 'and shoot to kill.'

Maria knelt down in front of them, showing them how to load and fire. 'These are *chassepots*,' she said quietly. 'We are lucky enough to have them. Most of the guardsmen are still using the *tabatière* system – a much heavier, less accurate weapon. Leslie, you first please.' She pointed to a thickset woman with a crooked nose and narrow eyes. 'Are you shooting Tommy again?'

The woman gave a vehement little nod. She would always be killing Tommy, she said. He was an American cockroach and needed to be stamped out. 'I will get him thwack in the nose just as he got me,' she announced.

And she did. She knelt down, one leg in front of the other, pressed the rifle butt very professionally to her shoulder, took aim and fired, hitting Tommy smack in the middle of his bulbous nose; and then, once again, in the middle of his minuscule manhood. 'Hah!' She gave a satisfied gasp as she surveyed the damage. 'Hah!' Then walked to the back of the queue.

Elizabeth's eyes were glittering as she watched, standing halfway between the women and the barrels. She looked more catlike than ever to Eveline with her silky hair and emerald eyes. And at the sound of each shot her back had arched up as Fifi's always did when she wanted to be stroked. Her fists were clenched at her sides and in the flickering light the tip of her tongue could be seen sticking out of half-parted lips. Like a cat, Eveline decided, watching a troop of mice.

A young girl came next, so small and light she could barely hold the rifle to her shoulder. It was obviously her first time. Maria had to show her the lesson all over again, explaining the technique carefully and considerately, gently pressing the gun into her hands.

'Who would you like to shoot?' she asked softly.

'I don't know,' the girl stammered.

'Why don't you choose?'

'I… I don't like to.'

'Why did you come here tonight?' Maria asked patiently.

The girl screwed up her forehead. 'I wanted to be able to defend my home and my little brother if the Prussians came.'

Eveline felt a pang of understanding. She would defend Jacques with her life if she had to. Not that he seemed to need it these days.

'Oh, come on,' cried Elizabeth angrily, a spot of colour appearing on each cheekbone. 'Have you ever been beaten?'

'No,' the girl whispered, looking terrified.

'Have you ever been raped?'

'N… n… no.'

'Has your father ever mistreated you?'

The girl shook her head as vehemently as Leslie had nodded. Definitely not. Her father was a good man, a grocer and even during these times of terrible hunger he had managed to provide them with carrots and potatoes almost every night for her mother to make a delicious stew with. She simply wanted to be able to defend the home if the Prussians came.

Elizabeth put up her hand. 'Enough! Alright, imagine this: the Prussians are beating at your door, they are going to kill your brother and rape your mother… what are you going to do about it?'

The girl stared at Elizabeth in horror, uttered a strangled little sound at the back of her throat then burst into tears. The gun fell from her hands and Maria picked it up and handed it to the next woman then led the girl sobbing from the room.

'Anyone else feel the same,' Elizabeth stood with hands on hips and glared about her, 'they had better leave the room. Right now. We don't want time wasters.'

One or two girls left, giggling – it wasn't their cup of tea, they much preferred sewing and cleaning for their men to this sordid spectacle; but most people stayed. It was as bad as the queue at Potin's, Eveline thought and she didn't know which was worse: queueing for food or queueing to kill.

Elizabeth was really getting into her stride now. She stood on the sidelines, goading the women on as they fired shot after shot at Andrés, Jeromes, Vincents and Guys or any name they particularly disliked.

'All Peters are bastards!' shouted one, though she hit a Vincent by mistake while another brought a rain down on Simon because 'it was the wettest name in the world'. A voluminous-looking woman overflowing in petticoats and bonnet streamers didn't fire at all but simply charged up to a Jerome and started bashing him in the balls with the butt of her gun. 'What they want to do to you,' she shrieked, 'is ungodly. Lord a mercy!'

'SATANS!' roared Elizabeth in agreement, clapping her hands and stamping her feet. 'Bravo, madame. Bravo!'

Eveline didn't know how she would react when it came to her turn and she could feel her stomach fluttering with butterflies. She didn't particularly dislike any names – none that were present in any case – and she had no desire to go for a phallically inspired doodle. Perhaps she would gun down a smirking face. One or two were quite life-like and they reminded her a little of her father after he'd taken a drop. Many's the time she would have liked to wipe the smile off his face…

'Be my guest,' Queenie was gurgling in her ear. 'Francis can take as many hits as he deserves as far as I'm concerned.'

Maria handed her a loaded gun and Eveline, keeping her body very straight, knelt down, aimed and fired. She felt the gun jerk in her arms and heard the reassuring smack of splitting wood. Her heart beat a little faster and a surge of hot blood coursed through her veins. She fired again at another smirking face and got him right in the middle of the mouth.

'Are you a slave in your own home?' Elizabeth was shouting from the sidelines.

Yes she was. A mouse and a slave. Well, not any more. With a gun in her hands she was all-powerful, omnipotent.

Mouse, am I? Slave, am I?

The violence inside her was like a dam bursting – it flooded through her body in warm, angry waves. 'Mouse, am I? Slave, am I?' she sang to the rhythm of the load and fire technique. She wasn't even surprised when a smirking face suddenly spurted blood from one of its eyes though many of the women behind her gasped.

'You've been bloodied!' Elizabeth whooped gleefully, racing over to the barrel and holding out her hands to catch a few drops. Then she walked solemnly over to Eveline and traced the mark of a cross on her forehead. 'You've been bloodied, *ma petite*,' she whispered, kissing her on the cheek.

Eveline smelt the familiar smell of wine and it brought her rapidly back to her senses. She watched the women crowd around the barrel, licking drips from their fingers – anyone would think it was the fountain of life – or crouching down and opening their mouths like a bunch of pickled herrings. Some even pressed their lips to the hole as if to suck the barrel dry. Eveline stood, feeling drained, a little ashamed and vaguely repulsed. Even here she didn't belong. It was like being with her father and his cronies when she was stone-cold sober – how stupid they seemed with their red faces and exaggerated gestures, their displays of emotion and heart-to-hearts that left you feeling awkward and embarrassed the next time you saw them. Here it was almost the same feeling: the women appeared half mad to her now, lunatic, demented, sticking their fingers in a barrel of wine like a group of greedy vampires – worse than Papa and his cronies!

She felt suddenly suffocated by the odour of wine, spent guns and sweating women. If this was her own little adventure she'd had enough of it. She picked up another gun and a National Guard uniform and made her way out of the suppurating basement, up the cold hard steps, down the corridor and past the room full of rugs like glowing sunsets and silvery deserts and the scatter cushions – pink, azure and rainbow hued. Elizabeth caught up with her at the front door and grabbed her elbow.

'Why so soon?' she demanded, raising a quizzical eyebrow.

'Intuition,' Eveline replied for want of anything better to say. And yet it was true in a way. Something in her heart or head had told her to flee, flee while she had the chance. There was an undercurrent between the women – and in herself – that she didn't understand and didn't care to understand.

Elizabeth's eyes crinkled up into a smile. 'Well done,' she smiled, kissing her on the lips, '*ma petite*.'

Her breath tasted like cinnamon and her hair felt like silk; and Eveline left the Rue de Turbigo with the faintest hint of regret for an opportunity missed. A trip not taken. An avenue unexplored.

Chapter fifteen

Eveline had left Jacques fast asleep – or so she thought – but as soon as she closed the front door behind her he was climbing stealthily out of bed, lighting the lamp and pulling on as many thick clothes as he could muster. Summer layers under winter layers. Vests under shirts under waistcoats under jerseys. Stockings under socks under short trousers under long. Gloves, mitts and scarf – he bundled himself up so much he looked like a little snowman – but no hat. 'Heads can swell,' the Professor had warned time and time again. 'Heads can swell and tongues turn black!'

He hadn't forgotten the brandy – to pour over blackened tongues and swollen heads. He'd packed it away in his satchel the night before along with a cushion to sit on, an opera glass stolen from one of the Brothers who liked to watch the boys from afar, and a teaspoon for handling the sand ballast. Eveline would miss it but it couldn't be helped. He was a man on a mission and the handling of ballast was a most delikat affair. Like baking a cake or bread – a teaspoon here, a teaspoon there of sugar, yeast, sand, air and you could rise or fall flat in a matter of seconds! His sister would understand that to be sure. The Professor had entrusted him with his apparatus too – an altazimuth for the axes, a sextant for the angles and a map used in Zanzibar! Jacques sucked on the words as if they were candies that gave off flavours unknown and undreamed. Altazimuth, sextant, Zanzibar! Bitter, tangy, strangely sweet.

Still he couldn't help feeling a little guilty about Eveline; and he sat down and wrote a note, explaining his secret mission as best he could, then looked around the room. He would tidy up. He would tidy up for her sake. It was the right thing, the proper thing, the brotherly thing to do. She was always complaining about his desk and under the bed. He lifted the lid of his desk and heaved a small sigh. It was cram full with odds and ends, lesson books and some of his most treasured possessions: a peachstone whistle, an owl's pellet, a shell fragment he'd found on the Esplanade des Invalides and half of Lippy Buggins' front tooth. He ran his fingers thoughtfully over the items and, deciding the peachstone whistle might come in very handy, stashed it away in his satchel, faithfully recording it on his weight inventory. *Two ounce mergency whistle*, he wrote under:

Balloon, netting, car – 700 pounds
Ballast – 1500 pounds
The Prof – 3000 pounds
Monsieur Renan (me!) – 3 pounds
Grapnel and rope – 50 pounds
Apparatus: clocks, barrow-meters etc – 30 pounds
TOTAL – too heavy. Far too heavy!

And that wasn't including the mail, the pigeons and Fifi. He always concluded the total was far too heavy though he never could add it up correctly. Addition had never been his strong suit. School, in fact, had never been his strong suit.

He was beginning to feel very hot in his bundle of clothes and he stared at his lesson books in irritation. How boring! Wool, the seasons, paper, silk, railroads, vines, honey and bees.

'Bees show us that we must love Work,' Brother Mathias had written on one of his assignments. 'And Work assures Success.'

It seemed so far removed from him now. School! How silly! Those days were long gone. He had simply, he told himself, outgrown them. Not that he had enjoyed any of it anyway. The only lesson he could remember was the one on Christopher Columbus who'd brought back chillies and parrots from America, amber, gold and red peppers. And Icarus of course. Icarus who'd wanted to fly, built himself wings and flown too close to the sun.

Luckily they were travelling by the light of the moon. The light of the silvery quivering moon. When the moon turns to green cheese, the Professor had said, we will go. It was mouldy and ripe as a Brie and he'd given Jacques the nod just yesterday afternoon. He padded over to the window and stared up as always at the heavens, the domain of gods and insects. It was a cloudless night – there would be no water vapour in the air – and full of stars. Calling at Little Bear Corner, he whispered to himself in an awestruck voice, Angel Gate, Lucifer Heights, Icarus Straits.

Then he looked down at the ground as if in farewell, at the neglected yard and the step Eveline scrubbed every week with a hard, bristly little brush, though it never looked any different to him. He felt suddenly guilty again, thinking about his sister. He was meant to be tidying his room.

He went back to work, fishing out the unpleasant little morsels that lurked in the dark beneath his bed: a rotten apple core which he threw out of the window, a bit of cobwebbed chocolate which he ate heartily, plenty of dust which he left well alone, and to his surprise a letter he had begun and then discarded to Amelia Botton. Amelia Botton! The name was like a long forgotten summons in his head. Amelia Botton! How many nights had he burnt up with the thought of her? He marvelled at it now. Amelia Botton who threw stones at policemen and ate sherbet with her eyes shut.

Dreams of Amelia Botton had brought him closer to doing the 'thing' than anyone else had before or since. The thing that made you gasp and which the Brothers warned made your eyes go bloodshot and your voice go squeaky. Lippy Buggins had done the 'thing'. He said it was better than liquorice and his eyes weren't bloodshot at all though his voice hadn't half squeaked when his tooth came out. He said Brother Mathias had shown him how – he was thinging all the time apparently. Brother Mathias' eyes, Jacques remembered now, had been very bloodshot indeed. He'd thought it was simply because he kept such a good eye on the boys through his opera glass.

He was older and wiser now. He was nearly twelve and a half. Hardly a child! Though Eveline seemed to think so. Only last year she'd taken him to see a Punch and Judy show and bought him a toy bucket and spade. Honestly! Wimmin! He'd learnt a lot about wimmin from his father and the Professor. They either died or were full of gas and you didn't want to get in a menagerie with any of them. Jacques didn't think Amelia would get gassy in a hurry (despite the amount of sherbet she ate) but he dismissed her now as a 'yoofull infatchooation'. He was older and wiser these days. Nevertheless he wouldn't have minded seeing her eat sherbet with her eyes shut one more time. Just for fun. For old times' sake. Maybe one day, if he were so inclined, he'd come back for her in a steerable balloon, pick her up from school and land her down on her favourite café where he could watch her eating sherbet to his heart's delight; then make a grand exit through the Arc de Triomphe, to the utter amazement of onlookers.

Jacques picked up his satchel and left his room behind without a wave, a backward glance or even a cheerio. He wanted to say goodbye to his father though – if he could wake him that is. The snores from the next room were loud and regular and Jacques didn't really fancy his chances.

Mistigris had taken to sleeping in a coffin in preparation for death and the next life. He had made the coffin in his few sober waking hours, having raided the slabs (much to Eveline's dismay) from the nearby cemetery of Lachaise. It was three-quarters finished and had no lid – fortunately even Mistigris didn't believe that practice for the next life involved sleeping in a coffin with a lid on top. He'd started an engraving too. '*Ici repose…*' he had begun. Here rests… but he hadn't been able to finish it because he didn't know whether to put 'the son of', 'the father of', or simply plain old 'Mistigris'. So in the end it just read: '*Ici repose*' and then a blank. He'd even begun to feel that the blank was more eloquent than any words would have been. *Ici repose* nothingness. *Ici repose* no more. *Ici repose* dust and ashes.

Jacques tiptoed close with the lamp and peered down at his father. Two bottles of wine sat beside him in the space he'd designated for 'otherworldly nectar' and a newspaper lay spread on his chest in place of a rug, the headline 'Paris in Peril' fluttering desperately up and down in time with each gigantic breath. Jacques took the two wine bottles into the kitchen, filled them up with the diluted raspberry juice Eveline kept for that very purpose, then returned them carefully to their designated place. Next he brought a blanket from his own room and laid it over the coffin lest his father wake up and feel the cold. He wondered if he shouldn't wake him now to say goodbye but his father looked so peaceful he decided against it. Instead he sat cross-legged by the coffin, staring at his father with a mixture of pity and affection. Once long ago he'd laughed and told jokes, made boats and battleships for Jacques to sail on the Seine; sold silver-tipped canes of myrtle and dog wood to old gentlemen in waistcoats. He'd told Jacques all about the properties of wood – their characteristics and personalities, textures and grains. How some were warm and yielding, others hard and stiff. Now he only worked in stone because it was cold and dead, so he said, just as he was. Jacques blinked away a tear, kissed his father on the forehead and stood up very straight, clasping his satchel.

He was a man on a mission. He had to go.

'Here Fifi,' he called to the little cat who'd been watching him all the while from her box in the corner. The cat leapt into his arms with a soft miaow and he stuffed her very gently into his satchel on top of the cushion, mentally adding her to his weight inventory.

Fifi – 4 ounces. Far too heavy!

He blew out the lamp, took one last look around the room and at his father snoring fit to burst in his home-made coffin. Then he stepped up to the front door.

He had just enough time to reach the Gare du Nord by midnight…

Chapter sixteen

Eveline gasped for breath as she read the note out to Alphonse for she'd run all the way to Brébant's without stopping.

'Calm down,' said Alphonse sternly, 'and read it again. Slowly!'

'*Dear Sis,*' Eveline repeated in a choking voice, '*I've gone on a secret mission to study the clips of the moon and take guvvermental desk-patches. And to rescue Fifi from the clutches of Monsieur Lafayette. He is always feeling her for jambonpoint and I don't like it one bit.*

Yours ever,

Your brother, Jacques.

PS: Do not blame Papa. He does not know.'

Alphonse shook his head thoughtfully. 'It seems quite clear to me that he's gone to the Gare du Nord.'

'How can he be so selfish?' cried Eveline, stamping her foot. 'If he's not going up in balloons he's running away. I won't put up with it any more. Last year I was having to go and see the Brothers every few weeks about him. They said it would be easier to teach the catechism to the devil. I hope he has gone off in a balloon. Serve him right. And taken Papa with him, coffin and all. Silly little fool! Does he think Monsieur Lafayette means it about the cat?'

Alphonse half smiled and patted her arm. 'Calm down. And think. When did you last see him?'

'Earlier this evening.' Eveline felt a stab of guilt and wished she'd never gone to the Rue de Turbigo. 'He was fast asleep. They were both fast asleep. Papa in his coffin, Jacques in his bed. I tell you they were fast asleep,' she almost wept.

'Yes of course. I believe you. Don't get yourself into a state. But this doesn't look like a spur of the moment thing to me. He's obviously been planning it for some time. Has he been acting strangely recently?'

'N… no,' said Eveline a little despairingly, not wanting to admit that she didn't take much notice of Jacques. He came and went as he pleased, as they all did. She put the food on the table and scolded him but she didn't do much else. She'd never done much else but feed him and scold him. No wonder he'd run away. A father who drank and a sister who scolded. It wasn't much of a life for a boy. And yet he had never complained. He was mischievous and disobedient but he had never complained. And she had thought, when she ever did think about it, that he was happy in his own strange way with his cat and his trains and his balloons. 'He's always the same,' she whispered now. 'Jacques is always Jacques.'

'What a dangerous assumption,' Alphonse murmured with interest. 'Are you telling me that you are always Eveline?'

'Yes. No. Of course not. I am older.'

'I see.'

He'd tied her up in knots and she realised how stupid she sounded. To her, Jacques was Jacques and Papa was Papa. A little boy and a drunk. Because that was what she wanted them to be. A little boy and a drunkard whereas she had leave to be different, to change, to evolve, to grow. She was guilty of the thing she hated most in Laurie – putting someone in a box and throwing away the key. Putting someone in a box for one's own peace of mind.

'Well, never mind all that now,' Alphonse said quietly, taking her arm so that she could keep up with his long, loping strides. 'We'll head straight for the Gare du Nord. We'll find him.'

They made their way to the station as quickly as they could, Alphonse leading her on a shortcut through back gardens, down narrow alleyways, over piles of rubble and walls so that she cut her hands and feet many times and ripped her dress. But she was glad it was Alphonse taking her and not Laurie. She felt a little guilty about it but she was glad that Laurie was still in hospital so that she could go to Alphonse without reproach. Laurie was not the best person in a crisis. He thought too much, analysed too much and in the end he usually did nothing. Alphonse just seemed to know without thinking. It wasn't that he reduced the complexity of things – far from it – but he was able somehow to cut a path direct to the core, the heart of a problem in a matter of minutes. It was a gift she recognised and appreciated, especially now. It was a gift, she guessed, of a natural leader. He didn't say much but when he did, you listened. She didn't know much about him but she didn't need to because she trusted him. It was a feeling that went beyond words, beyond thoughts even.

The Gare du Nord was lit up like a bandstand. People were milling about with lamps and candle torches and making one hell of a racket. A balloon had just gone up by the look of things.

'We've missed it,' cried Eveline, aghast, tearing from Alphonse's grasp and running headlong for the take-off point. 'JACQUES, JACQUES,' she shouted, gazing about her in bewilderment. The sky was a pure evil black with one or two horridly twinkling stars and the ground was scuffed where the balloon had been, the tethering ropes coiled like treacherous snakes. She grabbed somebody's arm. 'When did it go up?' she demanded.

'Only a short time ago, miss.'

'Who was on it?'

'A little boy and a big fat man.'

'N... not Mathers?' she whispered, her heart sinking.

'Who?'

'Mathers. A sailor. An old sailor.'

'I don't think so, miss.' The man scratched his head. 'They called him the Professor.'

Eveline blanched. 'The English Professor?'

The man's brow cleared. 'That's right. Do you know him? He was going up to study the eclipse of the moon. They say he's mad as a March hare.'

'And he's been to Zanzibar,' somebody piped up.

'I thought it was a little dwarf man with him at first then I saw it was a nipper. Couldn't have been more than ten. Some tearaway fleeing from home probably.'

Eveline didn't want to admit it was *her* home the tearaway was fleeing from; and she felt a lump come into her throat. Why had she ever gone to the Rue de Turbigo? she wondered. Why hadn't she stayed home and looked after Jacques? 'Was it a safe ascent?' she hesitated.

'Depends what you mean by safe,' the man recalled. 'They couldn't get any lift at first, the Professor's weight being what it is... in the end they threw out so much ballast it shot up like a fucking bullet, scusing the language. Like a fucking bullet!' His eyes shone at the memory. 'The Professor looked half out of his wits.'

Eveline wanted to shut her ears to it now but a little crowd had gathered round by this time and everyone was putting in their pennyworth. Someone said he'd heard the boy miaow like a cat he'd obviously been so frightened. Another said he'd seen him fall from the basket clinging on to a sack of ballast. The general consensus of opinion was that the Professor was some sort of lunatic and the boy an unfortunate orphan.

'Poor little mite,' a woman sighed. 'His mother will be turning in her grave if she's dead and if she's alive she oughtn't to be. Did you really say he shrieked like a cat?'

'Fifi!' Alphonse whispered in Eveline's ear and she almost but not quite smiled.

The crowd was mulling over the incident now, expressing concern for the adventurers by prophesying all the terrible calamities likely to befall them and the dire straits they would no doubt end up in. Eveline wanted to kick them all in the shins but she restrained herself by holding tightly to Alphonse's hand.

Alphonse led her gently away then because she was on the verge of hysteria. One or two people were giving her pointed glances, shaking their heads in disapproval.

'How can he go up there?' she blubbered as Alphonse half carried her out of the station, 'when sometimes he can't even sleep without a light.' She pointed up at the sky. 'It looks so black, as black as marble and he is only a little boy.'

'Don't forget,' Alphonse interrupted sternly, 'how skilful, competent and well practised he is, how impressed we were when we saw him rehearsing. And the Professor is an experienced balloonist whatever else he is. He will be back soon enough to plague you again.'

'But he is only a little boy,' Eveline wailed again.

'He is a young man,' Alphonse corrected. 'And one day he will tell his grandchildren how he flew over Paris with a lunatic Professor.'

That did the trick. The thought of Jacques as a grandfather made Eveline giggle albeit a little hysterically.

'Besides which,' Alphonse went on sombrely, 'maybe it is better this way. Who knows what will happen in the next few weeks. He's probably safer up there than down here. In fact I wish you had all gone off in a balloon.'

'What do you mean?' asked Eveline, alerted by his tone of voice.

Alphonse shrugged his shoulders. 'Paris is in turmoil,' he said simply. 'Anything could happen.'

Eveline wanted to press him on the subject but his lips were set in such a grim determined line that she didn't dare to.

They talked about the war then in general terms – of the possible armistice with Prussia and the disaster of Buzenval – and conversation quickly turned to Laurie who was still laid up in the Louvre which had recently been transformed into another hospital.

'He is a little ashamed,' Eveline admitted. 'He says concussion is hardly a war wound!'

Alphonse smiled. 'Is he still raving about the French Officer?'

'Yes, he seems to be. And Tessier. He says the officer shouldn't have taken Tessier's gun like that.'

'Maybe he needed it,' Alphonse remarked a little brusquely, 'more than Tessier did.'

Eveline was silent for a moment as a mark of respect. 'The doctor says Laurie will be better when he gets back to familiar surroundings. I'm to take him some of his books and paper for his letters.'

'Of course,' Alphonse grinned. 'Where would Laurie be without his books?'

Eveline sometimes wondered the same thing but she didn't want to admit it to Alphonse out of loyalty to Laurie. She no longer loved him – she knew that now – if she ever had but he was still a friend whom she wanted to defend. 'And what is wrong with liking books?' she asked almost playfully.

'Nothing whatsoever. Unless they take the place of reality.'

'At least he has a passion,' Eveline burst out hotly. 'At least he has a passion for something.'

Alphonse gave her an odd, serious little look for a moment. 'Yes,' he nodded. 'Some of us find solace in words, shadows, ghosts, things that don't exist…'

'And others?'

'Others have more prosaic needs. We are content with people and what we find in them.' His eyes resumed suddenly their merry twinkle. 'And you, Miss Eveline Renan? Did you find your passion at the Rue de Turbigo?'

He had a knack of turning the tables. Eveline knew that of old. Whenever you dug too close he fielded you off with a joke or a dry riposte. 'Sort of,' she shrugged. 'I don't know. I got a gun and a uniform.'

'Help!' laughed Alphonse. 'Eveline Renan has a gun and a uniform. Take cover everybody!' He almost shouted it into the empty street. 'Take cover everybody!'

He was ridiculous – but he made her laugh – and she knew he was trying to cheer her up and she was grateful to him for that. 'If you remember rightly,' she taunted him, 'it was you who encouraged me to join a women's battalion. Your exact words were: "Break free while you've got the chance else you'll be a little mouse forever".'

Alphonse shook his head gravely. 'If that's true it was mighty irresponsible of me. Mighty irresponsible.' He pretended to shiver and shake. 'But I must have been mad to ever call you a mouse.'

'You did!' she cried triumphantly.

'Mouse with a tiger's heart more like!' He brushed her fingers with the tips of his own. 'But you must be very fond of me to remember my words so exactly,' he teased.

She hoped he couldn't see her blushing in the darkness. 'I have the memory of an elephant,' she explained. 'I remember everything.'

'An elephant's memory and a tiger's heart all in the shape of a slender little mouse! What a girl you are Eveline Renan! Is this what Laurie means when he talks about evolution?'

It suddenly started to rain quite heavily and Eveline stared up at the sky in alarm.

'He'll be fine,' Alphonse comforted her, taking off his coat and wrapping it round her for she'd run out of the house wearing next to nothing. But it was coming down hard and pretty soon they were both completely soaked to the skin. They decided to take shelter in Laurie's rooms. It wasn't far and it would kill two birds with one stone, Eveline said, because she could get the books and they could wait for the storm to pass. At least it was warm and dry in there and Laurie wouldn't mind at all. At least she didn't think he would.

'D'you think he'll be alright?' Eveline asked as they ran, heads bowed, in the direction of the Rue d'Enfer.

'Who? Laurie or Jacques?'

'Both,' answered Eveline wondering vaguely what on earth she was doing. The night had been so strange already, full of unexpected twists and turns and she had the oddest feeling it wasn't over yet. A voice outside herself had suggested the plan of taking shelter in Laurie's rooms and part of her had looked on askance. Would Laurie really mind her going to his rooms in the company of his good friend Alphonse? She squashed the doubts with an invisible shake of the head. Of course he wouldn't. It was the sensible thing to do.

'They'll be fine,' Alphonse answered. 'If Laurie has his books and Jacques has his balloons they'll both be in seventh heaven. Wherever they are. It's you who needs a passion,' he added, gripping her hand so hard that she almost yelped out in pain. She turned to scold him but the look in his eyes made her giggle nervously instead. They were serious yet playful, fierce yet hesitant. His eyes are the key, Eveline told herself then as if at the birth of some sudden illumination. The eyes spoke everything his voice did not. Whenever I want to know him I must just remember to look in his eyes.

She was so busy looking into his eyes that she didn't notice the solitary figure beneath his umbrella gazing at them with interest from the far side of the street. And when they turned down the Rue d'Enfer the figure changed its course and followed closely after.

They tiptoed past the concierge who was sound asleep and always asleep. Eveline had a key but she didn't want any awkward questions about Alphonse. Dripping and giggling they crept up the steps and into Laurie's rooms where it was marvellously warm and dry and the cuckoo clock was just striking one. Alphonse lit the lamp and stared discreetly out of the porthole window while she dried herself off with a dirty old duster.

'What a night!' she chattered, smearing and smudging herself as best she could then going over to the bookshelf in an effort to select a book. She could hear nothing but the sound of her heart pounding and her fingers trembled as they ran over the titles. Molière's *Imaginary Invalid* – no that wouldn't do at all! Corneille's *Fantastical Illusion* – nor that! Racine's *Antigone* and other plays…

'What about Racine?' she called over her shoulder.

'Who?' teased Alphonse, presumably staring out at Miss 49 and Mr 50 or the blackness, stars and the square-topped belfry of St Jacques.

'Laurie loves his work,' Eveline muttered to herself, trying to remember what he'd said about it. Beautiful, tragic like a piece of Bach… all about fate and how we can't escape it. She pulled the book out onto her lap. Was there such a thing as destiny, as fate? Did every moment in the past lead up to this point? Did you choose your own destiny or did it choose you?

'Do you believe in fate?' she asked, twisting her head round to look at him.

He was standing staring at her with his back to the window. She looked quickly into his eyes. They were purposeful and determined as they always were yet oddly shy and passionate, and she saw with relief that they spoke everything she wanted to hear. She smiled to herself, still grappling with the idea of destiny. They had chosen to be here. They didn't need to be. It was only a spot of rain after all – he could have escorted her back to her father's house and probably should have. They had colluded in it – both of them. And yet it had seemed strangely inescapable too.

She smiled a welcoming smile and the thought of Laurie passed through her mind, but only for a moment.

'Fate,' Alphonse replied, coming towards her with his arms open wide, 'is what we make happen…'

Jacques soared above the clouds, grasping his satchel and grinning from ear to ear. The Professor was sound asleep, tired out with all his exertions and he, Jacques, was in charge of the balloon. All alone. Master of the skies, the heavens, of every little thing they flew over: palaces and prisons, chimney stacks and church steeples, hospitals, grasshoppers, sweet shops and trees. He pinched himself again just in case he was dreaming but the pinch hurt so much he knew that he wasn't. No dreams had ever been like this, even the ones of Amelia Botton! Fifi poked her head out of the satchel, gave a nonchalant glance in the direction of Neptune and Jacques gave her a reproving tap on the nose with the end of his peachstone whistle.

'Fishes and cream,' he promised her, 'when we get to America! Much better than a bit of scrawny old pigeon even if it does come from a line of noble lineage!'

Maybe some chillies for his father, a parrot for his sister, an amber-rated insect for Amelia Botton and a gold tooth for Lippy Buggins. Poor old Lippy Buggins! Poor old chap! Jacques hugged himself in delight, remembering the row of upturned faces that had stared as he soared, gaping and twinkling ever more distantly like pins in a cushion or glow-worms in the dark; and the hubbub of voices like school being let out, far far away… it was perfectly quiet and tranquil now as they sailed aboard a bed of cloud, through blackness and stars and over every little thing that had ever been since time began. He was leaving it all behind. The petty squabbles and the scoldings, the wars and the washing up. He was sailing over everything that anyone had ever taught him. The catechism and algebra, honey and bees. He was free, perfectly free. He could spit on it all if he chose to. Not that he would of course. He left that sort of behaviour to the likes of Lippy Buggins. Though it would have been fun to have spotted Monsieur Lafayette and dropped a gob on that boiled egg head of his. Maybe a bag of sand ballast just to teach him a lesson. A good clout from the heavens. Not that he would of course. He had more important things to see to like Zanzibar, America, the Orient, the moon…

Little did he know that his nemesis was down below pressed to the keyhole outside Laurie's rooms, peeping and peering for all he was worth, his bald head shining like a full moon itself; and as the stars grew paler and paler in the sky, his black eyes grew brighter until they fairly glistened.

Chapter seventeen

Brother Michael looked wilder than ever as he paced the floor of Bernadine's cell, stopping every now and then to cock his head and listen. He'd paced and waited for nearly two hours and out of those two, he decided then and there, three had been spent agitating in the armchair. Sometimes he pushed aside the dingy grey curtain to peer down the corridor at the warren of little cells but he caught neither hide nor hair of Bernadine or Bluebird, as he'd recently dubbed the infant Aggie. He hoped they hadn't come to any harm. It was a dark night to be out and about in the low dives and haunts of Montmartre.

He fell to reciting the *Confiteor*, the *Office of the Virgin* and a long Latin sentence in which he got completely lost. '*Sanctus, sanctus, sanctus,*' he mumbled, making the sign of the cross in the air. '*In nomine Patris*. In the name of the father...'

He wanted to say '*In nomine Patris, Filii et Spiritus Sancti*' but he couldn't get past '*In nomine Patris*'. The words got stuck in his throat. Those dratted miraculous wines of the steward had given him a headache indeed. Bloody fool, watering them down like a bunch of patio roses. He needed Dutch courage at this point not a headache and a fuzzy tongue. In the name of the father, he tried again – to no avail.

He'd determined to tell all – though it would cost him his black stockings and cassock. 'There will be nothing left of my religious life,' he said to himself, 'but a pair of black stockings and a worn-out cassock.' Still, conscience dictated that he reveal all, unburden his soul, loosen the tug boat of sin for the waves and the Lord to do what they would with. He had no doubt that the Lord would forgive him. It was the Lord's job to forgive. It was what He did after all. Brother Michael had concluded long ago that it was the Lord's job to forgive and the Mother Superior's job to punish. The thought now of what that Gentle Terror might do to him when she found out sent a shiver down his spine and the whole of his portly frame baulked so that he paused in the spirit of St Thomas Aquinas, one overly capacious boot mid air, mid step. Perhaps he didn't need to tell her after all. Perhaps it would be best not to tell her at all. She had plenty to worry about without adding his spiritual health to the list of her concerns. Indeed it would be kindest not to tell her. It would be doing her a positive disservice to tell her.

Yes, that was it! Brother Michael began pacing again, much relieved in heart and mind. To tell the Mother Superior of his wrongdoing would be the biggest wrongdoing of all. It might even be the straw that broke the camel's back for she was terribly overburdened with her shelves of confiscated property – the novels and bottles of anisette, fancy note paper and smuggled sweets – and spent longer and longer each day sorting through them, her whispers less and less audible, her face quite red and startled if you came upon her unawares. No, it would be quite improper, the most heinous crime of self-indulgence to loosen his little tugboat of sin on her waters. It was for the waves and the Lord to deal with. And maybe Sister Bernadine. She had a right to know and she wouldn't be too appalled. She had secrets of her own, so they said. Shady Lady. Woman Rumoured to have a Past. He would clear his conscience with her, she would smile, nod her head, and he would disappear like a cloud into the velvet of the night.

Yes, that was it! To disappear like a cloud into the velvet of the night. Like a ghost, a will o' the wisp, leaving no trace but a pair of black stockings and a worn-out cassock. They would grumble, curse, lament his departure but at least he would have followed the dictates of his conscience. Or would he? A nagging little voice told him he was a casuist of the first and worst order, that he must brave it out with the Mother Superior and face the consequences of his actions. Yes he must! No he mustn't! Yes he must! No he mustn't! He swung like a pendulum between a rock and a hard place. If he stayed what would they do to him? If he went where would he go? It was all very well disappearing into the velvet of the night but where did it take you? He'd gone astray once already in the velvet of the night and look what had come of that! He'd better just stay and face it out. An image of the Gentle Terror's face swum into his head, red and whispering. No he hadn't! He should go – sharpish! Why should he tell her anything? She only kept him here out of charity because nobody else would have him. His existence here was merely one of a Silent Reproach.

He threw himself into the armchair and flung his apron over his head, revealing a pair of black trousers patched in green at the knee. His existence had always been one of a Silent Reproach, ever since his days at the monastery or even before when his mother had washed her hands of him. Oh, she'd spun him a story! She'd even climbed into the monastery orchard and adorned the trees with sugared almonds and fruit, marzipan and candies to persuade him that it yielded good and sweetly things. He'd thought, at the age of ten, that he was entering the gates of heaven. Tennis and lotto in the sand, boules and skittles. His fall from grace had come in the end of year report when the Brothers had written: 'Little Michael has proved himself to be a proficient player of boules but is not at all useful in the classroom.' Not at all useful in the classroom. The words still stung him after all these years.

'Oh woe is me,' he spluttered, quite overcome with self pity. 'Why me? Why me? Why doesn't life go and tweak somebody else's nose for a change?' It had been tweaking his for as long as he could remember, which he believed accounted for its extraordinary shape and colour. Life had a nasty habit of coming up and tweaking you by the nose like a cheeky little prankster just as you were going along fine and dandy. In the end he'd tried to beat it at its own game, tweak life in the nose for a change and look what had come of that! He had better just go, like a will o' the wisp, a shade, a ghost, like a cloud into the velvet of the night.

'*Oh nomine Patris!*' he groaned with the apron over his head. '*Oh nomine Patris!*' he gulped, desperately trying to bring up the words like a cat straining to regurgitate a hairball.

Bernadine's eyelids drooped with fatigue as she listened to the comforting sound of little Aggie suckling at the young woman's breast and the not-so-comforting sound of the coffin maker up above tip-tapping his nails into soft, yielding wood, smooth and regular as the ticking of old clocks. Nailing time down for an eternity. His business was thriving, the young woman had told her, for typhoid was spreading like wildfire with all the unfiltered water from the Seine. Bernadine knew she was risking the baby by bringing her to such a place but what else could she do? She had no milk of her own to give her and no other means of getting it. And she had thanked her lucky stars and God when she'd come across the young woman, after a seemingly endless search, in the poorest, most dilapidated, inhospitable part of Montmartre.

Even now she couldn't believe it. Couldn't believe she was sitting here in a room no bigger that a nun's cell with almost as little furniture. A chair, bed, stove, the rest gone for food or firewood. It would satisfy the ascetic soul of even the most perfect of nuns. Not a sniff of indulgence to tempt the heart away from virtue. Small, bleak, clean and bare – except on the outside. The outside had filled her with terror when she'd first come upon it. A monstrous ogre of a building towering above her, five storeys high with fifteen blackly discoloured shutters and three disused shops on the ground floor. An old haberdasher's with an ancient umbrella still propped in the window like the broken wings of some enormous old crow, a coal merchant ransacked and ruined and a greasy eating house filled with sticky dust and grime instead of sticky buns and dumplings. She'd wanted to turn and flee back through the courtyard over the puddles, stinking heaps of rubbish, nappies and clothes plastered with filth. But something had made her go in, go on, up and up the staircases, round and round the corridors until she felt quite faint. They were narrow and gloomy and lit by a sputtering oil lamp or smoking candle now and again, like a star at the end of one's destination; but more often than not she got herself lost and had to retrace her steps past doors that were shut, blackened at the lock from the dirt of hands, and doors that were open and offering glimpses into lives that were strange and bizarre to her. Lives that made her squirm, turn red, avert her eyes or quicken her step. A woman in spangly garters lolling lazily on a bed with a man in nothing but his shirt-sleeves; a tall girl with a pail of water in front of a row of tow-headed children; a card game; a full scale beating; shoutings, coughs, mutterings, moans; a little old crone as yellow as wax, singing to herself and a couple of toy dolls; and the undertaker with a face like a Gruyère cheese, all dressed in black, grinning and tip-tapping at his wood. And then at last at the end of a seemingly endless corridor she'd found Anna. Anna sitting in her armchair and wringing her hands, her infinitely sad eyes fixed intently on the open doorway as though she'd been expecting her. As though she'd been expecting a strange nun to walk in carrying a hungry baby in her arms.

Bernadine smiled as the girl rocked and crooned little Aggie, putting her to the other breast with large and skilful hands. She was growing more attached to the baby each day – Bernadine could see that and it worried her a little. Sometimes when she sat cross-legged on the floor, almost invisible in the shadows, she tortured herself with the thought that she ought to just go, get up and leave the baby right here in this small bare, bleak room and large warm, comforting hands. But she knew she couldn't do it. She just couldn't. She'd made a promise to Agnes and to herself, and even if it had been the best alternative for the child she knew she still wouldn't have been able to do it. The emotions that had sprung to life since Agnes' death and little Aggie's birth were almost unstoppable. Like weeds that flourish when a stone is lifted from them. They choked everything in their path, every act of discipline she'd ever imposed upon herself, every rule, order, prayer, vow. She'd thought those emotions were long dead and forgotten but they'd simply been hibernating along with the snowdrops and primroses. Waiting for spring and the stone to be lifted from them. Waiting for time to start ticking again.

Tip tap, went the undertaker up above, his smallpox-ravaged face like a Gruyère cheese. Nobody can look at him, the young woman had told her, because his face reminds them of Gruyère cheese and it makes them feel too hungry. Bernadine strained her ears to the unfamiliar sounds of the building: the creaks, groans, mutterings and rumblings; the gurgling of little Aggie, the undertaker's tapping. One life ended; another just begun. In the street down below a drunkard was sobbing his heart out and the raised but muffled voice of the concierge was berating him soundly. And in the far distance she could hear a violin playing a quadrille for some revellers, clear and thin like the sound of a harmonica. She still couldn't get used to the noise, the chaos, the confusion. She'd skulked in the shadows of the convent too long, fearing the intoxication of full sunlight, steeling herself to take one step beyond its walls, its confines. Now she was out she felt smaller than an insect and more anonymous; cut off from the run of ordinary existence with its laughter, hope, tears… She'd seen the same look in the eyes of the poor or those who had suffered too much to find their way back to their place in the world. A little afraid, a little detached; wanting to join in but not knowing how. Or in the most extreme of cases they looked through you, past you, beyond you, liberated from the trials and tribulations, storms and vain delights. They simply awaited sleep. Awaited the tip tapping.

Anna's husband barged in then, brandishing a kitchen knife; and following closely after came a little blonde girl with her pinafore stuffed full of twigs and old leaves.

'They felled the old oak on St Michel,' she chirruped in front of her mother. 'The one we used to play hide and seek in. Papa dug out the roots and I took all the twigs I could see before anyone else could get them.'

Anna patted the girl on the head and exclaimed over the pinafore while her husband went to see what the nun had brought in exchange for his wife's precious milk. Bernadine thanked God that Brother Michael had provided her with a bunch of decent carrots and a few coins.

'Ten francs,' the man said, biting into a coin, 'would barely get you a cabbage these days.'

'Papa, Papa,' cried the little girl, tugging at his shirt which he was now wearing inside out to save on the washing. 'Shall I make the fire?'

'Hush Lalie,' Anna scolded lazily and pleasantly. 'Give your father a chance to catch his breath.'

The little girl went over to the fireplace and, kneeling down on the cold hearth, she emptied out her wooden treasure and began dividing it into piles of roots, twigs and leaves. It was obviously her usual job for she started singing a merry little tune as she did it and Bernadine's heart went out to her with her angelic face and her fierce little spirit.

'Has Gruyère got another?' the man enquired, sitting himself down cross-legged on the bed and tilting his head up to the ceiling.

'Three,' replied the young woman despairingly, tears springing into her eyes. 'Old ma Bru, little Emily on staircase B and Tisha who takes…who took in the ironing.'

'May they rest in peace,' said the man with a dull snigger, cleaning the blade of the kitchen knife with his handkerchief. 'Our father and all that…'

'Hush!' cried Anna with a fearful glance at Bernadine.

He held the knife up to the candlelight, twisting it this way and that then spitting on it to bring it up to a really good shine.

'Shall I blaze it up, Papa?' Lalie said softly from the hearth, almost to herself. 'Shall I blaze it up?'

'Don't you think,' the woman asked then, holding little Aggie up for her husband to see, 'that she has a look of Louis when she sleeps?'

The man's mouth tightened and he spat fiercely on the blade again without looking up. 'No I don't. And stop mooning over her, woman.'

Bernadine decided it was time to go and she got up with great difficulty, her legs all pins and needly from sitting so long on the floor.

'The nun wants to go,' the man announced rudely from the bed. 'Give the baby up to her Anna or I shall have to start upping the price of your useless milk.'

The woman smiled at Bernadine, her eyes big and pleading. 'Why don't you leave her here for the night. It will save you a journey,' she babbled. 'And it can't be good for her this late and so cold. And I can do the night feeds – you know how she hates the bottle.'

'Thank you,' said Bernadine firmly but with a rising sense of panic. 'But I must take her.' And she almost grabbed Aggie from the woman's arms and placed her hurriedly in the cotton shoulder sling she had devised for carrying. She didn't dare look at the woman for she knew the pain she would see; and she felt a little ashamed of what she was doing. She was almost doing to her what others had done to herself. But she had no intention of giving up Aggie. No intention at all. 'Here, take this,' she said guiltily, yanking the gold cross from her neck and holding it out as if it were some sort of compensation – though she knew only too well that it wasn't.

'I… I couldn't,' cried the woman, almost shrinking back from the object in alarm. But her husband had already leapt from the bed and was padding over in his holey socks, his churlish face almost smiling. 'That's more like the price of milk,' he muttered, taking the chain from Bernadine and holding it up to the light. 'You're welcome anytime, Sister.'

Bernadine nodded curtly and almost ran for the door, desperate to leave the scene behind her. She felt sorry for the woman and the child and even the man but she didn't know what else to do about it. And she wondered if she could risk coming here again.

'If I blaze it up really hard,' Lalie was asking sadly from the cold hearth, 'will it warm little Louis up in heaven, Papa?'

Bernadine bowed her head and scuttled down the corridor, almost fearing the man might come after her, brandishing his knife; and not daring to look through the open doors to the rooms that were full and teeming with life – though she caught a glimpse of the woman in garters yawning lazily in bed and the man in shirtsleeves pouring coffee. She felt suddenly old and tired with an accumulated fatigue of years and years and she wished she might bump into old Gruyère so he could measure up a coffin for her that very instant. And then, feeling the comforting weight of Aggie in her shoulder sling, she got a grip of herself. She had a baby to care for now. What else mattered?

She sped down the stairs as quickly and safely as she could and out into the courtyard. The moon was veiled in cloud like an old woman in mourning and the drains stank worse than ever in the stillness, black and profound. Clutching Aggie to her chest, she leapt over puddles which the lamp from the concierge lit with bright new stars. Strange and unfamiliar stars.

Brother Michael heaved a sigh of relief when he saw the two of them at the end of the corridor. Bernadine on the other hand nearly swore under her breath when she caught sight of him lurking about in the doorway to her room. Really, it was too much the way he paid her visits at any old godforsaken hour of the day or night, bemoaning this, confessing to that. Since Agnes' death he had practically confessed to everything under the sun including stealing peaches from the hothouse of the Tuileries as well as lacing the steward's porridge with pepper. She wondered what trifling misdemeanour had given him a case of insomnia this evening. She noticed he looked more perturbed than ever if that were possible – his eyes wild, his nose red and bruised as if someone had given it a good pinching. And while she groaned inwardly with utter weariness, she forced herself to smile outwardly with polite kindness.

'There you are!' Brother Michael let out another gigantic sigh. 'There you are!' He stuck his head up close to the infant and gave what he thought was a comforting grimace which luckily the child didn't see being fast asleep. 'I feared you had come to some harm.'

'As you can see,' Bernadine replied firmly, 'we haven't. What can I do for you, Brother Michael, at this hour?'

Brother Michael flushed at the vague reproach and bowed his head. 'A word if you please, Sister Bernadine, for a beleaguered soul. It takes one moment to confess a sin, a lifetime to redeem it.'

'Quite,' said Bernadine, beginning to feel a little annoyed for she was almost dead on her feet. She didn't want another discussion about sin and forgiveness at the crack of dawn; and she didn't want to hear about the Mother Superior's slow descent into madness, the steward's so-called miraculous wines or the fat, ripe peaches that grew at the Tuileries. None of it seemed to matter to her now. All she cared about was Aggie – keeping her alive, keeping her safe, keeping her well.

'Ignatius said what serves it to a man to conquer the world if he should lose his soul,' Brother Michael began hesitatingly.

'Quite so.' Bernadine slid the baby gently from the sling and swaddled her up tightly in another blanket like a little butterfly in a cocoon.

Brother Michael was pacing the floor now. 'Ever since Agnes died I have been thinking about the Virgin Mary. That Portal of Grace through which our Saviour entered the world. It was a ray of fecundation shooting from heaven to earth. Like a little sunbeam. It was one emission only,' he almost yelped. 'Ten seconds only! Like a little sunbeam! Even the Virgin Mary can lead you astray!'

'Quite so.' Bernadine laid the baby lovingly in the bottom drawer of the tallboy, marvelling at how much like her mother she looked with her rosy cheeks and her long dark eyelashes.

The old monk took a deep breath. 'I... I... am the father of little Aggie,' he whispered so softly that the words hardly left his lips, so softly that Bernadine didn't hear him at all as the infant hiccuped merrily in her sleep. 'Yes, dear,' she replied, believing he was confessing to some trifling misdemeanour and thinking (with an almost psychic flash) that he was not unlike dear old Agnes in that respect and what a good pair they would have made.

Brother Michael stared at her incredulously. 'You are not appalled?'

'Of course not,' she turned, smiling as the tears poured down his face. 'We are the sinners He lops and prunes. It is not the worst thing in the world. Here, blow your nose,' she added, handing him over a handkerchief, 'and don't upset yourself so. Sleep is a great restorer of body and spirit,' she reminded, a little slyly for her.

'But I must tell the Mother Superior.' He blew his red and swollen nose. 'Mustn't I?'

'If you must,' Bernadine half laughed. 'Though as you say, she is already tied up with all her confiscated property.'

'That's true.' He blew his nose again loudly but the tears still swam into his eyes. He was still in shock from what had just occurred. He had expected a dressing down at the very least, not this sublime goodness. This was goodness unparalleled. The goodness they talked about in the book of books; and he stared at Bernadine with undisguised admiration. She was a miracle of virtue, piety, love and compassion. She had set the standard of goodness so high that he could only stare up at it humbled and in awe. What a woman! What a nun! Giving off glows and hints galore so that the poor man felt that if he wasn't very careful he might go astray once more in the velvet of the night. He checked himself hard. He was littler than an ant compared to such greatness. Littler than a grain of sand. But he would come to deserve her in the end – little ant by little sand he would move the mountain of guilt and sin until he could raise his own bar of goodness one step higher.

He was filled suddenly with a sense of resolve, purpose, determination and he straightened himself up to his full height, mustering up all the spiritual strength that he could.

'I shall join the army,' he announced sombrely, much to Bernadine's astonishment.

'Yes dear,' she replied placatingly. 'I'm sure you will one day. But you had better go to bed first. Everything always seems so much better after a good night's sleep.'

Brother Michael held up his hand. 'Do not dissuade me, Sister Bernadine, out of your immense wealth of goodness and mercy. Do not try and dissuade me. I have made up my mind. I shall die for you and Bluebird if I have to.'

Bernadine had a horrible thought that he'd been sipping the miraculous wines again but she could smell no alcohol about him and in his own peculiar way he was in command of himself. She watched him kneel down beside the bottom drawer of the antique tallboy and with violently trembling hands make the sign of the cross above the infant's head.

'Your mother was a grand lady,' he whispered, smiling through tears. 'The Prettiest Perfectest Peach… and the only one who would ever hold her breath for me.'

His great head wobbled from side to side like a very old man's as he delicately caressed little Aggie's face. 'I give you leave not to live as a Silent Reproach. I give you leave never to let yourself feel belittled. Be somebody. Be anybody. But never live your life as a Silent Reproach.'

And then he got up and turned to Sister Bernadine who sat bemused and amazed at the edge of her bed; and he bowed deep and low to her like a man paying the warmest homage.

'*In nomine Patris, Filii et Spiritus Sancti*!' he recited with perfect inflection before backing slowly and with great dignity out of the room and (once he'd packed his few belongings) out of the convent and into the deep dark velvet of the night like a shade, a ghost, a will o' the wisp. And just as he wanted he left no trace but a pair of black stockings and a worn-out cassock; though a few days later a rumour reached the convent that a balding monk had feigned death by holding his breath and thereby escaped over enemy lines.

Chapter eighteen

'This is a disgrace!' shouted an irate-looking gentleman from the pulpit, matching each word, syllable for syllable, with a punching cut in the air. 'This is not an armistice, this is capitulation. We have capitulated to the Prussians even though General Trochu and that specious member of our Elected Imbecility, Jules Favre[17], have been telling us for months that we will never give in, never give up an inch of our territories, stone of our fortresses. Ha Ha! What they say and what they mean are evidently two very different things indeed. They have led us up the garden path,' he added, mixing his metaphors, 'like lambs to the slaughter.'

A woman with piled-up hair put her hand out to interrupt. 'General Trochu says he is the Jesus Christ of the situation. All I'd like to say is that if he's the Jesus Christ of the situation,' her eyes gave a dramatic sweep of the room, 'then who is the Judas, who is the Lucifer?'

'Well put,' the man from the pulpit applauded. 'I couldn't have put it better myself. If he's the Jesus Christ of the situation then I must be his mother!'

One or two titters met this as well as a few hear hears though a little old lady jabbed her son in the arm and enquired in a perplexed voice: 'What on earth is he talking about? Why is he saying he's his mother?'

'In 1792,' the irate-looking man bawled on, 'our forefathers fought all Europe without bread, without clothes, without shoes… and yet in 1871…'

'How do you know this, sir?' cried a dissident voice from the back of the room and everyone craned their necks to get a look at the upstart.

The man in the pulpit looked a little dumbfounded.

'Because the history books tell us? Because you see funny little pictures in history books? Were you alive in 1792, sir?'

The man in the pulpit looked deeply affronted.

'If you were, by my reckoning that makes you ninety-five at the very least, and in that case you are remarkably well preserved and I would suggest – *loud cheers* – I would suggest that you give your age-defying remedies to the old Emperor who is living out his days in England in semi senility.'

'No more Boney-parts on the throne,' a little man jeered, quite obviously tiddly. 'Let the Emperor enjoy the beautiful climate of England for a while. Maybe he could become an umbrella manufacturer.'

Hear Hear!

The irate gentleman stepped down, dusting his lapels and looking slightly abashed at the strange attacks and surprise interruptions when he'd only been speaking for the majority. The meeting had started off with a bang and it looked like it might explode by the end of the night. The church was packed to the rafters and everyone was making a din, airing their opinions, venting their spleen about a siege they had suffered, so it seemed, in vain. Lips breathed the words 'an armistice with Prussia' in dismay and disbelief even though the tatttered remnants of regiments were pouring back into the city, roaring drunk and causing mayhem.

'Our country, our families, our trades are ruined,' a beery-faced man spoke up then, a butcher by trade with great meat-hook arms. 'We've given up everything to fight the Prussians. We've been kept in suspense for four months and now this? To just give up?' His voice almost failed him. 'It makes me ashamed to be French.'

The house was divided on this. Some people wept in agreement; some caterwauled or booed unrestrainedly, unwilling to take the blame for the imbeciles up above. They were proud to be French and nobody better tell them otherwise. A glass was hurled in the direction of the butcher's head but it missed him totally and crashed into a wine bottle standing on the pulpit, much to everyone's amusement.

'No definite peace treaty has been decided yet,' put in a sensible-looking man in a tweed coat and hat. 'Remember that no peace treaty has been decided yet. Parliamentary elections must be held for the return of an Assembly charged with pronouncing on a definite peace treaty. Until then it is all speculation.'

'Rubbish!' declared a National Guardsman, fixing the tweedy gentleman with his eye and trying to stare him out of countenance. 'If you don't mind my saying so you're talking utter rubbish. Everyone here knows that this is capitulation pure and simple and the peace terms are more than shameful. We are to give up Alsace and Lorraine, pay an enormous war indemnity and hand over our arms and colours. Even the cannon that were paid for by public subscription. It's all over the papers.'

There were furious boos and hisses at this. The amount of hot air expended on the subject would have filled an entire balloon. No one was willing to give up the guns that the city had worked so hard to pay for and manufacture. They had sweated blood over them and blood would be shed if they were forced to give them up.

'Over my dead body,' somebody swore obscenely and his oaths were met with a stampede of delight.

Miss Grist, who was Tessier's replacement, pursed her lips and signalled for an intermission. While everyone else made a dash for the trestle table she duly wrote down in her little green leather-bound notebook: *This is Miss Grist signing off for an intermission at eight fifteen precisely.* She never partook of the 'entertainments' as she put it. She took her job far too seriously for that. She would sit through the whole of every break, straight backed and straight laced, poised and waiting for the moment she could write again in her little green leather-bound notebook: *This is Miss Grist signing in again at eight forty five precisely.* Occasionally a kindly soul would try and tempt her with a dry biscuit and glass of wine but she would always shake her head grimly and indicate the glass of water standing on the table next to the little green leather-bound notebook, though nobody had ever seen her even wet her lips with it. Everyone agreed she didn't have the heart of Tessier and they mourned his loss deeply, waxing nostalgic over his crazy doodles, symbols and flashes of inspiration, conveniently forgetting what a botch job he'd made of all the meetings. Even the ones who'd called him a limp leg and a dull wit now praised him up to the heavens. 'A very hard act to follow,' they would say, shaking their heads in regret at Miss Grist. 'A very hard act to follow!' Nobody gave her any credit for running the show with a firm hand and reworking the little green leather-bound notebook. But she didn't seem to mind. She obviously took pride in a job well done and sat alone on her stool beside the sacristy, a handkerchief tied under her chin, surveying the goings on in St Nicolas with eagle eyes and pursed lips.

Eveline brought a hunk of dark bread and a glass of wine back for Laurie who was bundled up in a back pew, still feeling the cold despite a church full of heated bodies. She and Alphonse had been cracking jokes with him all evening to distract him from Tessier and his own recent brush with death. He'd already taken a dislike to Miss Grist, more out of loyalty to his old friend Tessier than anything else, and he eyed her sullenly from beneath his woollen cap as he dunked his dark bread in the wine.

'She's doing very well,' he began with ostensible fairness, 'but Tessier joined in more. Tessier was more of a team player don't you think?'

Alphonse and Eveline exchanged a small smile. At least he was talking about Tessier without getting hysterical – that was a good sign. The doctor had said it would take a long time for such a sensitive soul to recuperate but he seemed to be getting there.

'I should go into hospital more often,' he said then, smiling at them both, 'if this is how I get treated when I come out! I like being waited on hand, foot and finger!' In truth he had been amazed by the solicitude of his friends and deeply touched by it.

Eveline blushed and patted him on the knee. 'What are friends for?' she whispered in a strange little voice and he stared at her in surprise. She'd been acting strangely ever since his spell in hospital. At first he'd thought it was her fears over Jacques but now he wondered if there was more to it than that. He'd never known her be so kind and considerate, almost tender in her dealings with him, thinking of every whim he might have even before he'd thought of it himself. And Alphonse, normally so aloof, had been dancing attendance upon him like a long-lost brother. He wondered suddenly, with a flash of suspicion, if something had gone on in his absence – and then he let the matter drop. That happened to him a lot nowadays and he thought it was probably a result of his illness. Thoughts came up then drifted off, floating to the edges of his brain. It was like watching a theatrical farce – a medley of characters chased each other across the little stage of his mind – garish, caricatured, grotesque – and he watched them go, sometimes with regret, though he never bothered to pursue them. And they rarely came back for an encore, even the most entertaining. He sat and watched from the gallery, more of an outsider than ever, more detached than ever before.

The three of them chatted on then about the meeting so far. The speakers had all been terrible, Alphonse admitted, grimacing at the memory of the irate-looking gentleman, though to be fair he had spoken for the majority. Laurie urged him to change his mind and speak himself that night but Alphonse shook his head. No, he would remain silent this evening as a mark of respect for Tessier, however much they provoked him! Added to which, the meeting was so out of control that no speaker worth his salt would dare take to the stage for fear of being dragged off it. The crowd wasn't listening to reason tonight – that much was clear already – and Eveline wholeheartedly agreed with him. Laurie sipped his wine thoughtfully, almost choking on one or two dark soggy crumbs and feeling more apprehensive than ever. He'd never felt this way in a meeting before and he'd been hoping it was simply another consequence of his illness but Alphonse had put his very own fears into words for him. Even Alphonse could see that the crowd was not the same. It seemed to Laurie like a wild beast, famished and mistreated, turning brutal and savage and he didn't want to be a part of it or get in its way. He was secretly glad that the war was over but he didn't dare admit it, not even to Eveline; and he shrank back in his seat, pale and afraid, fidgeting nervously with the edge of his blanket.

Miss Grist put up her hand to signal the end of the intermission and duly wrote: *This is Miss Grist signing in again at 8.30 precisely after an interval of fifteen minutes where there was some singing and much inebriation, a broken nose resulting from a fist fight and three spilt bottles of a red wine (Normandy variety).*

A sly little chap took to the stage then, his eyes darting about in his head like marbles. His hands trembled as they gripped the lectern and one or two members of the audience sniggered in anticipation.

'They've been secretly negotiating for weeks,' he began in little more than a whisper, his eyes bashing into each other then rolling away with the shock. 'Favre, Trochu, the lot of 'em have been secretly negotiating with Bismarck for weeks.'

'Speak up!' someone shouted. 'It's not a fucking confessional!'

'What was that?' asked the little old woman in the pew, jabbing her son in the back.

'He says it's not a bloody confessional,' a National Guardsman explained with a hint of irritation in his voice. 'It's not a confessional here, ma'am.'

The old woman looked more perplexed than ever before and she knelt down, clasping her hands together like a young girl in prayer.

Alphonse stood up, stamping his feet. 'This is gibberish,' he said angrily to his friends. 'It's like trying to keep a runaway train on the tracks. Let's get out of here.'

Laurie was more than happy to oblige and Eveline helped him up with his heavy coat and blanket.

'Before things turn nasty,' Alphonse finished, running his hands through his dark spiky hair and eyeing the crowd warily.

In Laurie's opinion things had already turned nasty. Fights were breaking out all over the place – in pews, in aisles, under stained-glass windows depicting gentle scenes of Jesus with a distaff, Mary with a crown of stars, Mary with a little lamb... Right hooks were being hurled as easily as insults and most people were on their feet, creating a furore with their neighbour. Miss Grist seemed to be the only one still seated, valiantly recording the minutes for posterity with a steady hand and pursed lips; and Laurie silently saluted her courage. The tiddly winking man had already been seized and thrown out into the snow to cure his wits and perfumed breath; and the crowd was baying for more blood, like a pack of dogs.

Alphonse gripped Eveline's hand and guided her firmly to the door with Laurie following closely behind, trying not to cry out at the pain of bruised toes and stepped-on heels. He overheard a girl whispering daringly to her friend that she didn't care about Mr Favre or Mr Trochu. All she wanted to know was when the food was coming in and he nodded in sympathy. What did it matter if the peace terms were atrocious – he'd lost his revolutionary zeal for good – if the people ate again, smiled again, were happy again, the boulevards busy and bustling again. He didn't want vengeance. Vengeance or justice even. He just wanted life to return to normal – to pick up Eveline every afternoon from the pâtisserie and get back to his poetry. Maybe taste a decent dinner. Take a trip to Toulouse.

He stared at the clasped hands in front of him and felt a pang shoot through him. What if life never did return to normal? What then? What if this was it? What if this was the beginning of the end for himself and Eveline? He stumbled after his friends, not daring to think the unthinkable and wishing he could turn off the little theatrical farce in his head. He was so depressed by the evening's events that he didn't notice Monsieur Lafayette waiting for them all at the door until the three of them had almost bumped into him.

'You, sir,' the old man accosted Alphonse without preamble, his eyes small as pins, his fat lip wobbling in agitation. 'When you were a waker-upper, sir, how many beauties did you wake up? How many did you put to bed? Mmm?'

'I beg your pardon?' asked Alphonse, staring at Monsieur Lafayette in astonishment, still gripping Eveline by the hand.

The old man looked at him in silence for a moment and Laurie was aware of the racket going on behind like a turbulent stream. 'I said, when you were a waker-upper, sir, how many beauties did you wake up and how many did you put to bed?' he repeated with undisguised malevolence.

Eveline turned to Laurie with a strange expression in her eyes and he had a feeling he was missing something vital and absurd like a jester running across the stage with no clothes on and giving the game away to the audience at the top of his voice.

'You may be a fox with a magnificent brush but sometimes the fox is outwitted by the tortoise!'

'Is that so?' Alphonse drawled, recovering himself sufficiently to speak.

Monsieur Lafayette turned to Laurie then and bowed his head. 'Your fine friend is a traitor. I give you fair warning. A veritable Brutus.' He tapped his nose. 'Watch your back!' And without another word he strode off into the church, leaving Laurie with the feeling that he was peering into the mouth of hell or missing another vital scene in this most peculiar of farces.

'What on earth did he mean?' he cried. 'The man's half mad. I've always said as much. You shouldn't let him in the house, Evie, even if he is an old friend of your father's. Alphonse Duchamp a traitor!' he giggled, clutching nervously at the scarf about his neck as they stepped out into the cold grey night. 'That's a good one! What does he think you are, for heaven's sake? A Prussian spy?'

Alphonse and Eveline bowed their heads, seemingly against the wind, though their hands remained clasped together, tighter than ever.

Chapter nineteen

March 10th 1871

Dearest Maman,
*   I am back on my feet again after a brief spell in the Louvre!*
(Armament shop turned hospital) An extraordinary place to convalesce. I
thought I'd died and gone to heaven when I opened my eyes to that angelic
ceiling. Can you imagine hospital trolleys being wheeled over bloodstained
marbled floors; and patient name tags hanging from the walls in a dusty space
where the Mona Lisa smiled or a La Tour cavorted? I was treated better than
any priceless antique, I am sure – buffed and polished until I felt quite rarefied.
Even now it makes me chuckle to think I convalesced in the Palace of Kings!

We lost some good men at Buzenval. It was, as you may have read, a
complete fiasco. I have come to the conclusion that death is meted out entirely
at random – some strange design beyond any natural human justice. The good
perish as easily as the bad, perhaps more so. Maybe it really is the case that those
whom the gods love die young. They certainly use us for their sport. Tessier was
the best of men...

Laurie broke off, undecided what to say. He didn't even know if he'd
already told her about Tessier. He quite possibly had for he'd written all
sorts in a state of delirium on the reams and reams of paper Eveline had
smuggled in. Poems, dreams, love letters, regrets and lists and lists of
things he wanted to do when he was well. God knows what else. He only
hoped he hadn't sent any of it or if he had that the balloon had gone astray.
Thoughts of balloons brought his mind back to Jacques and he wondered
if he'd told his mother about that. Or about the French officer. He sat

back and lit a cigarette with trembling fingers, gazing through the porthole window to the vast gardens by the belfry of St Jacques, which looked from this distance the same as ever though he knew them to be on closer inspection blackened and deserted. Nothing was what it seemed any more. Nothing worked as it should. Nothing behaved as it should. Everything was topsy-turvy, out of control, out of his ken. The whole world was in disguise in its giant theatrical production, at a masked ball, a fancy dress and he alone sat watching it. It was one of his worst nightmares – to sit alone watching the world, unable to penetrate its disguise: a hospital, an armament shop in the shape of the Louvre; a madman in the uniform of a French officer; a traitor with the face of a friend…

He frowned thoughtfully and picked at a sweet biscuit on the plate beside him, delighting in its crumbly texture and smell; and stretching his long legs luxuriously beneath his warm woollen dressing gown. It was good to be back. It was good to be back home in his own little room with his bed and his books, food and his own thoughts. He must take comfort in that at the very least. If he couldn't count his blessings now, when would he?

The amount of food entering the city from abroad is phenomenal. So far we have received 500 tons of corned beef, 26 tons of fresh fish, 70 tons of cake, 140 tons of butter, 1,500 tons of salt pork and 2000 tons of cheese!

You missed a treat on the first of March. Ha ha. The Kaiser and Bismarck doing their little triumphal march through the streets. It felt, that day, as if the city had died. No omnibuses ran. Fountains were stilled. No newspapers sold, no cafés open for business. Most people held their breath behind locked doors and shuttered windows, waiting for the dreadful event to be over. Bismarck apparently smoked a cigar by the Arc de Triomphe then strode off; and the Kaiser took the review of the troops at Longchamps.

There is much to be set to rights of course besides. There is still a burning anger in the city at the peace terms and the newly elected government set up at Versailles. How can we be led by a man like Thiers[18]? That silly little septugenarian who spent the siege in Tours, fattening up on macaroni! How can he know what we suffered here? Indeed he cannot know for if he did he would not be imposing such draconian measures on a city that has been to hell and back. To demand immediate payment of rent suspended during the siege is not only criminal but foolish. 150,000 bankruptcies have been declared already and there are more to come. If he wants a rebellion he is going the right way of getting one, for Paris is brewing for a fight.

The city smokes, steams, burns, shines, boils and bubbles just as Victor Hugo said it did! Dearest Maman, do you remember the days I spent in Toulouse counting the hours till I got here? Desperate to reach the city of light, to make my name and earn my fortune. The nights I spent reading poetry books and drinking coffee just because Balzac did it, sending myself quite lightheaded in the process! And here I am still in the thick of it as you see, in this bubbling simmering cauldron, waiting to make my name and earn my fortune. It is a place like no other – it hungers, sleeps, weeps, breathes… a giant living organism. Even its buildings are permeable, like great sea sponges, taking on the imprint of the thousands and thousands of souls that live here and have ever lived here since time began. It pulsates to a rhythm quite unlike the rest of France and we dance here to a different tune. If Thiers thinks he can play the Pied Piper, the rats might follow him but the rest of us will not.

Eveline is very quiet. I think she ~~feels guilty, is very guilty, is beside herself~~ fears for the safety of Jacques. We can only hope he hasn't succumbed to the high altitudes or an enemy bullet. Send a prayer up for him, Maman, when you can and tell Molly I expect a perfect rendition of oh let me see, the 'Moonlight Sonata' perhaps – a catchy little number if she hasn't heard of it – upon my return.
All my love now and forever,
Your son,
Laurie.

Laurie munched on a biscuit and stretched his legs out again beneath the dark woollen dressing gown. He wanted to take comfort in the fact that he was back in his own little rooms but even they seemed different to him now. Even his rooms were in disguise. His head was busy with thoughts of Eveline or more specifically with thoughts of Alphonse and Eveline. It was as if they'd flown away from him somewhere, like Jacques in his balloon, leaving him dull and earthbound. He ate a hunk of cheese, picking up the crumbs by pressing the tips of his fingers against them, his thin aquiline face serious and drawn. He wrote *Alphonse is well* as a postscript, then put his pen away, not knowing what else to say. The sun poured in through the porthole window, showing up, it seemed to him, the props of an empty stage: a solitary bookcase and bed, a solitary cobweb in one corner as big as the sail of a ship, a solitary mirror reflecting nothing but its own frame shimmering like gold dust, and a solitary character poorly drawn by an artist with hesitating and undecided fingers.

Part Three: Death, Life

Chapter twenty

Eveline looked at herself in the glass with approval. At first glance she might pass for a man, a rather effeminate young man certainly, with a slender figure and a delicate complexion but a man nonetheless. She swung her head from side to side, delighting in the shorn curls (she'd snipped them off herself) that framed her face like a little halo. She looked like some of the statues her father used to carve of cherubim and archangels and her head felt so light without the weight of the hair that she thought it might float off right through the ceiling and straight up to heaven like a miniature hot-air balloon. She smiled then, wishing Jacques could see her now, dressed up in a man's uniform. She had a feeling he'd be vastly amused by the whole spectacle – the little wretch. She was no longer angry with him for running away. She understood only too well his desire to break free, to escape; and she wished him Godspeed whenever she thought of him.

She tucked the brown woollen trousers into the high black boots and stuck her thumbs under the broad belt about her waist just as Maria at 21 Rue de Turbigo had done. She didn't look bad at all, she decided, quite dashing in fact! The trousers clung to her hips, moulding her soft, slender curves and she struck out her legs like a ballet dancer just for fun and the freedom of movement. She tilted her chin the way Alphonse did and posed with her hands on her hips, giggling to herself as she did it. All she needed was a pipe and a beard to pass muster in any men's club or regiment. And then her face turned serious for it was only now, in the full transformation of dress, that the endless possibilities opened up to her. She could go anywhere like this in disguise as a man, do anything, say anything, be anything she wanted. Not only was there freedom of movement, there was freedom of action, or so it seemed to her at that moment as she stared at the strange reflection in the glass. Herself yet not herself. It was like jumping into a different skin, and this new skin was no barrier to the outside world. This skin was a passport to it, to freedom, adventure, fun. It was the difference between a cocoon and a butterfly. No more being confined, muffled up, pretending deaf and dumbness. She could sing, shout, fly with the best of them, drink herself silly under the table if she felt so inclined, tread the boulevards at night with complete immunity, curse to the heavens without being frowned upon, grab life by the throat and take what she wanted from it without being seen as a whore or a witch. No more waiting for life to come to her. No more hanging around for Laurie to poke his nose out of a poetry book and remember her existence. No more hanging around for her father to poke his nose out of his coffin and demand to know the time or what was for dinner or whether the dreaded Madame Larousse had been after him again (as she had been many times since the ne'er to be forgotten Christmas dinner). No more hanging around for Alphonse to return from one of his so-called secret missions and regale her with selected details while she simpered at his feet like a lovesick puppy. This time she was ready for him. This time she was going with him.

The gentle rat-tat-tat of pebbles on the window heralded his arrival and she took one last look at herself in the mirror before striding over and staring out into the night. She could just about make out his shape tall and straight beside the front doorstep and she threw her handkerchief out of the window to signal she was on her way then scampered down the rickety stairs past her father who was moaning to himself in his coffin. Eveline's heart pounded with excitement in anticipation of Alphonse's reaction and when she opened the door to him he almost fell over backwards then recovered himself with remarkable aplomb, redeeming himself completely by uttering a long, low appreciative whistle.

'Our very own modern-day Joan of Arc! I think it suits you, Miss Eveline.'

She smiled and invited him in for a cinnamon cake and coffee, thinking ruefully to herself that it wasn't as easy as all that to get over the role of little mother. She'd been baking away all afternoon, delighted to be back in the kitchen with an abundance of ingredients; and the whole house smelled temptingly of sweet and savoury snacks, biscuits and warm loaves. Madame Larousse had turned up at around tea time, sniffing her head off and Eveline had given her a tray of currant buns much to her father's disgust. She hadn't gone back to work yet for the pâtisserie had been blown up during the bombardment and was still in a state of disrepair. She hadn't even thought she'd missed it but truth to tell she'd spent several happy days experimenting with strange combinations of flavours, textures and scents; and had a million and one ideas to go back to work with. She had a feeling a new gastronomic wave was about to hit the streets – after the four-month deprivation in taste and sense – and she wanted to be in on the crest of it. She'd rolled liquorice plaits, filled buns with lemon and lavender, even tried a sugarless marzipan dough, though that had not been an unqualified success. And yet she'd found great comfort too, baking the old traditional recipes like gingerbread and Easter biscuits, her fingers and mind revelling again in the repetitive and the familiar. I can bake, she'd said to herself, and be a soldier at the same time!

Alphonse didn't seem to be able to take his eyes off her as she moved about, serving him up his coffee with a sprinkling of sugar and a dollop of fresh cream; and she didn't know whether it was because he knew she was sweetening him up for something or because she really did look too good to be true.

'You've been busy,' he commented, sniffing almost as hard as Madame Larousse had done and she nodded in agreement. 'I could open up my own pâtisserrie with all the baking I've done! How much should I charge for a tray of current buns? I gave one away to Madame Larousse this afternoon.'

'That depends,' Alphonse replied cheekily, sipping his coffee with his eyes closed, 'on how good they are!'

'Oh, they're good,' Eveline replied, smiling at the closed eyes because everyone did that now, everyone drank real coffee again as if it was pure heaven. She wondered if it wasn't such a bad idea after all to open up her own little pâtisserie or even a café. All she had to do was get rid of her father's statues and coffin, sparkle the windows up a bit. She imagined her customers lining up with their eyes half closed to get a taste of her coffee and cake. She felt quite excited about the idea and chatted on merrily about it as she cut out a cinnamon cake for him. 'I could call it Eveline's. Or maybe Renan's. I like the sound of Eveline's – it's a good name for a café... Papa could make some chairs and tables, maybe do a bit of waiting...well perhaps that isn't such a good idea...'

'I have to go soon, Eveline,' Alphonse interrupted her, staring at the cake as if she'd laid some sort of trap for him or was trying to seduce him with it.

She took a gulp of scalding black coffee and almost yelled out with the pain of it. Why did he have this effect on her? Why did he still have such an effect on her? In his presence she became a jabbering lunatic, a silent wreck, a ball of frustration and resentment. They'd never spoken about the night they'd spent together at Laurie's though it lay there palpable between them, between the three of them if you included Laurie, as palpable as the cake he was guzzling now.

'Is it good?' she demanded almost angrily.

'It's good,' he admitted, wiping the crumbs off his beautifully sculpted lips with the back of a rough, workmanlike hand.

For her it had been a night of ecstasy and shame, excitement and betrayal and she wouldn't have taken it back for the world though she still didn't know what it might have cost her, where it was headed or what it meant to Alphonse. He came and went as he pleased, offering no explanations, no promises, no guarantees.

'For all I know,' she blurted out now in spite of herself, 'you really do have a mistress on the Champs Élysées, like they say you do.'

His brilliant blue eyes twinkled in amused astonishment. 'Who says?'

'Oh, people... well, do you?'

'I have neither the time nor the inclination for a mistress,' he replied sternly, pushing the cup and plate away from him as if they were diseased. 'And if you knew me at all, Eveline Renan, you would know that.'

'That's the point I'm making,' she responded quickly. 'I don't know you, don't know anything about you.'

Alphonse sighed. 'Is this the moment when we have the conversation about how many children we shall have, whether we shall take a town house or a pile in the country, whether I can keep you in the style you're accustomed to. If so, we had better get your father in here, if we can lug him out of that godawful coffin.'

Eveline caught his eye and, much as she wanted to keep a straight face, couldn't refrain from laughing out loud. The thought of hauling her father out of his coffin for such a conversation was too amusing for words, but she wasn't going to let Alphonse off the hook as easily as all that; and she said in a teasing voice: 'So you've had these conversations before then?'

'No.' He stared at her seriously and his eyes were warm as they searched her face. 'But many of my friends have and they say it is like speaking the last few words of freedom before the prison gates shut behind them.'

'How can it be a prison,' Eveline enquired a little irritatedly, 'if you're happy with what's there?'

'It will always be a prison – if you catch so much of a glimpse of another life behind the bars you will always think the grass is greener. You are just like me in that respect, Evie, whether you want to believe it or not.'

Eveline looked down at the coffee cup in her hands, tracing the rim with her finger. It was true she had chosen freedom over security, had chosen Alphonse over Laurie as much for the way of life he represented as for his startling beauty. She wanted that way of life for herself, that freedom, that infinite possibility and now here she was, doing what Laurie had done to her, trying to change him, tame him, domesticate him, chain him to her. She realised now that if she wanted him she must take him as he was. He would come and go as he pleased, making no promises, giving no guarantees and nor, for that matter, would she.

'When do we leave?' she asked then, raising her eyes to his and he looked a little surprised then pleased; and she was struck by the sincerity, the strength and calm of his face. 'Well, you're dressed for the part. Can you ride a horse?'

'Yes,' she lied and this time it was his turn to laugh out loud.

'Save me from the Renans!' he chuckled, throwing up his hands. 'One is a balloonist, the other sleeps in a coffin and the third is a magnificent horsewoman!'

To her astonishment he bade her stuff as much of the food she'd baked that afternoon as she could into the hessian sack he always kept in his pocket or about his shoulders; and she packed it deftly, tight as a drum, with layer upon layer of pastries, biscuits, cakes and iced buns (leaving one or two out for her father lest he wake hungry in the early hours) until it bulged out like a Christmas sack.

'Are we feeding the five thousand?' she enquired as he tightened the top and threw it over his back; and he smiled and said: 'More or less, the greedy beggars,' before kissing her in gratitude and pulling her out of the door behind him.

At first she thought she knew where they were going – they were heading for the Champ de Mars – but then as always he started criss-crossing down alleys, up side streets, taking short cuts over back gardens, through courtyards until her head was in a spin and she hadn't a clue where she was. She thought she knew the city like the back of her hand but now here he was magicking up a new one in its place. She didn't know this tree-lined avenue, these sunken houses, this strange little churchyard with the yawning graves. It was as if she'd stepped into someone else's dream and she rubbed her eyes, feeling a little foolish. Maybe it was just the night, the darkness that transformed everything for even Alphonse looked different – like a little hunchback with the hessian bag banging up and down on his shoulders. She caught a few whiffs of new bread and buns and wondered who the greedy beggars were. Surely not the horses! She didn't know much about horses – maybe they ate iced buns and marzipan dough as happily as grass but she didn't think so. She was about to ask Alphonse who the greedy beggars were when he suddenly pushed her into the graveyard behind a huge stone and put a finger to his lips. She hardly dared breathe as two men walked past, talking loudly in drunken voices and she felt Alphonse relax beside her, obviously relieved. He beckoned her on again and she crept close behind, not daring to make a sound or do anything that might give him cause to send her home again.

She padded along behind, puffing as quietly as she could and pleased to be dressed in thick trousers and jacket for the night was cold with a frost-tinted breath. Her toes tingled a little in the high black boots and her face felt quite raw but inside she was aglow with excitement. The girls on the Rue Ornano and La Païva would never do anything like this! They had their sales and their crinolines, balls and caviar but they didn't have this. For the first time in her life Eveline felt truly alive. She had a purpose; she had a mission – though admittedly she didn't know what it was yet. Something involving secrecy and darkness, that much was clear, as all the best missions did. Her father had been right when he said that anything of import always happened in the dead of night. How could it not? When everyone was fast asleep, tucked up in bed another world came out to play in the trees and the boulevards. How many times had she stuck her head out of Laurie's window, wondering what went on under the blackness and stars. And now she knew. She was a part of it. For once she was a part of it. Another world existed between midnight and the early hours, amidst blackness and stars, before disappearing again like a vanishing act with cock crow and daybreak. And she was a part of it….

Soon they came upon an open space – a large field bordered by a rough-hewn wall and she thought it must be their destination because Alphonse started talking to her again in a normal voice.

'Here we stop to pick up the troops,' he told her and she decided he must be half mad. Nothing here resembled a troop unless you wanted a troop of cooking fires, a troop of shiny pots and kettles, a troop of shadowy figures flitting about like bats or moths and a troop of two ponies – and if they were the greedy beggars then they really were greedy for there were only two of them and even to Eveline's unpractised eye they looked pretty stout and well fed.

'Are these the greedy beggars?' she murmured in a tone of surprise.

'Don't let them hear you say that!' grinned Alphonse, unlacing the top of the hessian sack as a fair-haired young boy approached them. 'Else they'll put you on the fire with the hedgehogs.'

'Hedgehogs!' cried Eveline in alarm, staring at the nearest campfire and the red faces dancing behind the flames like a bunch of little devils. 'Hedgehogs?'

'Alphonse.' The fair-haired young man held out his hand and Alphonse took it warmly. He looked vaguely familiar to Eveline but she couldn't quite place when and where she'd seen him. She watched him eyeing her warily as he accepted one of the iced buns she'd made that afternoon and slipped it into his pocket.

'It's alright.' Alphonse motioned with his head as if to say that his friend was safe. 'You can speak freely in front of… Yves.' Even in the darkness she could sense he was grinning wickedly and she wanted to give him a kick in the shins for it. 'How did it go, anyway?' His voice turned serious. 'Did he blab?'

'Easy!' The boy replied gleefully. 'Like a baby. He was desperate to get it off his chest. Three o'clock in the morning just as we thought. They're occupying the bridges, railway stations and the Place de la Bastille. And they're heading for Montmartre.'

'Which gives us,' Alphonse thought rapidly, 'three hours at least. And the girl?'

Eveline pricked up her ears.

'Up to her tricks as we speak,' winked the boy, 'though she wants more for it.'

'Oh?' Alphonse raised his eyebrows.

'Grooms don't smell too good apparently. And they treat their horses better than women.'

'Quite probably,' Alphonse responded with a chuckle. 'Did she say how much…'

'What girl?' Eveline interrupted, bristling beside him in the darkness, feeling ridiculous and transparent in her man's uniform. It wasn't so easy jumping from one skin to another.

'Oh, just an acquaintance of mine from the Boulevard des Italiens,' Alphonse said easily which didn't make her feel any better for the Boulevard des Italiens was a favourite haunt of women who sold their bodies. She would have had it out with him then and there but for the boy's eyes upon her, sniggering and faintly derisive, having clearly seen through her ludicrous get up. 'Perhaps Yves would like to try a bit of supper,' Alphonse half spluttered then, striding off with the hessian sack like a little Father Christmas and making her want to kick him in the shins again. 'I don't suppose he's ever tried hedgehog!'

She was still glaring as the young boy led her to the campfire and guided her down on a smooth flat stone. The Boulevard des Italiens was notorious, even worse than the Rue de la Vieille Lanterne for the women were younger, prettier, singers, dancers and the like. Her father had said he'd met her mother in the Boulevard des Italiens, saving her from a life of shame and debauchery, though Eveline had always thought it was just another of his stories.

She took a grim little gulp from the tin of coffee handed to her and scalded her mouth for the second time that evening. It was boiling hot, black and tasted of earth, twigs and nuts and she didn't think anyone would close their eyes drinking this little lot unless they were closing their eyes in disgust. She glanced around at her companions – there were four or five boys about the same age as the fair-haired young man, except for one whom she took to be the cook with his fat cheeks and glistening skin. They were eating merrily and chatting away quietly, wriggling their feet by the fire and cupping their hands round their coffee tins for warmth. The night was turning icy and she took another sip of coffee, thinking doggedly that when in Rome… Alphonse was still going from group to group, doling out her home-baked goodies and she felt a little cheated and taken for granted. Oh I'm good for baking, she said to herself sourly, but not much else by the look of things.

Alphonse was calling time by then and the select few were leaping proud and excited to their feet, grabbing extra hats and coats and gliding into formation at the edge of the field. One minute they were lolling by the fireside eating hedgehog and the next they were lining up by the wall as professional as any army Eveline had ever seen; and she realised suddenly where she'd seen them before. They were the pilfering sparrows at the back of Brébant's, the bin pickers and scrap merchants. She couldn't believe how different they looked. She'd dismissed them as waifs and strays, tearaways and criminals and now here they were taking orders from Alphonse with the grace and ease of a well-oiled regiment. They even looked a little fatter like turkeys that had escaped the Christmas nightmare and she bowed silently to the cook before getting up and joining the end of the line.

Those who had been excluded gazed from their campfires and raised their coffee tins with a mixture of envy and pride. Everyone wanted to be involved in the mission. Mission Pegasus as it had been nicknamed. It was the most important mission ever to be undertaken apparently and only the most daring, courageous and skilful had been chosen. Mission Pegasus had been spoken about for days in hushed undertones, whispered rustlings, secret confabulations. Even the flames crackled Pegasus, even the stars shone Pegasus, the bats screeched it, the whole night air stank of it. It was to be the last strike of the oppressed and the poor and the first strike, Alphonse had said, of the revolution. It would be the stuff of nursery rhyme and ballad, firesong and myth; but it would never go down in the history books. It could not exist in the history books except perhaps as a small dead moth, absurd and irritatingly stuck between the pages, having dared to fly out of the cold black night and into the warm drawing rooms.

'We shall not have the time,' Alphonse spoke quietly to the group of young men who were itching and impatient to be off, 'to clarify things later so I should like to run through them now if you don't mind. Sandy…'

The fair-haired young man uttered an eager 'yes'.

'You are to head for the Bois, of course. Try to avoid the Porte Maillote and Trocadero if possible and go by the quieter ways. Roger?'

Eveline heard a muffled 'yes' from the middle of the group but she couldn't make out who'd spoken.

'You are going to Vincennes. It is a long way but I think you have the stamina for it if your reputation precedes you accurately.'

Some earthy laughter greeted this as well as a few stamping feet for the night was freezing away from the campfires and they were desperate to be off. Mission Pegasus, the boots seemed to scrape. Enough of the chit-chattering. But Alphonse persisted. 'Ben's crew?'

An impish-looking fellow next to Eveline stuck up his hand, grinning from ear to ear. He was the youngest member of the mission and though he took his responsibility very seriously hadn't been able to stop grinning since finding out he'd been chosen.

'You are to come back here, past the old church as we rehearsed. On no account take the main routes and if you get into trouble, drop everything.'

'Yes sir,' said the boy, still grinning from ear to ear.

'And stop grinning at me like that,' smiled Alphonse. 'They could spot your teeth twenty miles off in a balloon!'

'No sir.' The boy valiantly tried to straighten his face without success and Eveline reached out and squeezed his hand for he reminded her a little of Jacques but he glanced at her in alarm and she dropped it quickly, remembering who she was meant to be.

'Alright.' Alphonse's voice came clear above the rising, buffeting wind. 'Do we have the sacks and the lead ropes?'

Yes yes yes! Enough of the chit-chattering, the boots seemed to stamp. Whoever do you think we are? A bunch of bumbling National Guardsmen? A battalion of oafs in the regular army? It is time. We must be off.

Alphonse suddenly grinned, his own teeth lighting up the night like a torch. 'All that remains for me to do is wish everybody good luck. If our cause is noble – and I believe it is – then it shall succeed. Tonight my friends...' he saluted the men, 'we ride.'

'Tonight we ride,' they repeated solemnly and Eveline's heart pounded with excitement as the boots began their march over the dirty, mud-clotted field. She turned her head for one last glance at the twinkling campfires and saw, beyond the red and leaping flames, that the men left behind were standing to attention, silent and in awe, their coffee tins raised aloft. Dashing the tears away from her eyes, she bent her head to the task in front. Mission Pegasus had begun and she was a part of it. For once she was a part of it.

It must have been well past two o'clock when they reached the Tuileries stables and Eveline could see from the night lanterns that Alphonse's face was tense and worried as he ushered them into the courtyard.

'The night groom may well be back soon from his... distractions,' he whispered urgently, 'and we must hurry.'

Eveline had figured out that the night groom's distraction was the girl from the Boulevard des Italiens but she didn't know what she thought about it yet and she didn't have time to think. Alphonse was leading them at a fierce pace over the cobblestones, fleeing from one little shadow to the other before creeping forward and beckoning them on again, past the mounting block and water trough, the night groom's quarters, dark and empty still, and the tack room smelling of boot polish and silver until they were all panting but safely under cover of the stable itself. It was a long, low airy building, softly lit and smelling to Eveline of warm bread and treacle. It reminded her a little of the pâtisserie for she'd never been inside a stable before and didn't recognise the smells of bran mash, oats and molasses, would never have dreamed that horses could be fed such things as bran mash, oats and molasses. The nearest she'd been to a horse was when one dashed past her on the Rue de Rivoli, blinkered and hooked up to a dainty little carriage carrying the likes of La Païva and men in top hats. Or, more recently, hooked up, red and bloody, in a butcher's shop.

Close to they looked enormous, like monstrous statues that coughed and wheezed – there must have been thirty of them at least, peering their long noses over the tops of their loose boxes or standing with one back leg bent and balancing on the other three, their heads almost touching the floor.

Sandy was already tying the hessian sacks around the feet of a big black horse who stood patiently for him, looking down at him with large inquisitive eyes.

'Make 'em tight,' Alphonse advised, 'or we shall wake the dead on these cobblestones. Ben?'

The impish young fellow stood to attention, still grinning.

'Keep an eye out for the night groom. The rest of Ben's lot take the ten horses at the far end. Two a piece, mind, we don't have time to take any more.'

Ben dashed off the way they had come while the rest of his men scooted over the flagstones, digging out headcollars and lead ropes and the home-baked goodies Eveline had made that afternoon. They ducked into looseboxes, click clucking like professional jockeys and holding out iced buns and jam tarts to distract the horses while they slipped on their headcollars.

'They'd turn their noses up at carrots,' smiled Sandy, moving on to another horse with his hessian sacks. 'They eat better than we do!'

'Of course,' muttered Alphonse, directing Roger's men to the remaining looseboxes. 'What do you expect? They bear Generals and Emperors into battle. They are the best-kept horses in Paris. Even where they are stabled is kept a secret and they are moved every few months to keep them safe.'

'Can I help?' offered Eveline for the place was a flurry of activity now and she felt quite useless standing around watching. She hadn't come to watch, she'd come to act.

'Help Sandy,' ordered Alphonse, striding off to the far end to open the exit gates; and Sandy threw her some hessian sacks.

She crept into a loosebox and knelt down in the straw beside a large grey horse. Its feet were black as liquorice and big as soup plates and she tapped one of them nervously. Nothing happened. She tapped again and pulled feebly at the tuft of hair behind the ankle. Still nothing happened. The horse stood, stubborn and placid, blowing gently down on her head.

'Tap the foot at the front of the fetlock,' Sandy grinned, peering at her over the top of the loose box. 'And he'll pick 'em up for you no fuss.'

Eveline tapped the front of the foot and instantly the horse re-balanced itself and lifted up its leg, revealing a half-moon-shaped, silver-coloured shoe. She slipped the hessian bag on and tied it up tightly before moving on to the next foot, feeling decidedly pleased with herself. How obedient the horses were. How beautifully trained. You tapped at their feet and their legs popped up like little Jack in the boxes!

She slipped into the next loose box, edging round another horse, tying its feet up tight in the sacks – putting on the mufflers as Sandy put it – as deft and sure as any professional horse stealer. Now she'd got the hang of it she hummed as she worked, marvelling at the beauty of these living, breathing statues. They'd seemed so different from the boulevards, careening along in their feathers and plumes but maybe she'd simply been confusing them with their owners or maybe carriage horses were a different breed entirely. These, after all, were inured to the battlefield. They didn't just prance over puddles and parasols, they stepped out to the rhythm of battle drum and bugle, tossed their manes in the line of fire, swished their tails at bullets like flies, stepped over cadavers and torn, broken limbs. Silver-haired and battle scarred, there wasn't much that could surprise them any more, even a girl messing about with a couple of hessian sacks. Some of them blew soft and gently on her hair, wisps of stray hay at the edges of their mouths, others stood calm and aloof, observing her knowledgably with their large liquid eyes as she hummed and hurried about their feet.

She was just onto her fifth horse – a giant chestnut-coloured animal with a back as broad and shiny as a mahogany table – when Ben came rushing in, the smile wiped right off his face.

'They are coming,' he uttered in a piercing whisper. 'Quick, quick, they are coming!'

Alphonse appeared out of the shadows of a loose box with a halter in his hand. 'How many?'

'I don't know,' Ben muttered helplessly. 'I just heard voices.'

'Right. Join your lot. And get going. Now. You know your destination. The rest of you follow one at a time. Don't panic. If they don't hear anything they're more likely to sit down to a game of cards than check on the horses. Sandy, Eveline, forget the hessian sacks.' As he spoke he moved rapidly towards the pitchforks hanging in a line above the food bins and, taking one down, began forking straw from an empty loose box onto the flagstones to deafen the sound of the horses' hooves. 'Eveline, take Apollo and follow Sandy.' His eyes met hers briefly and she smiled gratefully back at him. 'I'll join you as soon as I can.'

And they were off. The horses were off. Flying out of their stables with little jockeys on their backs as if they were heading for the racetrack at Longchamps. All they needed were colours and silks, candy stalls and roaring crowds to complete the picture. The boys crouched low, their knees high and their heads down to negotiate the exit gate and the horses surged forward like a wave, their ears pricked and twitching, sensing the excitement and adrenalin in the air.

Scarcely daring to breathe, Eveline led the chestnut horse out of his loose box, one hessian bag on its foot, cringing at the sound of the other three clip-clopping over the flagstones but Alphonse smiled and waved her forward. 'Vault on! Vault on!' he urged; but she couldn't. The horse was too big and his coat too slippery – like a mahogany table polished up once too often by an over-zealous housemaid. In the end, they had to give her a leg up and she half sprawled, half lay across the horse's neck as he followed the others eagerly out of the cosy stable into the fresh night air.

And then began a ride Eveline thought she would never forget, not even if she lived to be a hundred years old. She felt about a hundred years old in the middle of it and for a few days afterwards but she never forgot it.

She didn't turn round and look at Alphonse or wave goodbye to him for fear of sliding off in an inglorious little heap again; she simply twisted her hands in the luxurious mane and allowed the horse to have its head, following Sandy on the smoky-grey creature in front of her. Sometimes she felt like she was following a smoke signal as the horse in front weaved this way and that, silently drifting out of her line of vision but Apollo followed closely one step behind as he must have learnt to do in the battlefield. She could hear no sounds of chase or pursuit, only the faint clip-clopping of the horses in front as they fanned out to their separate destinations; and she breathed a small sigh of relief and loosened her grip on the thick chestnut mane. She hoped Alphonse had escaped too or at the very least hidden out of sight and she wanted to ask Sandy if they should wait for him somewhere but she didn't have the time to. They were already catching up with the rest of his men and he was spinning in and out on the smoky grey, urging them away from the Rue de Rivoli and Place de la Concorde and onto a grassy little path beside the Seine. She couldn't help but notice how beautifully they rode, without saddle or bridle, some of them leading a horse or two behind, guiding them solely with knees and voices; and she was ashamed to think she'd once labelled them tearaways, scrap merchants, pilfering sparrows at the back of Brébant's.

They streamed ahead of her along the little path beside the Seine and it was all she could do to keep her balance, bumping up and down at the rear end in a bone-shaking trot. Every movement the horse made seemed to send her more and more out of kilter and she tried sitting up straighter but that sent her dizzy and she was frightened an overhanging branch might knock her head off her shoulders so she went back to crouching forward, clinging on to the neck and thick wiry mane. Sandy shouted something to her but the wind tore it out of his mouth and all she could hear was her own laboured breath, the roar of the water and the horse's pounding feet. Whatever had possessed her to say she could ride? She managed to stay on as they negotiated small obstacles, puddles, bridges, sharp narrow alleyways, the horses gliding like ghosts past dark and shuttered houses, washing lines and trellised vines. Nobody was afoot. Nobody, not even a mouse was stirring, for they rode as soft as a mouse's dream or a prayer sent forth in sleep. Sandy was whispering to everybody that they didn't have far to go now, mainly to keep morale up, Eveline thought, for they were nowhere near the Bois de Boulogne.

'We're nowhere near the Bois de Boulogne,' she said indignantly, sitting up straight for dignity's sake and blinking her eyes wide open to distract herself from the fatigue that was threatening to overwhelm her and the pain that went from her legs to her shoulders. 'If that is where we are headed…'

'We are headed for freedom,' he replied cryptically and nonchalantly then cantered off before she could ask him to explain himself.

She dug her knees into Apollo's sides, desperate to catch up and suddenly furious with the euphemisms, the secrecy, the idiocy of the mission. Whoever heard of stealing a pack of horses in the middle of the night only to take them to freedom? Weren't they free enough with their jam tarts and polished hooves, cosy stables and warm sweet hay? She dug her heels in again querulously but the horse didn't respond. If anything he got slower and she watched the others streaming away from her, their tails flying out in the wind. She stared miserably after them into the darkness, banging uselessly at the barrel sides. What if her horse had gone lame? It suddenly occurred to her that Apollo might be lame. He'd lost his hessian sack ages ago and his stride didn't seem any different but his neck was hot and damp with sweat. She knew that they wouldn't come back for her if she got left behind. They'd leave her here in the middle of nowhere to fend for herself. Survival of the fittest Laurie would have called it. That was how they lived, how they survived, existing as they did under blackness and stars. She felt a rising sense of panic then pulled herself up sharply. She wasn't some damsel in distress needing to be rescued. She would follow on at her own pace, head for freedom and the Bois at her own pace. Even if she never got there at least she would have tried.

She spoke to the horse as she'd heard the others do, in a soft low crooning murmur. 'Just a few more steps,' she whispered, patting him on the neck, 'just a few more steps old man.'

His ears flickered back and forth at the sound of her voice and his pace picked up a little on the rough pebbly track. Encouraged, Eveline patted him again, reminded him he was a grand old fellow, a veteran soldier who'd taken Generals and Emperors into battle, who'd survived explosions and cadavers, whisked bullets away like flies. This in comparison would be a breeze. Just a short step out to the Bois de Boulogne, to freedom and to liberty. What horse wouldn't give its eye teeth for a holiday in the Bois de Boulogne? To be able to race under the canopy of trees, drink from the fountains and taste the tasty herbs and flowers the Emperor had planted, imported from abroad.

'You'll love it,' she whispered into the chestnut's ear. 'They may even have snowdrops at this time of year.'

The horse seemed to understand for he nodded approval at the sound of snowdrops and she giggled out loud, wondering if his name was Snowdrop and not Apollo after all.

'Snowdrop,' she kept muttering into the emptiness. 'We're heading for snowdrops and liberty.'

The wind had dropped by now, the clouds evaporated and the stars hung clear and icicle bright in the night sky. Was everything Alphonse did concerned with freedom in some way, she wondered. Freedom of choice for people, even animals. Freedom from family and friends, the mundane, the routine. Freedom to rustle up a little army in the night that appeared and disappeared silent and surprising as dewfall. Was freedom so intoxicating to him? She touched her face with her fingers and felt nothing but cold. She heard nothing but the sound of her indrawn breath and the horse's hooves on the road; and she felt entirely alone. Was freedom just another word for loneliness? She tried to imagine La Païva asleep in her golden bedroom and the shop girls dreaming of sales and crinolines; and she wondered if she would exchange her life for theirs now, at this very moment. Was luxury a freedom, as she had always thought, or just another form of aloneness? Freedom after all was hard, gritty, painful and uncomfortable. Maybe you couldn't get there on a feather bed. Maybe you had to get there on the back of a mahogany table!

She clasped her hands about Apollo's neck to stop herself from falling asleep and falling off; but the horse seemed to pick up its pace, sniffing the air and whickering softly as if he could smell the snowdrops just around the corner. 'Slow down,' shrieked Eveline as she lurched up and down in her bone-shaking trot. 'Slow down you idiot!' But the horse didn't seem to be listening now. He was careering along, his hooves making sparks along the road and she only hoped he wasn't about to bolt. The last thing she needed was him bolting back to his stable.

'We're heading for snowdrops,' she reminded him in an attempt to pacify, gripping as hard as she could with her knees and nearly unseating herself in the process. 'Not the battlefield!'

The horse suddenly slithered to an ungainly halt and began pawing the air with his foreleg. Eveline pushed herself up straight and peered about her into the darkness. What on earth had gotten into him now? And then she saw it – a shadow tall and straight leap from the hedgerow and she ducked behind Apollo's neck as if it might make a difference before realising instinctively who it was. How had he got here so quickly? Had he flown on a broomstick? Come in a cab?

'He knows you,' she smiled as Alphonse vaulted up behind her and took her in his arms. 'You smell like a horse...or a pâtisserie!' She didn't know what she meant or what she thought and she was too exhausted to care. She was tongue tied, hysterical, overwrought and all of a sudden blissfully happy. And she allowed herself to sink back into his warm reassuring arms as he moulded his body about hers and they rode on, hard and strong, into the darkness. And she dreamt she was riding every night with him hard and fast into the darkness and out the other side again to freedom and snowdrops...

Chapter twenty-one

Laurie heard the sound of the rappel through the fogginess of sleep but thinking he was dreaming turned over with a grunt, pulling the pillow after him. But the noise persisted, loud and insistent as a hammering on the door or a peal of thunder; and he sat up suddenly wide awake, his fair hair as tousled as a haystack, his soft eyes full of alarm.

There was no mistaking it – that sound. A sound that filled every heart with trepidation, proclaiming as it did that Paris was in danger and summoning every man and woman out into the streets. But what could it be? The war was over wasn't it? Had there been an insurrection? Had the day dawned at last on revolution? Laurie leapt from his bed and cast aside the curtains of his porthole mirror but he could see practically nothing for the morning was grey and misty. It could not be the dawn of revolution, he said to himself, for he had imagined that day to be bright and clear, a promise and a sign of good things and new beginnings.

He dressed hurriedly, pulling on his old uniform, dragging a comb through his hair and finishing off the remains of last night's repast – two eggs, a hunk of cheese, and the dregs from an old wine bottle. Then he raced down the stairs past the concierge who was surprisingly awake for once and smugly gloating with the news.

'There has been a collision,' he announced with just the right air of gravity, though his eyes shone at being the first to convey the tremendous events. 'Between the red National Guards and the regular troops.'

What sort of collision, Laurie wanted to know, but the concierge wasn't saying much more. He simply knew there had been a collision on the Buttes Montmartre between the red National Guardsmen and the bourgeois battalions or regular troops.

'I am no follower of Thiers,' he confided, his face waxing pale behind his cubicle of glass, 'but I am no hot-blooded revolutionary either. Not at my age. The best one can hope for at my age is sleep, food and a few good dreams.'

Laurie nodded politely and left the building, his thoughts in turmoil. If there had been a clash between the red National Guardsmen and the regular troops or bourgeois battalions then it was an insurrection of some kind. On this icy grey morning in the middle of March there had been an insurrection! He huddled into his greatcoat and made for the heights, stopping now and then to ask a passer-by for news, but nobody seemed to know any more than he did. People were heading in the same direction or milling about on corners, gesticulating with excitement. Women stood slipshod and bloomered on their doorsteps with their frozen pails of water; while children peeped from behind closed shutters. The mood seemed disbelieving, angry and celebratory all at the same time; and dogs were barking nervously at the relentless roll of the drums. A young man raced past, holding his képi up on the end of his bayonet. 'The red flag is flying in the Place de Bastille!' he shouted; and Laurie's heart pounded with excitement.

When he reached the heights via the Rue Marcadet, he could see little at first, for a huge and swelling crowd blocked his sight. He pushed his way through, catching a glimpse of a General on a white horse and a line of ragged and shambolic-looking soldiers surrounding the gun park and he knew in a flash exactly what was happening. They were trying to steal the guns! The government was trying to disarm the National Guard of its guns and cannon, the guns and cannon that had been paid for by public conscription and manufactured during the siege. Laurie gave a low, disgusted whistle. What idiots! Was Thiers so frightened of revolution that he had to disarm the National Guard? It was the one sure way of starting a revolution for the guns were sacred to the whole of the city not just the red battalions. They were a symbol of hope and suffering, of valour and determination; and he could see them glinting in between the chestnut trees of the park, polished and pristine as always, even in this dull grey mist. *The Kaiser* was there, and *Bill* and the *Savage Chieftain*, their barrels pointing down into the soft brown mud. He recognised *The Dancer* with its brightly painted wheels and *Butterfly* with her winged motif – two cannon paid for by a group of women from Mabille's – taking pride of place in the front line beside the *Kaiser* and the *Savage Chieftan*.

He pressed forward to get a better look at the General and the men who guarded the park, gaping inwardly at the government's foolishness.

It was one thing to secrete the guns off in the middle of the night and present the whole situation as something of a fait accompli, but to be still standing here at eight o'clock in the morning in front of a pack of civilians was another thing entirely. It was madness. Did they think they could get away with it? Did they think the crowd would let them pass? It was jaunty and bantering for now but it was a banter that could so easily flare into anger – he'd seen it before in the political meetings and he trembled at the prospect. Even the soldiers looked dispirited to Laurie, seemingly aware of their absurdity. They were trapped like bears in a net; it was stalemate, an impasse. They had come to get the guns and now they could not – it was as simple as that – without wreaking havoc on a crowd that was full of women and children, matrons and old men and swelling by the moment as the rappel sounded through the neighbourhood. One or two grinned sheepishly at the crowd when the General's back was turned or sloped off in the direction of the nearest café, fed up with the whole proceedings. Most of them looked pretty much on the verge of collapse, their faces blue with cold; and Laurie felt a little sorry for them, wondering how long they'd been there. The General was cantering up and down on his little white pony, lifting the fallen with the end of his bayonet.

'Never mind,' grinned an old man in the crowd to one who had been treated thus and was shaking his head like a dog and looking daggers at the back of the General. 'If you're lucky you'll be away by lunchtime.'

The soldier scratched his head and said he God only hoped so. His mate had had the sense to bugger off hours ago in the company of a girl from Mabille's just off duty no less. He was probably toasting his feet or something else by now the lucky sod. 'The General's an evil bastard,' he offered up suddenly and then shut up as the man himself cantered back on his little white pony.

'Stop fraternising, 206,' he barked, his yellow face pinched and alert. 'You're not here to make smalltalk.'

'Where are you taking the cannon?' the old man jeered then with a raucous laugh. 'Berlin? Take your time! No rush! When you're ready!'

'Old man, old man,' the General sneered in response, jerking his pony about with hard and heavy hands, 'why don't you get back into your armchair!'

The old man was startled into silence and somebody else in the crowd took up the fight on his behalf. 'At least he's not riding one! Where did you get that thing from? The circus?'

A roar of laugher met this little gem for indeed on closer inspection the pony the General rode looked quite unfit for military use. It was small and slender with a carthorse mane and tail and an odd way of splaying out its feet when it moved. It looked more like something a butcher drove or an undertaker.

'Have the rest all been eaten?' a woman cackled in delight. 'Or has Mr Tom Thumb[19] reduced them all in size for his own sake?'

The crowd was making merry now at the expense of Thiers and the madcap situation, already celebrating victory over the fools in government.

'Where is the little hero, anyway? Hiding under a blade of grass? He'd need a horse just to come over my knees!'

'What a mastermind! What a plan! Hey, I've got a plan. Better than Trochu's. Why don't you drag the guns off yourselves!'

It suddenly dawned on Laurie what was happening as he listened to the shouts. They were waiting for the horses! They were waiting for the horses to tow away the guns!

'How long have they been here?' he asked a woman next to him in astonishment.

The woman, who had a face like a little old schoolmarm, looked pleased to be asked. 'Well,' she began thoughtfully, 'I was up and doing my rounds at four o'clock in the morning – I live just opposite the Place Pigalle – when I heard this little riot so I imagine they were pushed out of their barracks at the crack of dawn. The trouble was that in their...' her lips chewed over the word, '...precipitousness to steal our guns, they forgot to bring refreshment for the men – look at them all dropping like flies – and, believe it or not, they forgot to bring the horses!'

'Forgot to bring the horses?' Laurie parroted in disbelief and the woman nodded in amusement. 'Right. They appear to be a little thin on the ground these days. Either they've all been eaten,' she chuckled, 'or simply evaporated! I believe that is why the General is mounted on little Bucephalus over there.'

What a superb farce, thought Laurie, standing agog at the ineptitude of the whole affair. It was just another superb little farce playing through his head though this time, it seemed to him, he was right in the middle of it. Almost an active participant. No wonder the men looked ashamed and embarrassed, not knowing whether to throw in the towel and tear off their uniforms or stand on guard as they had been ordered. He didn't envy them. The crowd was surging forward, a swollen river – there was barely a hand's breadth between the front of the queue and the line – and any moment now it was sure to burst and flood the ranks. The General kept trying to back his pony into the crowd but a few hearty thwacks from the angry mob sent the poor little animal careening off in another direction, much to everyone's amusement.

'Load your bayonets!' the General shouted, turning purple with fury. 'Load your bayonets.'

One or two feebly attached their bayonets but most of them disobeyed the command. Some even raised the butts of their rifles in the air to signify their disapproval, despite the General's threat to shoot any deserter in the back.

'Fix your bayonets,' the General ordered again, jagging so hard on the reins that the froth at the edge of the horse's mouth turned pink with blood.

'Ignore the circus master!' yelled the old man at the front, nearly losing his footing as the crowd surged forward; and the soldiers glared at the General sullenly, even derisively. Why should they fix their bayonets? They'd come to take the guns, not threaten civilians – old men, women and children. They had more of an eye for the women from Mabille's who were coming straight from work in their droves, glowing and garish as tinsel after a party, flaunting bare bosoms and bacon soup under the men's very noses.

'You wouldn't fire on us,' they wheedled, winding their way through the line, batting their painted eyelids.

'Not on your life,' a soldier replied jocosely, staring longingly at a tin of bacon soup.

The General suddenly lost his temper, charging a girl in a peacock-blue dress and knocking her to the ground. Scalded, she leapt up, shouting obscenities and spat in his face; and the scene suddenly became chaos.

Laurie wasn't exactly sure whether the crowd attacked the General or the General attacked the crowd but a few moments later he was dragged from his horse and borne aloft on the shoulders of two Guardsmen. Nobody stirred their stumps to help him. None of the men seemed to care that their General was being carried off like a prize piece of meat. Some even cheered or stuck their finger in the air at the yellowing face still bellowing orders and threatening court martials as it disappeared from view. One or two had the grace to look dutifully aghast but were prevented from following by the women from Mabille's with their tins of bacon soup. Laurie watched the crowd swallowing up its prey – 'Just deserts' somebody shouted, 'he's only getting his just deserts' – and the sun peered feebly out for a moment as if to herald the faint dawn of a promising new day. 'Wake up,' Laurie muttered to himself as he'd once bade fruiterers and fancy hat-box makers. 'A new day! Wake up!'

The rest of it seemed to pass in a dream, however, or maybe a nightmare depending on how you looked at it. The mob raced on down the dusty Clignancourt and Laurie was swept along like a piece of debris between the little old schoolmarm and a man with a lantern jaw. For the first time in his life he gave in to a sense of abandon, a loss of control, allowed his identity to merge with this seething mass of humanity. For the first time in his life he was free of all logic, all rational thought. In the anonymity of the crowd he was free of himself, yet a part of every other: every grimace, roar, caterwaul and wail, every gap-toothed mouth and callous shout. Free of himself yet bound to every other and subject to one will, one merciless intent.

'Where are they taking him?' whispered the women on the doorsteps of the Rue des Rosiers, a little washing line of women, clean and brightly smocked. It was a pretty, green-leafed street, the Rue des Rosiers, largely untouched by the Prussian bombardment and made up of painted houses and law-abiding citizens. The sort Laurie had woken up in the early hours for it was a long walk from here to the bustling heart of the city. Many of them had heard the rappel and covered their ears or hidden under their beds; but this wild procession passing by right before their eyes had brought them out by the dozen. They hung out to dry on their doorsteps, poking fun at the crowd. *My, but didn't revolutionaries come in all shapes and sizes: doddering old granddads, mop-haired gangly youths, dirty prostitutes dressed to kill... What did they think they looked like, screaming like banshees and brandishing their rifles. As for the General frogmarching along poor thing. With his black eye. Quite a dish, no doubt, without it. Bellowing orders to no one in particular...*

'He can give me an order,' declared one bright smock, staring at the General's long and dazzling sword, 'any day of the week!'

The crowd rushed on pell-mell down the street, Laurie still wedged between the little old schoolmarm and the man with the lantern jaw. The little old schoolmarm was working up a sweat.

'Listen everybody,' she kept yelling, as if she were trying to educate the lot of them. 'Listen everybody, the people have won, you fools, the people have won!'

'The people have won!' Laurie echoed in delight, filled with a sudden sense of elation. It was true. The people had won. They had toppled a General and confounded a military manoeuvre. They had risen en masse to defend their rights, taken power into their own hands. For the first time in his life he was experiencing events as they happened, not reading about them second hand in history books (and yet, what a letter to his mother it would make!). As the sun pouted down on the Rue des Rosiers, he realised the city was in the grip of transformation, in the grip of revolution. Right here. Right now. He smiled at the thought that Alphonse was missing out on the action for once. For once Alphonse was in the wrong place at the wrong time and he, Laurie, was right where it mattered.

'Chop the rat's head off!' the lantern-jawed man yelled then, bringing out a mouth organ and blowing a few dirgeful notes on it; and Laurie, flinging his cap in the air and giving vent to months of pent-up frustration shouted with him: 'Chop it off! Chop it off!'

They bundled the General into the old National Guard headquarters at number six Rue des Rosiers, a homely little house kept in ship-shape condition by Madame Victoire, wife of the late and notorious Commander Bernard Victoire... It was the sort of house, Laurie thought, that Eveline would have liked, with its wooden shutters, vegetable plot and marked-out flower bed. One or two National Guardsmen were positioning themselves in the garden and around the building to prevent the crowd becoming too unruly and making a forced entry.

'We are awaiting further instructions,' a bulky fellow called Lacroix informed them, raising his voice above the clamour. 'The General is a prisoner, a prisoner of war if you like, and a potential hostage to bargain with Thiers over. So I'll thank you all to keep your distance.'

The crowd made it quite clear that it didn't give a jot about further instructions. They'd had enough further instructions to last them a lifetime. They were giving the lesson book today; and they meant to set an example.

'Let the rat out, citizen,' someone shouted menacingly, 'and I'll give him further instruction!'

'Keep back, keep back,' Lacroix growled uneasily as more and more people pushed their way into the garden and the crowd surged forward almost up to the doorstep. And he fired a few shots into the air in an attempt to quell the uprising.

Madame Victoire (who kept the downstairs spick and span in exchange for living free in the upstairs) was about to make herself a nice pot of English tea when she heard the commotion and, clutching a little china cup to her chest, she dashed over to the window to see what was happening. She nearly fainted away at the sight of the rabble in her well-kept little garden. 'Bunch of rascals!' she muttered to herself, pressing her nose against the pane to get a better look. They were doing untold damage to the cabbage patch, the flower bed looked to be utterly ruined (and the buds just budding) and a little unmentionable was making merry on the lawn with a handful of mud. The sight of a couple of uniforms reassured her somewhat until she saw one of them having a go at the windows – windows she'd sweated buckets over – with a large lump of wood. She'd kept the downstairs clean hadn't she? Ruined her knees on that stone cold floor, kept the garden immaculate… all in exchange for this little pigsty. She clutched the china cup to her chest and strained to hear what was being said amidst the cacophony.

'Let the rat show its face,' she thought she made out and she bristled visibly. Rat! What rat! She'd know about a rat if there was one in the vicinity. She peered out again in mild surprise, scrutinising the thin and emaciated faces. Were they still hunting rat, in any case, for food? She'd heard about such goings on in the poorer quarters when food was scarce but now when food was plentiful? Surely not. Rat hunting in the Rue des Rosiers didn't seem possible unless they were taking it up as a hobby, a sport akin to fox hunting in England. She tried to remember what her late husband had said about fox hunting in England. 'Merciless to the end,' she thought she remembered, 'but there are worse things at sea.'

The kettle boiled furiously behind her, gently misting up the pane and she wiped the steam away with her finger, her fist and finally the whole of her sleeve, transfixed by the scene outside. It was chaos. The rabble was flinging anything it could think of at the windows – rocks, branches, even bayonets – and the noise was deafening.

'Flush the rat out,' somebody roared and a great cry went up. There was a sudden crash followed by the sound of boots stampeding over a stone floor – the stone flag floor she had ruined her back over – and she dashed across to the door to peer down at the downstairs. She was just in time to catch sight of a man sitting quietly in the armchair by the fireplace, his head bowed over the empty grate as if silently contemplating his fate. He must be the rat, she muttered to herself before bolting her door and rushing back over to the window. Another venomous cheer went up as the General was dragged out into the garden; Madame Victoire felt cold. What had he done to deserve this? They were even taking his money off him! She distinctly saw him hand a bag of money to a National Guardsman. How despicable. It was the last time she'd clean the downstairs for that little lot. They could chuck her out on the street if they wanted. She pressed the china cup absently to her chest, thanking her stars that her husband had left her with a small but manageable pension. At least she wouldn't have to eat rats! She thought the General looked very handsome in the sunshine, his medals glinting. Most dignified, the way he held himself. Tall and erect – not unlike her husband in that respect… the first shot took her quite by surprise and she thought the

General had simply fallen. The second, third and fourth, fired by anyone, it seemed to her, who had a gun, left her in no doubt whatsoever and she stood trembling at the window, her face white with shock. The kettle shrieked merrily behind her as she kept wiping blurrily with her sodden sleeve, desperately trying to remember what her husband had said about executions in England. 'Merciless to the end,' rang a bell in her head, 'but there are worse things at sea.'[20]

Laurie found himself outside the Renans by nightfall, rubbing his eyes as if to dispel the dreadful events he had witnessed. It had been like a dream – one you couldn't wake up from – and yet, in his dreams he was always a hero, never a party to murder. It didn't seem possible that only that morning he had woken up to the rappel. A lifetime surely had aged him since then. A lifetime in one crowded day. He rapped dully at the front door, hoping against hope that Eveline would be there but the familiar voice of Mistigris bade him come in.

'If I turn my back for a moment,' the old stonecutter explained cheerfully as Laurie entered, 'Madame Larousse is bound to cheat!' He indicated the chessboard sitting on the table between himself and the infamous lady who, strange to say, seemed quite tickled by the remark, helping herself to an enemy pawn with a satisfied little grin.

Laurie waved away the apology and stood aimlessly staring about him. It was true what Eveline said about the statues – they did look just like bodies in the morgue. And yet, he thought gloomily, everything after today would look like a body in the morgue to him. Even Madame Larousse in her purple hat. Especially Madame Larousse in her purple hat. Mistigris was wearing a tattered old dressing gown and he kept batting his tassel in front of Madame Larousse as if trying to hypnotise her out of her tactics. They were evidently ensconced in the game for they fell into silence as if forgetting they had a visitor; and Laurie stood hesitatingly in the shadows, waiting for somebody to say something.

'Is Eveline with you?' he ventured at last as the minutes ticked by.

'Eveline?' Mistigris started up. 'Is Eveline with you?'

'N… no,' stammered Laurie. 'I assumed she was here.'

'Poor old fellow,' Mistigris whimpered then, referring to himself. 'Poor old lad, poor old lad. They have all deserted him: wife, son, daughter who is not his daughter.'

'*I* have not deserted you,' interposed Madame Larousse, rapping her knuckles on the board to bring his attention back to the game; and Mistigris winced and took a long slug of gin.

'Is Eveline not with you?' Laurie repeated, a note of alarm in his voice.

'No, she has deserted me too. She went off with that fine friend of yours the other night and hasn't been back since, not even to feed her dear old papa.'

Laurie's heart flickered uselessly like the embers of a dying fire. This is revolution he kept whispering to himself, and he felt completely numb.

'*I* have been feeding you,' Madame Larousse reminded gently; and Mistigris winced again and took another long swig of gin. 'I hear there has been a kerfuffle out in the streets,' he added, changing the subject quickly.

Laurie almost smiled at the word. A kerfuffle, yes. There had been a kerfuffle of a sort. The government had fled Paris. The city was an open space. She was anybody's for the taking.

Madame Larousse made a noise somewhere between a snort and a chortle.

'A Commune is now inevitable. Paris will have its Commune at last.'

Mistigris stared at the boy's intense little face. 'And what is a Commune exactly?'

Laurie half smiled again through tears. 'Something Alphonse and I have dreamed about. A government based on the rights of the working man. A government based on the people…'

'Ah.' Mistigris was losing interest and he went back to the game, his eyes suddenly gleaming with triumph. 'I can take you from behind, my dear, with my great big Bishop or direct from in front with my simple little pawn.'

'…a *revolutionary* government,' Laurie finished in an effort to convey the enormity of the day's events.

'Dirty beast!' Madame Larousse shivered across the brightly painted chessboard. 'What a dirty beast!'

Chapter twenty-two

Bernadine couldn't sleep, hadn't slept in weeks…. She knelt, in a state of undress, before the statue of the Virgin Mary that stood on her desk beside a calendar naming the month, year and saint of the day. (Saint Antony finder of all lost objects – pincushions, thimbles, keys and the like – but not people. Never lost people. It was God who found people and when he found them He kept them.) Bernadine frowned and raised a hand to her forehead. Thoughts lay too heavy upon her tonight. Too heavy for sleep. She listened to the rain patter softly over the rooftops – like the marching feet of some angelic little army – and unlaced the drawstring at the top of her stockings, peeling them carefully over her legs so as not to get any more holes in the toes. She stuffed them into her worn black shoes and folded her chemise neatly on top, smiling at the care with which she handled her clothes, despite her overwhelming fatigue. Everything in its rightful place. A tidy wardrobe is a tidy mind. A woman needs a man to govern her or a wall to contain her. She shivered and quickly pulled on her nightdress but not before catching sight of her naked silhouette against the wall, thin and wavering as the taper itself.

She threw a blanket over Aggie slumbering peacefully in her makeshift hammock and began pacing the narrow dimensions of her cell. Everything was changing. Her head was a whirlwind of fear and uncertainty and she didn't know which way to turn for the best. She even missed Brother Michael and his rather dubious counsel on nights like this and that was saying something! She smiled and listened to the April rain, trying to take stock of her situation. It was clear that the convent was no longer a safe haven, that much was true. If it ever had been. The wall that contained her was crumbling by the second under the new revolutionary

Commune. Religion was in disgrace apparently – in cahoots with Versailles – and cries of '*À bas les prêtres! À bas les couvents!*' could be heard on almost every street corner. One member of the Commune had even issued a warrant for God's arrest because he lived everywhere and was therefore a vagrant! Half the clergy had fled for their lives, donning wigs and legal frock coats as a form of disguise; and several convents had been attacked by fanatical Communards.

'Ravaged by revolutionaries,' as the Mother Superior had put it in a breathless little whisper the other night at Vespers. 'Oh ye virgins beware, beware. What an ending! To be ravaged by a red hot and bothered revolutionary!'

It was as if the whole city had gone insane. As if everything that had lain quietly dormant for years was pushing up from underground with the shoots of spring; and bursting out into flowers of madness.

She decided to get herself a glass of water and maybe some tincture of valerian if Brother Michael had left any in the store cupboard. She must keep her strength up now, if only for the sake of little Aggie, and the nights without sleep were starting to take their toll. She crept out into the passageway and stared up and down at the warren of cells. There was no sign of life in any of them, no sign at all and she turned suddenly on impulse and went back for Aggie, scooping her up into a cotton papoose and hitching her over her shoulder. She was heavier now and Bernadine's back bent under the weight as she made her way out again.

It was cold and dark and she wished she'd had the sense to put on a dressing gown and shoes, but she carried on towards the chapel, hoping the infant wouldn't wake and cry out. The chapel was warm from the press of frequent bodies and a little light illuminated the main altar, still clothed in sumptuous purple from the Easter celebrations. A few painted eggs sat amidst a pile of hymn books and Bernadine stepped forward to take a closer look. She'd always loved Easter, ever since she'd been a little girl. The Easter story, she'd told her father, was the best of all because everything that seemed to be dead came alive again; and time that seemed to have stopped in the winter months started ticking again with the clean white snowdrops. 'That is a story of dissembling,' her father had responded wearily, 'because nobody who dies ever comes alive again and time never stops ticking, not for anyone.'

As Bernadine turned to look at the eggs she felt a sudden pain in her foot and, thinking she'd stepped on some broken eggshell, cursed out loud in aggravation. How clumsy the novices were and frivolous with their stupid painted eggs – their dots, stripes, smiley faces, silly little trees. When had any of them last seen a real tree for goodness sake? When had any of them last seen spring in all her glory, shut up here in this godforsaken prison where the changing colours of the altar cloths substituted for the changing colours of the seasons. She caught her breath at her own blasphemy and dropped to her knees, her long thin fingers tremblingly feeling for bits of egg shell and coming across shards of flask and broken glass instead. Someone had knocked over the altar cruets! Some idiot had knocked the altar cruets over! She got up, her right foot sticky with blood and hobbled off towards the kitchen, cursing under her breath again. She'd have to clean up this little mess in the middle of the night and all she'd wanted to do was get herself a glass of water.

At least the kitchen was warm from the heat of cooking and she looked about in search of her valerian and a dustpan and brush. The place was a tip. The steward had left spices everywhere and crockery sat unstacked and greasy looking. *Everything in its rightful place...* No wonder Brother Michael had gone round the twist. Even the cupboard where the consecrated vessels were kept looked as if it had been ransacked, its door ajar, half hanging off its hinges. Whoever had done such a thing? She held the taper above her head and almost cried out in alarm. The cupboard was empty! Somebody had made off with all the consecrated vessels as well as the silver chalice and candlesticks that had been hidden in there for safekeeping.

It was then she heard a noise in the cellar. She shrank back, snuffed out the candle and quieted little Aggie who was stirring restlessly in her sleep. There it was again: a scratching, scraping, crash and a bang. Her mind raced. It could, of course, be Brother Michael back from his spell in the army but she didn't think so somehow. She had a feeling he'd left the city for good. It could even be the steward working late, catching up on this ungodly mess but that didn't seem very likely either. As her eyes became accustomed to the darkness, she detected a glimmering light coming from behind the cellar door. There was definitely somebody down there. She spun the papoose around to the front the easier to protect little Aggie and, shutting her mind to what the Mother Superior had said about red hot and bothered revolutionaries, she pushed through the door and bent down over the gaping hole.

'Brother Michael,' she shouted confidently into the blackness, 'are you down there?' She didn't think for one moment that it was he but she felt the subterfuge was justified in the circumstances; and the trespasser – if that's who the body was – might be a little unnerved to hear that a man was in the building. 'Brother Michael,' she went on nervously into the silence.

There was no reply. The glimmering light flickered for a moment and then stood still. Bernadine, more irritated now than scared, clambered down the top few steps, ducking her head to avoid a low beam and straining to see around empty crates and wine boxes.

'Who's there?' she demanded angrily. 'Who's there?'

The light shone tantalisingly at the far end of the cellar, casting shadows on the walls of monstrous wine bottles and grotesque jam jars. 'Who's there?' she demanded again.

And then she saw him. The ghostly figure of a Bishop bent over a crate of wine. Her heart stopped and she felt a rush of blood in her ears like the pealing of a hundred church bells. Could it be he, after all these years? She clutched Aggie tightly, almost crushing her to her chest as she climbed down the last few steps.

'Ernest?' she faltered. 'Ernest?'

The figure turned at the sound of the voice and raised a lantern in the air. Bernadine strained her eyes to see. *His garments shone white as light and when they saw him they worshipped him but some doubted...* could it be he, after all these years? After all these useless, fruitless years had he come back for her as he promised he would? 'Ernest,' she faltered again, then (as she allowed herself to believe it was he) in joyous disbelief: 'Ernest?' And as her feet flew over the cold dank floor, her mind flew back to the night they had lain in incense of lavender, the rose all thorn and crimson petals, the ha-ha overgrown with stars.... Quite the theologian, he had said the day they first met (the day the very flowers had caught their breath) and she had blushed, oh she had blushed deep...

'Green!' said the Bishop in a slurring tone. 'Green she was and bloated when they fished her out of the Seine.'

Bernadine stopped in shocked astonishment and rubbed her eyes, her body drooping with fatigue. Had she been dreaming? Was she dreaming still? She stared at the figure in utter bewilderment.

'Another one?' the stonecutter remarked, absurdly pompous in his ornate costume, pointing at Aggie sleeping soft in her papoose. 'You must breed like rabbits down here. In the dead of night I shouldn't wonder!'

It was all Bernadine could do to hold herself together. To stop herself hitting the man or bursting into a fit of hysterics. It was all she could do to ask in an even-tempered voice: 'What are you doing here at St Joseph's in the middle of the night, Monsieur....' Realising she didn't know his real name she found herself saying: 'Monsieur Mistigris.' It was the last straw. It was the straw that broke the camel's back and she burst out in nervous laughter. 'Monsieur Mistigris. Monsieur Mistigris.'

'Governmental decrees[21]!' the old man stuttered, holding up the statue he had made and never been paid for, the statue Brother Michael had thrown into the cellar with the other broken bits of religious paraphernalia. 'Up with the Commune! Down with the Bishop! Up with the Good Lord! Down with the Bad One!'

He was certainly mad. In a court of law he would be judged insane. Drunk and insane. But it was small comfort to Bernadine who stood with trembling limbs, her heart still thumping horribly out of rhythm. It was too cruel a joke. It was too cruel a joke to play because for one perfect moment he had made her believe that life was worth living again, that time had started ticking again with the nice clean snowdrops. How stupid of her to be fooled by such an illusion! Her father had been right all along – anything truly dead never came alive again and time never stopped ticking, not for anyone. It was she who'd stopped ticking, not time, she just hadn't realised it. She'd stayed put, suspended in her vial of holy oil and time had just got on without her.

'You should have been paid for it,' a part of her went on with impeccable politeness while the other part simply wilted. 'The Mother Superior should have paid you for it.'

Mistigris shook his head sadly. 'It's a little much when the Virgin Mary ends up in a cellar. She should be on the altar with the other holy relics. Dear dear dear. I had to fish her out of the rubble back there like a little mermaid. Green! Green and bloated among the reeds and the water lilies.'

Bernadine didn't know how to respond. Her impeccable politeness had gone. All she could think was that her hopes and dreams had collided in the ridiculous creature in front of her and she felt suddenly pale and conspicuous in her white cotton nightdress like the mushrooms that grew in a corner of the cellar. Growing thin and transparent, etiolated in the darkness. Never setting eyes on the sun.

'Green as a pea,' Mistigris went on, swinging the lantern in front of her as if to get a better look, his robes flashing like fire in the light.

Where had he got them from, Bernadine wondered, in any case? Had Monsieur Lafayette lent them to him as a joke? Some sick and mischievous little prank? She suddenly lost her temper. 'When you come to think of it, monsieur,' she began bitterly, 'the Virgin Mary gave birth in a stable so it is singularly appropriate that she ends her days in a cellar.' And with a deft movement she grabbed the statue from the man's hands and threw it back into the rubble on the floor.

Mistigris stared at her in astonishment and the baby, disturbed by the violent action, started to cry in the cold night air. 'Hush Aggie,' mumbled

Bernadine, overcome with shock at her own little outburst and swaying self consciously from one foot to the other in an effort to quiet her.

'In the dead of night I shouldn't wonder!' Mistigris said gruffly, peering at them both with a comically morose look on his face. 'Everything comes to light in the dead of night. But I never needed paying for her.' Tears suddenly poured down his cheeks. 'I swear by any angelus you care to mention, Sister, that I never needed paying for her. Down with the Bishop! Oh down with the Bishop!'

'I believe you,' whispered Bernadine, still swaying from foot to foot. He was certainly mad – a cuckoo in borrowed plumes – and she wished he'd just go and leave her alone. There was so much to do! She must feed little Aggie, sweep up the altar cruets, get herself a drink of water, bandage her foot. So much to do and so little time. Time. Time that never stopped ticking, not for anyone it seemed. She must tend to Aggie's grave with her sturdy secateurs, lop and prune her dear little garden, plant some spring onions, maybe pansies for remembrance… She watched the stonecutter make his way a little clumsily up the steps and part of her must have wished him a polite goodnight. She watched him disappear with his tilting lantern, leaving her still rocking in the darkness. She must keep herself busy at all costs! She must keep her mind occupied if only for Aggie's sake! *Until the day breathes again*, another part of her whispered. *Until the day breathes again and the shadows flee away…*

Chapter twenty-three

Alphonse's name was on everyone's lips. It was rumoured that he'd singlehandedly started the revolution though nobody quite knew how he'd done it. Alphonse himself maintained a dignified and resolute silence upon the subject which only added flame to the rumours. Laurie was perhaps most confounded, most confused of all, wondering why he'd been left so completely in the dark. He wanted to ask his friend outright about the events of 18th March but didn't have the heart to, fearing to hear the reasons why he had been excluded.

He realised now, taking another swig of wine, his head thumping, that he had never really confronted anything. He'd never quite looked life in the eye, he took shy peeping furtive glances at it and even that was too much for him. The corner of his eye acted like a telescope, honing in on little things, magnifying them out of all proportion so that he never saw the big picture. He should have swivelled his head more. Even now, at this very instant, he was waching Eveline out of the corner of his eye watching Alphonse heading for the platform. Alphonse kitted out in evening dress – white gloves, silk cummerbund – every inch the hero. There were sharp intakes of breath on his left – a woman (a launderess he guessed) was also watching Alphonse heading for the platform. Eveline couldn't take her eyes off him, valiantly trying to make light conversation in an effort to cover up the fact that she couldn't take her eyes off him.

'Honestly,' she was saying, patting his hand in a sisterly gesture, 'Papa's gone completely mad, once and for all. He and his cronies stole some theatrical costumes from the Jesuit school on the Rue de Rivoli. I came home the other night and found him dressed as a Bishop, Madame Larousse as a nun! Can you picture it?'

He turned to look at her. She was wearing a dress for once instead of the trousers that had become de rigueur for her. It was soft green, flowed over her body like water and she reminded him of a sea nymph or a woodland sprite. Her hair bright gold fire about her face, her skin so translucent you could see the veins beneath. *He stared in awe at the trembling leaf, her veins on fire…*

'He's thinking of extending the coffin to make room for his mitre…'

Or should it be: *His veins on fire…*

'I think he's stolen more than theatrical costumes though. I found a silver chalice in his pocket.'

It was too much for him. She burnt his eyes. He had to turn away again. 'Oh dear,' he said flatly, taking another swig of wine. There were shushing whispers from behind. Alphonse Duchamp was about to speak. Alphonse Duchamp the revolutionary. Oh yes, they all hung on to his every word, wanted to know his opinion on everything under the sun from the colour of wallpaper to the Apocalypse, boils to Bismarck. It would have been mighty sickening, Laurie thought, if he hadn't been his friend. The shushing whispers dug into his back: Alphonse Duchamp was about to speak.

'We have a Commune!' he said simply, stretching out his arms as if to envelop the whole audience. After the thundering applause had died down he went on: 'The Communal revolution begun on the 18th March by popular initiative signals the end of the old clerical and governmental world, of militarism and bureaucracy, exploitation, privilege and the start of political unity.'

'What unity?' somebody shouted out. 'The members of the Commune are at each other's throats already as far as I can see!'

Alphonse looked a little taken aback though nobody but Laurie would have noticed it. It was the way he lifted his shoulders a fraction and ran a hand through his hair. 'The Commune took over the reins of power at a gallop,' he countered firmly. 'The ride is bound to be a little bumpy to begin with.'

'That is his way of admitting he stole the horses,' the laundress whispered to her friend who Laurie decided was undoubtedly a boot stitcher. 'He hides his light under a bushel, that one. You have to read between the lines with him.'

'Is that his mistress?' the boot stitcher murmured curiously. 'The one in the green?'

Laurie frowned and took another swig from the bottle. He was beginning to feel ill with all the wine he had consumed. He wished he could shut down his telescopic eye and frightful tendency to eavesdrop but he didn't think that he could. He should have been a spy though he didn't know which side he would be spying for.

'Bumpy!' scoffed the man in the audience. 'I should say it's bumpy. We've practically got a civil war on our hands.'

Alphonse smiled. 'This is transformation and transformation is always difficult. We are so used to the habitual, the routine, that we fear change, even change for the better. But these are the birth pangs of the revolution, my friend, and birth pangs are painful, laborious, even bloody. Do not forget, however, that the end result will be glorious.'

The boot stitcher leaned over and whispered to her friend. 'Is that his way of admitting his mistress is with child?'

Laurie stood up, trembling violently. He felt so lightheaded he thought he was going to faint. Is it true, he wanted to shout at the top of his voice. Is it true that you and Alphonse...

'Are you well, Laurie?' Eveline cried out in alarm. 'Are you quite well tonight, Laurie?'

'Quite well thank you.' Laurie sat down again with a thump. Perhaps it was best not to hear it articulated. It was best not to hear it articulated that Alphonse loved Eveline and Eveline loved Alphonse. Better to keep looking at it out of the corner of his eye.

The legendary Mabille got to her feet then, prodded on by the girls in her charge. 'Is it true,' she began in an embarrassed and quavering voice for despite her vocation she was prim and proper as a high court judge. 'Is it true that illegitimate companions and children of National Guardsmen killed in action are to receive the same pension as the legitimate companions and children?'

'Yes it is true,' replied Alphonse, his eyes frank and smiling. 'The Commune recognises partnerships between men and women other than marriage.'

'Marriage is a crime!' a young girl piped up, as dainty as a ballerina. 'A crime against morality!'

Hear Hear! There was more thunderous applause at this. *All for the free women*, came a chorus of shouts from Mabille's corner. *None for the slaves!*

'All for the free women!' Eveline repeated a little hesitatingly though nobody but Laurie would have noticed her uncertainty. 'Marriage is a crime against morality!'

Miss Grist, head bowed, was writing as fast as she could. A glass of water stood on her desk, untouched as always and somebody had mischievously placed a cream cake right under her very nose to tempt her into what she would have called a 'dereliction of duty'. It sat there oozing sugary nonsense and her mouth twitched now and again at the sight of it.

Marriage is a crime against morality, she wrote, pressing so hard with her pen that the nib broke. She cried out in dismay. This was a catastrophe indeed for she hadn't brought another.

'BREAK BREAK!' she called out in a shrill and flustered little voice, raising a skinny arm in the air. 'I need a new pen.'

'Not a patch on Tessier,' Laurie murmured to Eveline who nodded in agreement. Tessier had always brought an array of coloured inks for his doodles and symbols which was why he'd always taken so long over the affair and been forced to concoct the system Léon in the first place. But to forget an extra pen at a political meeting – *that* was a crime against morality.

Miss Grist, waiting for a new pen to be brought, was beginning to agitate over the fact that she couldn't write down that she couldn't write anything for want of a pen. It played on her mind that even when she got the new pen she'd have to write down that she'd had to stop writing for lack of a pen, what had happened in the interim and that she was able to start writing again because so and so had brought a replacement. As the minutes ticked by with nobody seemingly able to produce the right equipment – someone offered up a ruler, another a protractor – Miss Grist got so het up that she took a great bite out of the cream cake in front of her, gulping it down with an oddly bobbing little action.

'Miss Grist is eating cake!' somebody gasped as if mortally offended. 'Miss Grist never eats cakes!'

Poor Miss Grist. Her face suffused with blood at the reproachful glances cast in her direction; and mayhem might have ensued if a scholarly looking gentleman hadn't suddenly turned up with a pencil and the rather unjust little quip that if Miss Grist would deign to stop eating cakes they might get on with the meeting.

The mood became quite revolutionary after that. The sight of Miss Grist eating cake turned everybody's head, even more than Alphonse's speech. Someone proposed chairing a debate on whether the rich should be made to give back what they owed to the poor or simply be exterminated.

'Make them give back what they owe,' suggested a grisly looking fellow with an eyepiece, 'and then have them all exterminated – along with priests and nuns!'

There was laughter at this. Everyone agreed that the dandies who paraded along the boulevards with their pince-nez and kid gloves should be made to dig up the pavements in the fight against Versailles. There was even talk of blowing up the city rather than letting the old government back in.

'I should set myself alight,' went on the grisly looking fellow, his eyepiece twitching, 'rather than let Tom Thumb back into town.'

'I should set myself AND my children alight,' a passionate-looking woman declared, going one stage further, 'for the sake of the Commune!'

Tremendous applause at this. What an example! What a woman! Everyone was suddenly eager to sacrifice their nearest and dearest on the altar of the Commune.

'I should set myself, my sister and my canary ablaze!' a little old woman puffed, slyly watching Alphonse descending the platform, 'if it would help the revolution.'

'Thank you, madame,' Alphonse responded, looking her straight in the eye, 'but I don't think that will be necessary.'

An elderly gentleman suddenly sprang on to a pew, waving a bible. He was often at meetings and most people usually tried to ignore him.

'REVELATIONS,' he began with a roar.

The whole church yawned in unison. Honest to goodness. Take him away somebody, please do, and string him up. They'd had God rammed down their throats for eighteen centuries and that was more than enough for any of them.

Laurie, having drunk nearly three entire bottles of wine, was feeling strangely elated. Tears of joy pricked at his eyes as he looked around at the gathering. He had never felt so at one with humanity, so at peace with himself and mankind. It was like dreaming the most wonderful of dreams that one fought to recall upon waking. Like singing the most eloquent of songs in sleep that you couldn't retrace in the mornings. His heart flew out to the people around him: the sinners and villains, heroes and ragamuffins. He would share himself with them all tonight. He would share his soul for once in his life. He staggered to his feet, waving away the worried protestations of Alphonse and Eveline and laughing outright at their suggestion that he ought to get some bitter coffee down his neck. There was nothing wrong with him. He was just dandy thank you. They were the ones slurring their words by the sound of things! He lurched out of the pew, waiting for the sharp intake of breath from the laundress on his left for he could still cut a figure with the best of them in his finery for the evening's entertainment – white gloves, blue cummerbund – quite a heart-throb in fact. He propelled himself up the aisle, beaming at the faces smiling back at him red hot and glowing in the lamplight. All here in their common humanity. All here for the one idea – to celebrate the revolution. It was glorious indeed!

He stepped up to the lectern and clung on tight as the bloodshot faces swum beneath him and the stained-glass panes frowned down at him. Mary with a distaff, Mary with a little lamb… He spied Alphonse gesticulating violently at him to come down. Good old Alphonse! Always there to save the day. Always there to play the hero. But he needn't have worried. Laurie was in fine form tonight. He'd never felt such a surge of inspiration, such an outpouring of emotion. It was as if he'd tapped a wellspring inside him, a little wellspring of words to anoint his fellow men with.

'*Homo sapiens*,' he began, quite off the cuff and impromptu, '*are really at the Vatican*

God no hope

Look where we're at again!'

The audience approved. It was in the mood for a bit of recitation. Just what the doctor ordered, especially after that raddle-headed religious nut.

'*Little Thiers*,' Laurie went on, gaining confidence, '*has got no ears!*

Trochu's plan

Went down the pan.'

The hail of applause was music to his ears and he grinned in delight. He was on fire tonight! The words were coming thick and fast, leaping into his head like bright green frogs. He glanced meaningfully at Miss Grist as if to say that she better be getting this down, pen or no pen. It might very well end up in Volume Two by Laurie Marçeau, working title: Gods and Monsters.

'*The Ichneumonidae*

Are very greedy

Said the caterpillar host.

That a cat should play with mice

Ain't very nice

Darwin wrote.'

Nobody had a clue what *ichenondiae* were but they cheered even harder to make up for it. One woman went so far as to say she'd had them in her privy and Mr Darwin knew what he was talking about alright.

'Is he the one who married a monkey?' the grey-haired little woman asked, craning her neck to get a look at Laurie.

'Hardly!' scoffed the stately matron beside her. 'He said that as a race we humans are descended from monkeys.'

'Adam and Eve were monkeys?' The little old woman patted her hair with a startled look.

'Well, in a manner of speaking, I suppose. As a species we are constantly evolving.'

The little old woman gave a solemn nod. 'No doubt about it,' she puffed. 'No doubt about it. You've only got to look around you.'

Laurie didn't know how he'd got from St Nicolas-des-Champs to the Tuileries but he found himself a little while later ensconced between his friends on a seat in the Salle des Maréchaux. His head was still spinning with drink and the four cups of coffee Eveline had brought in an attempt to sober him up. He had a feeling he'd done something vaguely reprehensible but he couldn't think what and he was still too elated to care. He crunched on a nut brittle and listened to the violin tuning up behind the curtain, the people rustling into their places behind him. He was looking forward to the evening's entertainments – a concert in aid of widows and orphans. There were to be a few amateur-dramatical turns, a juggler apparently, La Bordas herself and some poetry reading. He hugged his knees in anticipation and watched the ushers in their white gloves handing out tea served with sugar, lemon and Normandy cream. It was all very civilised, he thought wryly, considering there was a war going on. The main attraction of course was the Tuileries itself. For fifty centimes anyone off the street could come and satisfy their curiosity as to how the other half had lived. Red flags had been stuck in the cheekiest of places to emphasise the point that the Tuileries was now the property of the Commune or rather the people; and posters reading 'the gold that drapes these walls is your sweat and toil' adorned every bit of marble and gilt. People were lining up in droves to see where their sweat and toil had ended up. Women fingered the satin sheets the Empress herself had slept between, dabbed their necks with her bottled perfume, riffled through her stockings and political dresses; children pressed the bells that went through to the servants' quarters; and men gazed up at the chandeliers or pointed out to one another where they lived on the replica floor map in the Emperor's study. It was accurate in every detail apparently, right down to the flower stalls on the Madeleine and the curving loops of the Seine; and it was changed every year to keep it up to date with modern development. Laurie tried to imagine the poor old Emperor in night cap and slippers traversing the streets of Paris in his room before ringing for cocoa and bed. Now he was traversing the streets of London for real in complete anonymity.

Laurie accepted some tea with lemon and cream, much to Eveline's disgust. 'You'll give yourself stomach ache,' she chided. 'Lemon and cream curdle in the stomach.' But Laurie didn't mind. The concert was about to start and he wanted to be refreshed for the performances. 'Anyway,' he said with an all-inclusive grin at Alphonse, 'it can't be any worse than mouth warmer!'

Alphonse made a grimace and Laurie laughed out loud. It was good to be with his friends. It was good to be with his friends on such a memorable occasion. The Tuileries open for the public at large. It was everything he and Alphonse had dreamed about.

'Has it all been worth it, my friend?' he asked, vaguely gesturing with his cup.

Alphonse started a little though no one but Laurie would have noticed it. Something flickered into those bright blue eyes and then disappeared again like the ripple of a stone in a bright blue lake. Laurie suddenly realised that he had misunderstood the question. He had misunderstood the question and given a different answer. And Laurie knew. He had seen into the soul of Alphonse the hero, Alphonse the enigma. And he knew that Alphonse knew that he knew.

The curtain went up then and a man rushed on stage with a small prop for the first act. Laurie felt as if he were watching the workings of his own mind as a variety of characters raced on and off in different guises. There were tumblers and acrobats with sleeked-down hair and well-oiled bodies who somersaulted and cartwheeled their way around the stage; a violinist with a wild moustache and a plaintive tune; and a juggler who could juggle anything in the universe apparently, anything the audience cared to throw at him. Someone threw a hat, another a scarf and he juggled these without shifting an inch from his jewel-coloured carpet. A man threw a shoe at him then and a boy his penknife and even these he managed to juggle without batting an eyelid. Laurie was astounded and Eveline said she wished Jacques was there to see it. 'He would have loved it so,' she sighed, wiping a tear from her eye.

'He'd have thrown a balloon at the man!' smiled Alphonse, watching the people foraging in their pockets for something more testing than a shoe and a penknife. A cushion was hurled from a velvet bench and a rotten-looking orange but luckily for the juggler his time was up for La Bordas herself was waiting in the wings.

She sashayed onto the stage draped in a red flag and little else and a frisson of anticipation went through the audience. Acrobats and jugglers were just the starters. La Bordas herself was the main course, especially when she sang her version of *La Marseillaise*.

'I won't be singing *La Marseillaise* tonight,' was the first thing she said in her usual steely voice; and the audience groaned with disappointment. She always sang *La Marseillaise* – it was her trademark song so to speak. 'The last time I sang *La Marseillaise*,' the great singer explained, 'the Prussians were at the gate. Now it is our fellow countrymen and I cannot in all conscience sing it tonight.'

The audience was keen to show its sympathy. Of course. What a predicament for such a temperamental soul! Whatever she chose to do would be fine by them (so long as she sang *La Marseillaise*!). No no but really, she couldn't. In all conscience she could not sing it tonight. If they didn't mind she would recite a poem by Victor Hugo. And much to Laurie's delight she did. She recited *Le Lion Surpris* with, on the whole he thought, much feeling though perhaps not with the political impartiality she might have hoped for. He wanted to put his arms round Evie's shoulders during the savage attack but he pressed his hands to the velvet bench to stop himself doing so.

A young girl came on in La Bordas' shadow and most people expected to be bored. Dressed in a simple cotton frock she looked as frail as a grey-winged moth, her hair catching the light in the candelabra. She cast a quick, scared look around the room and then, clutching her hands together in front of her, she suddenly broke out into song, her voice soaring up into the golden-tableauxed ceiling. She sang about remembrance and everything past as if her soul held all the longing that had ever been and ever would be… and you could have heard a pin drop in that vast quiet multitude, in the Salle des Maréchaux… just a girl singing her heart away like a bird in a gilded cage.

> *J'aimerai toujours le temps des cerises*
> *Et le souvenir que je garde en coeur.*[22]

When it was over Laurie got up to go because he just couldn't bear any more after that. The song had pierced his heart and he wasn't quite sure if he'd been very happy and was now very sad or had been very sad and was now very happy. Alphonse protested at the sight of him making ready to depart.

'We've only just begun,' he said, gesturing vaguely around the room; and this time it was Laurie who misunderstood.

'Yes,' he said seriously. 'We have only just begun and yet already it feels like an ending.'

'But the best bit's next,' Eveline chimed in, patting his arm in a sisterly gesture, a little too sisterly by half. And he gazed at the woman who reminded him of a sea nymph or woodland sprite, a slender tree, a translucent leaf. For her the best bit would always be next; but for him it was over, past, a memory to hold in his heart.

'You were right, I'm afraid, Evie,' he said with a rueful smile, 'the lemon and cream has done for me it seems!'

'Then we will all go,' Alphonse announced firmly, fishing beneath the velvet bench for his hat and coat.

'Please don't,' muttered Laurie, holding up a hand because he just couldn't bear any more of it. He didn't want a long walk home full of explanations and reassurances, didn't want to hear in excruciating detail how Alphonse loved Eveline and Eveline loved Alphonse. He had seen it in the frank blue eyes of his friend. He didn't want to see it again.

'Well, make your minds up!' came a disgruntled voice from behind and the three of them, catching each other's eye, burst out into crazy laughter, an awkward embarrassed exaggerated laughter that united and parted all at the same time. Three children of the revolution, thought Laurie, in the Salle des Maréchaux, a baker and two waker-uppers in the palace of kings. It was everything he and Alphonse had dreamed about. And he left after saluting a silent goodbye and made his way out into the warm spring night though for the first time ever the streets of Paris left him cold and the city of light felt dark to him.

Chapter twenty-four

'Frogs and tulips!' muttered Monsieur Lafayette as the banging on his door grew louder and louder. 'Hell's bells! Hold your horses!' He pulled off his nightcap, put on his dressing gown and padded to the door on his thick-soled feet, pressing a pin black eye to the peephole. A malicious little smile suddenly stole across his mouth; and he rubbed his hands together in delight before drawing back the heavy bolts.

'Well, well,' he said to the hooded figure on his doorstep, 'I thought it looked black enough to rain a few priests and nuns!'

Sister Bernadine stepped over the threshold, sopping wet and dripping rivulets, her cloak bulging oddly over the form of little Aggie. The nun looked paler than ever, her face almost ghostly in fact and contrasting sharply to the trellis of curls that clung in red clusters to her forehead and cheeks.

'No umbrella?' the herbalist ventured in a conversational tone as if having a nun after hours in the middle of his shop was a commonplace social event. 'You must be chilled to the bone!'

'N... no,' stammered Bernadine a little confusedly, gazing about her in dismay. She lowered her hood and opened her cloak to check that the infant was perfectly dry then sank down on a chair beside the counter.

The shop was full again. Brim full with coloured bottles and dried herbs: mallow, comfrey, elderberry and thyme; and the jars were stuffed once more with pounds and pounds of shrimp sugar, marzipan, chocolate shoe laces, caramel cigars, barley twists, gumdrops, almond brittle and peppermints... everything the sweetest of teeth could desire.

Monsieur Lafayette, delving about in a cupboard by the counter, brought out a brown decanter and two small tumblers. 'An apple brandy,

Sister?' he offered with a sly little grin. 'I won't tell if you won't. Perhaps a rum baba to go with it?'

Bernadine shook her head, uncertain how to begin. She almost wished she hadn't come and yet she knew at the same time that she had to confront it once and for all. She couldn't carry on with the uncertainty, the not knowing, the hypotheticals and the question marks. Clutching the string of rosaries sewn into the lining of her pocket, she steeled herself to speak.

'Did she live?' she uttered in a peculiarly loud and uneven tone of voice.

Monsieur Lafayette tapped his glass and swirled the brandy around with a delicate flick of the wrist. 'Very voluptuous,' he murmured dreamily, taking a sip and smacking his lips. 'Almost titillating to the tastebuds. Apple is the most pleasant of fruits and yet, of course, the most ambiguous. Think of Eve, my dear, before that fatal scrumping... your Ernest was partial to a drop. On the quiet naturally.'

Bernadine started and a flush began to creep from her neck to her chin.

'Funny little man,' Monsieur Lafayette went on, bringing his chair so close that she wanted to recoil. 'He always reminded me of a hungry boy staring at a jam sandwich. I wonder what he made of all that bare flesh in Africa. Jam sandwiches galore, I should say! Just like her mother,' he added, touching the infant's downy hair with his yellow-stained fingers. 'An uncanny resemblance.'

'You have not answered my question,' Bernadine said accusingly, fighting the urge to flee then and there.

'Oh but I am answering your question,' replied the herbalist a little obliquely. 'The church talks in riddles so why shouldn't I? It is all metaphor after all. We are talking are we not of the daughter you did not have... and a Bishop who was sent to Africa simply to tame the barbarous natives and flesh-eating crocodiles. I wonder what became of him...' Monsieur Lafayette mused vaguely. 'They probably ate him alive. Put him in a pot. I know my wages dried up.'

'So you *were* blackmailing him,' Bernadine said with a note of resignation. 'I thought as much.'

'Earthly repentance you might say,' Monsieur Lafayette replied icily. 'Put it this way, he valued my silence. Besides which it takes a lot to clean up that sort of mistake.'

'You drove him away,' Bernadine cried scornfully, 'with your demands.'

'Hardly! I'm not that powerful, my dear. I'm afraid his superiors got wind of – oh must we use metaphors again – his *transgression* and that was the end of that. They sent him off to the depths of Africa to spread the good word. I imagine he spent most of his days reading the bible to those flesh-eating crocodiles. Until even they got sick of him. What a spectacular instrument of God he turned out to be!'

Bernadine covered her ears. 'I should not have come to torture myself so. You have no right to judge, monsieur. Ernest was worth a thousand of you,' she added bitterly.

Monsieur Lafayette gave a coarse laugh. 'Was he now? Well, you should know, my dear, though I don't believe you've had the opportunity to make a comparison. More's the pity.' And he leered at her with his pin black eyes, his boiled head gleaming like an egg in the lamplight.

She shrank back a little farther into her seat, wondering what to do. She wasn't exactly scared of the man; she disliked him more than she feared him. But she knew what he was capable of and she had Aggie to think of too. She almost wished she hadn't come but she had to find out the truth once and for all. St John, chapter eight: *And the truth shall set you free*, sang a voice in her head. *The truth shall set you free.* She had tried to move on, make her peace with the Lord and the Mother Superior, go back to her calling, step into that more rarefied air, leave the past dead and buried at her feet. But the past didn't stay where it should. It sprang up again and again with the snowdrops and primroses; sprang up again and again like a resurrected shadow over the present.

'Or are you too high and mighty for a Modeste?' Monsieur Lafayette was teasing. 'Now that you have had a Bishop.' Snapping his fingers in front of her: 'You were drifting off, Bernadine. You really ought to get out of those wet clothes I'm sure, else you'll catch your very own death and what would the Lord make of that? I have one or two dry items you could use and I could hold the baby while you dress…'

'N… no,' stammered Bernadine violently, watching him go over to the counter and help himself to a slice of rum baba, delving into the rum-soaked sponge with a huge silver spoon. She was beginning to think he wouldn't tell her anything. He would go on playing cat and mouse with her for as long as he wished then let her go. What did *he* care? He had nothing to lose – if Ernest were really dead. Nothing to gain perhaps but nothing to lose either. He could make up whatever he liked – say the girl was in Timbuctoo – to suit his own design. How could she have been so blind? So blind and so stupid as to come over here without any sort of plan. The incident with Mistigris had sent her over the edge, she chided herself silently. How stupid to race off into the night like that in search of the truth. You never found the truth when you looked for it; it hit you unawares like sunlight through the trees or a face in a dream. Hadn't she learned anything in all these years? Surrender to the moment and the truth will be revealed. That's all she had to do. Surrender to the moment and the truth would be revealed.

She smiled serenely, with a certain amount of difficulty, and loosened the bonds on the cotton papoose. Little Aggie was wide awake and staring inquisitively at the colourful jars behind the counter. Monsieur Lafayette, noticing her reflection in the fly-spotted mirror, enquired with a wry smile: 'Would she like a chocolate shoe lace or a caramel cigar? They were her mother's special favourites if I remember rightly.'

Bernadine shrugged. 'Why not?' she smiled sweetly. 'It can't do her any harm.'

He brought one of each, crouching down beside the infant and dangling them into her mouth as if he were feeding worms to a bird. 'I expect you were rather pleased,' he chatted cosily to the nun, 'when the Cannibal's Delight popped her clogs. No offence meant of course – she was a valued customer, poor woman – no doubt eating the wildflowers by their roots at this very moment as fast as she is able. But the infant is some sort of compensation to you is she not?'

Bernadine smiled blandly though her heart wept at the betrayal. *Forgive me*, she cried silently. *Forgive me my dear, kind, brave, best friend.* 'In a way you are right, monsieur,' she spoke carefully. 'The infant is a compensation of a sort. A chance to redeem.' She paused. 'I don't expect I shall ever meet my own daughter… but I am sure that you found a good home for her where she was well loved and looked after. I am sure that Ernest's trust in you was not misplaced.'

'Oh my dear,' the confectioner's eyes twinkled in delight. 'You've set my pulse racing with that fine speech. You could tempt the birds from the air, you really could. I can see why Ernest fell so sharply from grace.'

Bernadine smiled grimly.

'I can even see,' Monsieur Lafayette went on, 'why you fell for him. Power is a strong aphrodisiac at any age. The Bishop with his mighty staff… but what I cannot understand…' he stopped to wipe the little chocolate-stained mouth, 'is how you could continue to live a holy life after committing such a terrible – oh let us call a spade a spade – sin.' He almost hissed the word out. He lingered on it, revelled in it, luxuriated in it, lavished every nuance of feeling on it as if it were a pet.

Sin. The word reverberated round Bernadine's head, knocking into other words like shame, love, duty, despair. She felt as if he were holding her heart in the palpitating mid air to see if she could cope without it. She couldn't. He had won. He had defeated her. If that is what he had wanted he had succeeded for she had no answer to that simple question. With great difficulty, she could have said or, in the hope that the Lord is a merciful one. For that was how she continued to live, day after day. In the hope that the Lord was a forgiving Lord. In the hope that the Lord was a merciful one. She bowed her head, mumbled a prayer, clutching on to Aggie with trembling fingers. 'If you could just tell me her name,' she pleaded, her eyes wet with tears. 'That would be something, if I just knew her name.'

Monsieur Lafayette got up, his joints clicking, and helped himself to another apple brandy. 'Funny thing, the memory,' he mused, adding a spoonful of sugar to the glass. 'A most temperamental organ, I must say. I swear it likes a little game of hide and seek or after dinner-charades. For the life of me I cannot recall my mother's face and yet the voice of my first wife is clear as a bell or should I say a seagull. Shriek shriek shriek. Peck peck peck. I can hear it now at this very moment but the face of my mother is quite gone from me. What do you make of that, Sister Bernadine?' He put up his hand. 'No, no, don't answer. I know what you're thinking. You're thinking it is simply a matter of chronology but that is not it at all. My wife ran away many moons ago with a wolf whereas my poor mother passed away only last spring. The only conclusion I have come to is that the memory is a most temperamental organ. I'd like to take it out and give it a good shake sometimes – like a baby's rattle.' He smiled in the direction of little Aggie. 'I have one or two tricks up my sleeve, however. Wine sometimes can lure it out of its hiding place. A little music, an unexpected smell. The scent of lilac for example and I get a glimpse of my mother's eyes – no more mind, just her eyes. A whiff of old cabbage and I see the whole of my wife's – well, yes never mind…. In the arms of a good woman I believe the organ could reassert itself, function perfectly. In a moment of passion I am convinced I could recall every detail of a person from their name right down to the colour of their teeth.'

Bernadine, suddenly understanding what he meant, gasped in horror. 'Even then,' she almost spat at him, 'you would not tell me.'

Monsieur Lafayette drained his glass in one fell swoop, even the undissolved sugar at the bottom. 'The question is,' he teased, towering over her in his long silk dressing gown, his ugly toes peeping through the fringe at the bottom, 'could you live with the possibility that I might have done?'

Bernadine strove to gather her thoughts, not knowing what to do or where to look. Could she live with the possibility that he might have told her everything? Of course she couldn't! He had won. He had beaten her. If that is what he wanted then he had succeeded. Three cheers for

Monsieur Lafayette! In a bid for time she placed little Aggie in the cotton papoose and slung her safely to the back of a chair; then she got up and nervously smoothed her skirts, realising for the first time that her legs were freezing cold. Surrender to the moment, sang a voice in her head, and the truth will be revealed. She stamped her feet to encourage the blood flow then sat abruptly down again, closing her eyes in despair. She could hear the confectioner crunching on a boiled sweet and it burst upon her with the awful clarity of some startling new dawn that this was to be her final punishment, her final degradation. The Lord it seemed was not a merciful one. The Lord was not even – far from it – a gentleman.

'Very well, monsieur,' she said in a barely audible whisper, her eyes still closed. 'As long as you promise to keep your side of the bargain.'

'I'm a fair man,' Monsieur Lafayette assured her though she didn't see the look in his pin black eyes, didn't see him scuttling about freshening his breath with a peppermint drop, pushing aside the fabled curtain that separated one half of the room from the other and revealed a dirty mattress and oddly placed stool. Didn't see him wet his moustache in the fly-spotted mirror with a bit of saliva and yellow-stained thumb – generally making himself a little more palatable. She didn't see any of these things as she sat in her silent shifting darkness. Only when she felt his hand on her arm and the heat of his breath against her cheek did her eyes open wide in alarm.

When it was over Bernadine dressed as quickly as she could, her limbs trembling so violently that she ripped a hole in her thick black stockings. Her clothes felt stiff and heavy on her flesh and she hobbled over to Aggie, hardly able to bare the weight of them. With an enormous sense of relief she saw that the baby was sleeping soundly, innocently, quite undisturbed by the night's goings on, her red mouth still a little chocolate-stained at the edges where Monsieur Lafayette had smeared his thick yellow thumb. It had been a small sacrifice to make, she decided, gazing intently at the rosy cheeks and thick black eyelashes. A small sacrifice to make in exchange for the truth. The truth, after all, was meant to set you free.

'Will you tell me now?' she demanded as Monsieur Lafayette reappeared from behind the curtain, readjusting the cord on his long silk dressing gown. There was a note of desperation in her voice. 'Will you keep your side of the bargain?'

The confectioner nodded, smiling. 'Modeste Ignatius Napoleon Abëlard Lafayette is nothing if not a man of his word… and after that…' he smiled lasciviously, taking a long cigar out of the wig box on the counter, 'how could I refuse? I can tell you straightaway she is as beautiful as her mother. A plump, ripe strawberry, ready to be plucked. On the way to going a little rotten around the edges and all the better for it in my opinion. They're no good to you hard and greenish, no good to you at all. You want 'em red and juicy – perfect with a sprinkling of sugar and a dash of thin cream.'

It will not have been in vain, Bernadine told herself valiantly, her stomach lurching and shuddering like a ship being wrecked upon the rocks. *It will not have been in vain.*

'She's broken one or two hearts already – even at her tender age. She does not know her own power as yet. A man only has to look at her and he practically falls simpering at her feet.'

'Oh,' was all Bernadine could think to say and as the questions flooded into her mind she asked eagerly and almost without pausing for breath: 'Does she know who she is, I mean the circumstances of her birth? Did she stay in the city or was she sent away? And her parents? Were they good to her? Did they treat her well?' There were so many questions she wanted to ask, they tumbled over each other like a horde of merry children, shrieking in their shrill insistent little voices. *Does she like the colour pink? Are there freckles on her nose? Does she wear her hair curled or straight? Does she sew or cook, pass the time with walks and books? What does she eat for Sunday dinner? Does she have a favourite flower?*

Monsieur Lafayette puffed thoughtfully on his cigar. 'No, she does not know the circumstances of her birth for I do not believe Ernest would have wanted it. He would not have wanted her to have ideas above her station. He was, despite everything, a humble man, was he not?' He paused and Bernadine nodded impatiently. 'She is a veritable rose upon a dungheap however. She does not fit in. Being the daughter of a nun and a Bishop she has an otherworldly quality about her. People notice... her parents on the other hand know exactly who she is. They were only too keen to accept the progeny of a Bishop in exchange for one or two shiny boys.' He rubbed his forefinger against his thumb to indicate the financial nature of the contract. 'I am sure they loved her. Her mother passed away a little while ago I'm afraid. She was that most lethal combination in a woman – a strong will coupled with fragile emotions – I do not think she ever came to terms with having a nun's daughter in the household, being a... these dratted metaphors... fallen woman herself. Her father, the old fool, loves her more than life itself.'

This was all good news as far as Bernadine was concerned. Better even perhaps than she could have hoped for.

'He is scared stiff of losing her. He believes that if she found out the truth... I have told him many times that her secret is safe with me. I shall not breathe a word of it to any living soul, present company excepted. My lips are sealed as the tomb.'

Bernadine shivered ever so slightly as if the most delicate of winds had fanned over her grave. She did not want to cause trouble between the girl and her father. She had simply come in search of the truth. 'I do not intend to say anything,' she began and was immediately interrupted by Monsieur Lafayette.

'Quite so, quite so, I should not have told you otherwise. No point digging about like dogs with a bone. The girl is fine as she is though as I have told her father many times she needs the steadying guide of an older hand to keep an eye on her, keep her secret safe; keep her on the straight and narrow. The thing is, my dear,' he sucked long and hard on his cigar much to Bernadine's irritation for she was beginning to feel quite faint with all the smoke in the air, 'to use a metaphor you might like to ponder, I have nurtured her since she was a tender shoot, fed and watered her, seen her flower, potted her on so to speak. There is no one more qualified than I am to keep her safe, keep an eye on her; keep her from following in her mother's footsteps.'

'Which mother?' Bernadine asked a little sarcastically for her and the confectioner chuckled good humouredly, his black eyes narrowing, if that were possible, in appreciation of the joke. 'Which mother you say? Ah, that is one I shall have to ponder. Which mother indeed! A sister of the Boulevard des Italiens and a Sister of St Joseph's? Never the twain shall meet, eh?'

She had asked for that. She had walked right into it with her arms outstretched. Not that it mattered of course for what he alluded to was the truth. There was no difference between herself and a girl from the Boulevard des Italiens. No difference at all except for one important point. A girl from the Boulevard des Italiens was probably a good deal more honest.

'Come to think of it,' he winked, 'on that particular score either mother will do. Her late mother might have had one or two more tricks in the seduction stakes but I am a man of simple pleasures at heart am I not, my dear. Hee hee! Nothing unusual in that department! No, I can honestly say that if she inherits one or two... er... qualities of her natural mother she will do just fine for me.'

'What in God's name do you mean? *She will do just fine for me?*'

'She will keep me young, keep me spry; keep me on my toes. A lively girl like that will keep my pecker up so to speak. What do you think, Sister

Bernadine – will the daughter of a nun and a Bishop do for a Modeste? I see you are a little perturbed by the notion. Don't be. Don't be. I have convinced her father of the rightness of the match. He was a little dubious at first, naturally. But the thing is you see,' he whispered, bending forward, his bald head gleaming in the lamplight like the golden dome of the Invalides, 'the closer she is to me the easier it is to keep her secret.'

Bernadine felt suddenly as if she were drowning. 'You are blackmailing him,' she gasped weakly, hardly able to breathe in her heavy, sodden clothes and the thickness of the smoke in the air. 'You are blackmailing him!'

'Oh you nuns!' Monsieur Lafayette smiled, jumping up and pacing the room. 'What a dramatic little lot you are! If it's not blackmail it's rape and abortion. When I come to think of how many of you I have served over there ...' he indicated the curtain behind which lay the dirty mattress and stool. 'Why I should be made an honorary saint myself. Saint Modeste Ignatius Napoleon Abëlard Lafayette. It has a certain ring to it does it not?'

'She cannot love you,' Bernadine insisted, shaking her head like a beaten dog. 'I do not care what you say, Monsieur Lafayette, she cannot possibly love you. You are deluded or mad or both. You are so old and...'

'Oh my dear, but you are forgetting the attractions of an older man – you were taken in by them once upon a time yourself were you not? The experience, the... er... technique... Besides which, in case you haven't noticed, we are in the middle of a civil war. The young men are dying like flies. When they have all deserted her or come a cropper – and mark my words that is exactly what will happen – who will be there to pick up the pieces? Who will be there to mend her broken heart? Why, her dear old friend Monsieur Lafayette of course! She will look upon him kindly then I am sure of it. It may take a little time, I grant you, but in the end, one way or another, I will make her the next Madame Lafayette.'

Bernadine staggered to her feet, clutching on to little Aggie. St John, chapter eight: *And the truth shall set you free*, mocked a voice in her head. *And the truth shall set you free. And the truth shall set you free.* She caught sight of herself in the fly-spotted mirror – a small white cloud next to a jar of colourful sweets; and she deduced that the white cloud must be her own face.

'Madame Modeste Ignatius Napoleon Abëlard Lafayette! It has a certain ring to it does it not?'

A dash of sunshine and she would evaporate completely. A puff of wind and she would skedaddle up to heaven or down to hell maybe. But she had Aggie to think of now. She pulled her cloak tight about the cotton papoose…

'Shall I send you an invite when the time comes? No don't be alarmed. You could come in the guise of an old family friend – meet the folks so to speak – nobody would ever suspect a thing. Oh, must you go so soon? I feel as if we were only just getting to know each other – in the biblical sense that is. Do you think it is wise to venture out on a night like this in those wet clothes? I fear you will catch your very own death and then what will become of you? Why don't you stay the night – only too happy to oblige – you could take the mattress, I could take the stool… Why you look quite terrified, my pet, like a tiny little rabbit that's just seen a ghost. Is Ernest out there on the doorstep waggling a finger at you. Or something else entirely. Very well then, a nightcap perhaps, to send you on your way and toast your daughter's impending nuptials. Good gracious me I've just had a thought – by the end of the year you will be my new mother-in-law. What a delicious prospect! Better pins than the last one I must say. Quite swollen up at the end poor duck, with the gout. Too much offal apparently. Lungs, heart, kidneys you name it. Treacherous for the legs! Oh you are a spoilsport Sister Bernadine, but if you must you must I suppose. It's been a quite delightful evening for my part I have to say. Come come my dear, there's no need to cry like that, no need for it at all. Your daughter's in the safest of hands and it makes you look rather haggard. Cheerio.

'By the way,' he added, as Bernadine fled out of the yard and into the night which was greying now with strips of dawn, 'you forgot to ask her name.' But the wind and rain tore the words from his mouth and the nun, full of anguish, did not hear him.

'It is Eveline,' he smiled, rubbing his hands with glee. 'Your daughter's name is Eveline.'

Chapter twenty-five

19th May 1871

Dearest Maman,
            I received your last letter with great delight. It arrived in the most convoluted of ways as all letters seem to these days. I believe it travelled down the Boulevard du Montparnasse, around the Place de l'Observatoire, over the Seine by the Pont des Arts, past the biscuit factory on the corner and in a semi circle back to me! You are wondering how I know all this. Well, on your next trip to Paris I shall show you – but for now let us just say Detective Claude eat your heart out!

At least it arrived safe and sound and has come to rest on the mantelpiece under the cuckoo clock. I must have read it a hundred times, indeed ~~do not laugh, maman, I have the strangest feeling that if I do not read it every hour upon the hour some frightful calamity shall befall me. My mind, it seems, is up to its old tricks again. It is late and~~ *You made me quite homesick, maman, with your description of the church bazaar and your dew-laden walks through the meadow with Molly. Does she still believe every hollow tree is the abode of some Ariel or wood-land fairy? Sometimes I wish that I still did. Well done on raising such a vast sum at the fête – I told you your knitting would come in useful one day, maybe not for hats and scarves but for an ancient church spire, well yes I can believe it!*

There is a festive air in the city at the moment, almost carnivalesque in fact. I think it is because there is a tacit understanding that we live on borrowed time and must therefore make the most of it. Rumours abound every hour or so that Thiers and his government have re-entered the city and will take possession again by nightfall... So in between our carousing we build barricades as fast as we can go with any material we can lay our hands on. Every quartier has one unique to its inhabitants. The other day I spied one on the Rue du Faubourg (the one where you love the cheesemonger so much) made up of an upturned old omnibus, wardrobe, flower pots, wheelbarrow, and four rounds of cheeses! (The stench alone should stop the Versaillais in their tracks!) My own hands are red raw from filling wine and beer barrels with pebbles and earth (Yes, yes, I know what you think of the area I live in) so do not be alarmed, maman, if you find a drop of blood on these pages. I bandage them up, in any case, every night in my spotless white evening gloves.

Do not think however that I while my time away with manual labour and dancing. Oh no, not at all! My work is going full steam ahead I am pleased to report. (My thoughts on Darwin and evolution are coming together nicely; and recently I have been toying with the idea that gravity and consciousness are somehow connected. When we sleep we fall down, for example, do we not? But more of that perhaps in another letter.) I am sure that by the end of the year I shall be entirely self supporting ~~so you must not send me any more money, maman~~ *You are very naughty, maman, sending me so much money. I am sure you cannot afford it. And in any case, aren't writers meant to teeter on the brink of starvation, fleeing from one bad debt to another? Look at Balzac! Or better still, live and die in abject poverty only to make a posthumous fortune for their dear old maman and sister when a manuscript is unearthed from under the bed… (Look out for one entitled Gods and Monsters if such a thing should ever happen to me!) I hate to think of you scrimping and saving, ekeing things out for little Molly. She must definitely continue with her piano lessons at any rate. Tell her I expect a perfect rendition of 'Für Elise' on my return now that she has mastered 'The Moonlight Sonata'. Beethoven composed it while sitting up a chestnut tree apparently!*

Laurie paused and looked about him. Mabille's was filling up fast it had got so late or rather so early. He noticed out of the corner of his eye a waitress hovering nearby with a tray and he pushed away his plate, smiling benignly, to signal that she could collect it.

'Did monsieur enjoy his food?' she asked politely, sweeping up with a dirty napkin.

Monsieur did, Laurie wanted to reply out of sheer impishness but instead he smiled again and nodded his head, though when he came to think about it he suddenly realised that he hadn't. Hadn't enjoyed it one little bit: the peas had been hard as bullets, the gravy thick and greasy tasting and the beer flat and horribly warm. But then again people didn't come to Mabille's for the food.

'Are you writing a letter?' th e girl asked then in an effort to engage him in smalltalk. 'I love writing letters though I'm not very good at them. Sometimes I practise in front of the mirror. Is it to your sweetheart?'

'My mother,' Laurie corrected, a little intrigued by the image of the girl practising her letter writing in front of the mirror.

'Ah.' She seemed to cogitate for a moment before casually mentioning a sum of money as if she were offering up some sort of dessert.

Laurie, somewhat taken aback, asked her to repeat herself.

'I shan't go any lower,' she warned with a determined tilt of the chin. 'Any lower than that and all you'll be able to do is look.'

Laurie shook his head wearily, running a hand through his hair the way Alphonse did. 'Not tonight I'm afraid,' he muttered awkwardly, not knowing what else to say and wishing he'd never come to Mabille's. He'd only wanted a bite to eat, a breath of fresh air, a break from the monotony of his stuffy little rooms. With an air of exaggerated preoccupation he picked up his pen as the girl flounced off and carried on a little self consciously with his letter.

I expect you heard about the Vendôme column[23] or – as the Commune puts it – that symbol of brute force and false glory. Not so false, I don't believe, for the old fellow standing next to me, his medals displayed across his chest. He was shaking like a leaf when they pulled it down, no doubt remembering his fallen comrades. It was a terrible anti climax in the end actually. After an inordinate amount of heave hoing and see-sawing it fell with the feeblest of clatters like a little piece of stage scenery and it was quite hollow inside (apart from its staircase) as if it had been gnawed out from the middle by a horde of hungry rats, horses, Ariels, woodland fairies – allow Molly to delete as apppropriate! I wish I'd gone up it of course, now that I've lost the chance forever. I met a woman in the crowd who said it was just like going up to heaven. Fifty centimes and a little lantern, she told me. 'What a view of Paris. It made my blood run cold!'

It was no good. He couldn't concentrate. The waitress whom he'd slighted was giving him the evil eye from behind a majolica plant pot and the place was filling up so fast he could barely hear himself think. He'd wanted to describe the quality of the light when the column fell, the strips of paper pasted over the windows in the square, the looks on people's faces. If he'd been an artist he'd have sketched the column as a dark flat shadow on the ground, criss-crossed with the shadows of women and children, the sun a fiery ball in the corner of the sky to symbolise perhaps the empty glory, the harshness, the cruelty of war. But he wasn't an artist, he was a poet and he couldn't even write a letter in this dreadful din.

He got up, pushed back his chair and struggled through the throng milling out onto the terrace. It was a night for dancing – warm, muggy with a wind that might have come out of Africa. It felt to Laurie as if a storm were brewing and he watched the couples pushing back the tables and chairs with a familiar sense of despair. He had no one to dance with now.

He decided to take a circuitous route home. He would fashion the letter in his head and when he got home he could copy it down direct. Yes, that was the ticket. Kill two birds with one stone: enjoy a stroll through the city and write a letter at the same time. Why hadn't he thought of it before instead of going into that low dive, Mabille's. He marvelled now at the girl's impudence, wondering what sort of impression he must have made, sitting alone at the table writing a letter to his mother. She must have thought him an incredible dandy, approaching him like that, with bags of money to throw around. How ironic. He grinned wryly to himself, vaguely flattered and yet repulsed all at the same time and wishing suddenly that it would rain, pour down so that he could feel the droplets on his hair, his skin, the tips of his fingers. There was nothing he liked better than a violent thunderstorm – the way the lightning illuminated the city, almost setting it afire, the thunder roaring like the voice of Zeus. Sometimes he got so charged with energy in the middle of a storm he threw himself out down onto the street in his nightshirt and stared at the sky just to be a part of that power, that magnitude.

I would have a tranquil revolution, he went on calmly, fashioning the letter to his mother in his head. *A revolution of the spirit if you like, untramelled by priests and religion of course. Just a stepping forward in consciousness. No more killing or revenge. (How hard not to take revenge when someone has hurt you, not to remain bitter for the rest of your life. It is a courage of discipline and restraint, something perhaps that I can aspire to.) The law of hostages is a monstrous law – to kill three Versaillais for every Communard – it is an unprecedented escalation of violence. This whole thing is a runaway train, maman, and I do not know where it will end. We must just sit tight I suppose and ride it out. The Commune has conscripted all men between the ages of 19 and 55 to march against Versailles. You may imagine what that has done for the city. People are coming up with the wildest excuses: one man said he couldn't possibly fight because he only fired up into the air, another said his shoes were too tight to march anywhere! Many are obtaining passes and heading for the town of Saint Denis. Yes, maman, I know what you are thinking but I cannot leave. I came here for an adventure and my goodness I found one! I intend to see it through to the end. I do not mind admitting however that I am a little ~~afraid~~ nervous of the final confrontation.*

Eveline is well. She is happier perhaps than she has ever been. ~~I think I have lost her to a better another man~~. I think that she has found herself and for that I am glad.

Laurie's emotions brought him to a standstill in the middle of the Boulevard du Montparnasse. He wished it would just rain down, pour the sweet warm rain down upon him, wash away the grime from his eyes, his lips, the palms of his hands. His mind was so disjointed tonight he couldn't think of anything else to write. He racked his brain for amusing anecdotes he had heard or read or made up even; but he couldn't recall any. A nagging little voice told him he had better get home before another hour struck else surely he would meet with some terrible calamity. Laurie sighed. The circuitous route he was taking home in order simply to thwart his obsession wasn't fooling anybody least of all his own head. He stared up at the sky waiting for the storm. Any moment now it would come. Any moment now.

Even as a child he'd tested himself in the most perverse and ridiculous of ways. Tucked up in bed half asleep he'd suddenly decide he must touch the garden gate to ensure the safety of every member of the household including the little dog Posy. Or he'd have to skip all the way to school else meet with a setback in his spelling test. He wondered now if it was an exaggerated reaction to his father's illness and death. Some mad peculiar grief sublimating itself in the demon voices.

He tried to distract himself by counting the steps up to the old soda factory on his left. *One two three four…* He and Alphonse had shared a soda on those very steps, a bottle of cherry soda and a box of almond paste. He could remember the day quite clearly, a sunny day in autumn soon after he'd arrived in Paris. Alphonse had shown him the sights, shown him around, shown him his favourite spots and haunts, got him out of one or two scrapes. *Five six seven eight…* Alphonse the brother he'd never had and always wanted. The audience was closer now, clapping vociferously up there with the gods who flashed their binoculars and little pince-nez at him. If he made a quick dash he might just be in time for – *nine ten eleven twelve…* There were thirteen steps exactly up to that little old soda factory where he and Alphonse had shared a cherryade one fine clear autumnal day. Unlucky for some… Laurie stood white faced and taut as a bow, battling with the elements that raged within his head; and as the cloud burst its sweet warm rain down upon him he suddenly broke into a run.

Chapter twenty-six

Eveline was sleeping fitfully through the storm until the loudest clap of thunder she'd ever heard in her life woke her up completely; and she leapt out of bed, almost tripping over her nightgown, to shut the window that had blown half open. It was then she saw Alphonse – lit up for a moment as if it were day – standing on the doorstep and holding a hessian sack over his head to protect himself from the rain.

'I'm almost hoarse from shouting your name,' he called up grimly, peering out from under the sack. 'Hurry up, for goodness sake Evie, and let me in.'

There was something in the tone of his voice that made Eveline decide to obey, though a part of her wanted to let him dangle out there in the thunderstorm as he had left her dangling for the past few days. She wondered for the umpteenth time as she scampered down the stairs, her heart beating uncontrollably at the unexpected sight of him, where he'd been and what he'd been up to. She hoped it was simply political business that had kept him away for so long.

She tiptoed over to the door and quietly slid back the heavy bolts, careful not to disturb her father who was slumbering peacefully in his coffin, seemingly oblivious to all the commotion. He looked quite peculiar crammed up beside his statues, like a freshly dug corpse in the Père Lachaise amidst a sea of grinning headstones; and in the lurid light of the storm even the bottle of otherworldly nectar took on the slightly sinister aspect of something left behind after a ghostly repast.

'What is it?' she demanded a little coolly as Alphonse barged past her, almost soaking her to the skin with a single brush of the arm. His hair stood up in black wet spikes like little exclamation marks about his cheeks and his face was white as a sheet. Without answering her he went over to the sink and proceeded to wring out the hessian sack as violently as if he were wringing someone's neck. He seemed quite unable to speak – as if he'd lost his voice for good – and Eveline watched for a moment, alarmed, before stepping up and tapping him on the shoulder.

'What's the matter? What's happened? You're scaring me with your silence. Here, give me that,' she added quickly, as he made a bungled attempt to lay the hessian sack out over the warm oven; and she deftly whipped it out of his fingers and hung it on the line Mistigris had devised for the purpose. Then she led him gently to the dining room table and pulled a chair out for him. She was shocked to see by the light of the lamp that his eyes were quite bloodshot as if he hadn't slept for weeks and his face was as crumpled and lined as an old man's.

'You can't come here looking like that,' she cried suddenly, her concern spilling out into anger, 'and not tell me what has happened. Have you been in a fight? For goodness sake say something!'

'I'm sorry,' he spoke at last and the note of despair in his voice was unmistakable. 'I didn't mean to scare you, Evie, it's just that, well, it's over, we're doomed…'

Eveline's heart leapt into her mouth…

'…The Versaillais have entered the city and…'[24]

She bit her lip with relief because for one appalling moment she'd thought he meant that *they* were over, finished, doomed.

'Passy and Auteil are occupied already. It is only a matter of time before they reach Montmartre and Belleville. There is no time for an offensive action. We are caught like flies in a honey trap and in the end it will be every man for himself.'

'But the barricades?' Eveline stuttered. 'We will defend at the barricades.'

Alphonse gave a dry little laugh. 'Have you seen them? The last one I clocked consisted of a garden bench and a chaise longue. The only way that'll stop 'em is if they feel a little tired and fancy putting their feet up for a bit. No, it is a lost cause I'm afraid, Evie.'

She stared at him in amazement, unable to believe her ears. This was Alphonse Duchamp the revolutionary talking like an old woman, talking like the bitter, cynical hecklers at the political meetings. Where was his moment of transformation? His tearing destiny his way? She held out her hands, palm upwards, hoping to knock some sense into him. 'Look at these you idiot. They're red raw from piling pebbles into beer barrels, carting lumps of wood about like the rest of Paris, even the children. Are you saying we've wasted our time?'

'Beer barrels – that'd be right. No wonder they say we are a city of profligates and…' he peered over at Mistigris '…drunks!' At that moment her father gave an extraordinarily loud snore and at any other time they would have laughed together. Alphonse went on bleakly: 'Time after time we petitioned the Committee of Public Safety to build a coherent system of barricades, not this piecemeal nonsense. But they were too busy with their ideals…'

'But we will fight them,' Eveline insisted, a little nonplussed. 'We will still fight them?'

'Oh yes, we will fight.' Alphonse gave another one of his dry little laughs. 'The hour of revolutionary warfare has struck. Soon the bells will toll, the bugles and the drums, to call the people of Paris out to arms. To arms! We will fight at the barricades as we always do, like animals defending our territory, our little patch.'

His voice was heavily laid with sarcasm and Eveline turned away in fear and disgust. She didn't understand him tonight and it made her afraid of what was to come. He reminded her of her father when he was drunk, when everything she said, every reassurance she gave, simply fell on deaf ears; but she decided to deal with Alphonse exactly the same way as she always treated her father. She left him alone for a while slumped in his chair and moved about the kitchen, brewing up some old coffee, bringing out a milk pudding and some oatcake biscuits. The biscuits were a little stale but mixed in with the milk pudding they would be passable enough…. She thought of the troops pouring into the city at that very moment and she shivered in her nightgown, becoming aware once more of the storm rattling around the house, the wind whistling down the chimney like a draughty Father Christmas and rapping at the panes like Madame Larousse on the look-out for grub. It would be a fine thing, she laughed to herself, if the chimney were to fall in right now on top of them all. Crashing down amidst yellowing stucco and overgrown vine, saving Thiers and his lot the job. At least her father was prepared for his trip to the next world, having practised for so long. She smiled fondly at the sound of snores from the other room and her thoughts flew to Jacques. Thank goodness he was far away from all this, the little wretch. He'd have managed to get himself killed one way or another, she supposed, if he'd stayed.

She piled up a tray with the coffee pot, milk pudding and oatcake biscuits and gazed with affection at the tiny kitchen. Now that she faced the possibility of losing her home it suddenly became the dearest place on earth to her. Forget the Rue Ornano with the sales girls twitching behind their lace curtains and the apartments on the Champs Élysées where La Païva bathed in golden bathrooms. (Well, maybe the golden bathroom would be nice but...) *This* was what mattered. This home. Her home. She would protect it with her life if she had to. Keep it safe for Jacques' return. Keep it just the way it was. A thought suddenly struck her and she spun round to face Alphonse, almost dropping the tray on the floor and startling him out of his gloomy thoughts.

'Hold on a minute,' she cried. 'Think about it. It'll be like last time when they tried to take the guns – they won't fire on their own countrymen. They won't attack their own city, their own homes even. How could they? It would be like turning against your own family, tearing down the place you were brought up in. They will come and they will realise that they cannot do it.' She was convinced then that she was right for it was inconceivable to her that anyone could come and see the great parks, the grand boulevards, cafés and operas, hear the rustling of the Seine beneath the old stone bridges and not be bewitched by it all. She who'd never had much time for the capital, well, now she could write a tourist book on it.

'I'm not so sure,' Alphonse responded quickly as if he too had weighed the possibility and come to the opposite conclusion. 'Thiers has recruited rurals and prisoners of war that Bismarck has released for this express purpose. Who knows what lies he has fed them. We are savages, animals, half mad anarchists – that is the line he will be taking. They are coming to save Paris from destruction – don't forget the Vendôme column – they are coming to save the good citizens, the wealthy bourgeoisie.'

'I still think I'm right.' Eveline shook her head stubbornly; but Alphonse hardly hearing her went on grimly: 'Oh, they mean business this time alright, there's no question about it. And everybody knows it. The Commune is starting to disintegrate already, its members fleeing while they've got the chance. It's the man in the street who will suffer: the ordinary man in the street. Many are getting rid of their guns and uniforms – I came across a pile by the Trocadero – pretending they had nothing to do with the Commune. There have even been denunciations...'

'What denunciations?' asked Eveline, alarmed.

Alphonse put his head in his hands and spoke in a flat, toneless voice like a little boy reciting his times table: 'A. Saracen, carver, Rue de Jessaint, 14; Gelez, civil servant, Rue des Boulangers, 22; Pindy, joiner, Passage Raoul, 10...'

'Stop it! What are you saying? Who are these people?'

'D. André, machinist, Rue Neuve-des-Boulets, 6,' he went on

mechanically. 'Bucolin, painter, Rue Saint Michel, 34…'

The storm crashed overhead and Eveline shivered again in her nightgown. 'Why are you saying their names like that?' she cried though she was beginning to understand why. 'Stop it Alphonse for God's sake. Who are they anyway?'

'Friends mainly. I have eaten with most of them, I know their families. André Saracen for example lives in a couple of pokey rooms with a crippled wife and two robust little sons. I count him one of the best. Père Bucolin, Vincent Bucolin is a fascinating character. He used to sleep on a decrepit old barge on the Seine. He is a great painter; I think one day he could produce a masterpiece. You should see his painting of the Seine below the Pont Notre Dame. Even his detail of the strewn flowers on the water on market day is…' Alphonse's voice tailed off distractedly and Eveline poured the coffee with trembling fingers, waiting to utter the question that had been on her mind from the outset. 'Is your name on the list, Alphonse?' she said in the end as lightly as she could. 'Are you one of the… marked men?' She strove to see his expression in the lamplight but the shadows connived against her, revealing simply one bloodshot eye that didn't meet her own.

'There are many names,' Alphonse sighed and she could tell from his voice that what she feared was true. His name was on the list. At the top probably. 'Men will betray their brothers to save their own skins at times. Not all men of course but… luckily for me I have no permanent address. They will have a job to find me.' He grinned suddenly, more like his old self and Eveline smiled in relief.

'You're safe then?'

'More or less. They may try and visit some of my old haunts and…' his face suddenly blanched. 'They may come and look for me here. It is not impossible that they will look for me here.'

'It doesn't matter,' Eveline reassured him, glancing nervously in the direction of her father. 'It doesn't matter at all. If they come here Papa and I will send them on a goose chase to the Gare du Nord or some make-believe street. Here, have some of this.' She doled the milk pudding out into two large bowls and jabbered on quickly: 'The biscuits are a little stale I think but it's all I can do to keep Madame Larousse's hands off them. I don't know where she puts it all, she's thin as a rake or a little bird. She reminds me of a bird with those feathers she wears in her hat. I think Papa is a little besotted, you know, in spite of himself…'

'I have been so stupid,' Alphonse groaned on in an appalled voice. 'I should go now, immediately.'

'Eat!' Eveline commanded sternly, deciding to take control of the situation as she did with her father when he was drunk; and she even muttered grace under her breath out of superstition or habit or both. 'Forwhatweareabouttoreceivemaythelordmakeustrulythankfulamen.'

They ate as the storm passed, Alphonse's mood lightening with its passing. It seemed to Eveline as she sat there watching him, that he was somehow connected with the storm, that he had come in with it and would one day leave with it, causing devastation in his wake; and then she laughed at her own melodramatics. At least he looked a little more human, having downed five biscuits and most of the milk pudding, despite having said he wasn't the tiniest bit hungry.

'You put Madame Larousse to shame!' she laughed at one point and he gave the sprightly retort that that indeed was a frightening thought, more frightening even than the Versaillais entering the city.

'What will you do?' Eveline asked him seriously then, leaning forward with her chin in her hands. 'What will you do now?'

Alphonse shrugged. 'Fight at the barricades I suppose like everybody else though we don't stand a cat in hell's chance. We might as well wave the white flags now, save ourselves from being slaughtered.'

Eveline felt the faint stirrings of anger in her stomach and she stood up, straightening her chair back noisily. 'I don't know why you just don't get rid of your gun, your uniform and that... stupid hessian sack. Take a trip to the Trocadero and dump them there with the rest. You're just as bad.'

'What do you mean?'

She ignored the flash of annoyance in his eyes and went on candidly: 'All your defeatist talk. You should hear yourself. I thought you believed in the Commune, the revolution. Now I'm not so sure.'

'Of course I do. What are you saying?' Alphonse's face clouded with anger. 'Are you calling me a traitor?'

'More or less,' answered Eveline, aware that she was using his own speech mannerisms and turns of phrase. Is that what you did when you loved someone? Did you emulate them so entirely, so unconsciously? If so she didn't much like it. 'In word if not in deed. You sit here mourning a load of men who haven't even died yet, a battle that hasn't yet been lost. Why don't you do something about it? Why don't you go and warn Monsieur Saracen or whatever his name is and his crippled wife as you put it. Or that fascinating creature who sleeps on a barge – why don't you wake him up like you did me so that he can go and hide somewhere and maybe one day produce that famous painting... and those useless barricades that I have ripped my hands over – I'm sure we have a few hours to spare before we all get slaughtered so why don't you build them up a little higher? Fetch some more furniture from the old department stores on the Rue de Rivoli. A dining-room table would stop a few bullets I should think. Or take some of father's statues to scare them out of their wits but don't sit here saying it's all finished before we've begun.' He'd got to his feet now and was towering over her in fury but she stood her ground as she always did with her father, completely unafraid of him. 'You're always preaching from the pulpit, Alphonse, about the moment of transformation. Well, this is it. Right now. Your moment of transformation. Why don't you take it?'

She thought for a moment he was going to strike her but he turned and blundered over to the window, staring out of it for what seemed like an eternity. The rain fell in sullen drops and Eveline stood shaking in her nightgown, wondering if she'd pushed him a little too far. She'd never spoken to Alphonse like that, never spoken to anyone like that for that matter and she wasn't at all sure now if what she'd said was justified. It was just that the sight of him so beaten and vulnerable had annoyed and frightened her all at the same time. She prayed he was back to his old self again, that she had brought him back to his old self again and she stood waiting, heart in mouth, trying to read the signs in the line of his neck, his shoulders, his strong, straight back. In the end she needn't have worried for he turned and smiled the broadest of smiles, his teeth gleaming white against his sunburnt skin.

'You must like me just a little bit,' he joked gruffly, 'to remember what I say so perfectly.'

She gave an audible sigh of relief. 'Just a bit,' she smiled happily. 'Just a bit!'

'You're a mouse with a tiger's heart,' he chuckled, stepping forward to kiss her on the cheek. 'We need a secret weapon like you at the barricades! Maybe not in that nightgown however. I don't know about your father's statues but the sight of you wielding a gun in that flimsy thing would scare us all witless, even the sturdiest Communard.' He added gently, his eyes full of emotion: 'If you're coming you better hurry up and get dressed hadn't you.'

She sped upstairs two at a time before he could change his mind, her heart swelling with pride and excitement. He had come to her in his darkest hour and she had strengthened his resolve, turned his mood around; and now he was asking her to fight with him at the barricades. She had never felt so powerful, so strong, so assured in her own being. She would fight on an equal footing with the men to defend her home, her father, her own personal freedom. She who had never much cared for these things, now they seemed to her the most important things on earth.... She pulled out the brown and red striped uniform (the one she had taken from the Rue de Turbigo) and dressed in it hurriedly, her mind whirring with apprehension. Would Maria and Elizabeth be at the barricades? Maria with her great thumbs hooked under her belt, Elizabeth with her cat-like tongue. This time they would be aiming at real faces not beer barrels, real men not doodles. Michaels, Antonys, Jeromes in the flesh. Other people's sons, brothers, husbands, fathers... She shivered as she tied up her thick heavy boots and thought of her father in his home-made coffin and Jacques... Jacques? Where was he now? She picked up a pen and scribbled a note as fast as she could, tears spilling out onto the paper.

Dearest Papa, it read smudgily, *Please stay in until the fighting is over. Do not venture out until there is calm. I do not want to lose a dear father as well as a dear brother.*

Then she knelt by the bed and brought the rifle out from its hiding place (the one she had taken from the Rue de Turbigo) and the little pouch of cartridges which she tucked into her pocket. The gun was heavy and well oiled and she slung it over her shoulder, checking its position in the long mirror behind the door. It hung a little low on her side and she adjusted it accordingly.

'Mouse with a tiger's heart,' she whispered at her reflection. It wasn't a bad thing to be. Better than being one of those shop girls on the Rue Ornano with their crinoline curlers and tearing silk voices. What would they do when the tocsin sounded? Peek from behind their twitching lace curtains...? Eveline rammed the hat down hard on her head, over the short red curls and, taking one last look in the mirror, she leapt down the stairs two at a time before Alphonse could change his mind, the rifle banging sharply and violently against her ribs.

Chapter twenty-seven

It was in the sweet clear calm of a dew-laden dawn that Bernadine decided to leave the convent. In truth she'd decided months ago, ever since Aggie died she'd been toying with the idea – to leave, to run away, to start a new life somewhere – but only now, in the strange serenity after the storm, did her ideas crystallise into a distinct plan of action.

She would make her way to Rhône, the place of her birth and early childhood. Perhaps an elderly relative would take her in if there were any still living. And if not, well, she would take up a position as a seamstress, dressmaker, a governess even. It wasn't too late to start again. She wasn't too old to try her hand at something new.

Her eyes swept the room that had been her home for twenty years: the little bed where the baby slept, tired out at last on sheets of unbleached serge, the old armchair and worktable, the bare walls and rugless floor. The room seemed so sad and empty to her now whereas once upon a time she had revelled in its bleakness, delighting in paring herself down to the bone for the sake of the Lord, for the sake of her vocation.

Was it all a delusion? Had she ever done anything more than hide away in a gloomy prison, fearing to take her place in the world? Even before Ernest had she ever truly believed? It seemed doubtful to her now. Somehow it seemed quite doubtful to her now that she had ever believed with the blind unswerving faith required of a nun; and she fought to remember her days as a novice, at the start of her vocation, but her mind drew a blank apart from one or two fleeting images... the starchy rustle of the Mother Superior and the little piece of paper that protected her finger on the breviary page, the taste of chilled cocoa on feast days, the terrible hunger pangs of Lent, the discipline of lying on hard, bare boards without turning or murmuring, and the sweet release of sleep when it came...

The baby whimpered softly in hers and Bernadine sat very still, hoping against hope that the child wouldn't wake up. She'd only just got her off and the thought of any more singing, soothing, rocking, was almost too much for her tonight. The fruits of sin, as even Bernadine referred to her sometimes, was getting more difficult by the day and the nun was at her wits end with the seemingly incessant crying, the mess, the chaos, the trail of destruction the baby left in her wake. In the early days she'd mainly slept and Bernadine thought how easy it was to look after a child – you fed and watered them, they gurgled and smiled. Now it was a different matter altogether – they wailed and crawled, howled and explored, seeking out the most dangerous of places without the slightest sense of fear, the slightest hesitation. There was a lesson probably in that somewhere. They were the centre of their own little universe, the sun around which you spun; and Bernadine was sick and dizzy with it all. Sometimes she even blamed Agnes for dying and leaving her with this horrifying little burden. Other times she blamed the child for disrupting her existence, for making her feel emotions she didn't want to feel, for creeping in and invading the solitary space of her heart.

The baby rolled in her sleep, almost falling off the bed and Bernadine started up in alarm. You needed eyes in the back of your head to look after a baby. Eyes in the back of your head and twenty pairs of hands. Even the Lord, she thought wryly and a little blasphemously, didn't have enough eyes and hands to keep track of all the mischief a child could get up to. In ten seconds flat. Only yesterday Bernadine had left for what couldn't have been more than a minute or so and returned to find her sewing kit tipped up on the floor, the fruits of sin wallowing gleefully amidst coloured thread, pins and needles, scissors and bobbins and sucking on a silver thimble for all she was worth as if she were sucking on a sugar plum candy; and then when Bernadine, a little vexed, had packed up the sewing kit, the child let out a storm of weeping as if her whole world had split asunder. Her bible too (Bernadine's only other treasured possession) had not gone unscathed. Habakkuk had been masticated to bits, the Book of Job shredded to ribbons and the future of Proverbs was decidedly at risk from the baby's single, serrated, razor-sharp tooth.

She almost suspected the Lord of playing a little joke on her. Providing her with this child when her own was lost to her for good. Not as a reward but as a punishment. Not as compensation but as penance. Her trip to Monsieur Lafayette's had not gone unnoticed, she felt quite sure of that, by the Lord and his spies. He may not have eyes in the back of His head but He was peering round every dark street corner, hiding under the bed, on top of the wardrobe – just like the bogeyman. Ready to pounce when you did something bad. Well, she wasn't taking it any more, she wasn't playing scared any more. She was leaving the lifeless shadow of the convent, stepping into the sunshine and the flowers, and she was taking Aggie with her.

It would be better, she told herself now, when they were far away, in a new place, though a part of her wondered how it would be better, why it would be better... In Rhône there were open fields and ponds full of rushes and ducks, children with skipping ropes, a grocer selling pumpkins like beaming jack o' lanterns or Cinderella carriages, sparrows in the town square at dusk, a carousel on market days and her father's dusty shop full of antiquated clocks all chiming peculiarly out of time – to show off their voices of course. There were grandmother clocks and grandfather clocks, carriage clocks and travelling clocks... brass, silver, gold, ormolu... monogrammed, engraved, jewelled, enamelled.... There were ones that went a little too fast (dust in the innards her father always said) like breathless ladies wanting to catch the omnibus and others that went a little too slow (pendulums awry) like portentous old men who've just had lunch. And there was one kept especially for her, its hands stuck just before midnight to remind her there was always time to escape her own life.... But best of all her father in his oily apron, looking up with a slightly bemused air as if to say 'where has the time gone'.

Where had the time gone? In the discipline of every minute, every hour, every day, every week, every month, every year? And suddenly two decades had passed right before her eyes. The shop had long gone of course as had her father and mother. It had turned into a tinsmith's, then a shoemaker's and finally a haberdasher's until he too disappeared. Her uncle had written her: *the haberdasher has a vineyard now, in Provence I believe*. As if she needed to know that! As if she wanted to know that! And yet of course she had remembered it. The trivial stupid things you remembered. *The haberdasher has a vineyard now, in Provence I believe.* Maybe it was all changed. Maybe the sparrows no longer collected in the town square at dusk. Maybe the pond had been dug over or drained – children had drowned there once upon a time. Maybe the carousel never came any more. Maybe the place existed in memory only.

She stared around the room again, at the dear and familiar objects and she quavered then at the thought of leaving it. To step out into the big wide world for good with no possibility of returning? What folly was that?

To leave a place that had been a home for the past twenty years for a place that might only exist in the memory? And how would she get to Rhône in any case? By train? Did trains run any more under the revolutionary Commune? How would she get a ticket if they did? She had no money. All she had was the locket and ring her father had left her (for such an event as this), her sewing kit and bible, the lay clothes she had come in – a white blouse and grey tunic, a child's uniform really and she wouldn't fit into *that* any more. The obstacles mounted up one by one in her head, stacking against her decision and she lay back on the bed exhausted, her body rigid and stiff beside the sleeping baby's.

How ill equipped she was after all to take her place in the outside world. She didn't even know the geography of France, didn't know if Rhône was East, South, West of Paris. She wouldn't have been able to pick out France on a map, or China, India, Africa, Japan. The only layout she understood was that of the chapel and convent garden. She hadn't stepped foot outside these walls for nearly twenty years, apart from her trips to Monsieur Lafayette's, to fetch Aggie's milk, one or two teaching duties…. How could she possibly be expected to understand the goings on of the modern world? She would be laughed at, ridiculed, vilified – an ex nun who couldn't point France out on a map, with a baby in tow. How could she possibly find work like that? It was far too late to start again. She was far too old to try her hand at something new.

She tilted forward, ignoring the pain in her neck, and took a few drops of valerian tincture from the bedside table to calm her nerves and soothe her head. (She was always getting headaches these days. She thought it was probably to do with the baby – the endless crying, chaos, sleepless nights.) Then, taking up her bible she read from Deuteronomy for a while as the light came in through the small high window. A verse she came across kept sticking in her mind, troubling her a little though she couldn't think why.

These forty years the lord thy God has been with thee, thou hast lacked nothing.

Her mind kept going over and over it and in the end she decided it was too late to read and besides, her eyes were tired and straining over the thin, fine print. She tucked the bible under her pillow and gazed instead at the light coming in through the window, streaming in with the limpid gaiety of spring (where everything dead came alive again, where time that had hibernated through the winter months started ticking again with the clean, white snowdrops), creating shadows on the walls of bars and trees, illuminating the carmine engraving on the walnut tallboy… the

Immaculate Conception... she marvelled to think the fruits of sin had ever slept in the bottom drawer amidst shoe polish and laces – she couldn't stuff her in there now if she tried, the baby had grown so enormous under her very nose! A thought struck her then and she smiled with pleasure. She would have to buy clothes for her soon: dresses and petticoats, ribbons and slippers, a well-soled pair of boots for the winter, a woollen cloak and scarf; a bonnet and cotton frock for the summer.

It was fun to think of the things she would have to buy or make for the baby. Books, toys, games, clothes. It was like going back to one's own childhood when everything was simple and innocent, when the world was a big wide place to explore without the slightest sense of fear, without the slightest hesitation... it wouldn't be so bad away from the convent, Bernadine told herself. She needn't be afraid. What was she leaving behind after all? Bare walls, a rugless floor, a life of sin and compromise and denial, of smuggled joys and delights like silver-wrapped chocolates in Lent, a life of preparing for salvation, for some shining illumination. Well, she hadn't been blinded by it yet and she hadn't been saved yet. Of rationing herself in the belief presumably that one day she would run out; of giving herself away in bits and pieces here and there like the body of Christ to be swallowed down with a glass of wine by some dreadful fellow in a pork pie hat; of saving herself up to spend presumably in the hereafter. Well, what was the point of that? It was like keeping your best dress in the wardrobe for a party you might never be invited to. It was all very well thinking what a whale of a time you were going to have when you got beyond the pearly gates with the angels, the archangels and all the company of heaven but what if you never got there? Then what? Better to wear your best dress every day of the week so if the Lord stole in like a thief in the night, like the bogeyman himself, you were ready and waiting for him. No need to change, powder your nose, drag a comb through your hair. Just a seamless transition from one party to the next. And if he never came to call it didn't matter anyway because you were having your very own ball right here on earth.

From now on she would have her very own ball right here on earth, out there in the sunshine and the flowers.

It was going to be a glorious day. She could tell by the light coming in through the window that it was going to be a glorious day. Fresh and clear with a bright blue sky, one or two white scudding clouds. The sort of day you could smell wild violets in the air, thickets of lavender and juniper bushes. She leapt off the bed as softly as she could and stood for a moment in the path of the sun as it forged its way in through the bars on the window. Even at this hour it warmed her skin; in the heat of the day it would be burning hot. She dug out her old umbrella from the bottom of the tallboy, a pair of sturdy shoes and one or two essentials for herself and the baby; and she assembled the little collection on the worktable. Then she gathered together the sewing kit that Aggie had left in a heap: scraps of wool and coloured threads, needles, thimbles, pastepot and darning egg, and packed it all up in her horsehair basket, checking to see if she could lift it singlehanded for in the other arm she would be carrying the baby. Yes, it was fine, heavy but manageable. All she had to do now was ask the Mother Superior for a reference and the safety box that contained the locket and ring her father had given her as well as the clothes she had entered the convent in – not that she would fit them now of course after nearly twenty years and a baby in between.

She saw herself every step of the way in her imagination: saying her farewells in the dear little garden (as the nuns padded softly off to Lauds) to Agnes and her own lost daughter for now she must put them both to rest for good. She must squash all thoughts of her own lost daughter for the sake of little Aggie. She must step into a new life, shed the past like an old skin, like a butterfly did. She saw herself entering the Mont de Piété and exchanging the ring her father had given her for a few gold coins, just enough for her fare to Rhône, mind. Any more than that would be unwise. And she saw herself boarding the train, taking a seat in a corner by the window so that she could watch the countryside slipping by at a rate of knots as the train flew on into the future, through cities and hamlets, villages and towns…

Goodbye, she whispered, blinking in the sunshine that bathed the cell in bright golden light, the cell that had been her home for nearly twenty years. Tears suddenly shone in her eyes. *Goodbye*.

Chapter twenty-eight

Laurie almost jumped out of his skin at the sound of the tocsin. He sat upright in bed, listening to the church bells pealing, the drums and bugles thumping and blaring, the voices shouting 'Aux armes, aux armes... to the barricades, the barricades'.

So the city had been breached then, the defences broken through by an enraged and avenging army and this was to be the final confrontation. He tried to drive all thoughts from his mind for he knew that once he started thinking he was done for. Once he started thinking he wouldn't be able to move. Just act, just act, he told himself curtly, getting out of bed and slowly and with much deliberation cleaning his teeth and washing his face from the little carafe on the table. He dressed carefully in his military uniform, preparing himself for battle bit by bit, even picking out a new handkerchief and putting it in his pocket, spitting on his boots to bring up a good shine. He found that if he concentrated on the detail of what he was doing he could keep the fear at bay. He cut himself a slice of chicken pie, feeling he oughtn't to go out on an empty stomach, and munched it standing up, unable to sit still for a moment. Better for the digestion in any case, he decided, catching sight of himself in the gilt-framed mirror, his jaws working mechanically on the pie, the expression in his eyes calm and detached. He knew that look of old. It was the mask he put on sometimes to face the world and it meant he was churning up inside. It reminded him of a poem he'd read once that began: *The stone cold faces are the ones that are feeling*.... Nine times out of ten it was true. The more impassive the face the more extreme the disguise.

The bells of Saint Jacques rang out sonorous and clear through the early morning, summoning people, so it seemed, to a frenzied church service, and then suddenly stopped mid chime as if the ringers had been peremptorily shot or simply run out of breath. Laurie paused, mouth full of chicken, waiting for the bells to resume and when they did not he stuck his head out of the window. Nothing seemed changed. The square-topped belfry still stood in the distance like the castle piece in a chess set, the fields about it blackened and deserted though one or two clumps of foliage had sprung up recently in the wasteland. He dropped the remains of his pie crust for the birds and Mister 50 then pulled his head back in. The drums and bugles were still blaring and thumping away, it was only the church bells that seemed to have given up the ghost. How strange! It was as if...

Just act, just act, he reminded himself sharply, taking a swig of water and swilling his mouth out. He mustn't start thinking at this juncture. Once he started thinking there was no way back. No way forward and no way back. Picking up his gun he left the room quietly without a second glance, taking himself by surprise so to speak, and marched down the stairs *to meet his fate.* The concierge had done a disappearing trick already – the cubicle of glass was quite empty apart from the leather chair, brown beer bottle and the keys all higgledy-piggledy in a cardboard box. He'd made a very poor show of keeping the place tidy, Laurie thought a little bitterly, noticing that the cubicle of glass was covered in a pattern of frosted stars. Why had he never noticed that before? It was a small trivial thing perhaps but he felt that he should have noticed it before now, having lived in the building these past two years.

It just showed. It just showed how subjective reality was. You could go through life seeing only what you wanted to see. He hadn't wanted to see the star-patterned glass before because he'd wanted to see the concierge and now the concierge wasn't there at all he'd wanted to see the star-patterned glass. It was a question of emphasis. A question of detail. And if everyone saw a different detail then it inevitably followed that everyone saw a slightly different world. There were as many different worlds, in effect, as there were people.

He didn't know if it was a wonderful thought or an appalling one but it amused him to think he'd been concentrating on the detail to stop himself thinking – how ironic was that – and he stepped outside with an unusually cheerful demeanour. The smell hit his nostrils almost immediately – a mix of smoke, gunshot and burning varnish – and he covered his face with the handkerchief for a moment, taking in short raggedy little breaths to get himself used to it. The smell hadn't penetrated his rooms, that was for sure, so he deduced it was coming on a north-westerly breeze from across the Seine which tallied, in any case, with the sound of gunfire. The drums and bugles could be heard in the opposite direction, moving away behind the Rue d'Enfer, warning each street, each arrondissement in turn.

He congratulated himself on his observational skills and decided to head towards the Place de la Concorde. If he hadn't joined up with a fighting party by then at least he would get some news for ever since the Prussian war people had gathered at the Place de la Concorde for a daily news bulletin. He had no intention of trying to find his old company – if it still existed – but he wanted to know if a concerted attempt was being made to defend the city.

He stepped smartly up the street, intrigued by the women scuttling home from market, their bags laden down with provisions. Everyone had heard the tocsin, everyone was diving for cover or making ready for an attack. Shutters were going up on the windows of the squat little houses, causing an almighty din of hammering, mothers were hustling their children in from play and it was strange to see them being shooed in like hens on such a beautiful May morning. It didn't seem fair to Laurie that the children of Paris were still in danger and he smiled at a little boy who was hanging on to the railings to watch him pass until his mother came after him with the broom.

'I'd make a run for it if I was you,' she called out to Laurie in a tight voice, 'while you've got the chance.' And Laurie bowed and half smiled an acknowledgement. He had no intention of making a run for it as she put it though his heart beat a little faster at her words and he prayed suddenly for the courage of Alphonse, of anybody but himself. He should like to make his mother proud. An image of her delicate, vulnerable face swum into his head and he imagined himself coming home a little battle scarred and world weary, full of tales to tell, a manuscript of poems tucked into a sack on his back (a little like the sack Alphonse always wore). He always imagined himself coming home a little battle scarred and world weary or setting off at the train station on some daring adventure as only sons and elder brothers were duty bound to do.

His first test came around the very next corner – a pair of boots were sticking out of the fountain on the Rue du Temple and Laurie, fearing someone had slipped in whilst taking a drink of water, rushed over to help them. The water was streaked with blood and the man was half submerged, his head propped up against the central statue. Laurie clambered in, trying to get leverage under the man's shoulders but he was hindered somewhat by the waterlogged clothing and the body kept slipping out of his grasp. In fits and starts he dragged him to the side where, taking the man by the collar, he managed to heave him over the edge until he lay outstretched at the foot of the fountain. He was quite obviously dead and Laurie, panting and soaked to the skin, stood staring at the corpse in dismay. Whoever could have done such a thing and for what purpose? He was old, a civilian, quite obviously unarmed. Had he been shot at the fountain taking a drink of water? Or dumped there afterwards? Laurie glanced suspiciously up at the brown squat houses but nothing looked back apart from opaque shutters. There was an eeriness about the whole scene that made him want to leave in a hurry. Retrieving the cap he'd spotted by the side of the fountain he placed it gently by the man's feet and walked away, anxiously fighting the urge to look back over his shoulder. His thoughts flew unbidden to Tessier and he tried to distract himself by counting the trees that were budding or in bloom along the street. There was a cherry tree, a chestnut tree, a copper beech. Amazing to see how they were recovering after the onslaught of the siege when almost every living thing had been cut down to burn. It lifted his spirits a little to think that even the trees were fighting back.

An omnibus rolled up, full of grinning National Guardsmen, and stopped to offer him a ride but Laurie declined politely, a little repelled by the fanatical look on the men's faces. One was wearing his gun tied about his neck like a giant crucifix and Laurie's eyes kept going back to it again and again as they chattered excitedly. 'Your best bet's Rivoli,' they advised him, finishing off each other's sentences in their eagerness.

'Quite a little firework display there...'

'... already. We're heading for Haxo. Might get a little...'

'... hot!'

Laurie nodded. He knew that one. It had been in the papers. Built by Gaillard, Director of Barricades, it was eighteen feet high and fifteen feet deep with parapets and loopholes for the machine guns and cannon. 'That should hold out a while,' he commented, shading his eyes with his hand against the sun so he could see into the omnibus. 'How far have they got anyway?'

One of the soldiers scratched his head. 'Passy, Auteuil, all the bourgeois districts. Those buggers...'

'...they wanted to be rescued. Welcomed 'em with open arms probably. *Ooh, save us, ooh deliver us!*'

They all laughed at the imitation of a bourgeoisie housewife and a little bottle of brandy was passed round to warm the guts up. For a moment Laurie missed the camaraderie of his old company – of Joubet,

Bidulph, Tessier and the like – he'd been on his own so much lately; and he wondered suddenly if he mightn't join up with the little band after all.

'Hop on! Hop on!' they urged him when he said that on reflection he might go as far as Rivoli with them; and willing hands helped him aboard.

His clothes started to steam in the fug of the omnibus and the man with the gun necklace joked that it was a little early in the season for bathing. Laurie related his ordeal in the fountain on the Rue du Temple and one or two of them listened half heartedly though most were intent on the ever-approaching sound of gunfire.

'The Rue du Temple, you say?' a man called Bibi asked when he'd finished and Laurie nodded his head. Yes. Yes, it was the Rue du Temple.

'I've a friend lives there. Number 32. An old man you say?'

Laurie nodded his head again. Yes, he was quite old. Definitely old.

'It wasn't him then.' Bibi scratched his head. 'It can't have been him then.'

'I shouldn't think so,' Laurie offered up reassuringly. 'He was a grey-haired gentleman.'

Someone put in at that point that looks were no bearer of age. In his experience looks were no bearer of chronological age. He'd known virgins that looked like grandmothers and grandmothers that looked like virgins. Indeed his only living relative was approaching eighty and still had the apple cheeks of a twenty-year-old tart!

'A twenty-year-old apple tart?' someone heckled. 'She must be flaking!'

'You haven't banged her have you, Nimbus? Your only living relative?'

'Course he has. Look at him. It's written all over his face. He'd bang anything that still moved, that one.'

Laurie smiled at the jibes that flew between the men – it was just like old times – and he settled back in his seat as the omnibus rumbled on. He half expected to see Coupeau dancing a salacious little jig at the back of the vehicle or Joubet leaping out in front of him with a pack of cards, a doleful smile on his face. He'd been on his own so much lately that it was pleasant to relax in the company of soldiers with their banter, their bottles of brandy, their rough bravado (what he had taken for fanaticism, he now realised, was simply a rough bravado). He took a tot himself when the bottle was passed round, pronouncing it very good indeed, much better than the mouth warmer he'd suffered at the ramparts.

'To victory!' someone toasted all of a sudden and the sun-filled vehicle echoed with cries of 'To victory! To victory! Over the forces of tyranny!'

'Every barricade we hold, *mes enfants*,' Bibi began solemnly and heads nodded vigorously in response, the men understanding implicitly what he meant. Every barricade that held was a chance. A chance for victory.

'To the barricades!' cried Laurie, rising a little unsteadily to his feet as the omnibus rattled over some cobblestones; and the men roared 'the barricades, the barricades', making as much noise as they could with the butts of their rifles and boot-clad feet. Anything to drown out the boom of cannons, the awkward silences, the drum-rolling hearts...

He was sorry when they dropped him off on the crest of Rivoli and he climbed down amidst a rather forced hilarity and cries of 'Don't get too warm, Laurie. Don't get too warm.' He shivered and looked about him as the omnibus disappeared out of sight. A pall of grey smoke was drifting over the brow of the hill and if he screwed his eyes up tight he could make out the figures crouched by the barricade at the bottom; now and again popping their heads over the top to fire a volley of shots. The Versaillais looked even smaller in comparison but Laurie knew that to be an optical illusion for the road dipped a little where they were entrenched – many a carriage had come to grief outside Ma Gorot's little tripe and paper shop. It was a good place for a barricade, he decided on reflection, blocking access as it did to three main roads and being halfway up a hill – the encroaching army would have to make a serious dash to overcome it and would be terribly out of puff when they got there. The only danger lay in their making a detour via the Boulevard Sébastopol and coming down upon the barricade from above, as Laurie was doing. He glanced stealthily over his shoulder just in case but there was nothing but a group of men dragging a gun and a few boys armed with sticks.

He walked purposefully on towards the barricade, his right hand gripping his chassepot rifle, his left hand nervously dusting off the lapels of his uniform. The sun gleamed down through the puffs of smoke, onto his fair, bright hair and grimly determined face. He buoyed himself up as he went with sentences in his head such as *he showed great daring and presence of mind... those who saw him remembered his courage...* In a moment he would have to go on all fours. By the cluster of shops at the bottom he would have to go on all fours for by then he would be perfectly visible to the enemy. It would be sheer recklessness to continue on foot. He had it all figured out in his head. By the cluster of shops he would drop to one knee, take stock of the situation, make a dash for the barricade under cover hopefully of a volley of shots.

His heart banged painfully against his ribs and he nearly tripped on a bit of paving that had been ripped up for the barricade. That would be just his luck of course, he thought sourly. To trip and twist an ankle at this particular juncture. To come to grief as the carriages did outside Ma Gorot's, be bandaged up in liniment and horse bandages (it was said she kept a jar of liniment and stack of horse bandages in her window for such an emergency). He stepped a little gingerly after that, almost wishing he'd stayed on the omnibus with the bluff and merry band of soldiers. Why did he always take the most perverse course of action? Why did he do something simply because he said he was going to do it? He had no especial liking for the Rue de Rivoli. If he were going to lay his life down for a part of Paris it would be for the cathedral of Notre Dame, Balzac's tomb in Père Lachaise perhaps, even stretches of the Seine between St Louis and the Cité – for those were the places he cared about, not the Rivoli with its manicured houses and smart-fronted shops.

He must have been fifty yards from the barricade when a burst of gunfire brought a ton of leaves raining down on his head from a nearby tree and he dodged instinctively, feeling a little foolish, dropping to one knee and throwing a hand out for support onto the uneven surface. The men with the gun overtook him at a run and he pretended to fiddle with his boot for a moment, not wanting to meet anybody's eye but a jaunty voice called out '*citoyen*' and he had to straighten up and respond with an enthusiastic '*vive la Commune*'. He could see the barricade quite clearly now – a sturdy affair of eight feet or more made up of carts and meat slabs, sandbags and paving, a red flag wedged on top to signify allegience, of course, to the revolutionary government. The men were hopping up and down on sandbags or crates and popping their heads over the top to fire because there were no loopholes in the barricade to poke their rifles through. A glaring omission in Laurie's opinion. If he'd been Director of Barricades he'd have ordered all of them have loopholes built into their design for cannon, *mitrailleuse* and the like. You needed to be protected yet able to fire; to be able to see yet not be seen. You needed to be the invisible enemy. Like God perhaps. Like Buzenval.

An image of Tessier's macabre dance of death swam into his head and he had to steel himself to inch forward even a few more steps. The noise was deafening now for the high buildings on either side of the street created a tunnel of sound and to Laurie the rifles sounded like cannon fire. He wondered momentarily if the people in their manicured houses had had the sense to put away their books and pictures for safekeeping, their precious objects and artefacts. The smoke was tickling his nose and eyes again and with the sun beating down on his head he felt he might just vomit up the chicken pie he'd eaten for breakfast. (That would be just his luck of course to vomit up the chicken pie he'd eaten for breakfast.) He wanted to run away, to hide, at the very least be sick in private but any moment now he would be visible to the enemy, would have to drop to one knee, take stock of the situation, maybe crawl forward on his stomach to reach the barricade. That was the plan. That was the strategy. It was all figured out in his head. Any moment now he must do it. By the florist's, by the dyer's, the butcher's or the pâtisserie… just act, just act, he told himself sternly but at the very last moment instead of dropping to one knee he ducked into the doorway of the butcher's, his heart beating madly, his hands thick and clammy with sweat.

He pressed his head against the pane to cool himself down and unbuttoned the top of his uniform to give himself some air. It was like a stranglehold upon him, that uniform, and he wrenched off a button in a desperate struggle to be free of it. (What is the point of a uniform, sang a voice in his head, when you have no intention of fighting.) The boys raced past him waving their sticks and skipping the stones that ricocheted from the top of the barricade and he felt a creeping sense of shame for they were fourteen at best and he was twenty-one. And yet, of course, it is a game to them, he told himself, they do not understand that it is truly a matter of life and death. He peered in through the window to give himself time to get the courage up to proceed: the hooks hung empty of carcasses, the cattle market of La Villette having shut some weeks ago; and the butcher's red-and-white-striped apron lay in a crumpled heap on the counter as if he'd left in a hurry. Everybody must have left in a hurry.

He could see the gun being manoeuvred into position out of the corner of his eye and a cheerful shout of 'that'll hold the buggers off for while' penetrated his weary thoughts. He supposed it would hold out for a while but in the end the barricade would fall, he felt quite sure of that. All over Paris the barricades would fall like a domino set – at the bridges, the railway lines, on the squares and the boulevards. He stared out at the scene from his perfect hiding place and his heart suddenly filled with an enormous sense of pity for himself and the rest of humanity that it should come down to this. That it should all come down to this. Three times he ordered himself to step outside the doorway and three times his foot came back as if pulled by an invisible string – and yet of course even that was dishonest for it was his own will pulling it back, his own fear, his own pathetic lack of courage. He felt his mind receding, drifting away somewhere hard and cold – a land of bright icicles and glittering snow though outside it was hot as hell, his body blazing.

He knew then that he was going to run away. His body would follow his mind as surely as night follows day. However long he stood cowering in the doorway wrestling with his conscience in the end he would run away. It was an instinct for survival. Darwin would have approved of it. With one last glance at the men and boys fighting for their lives and the tiny figures of the enemy outside Ma Gorot's tripe and paper shop, he turned and crept away from the barricade, scuttling from one dark shadow to another until he was at a safe distance from the fighting. He half expected somebody to call out his name (half expected it, half wished it), grab him by the arm and propel him backwards, arrest him on the spot as a traitor to the cause but nobody even noticed his going. In the maelstrom nobody noticed. He could have torn off his clothes and danced naked in the smoke and no one would have batted an eyelid. It was surprisingly easy to run away but then he knew that already. He knew that of old.

He bolted for home, running like a fugitive through the city that he loved and his breath came in great tearing sobs. He ran through streets he had meandered along on solitary walks or with Alphonse and Eveline, streets that bore the imprint of the hundreds and thousands of souls that had been before him and would be after him, past trees that were budding or in bloom, fighting back after the onslaught of the siege; and he ran past white, scared faces reflecting his own and fountains he had laughed beside on hot summer days and dangled his feet in. He had walked these streets in all seasons: in the biting cold of winter when even the Seine came to a standstill, the falling leaves of autumn when the wind whispered of winter and secrets and long-since-forgotten things, hot sultry summer nights when music lilted with the breezes over the boulevards and on a day like today in the giddy momentum of spring. He knew these streets better then any cartographer did – and yet he couldn't bring himself to defend them. It was monstrous to him that he couldn't bring himself to defend them, though a little voice in his head justified his course of action as cleverly as can be. Why should he put himself in harm's way for the sake of an idea? Why should he see his own flesh torn and bleeding for the sake of a principle? A revolution?

He was sick at heart when he reached his rooms and he raced up the steps and flung himself through the door and onto the floor, curling his knees up into his chest and rolling about from side to side like a wounded animal or a child in distress. He rolled right into his bookcase and he gazed up with sudden hatred at the books that lined the shelves in their serried little ranks. Books about daring and courage, love, duty, passion, friendship – all the fine things a human life was made up of. How they had lied to him, those books. He clawed them down one by one, ripping their pages with his long delicate fingers and breaking their spines until a host of jumbled-up words lay scattered on the threadbare carpet. How they had laughed at him, those words. It was all so easy in words to do the right thing yet so hard in reality. *Dearest Maman*, he began in his head, wondering what on earth he could ever write next. From now on what on earth could he ever write next? And he wept silent tears of shame and despair, wishing he was somewhere other than he was, wishing he was someone other than he was.

Chapter twenty-nine

'It is like Rome under Tiberius!' finished Monsieur Lafayette, pouring himself a glass of otherworldly nectar with one hand and wiping a handkerchief over his face with the other. 'The sights I have seen out there would make your hair stand on end. I swear it is like Rome after the barbarians.'

Madame Larousse gave a dreary nod while Mistigris, having made a foolish manoeuvre with one of his pawns, was hoping against hope that his opponent wouldn't notice and answered a little distractedly: 'Rome under Tiberius, you say? How dreadful. And you saw a body too? Your turn, my dear,' he added hurriedly in an effort to rush Madame Larousse into making a mistake.

'Oh, hundreds,' Monsieur Lafayette exaggerated. 'All over the place. There are corpses here, there and everywhere, many of them dismembered. It was hard to tell which wrist went with which ankle, which arm with which body etcetera. It was all most gruesome.' His eyes bulged like a toad's at the memory and Mistigris, sitting back in his chair, regarded him afresh, the game forgotten.

'Generally speaking,' he offered up, his interest piqued, 'nature adores symmetry. She has her aberrations of course but generally speaking she is fond of symmetry and proportion. We as artists try to replicate that.'

Monsieur Lafayette cast a doubtful glance in the direction of the statues in the corner but maintained a tactful silence.

'It would be most uncommon in nature to find a delicate wrist and large ankle on the same body. Or a sturdy shank and a fragile shoulder blade. It is the overuse or misuse of a part that causes it to swell or grow, become misshapen.'

Madame Larousse gave a coy little laugh, her eyebrows twitching ominously beneath her velvet hat. She picked up her knight, gripped it to her chest for a moment, waved it about in the air as if she were going to make a move then put it back down in the same place with a jabbing little thud.

'Soup for dinner,' she said waspishly. 'Skate and ginger if you must know. On the boil as we speak.'

Mistigris murmured a faint 'delicious' while the herbalist gave his most menacing of smiles. 'Well, my good woman, let us hope that a shell doesn't explode nearby as it did the other day when I dined with my old friend Burty. There we were minding our own business settling down to starters when a shell exploded in the garden. We were shaken on our chairs. The table rocked, the bowls rocked, the guests rocked. Colonel B's moustache was quite bespattered... Lady Wentworth's fan was utterly drenched. Burty kept lapping on quite calmly of course...'

'Did he now?' Madame Larousse stood abruptly, her hat quivering, her face crimson.

'... when he'd finished his last mouthful he said, quite matter of factly: "I must have a word with cook about the soup. It seems a little heavy on the salt this morning." That is the British sense of humour you see. A little dry, a little understated. Lady Wentworth was a sport I must say. I believe she was soaked right through to her undergarments... yes my good woman,' Monsieur Lafayette addressed the still quivering hat and crimson face. 'Are you going to cut and run with that little word too? *Undergarments*. We all wear them, even you. Stop lowering your eyelashes like a nun who's just seen a statue. Weren't you married to a grime merchant for nearly twenty years? Didn't he get a peek in your little coal hole once or twice poor man? Or was he afraid of the dark? Yes, that's it, my dear, run along to the kitchen with your little red nose in the air, it's most fetching I grant you... How on earth do you suffer her?' he added unkindly to his old friend Mistigris who was looking quite flustered by the whole conversation. 'You're right under her thumb these days let me tell you. You're a changed man. I barely recognise you in that dapper little waistcoat. And have you really given up the grog for her?'

Mistigris nodded soberly. 'Indeed I have. More or less. Theodora – for that is her name, what do you think of it – *I adore Theodora!* – is of the opinion that I just needed a little encouragement.'

'Fancy that.'

'That's all the old fellow needed, just a little encouragement. Not too much to ask is it? I'm sure I never got any from Jacques or Eveline. In fact I'm inclined to believe now that they conspired in keeping me on it for their own purposes.'

'I hardly think so.' Monsieur Lafayette quietly demurred, lighting up a cigar and puffing silently over the heads of kings and queens, bishops and knaves. 'Eveline has always been most solicitous of your health. She's been a good daughter to you, Renan.'

'Oh, Eveline!' cried Mistigris, throwing his arms out so hard he almost knocked over the chessboard. 'Where is she now? Who is it stirring the soup at this very minute? Who has cooked it? Who is about to serve it up? Not Eveline, no, but Theodora of course. Eveline has gone off to fight at the barricades, leaving her old father to fend for himself...'

The expression on Monsieur Lafayette's face changed from one of vague boredom to one of intense concentration.

'Oh yes indeed, left me in the lurch without a second thought. If it wasn't for Theodora, bless her soul, I shouldn't have even been fed and watered. It was she who found the note, didn't want me to read it at first, fearing it would be the final straw, the straw that broke the camel's back.'

'I didn't want to be the one,' Madame Larousse put in from the kitchen, a sanctimonious expression on her face, 'to wield that straw.'

'Oh, Eveline did that. Killed me with her little note. Stone dead. Just as Jacques did. Couldn't bear to tell me face to face I don't suppose, her poor dear ancient old Papa.'

'May I see it?' Monsieur Lafayette asked gruffly, on his feet now and pacing the room in agitation.

'See what?'

'The note, of course. May I see Eveline's note.'

'Oh, it is ashes now, as it deserves to be. Theodora and I put it on the fire last night.'

'You bloody fool, Renan!' cried Monsieur Lafayette scornfully and a spasm of anger passed over his face. 'Sitting here playing chess and drinking soup when your daughter is out at the barricades! Have you heard nothing of what I've been telling you? It is a mass slaughter out there. It is your daughter's corpse you'll be identifying in the morgue, *her* delicate wrist matching *her* delicate ankle... your daughter, Renan, *your* daughter.'

Mistigris shifted uncomfortably in his seat, looking to Madame Larousse for reassurance but she was watching Monsieur Lafayette, her eyes wide as saucers. 'So that is how the land lies,' she mumbled to herself, a triumphant little smile twitching about her mouth as he blundered off to the fireplace to search for the remains of Eveline's note, even getting down on all fours to fumble about in the grate with the rusted old poker.

It was so rare to see him so discomposed and in a sweat that the two of them were at a loss to know what to say.

'It's no good your doing that, Monsieur Lafayette,' Madame Larousse called out a little unnecessarily in the end for by that time he was on his feet again and dusting off his knees, 'for we put the note on last night's fire and those are this morning's ashes.'

'Very well.' He looked up at them in defiance and it was evident that one or two tears must have astonishingly squeezed themselves out of his pin black eyes for his cheeks were streaked and shiny looking. 'I shall find her on my own with or without a note.' And he was on the point of fetching his hat and coat when a soft and deliberate tapping on the door made them all turn around in surprise.

The young corporal, following close at his captain's polished heels, only hoped that this would turn out to be the right house. He'd lost count of the buildings they'd searched, the sheds and gardens, attics and cellars. The captain had even made him put his hand into a dog kennel lest the criminal be crouching there in the darkness. It had been a humiliating experience and one the corporal wasn't likely to forget. His hand still ached painfully where the mongrel had bitten him and he flexed his fingers worriedly now and again, fearing he may have broken a metacarpal. If only he'd kept on with his medical apprenticeship instead of joining the army – but it was too late for all that now. He had a wife and young son to support in the country and he must just make the best of it. He sniffed miserably as they entered the kitchen and the smell of soup made his throat ache almost as much as his hand.

It didn't look too promising to begin with – three old people about to eat their lunch. It didn't seem the sort of place a hardened revolutionary would hide out. Not that the corporal knew much about hardened revolutionaries. This one, apparently, was as dangerous as they came and orders were to bring him back dead or alive. Alive preferably but dead otherwise. Thiers himself had offered up a large reward for his capture and many a soldier was hoping to supplement his wages by tracking down the 'iceman'. The problem with the iceman was that he melted in the sunshine, completely disappeared. Nobody seemed to know where he lived, what he ate, who he did or didn't sleep with. Every lead anyone touched went cold. The corporal sometimes wondered if the man really existed, if he wasn't just a figment of the government's imagination, some paranoid fabrication. The whole civil war in his opinion was paranoia from start to finish and he almost wished he hadn't come on this wretched manhunt. But the captain had begged and pleaded with him and you didn't say no to the captain.

He'd wanted someone with psychological skills, someone who could tell when a man was lying, was medically ill, off his head or simply faking it and though the corporal said so himself he fitted the bill perfectly, having studied such things during his medical apprenticeship. The bald-headed man right now for instance was decidedly faking it, smoothing his features into an expression of obsequious alertness, toadying up to the captain with hand outstretched, thankful apparently that the forces of order had arrived in the nick of time. The captain was having none of it of course. The old fellow by the chessboard seemed genuine enough, his face white and scared looking. The woman, the corporal noted, was sly and needed watching. He stationed himself by the door as always while the captain did his usual thing of scouring the room with his gimlet eyes and making the occupants feel like dirt – all in complete silence. The captain did everything in complete silence or so softly you could hardly hear him. He washed softly, walked softly, ate softly, killed softly. He was murmuring now in a very low tone, stating their business and who they were searching for and the three old people were physically straining to hear him, a look of terror on their faces. It was the most terrifying thing in the world, not being able to hear someone. That, the corporal knew, was a psychological fact. It left you in the dark, uncertain, and uncertainty made the pulse rate soar. He stared closely at the three of them, gauging their reaction. The bald-headed man's was the most intriguing. He definitely knew the name – though that was hardly surprising – for everyone more or less had heard of the iceman. But there was more to it than that: the shaking hands, sudden pallor and perspiration indicated the name meant something to him. They were physical manifestations of an inner turbulence. The corporal knew a lot about inner turbulence; he'd once witnessed a man's heart literally bursting through inner turbulence and it wasn't an experience he was likely to forget. The old man by the chessboard had stood suddenly and was asking for the iceman's name to be repeated. The captain obliged, lifting his voice maybe a semitone higher and the old man collapsed back down on his seat with a look of dismay on his face.

'He's a friend of my daughter's,' he admitted immediately with painful honesty. 'They have gone off somewhere, they have disappeared together – at his behest no doubt. I did not know...' he looked at the old woman for support. 'Did you know that he was a *criminal?*'

The captain was cracking his hands with glee – a sound the corporal always associated with the agonising crunch of a snail shell underfoot – at the unexpected good news. It was the best lead they'd had so far and he would stop at nothing now, he would turn over the house until he'd turned up a button, a shoelace, anything belonging to the iceman. The corporal sniffed miserably at the sight of the coffin in the corner – no doubt the captain would make him put his hand in *that*, lest the criminal was hiding there in the darkness. He decided to try and catch the old bird's eye when he got the chance and cadge a bowl of soup off her. That wasn't too much to ask surely. Let the captain run about in damp chilly cellars, stick his hand into coffins and kennels. *He* was having no more of it. He tried valiantly to catch the old woman's eye but she was gazing fixedly at the captain.

'Highly original piece of furniture,' the captain murmured in an undertone, kicking the coffin with a polished toe. 'You, neither of you are men of the cloth so why the crozier, bishop's hat, religious ornamentation? Were you hoping to disguise yourselves as members of the clergy to evade capture as revolutionary Communards?'

'We are about as revolutionary,' the bald-headed man, seemingly unfazed by the rapid line of fire, put in blithely, 'as cats in the sunshine.'

'Cats,' the captain raised his voice a fraction along with one pencil-thin eyebrow, 'with mice are about as revolutionary as it gets. I met a red the other day dressed as a priest and let me tell you I saw through him immediately. I have seen better acting at the *Alcazar*. Are you telling me then that these items are theatrical props?'

There was the faintest glimmer of hope in the captain's voice and the corporal sighed audibly with exasperation. The theatre was the captain's greatest passion, his grand passion, his one and only abiding passion. That apart from money and only money insofar as it enabled him to go to the theatre as often as he liked which, it seemed to the corporal, was once a night at the very least. It was all he cared about, all he talked about. He had no wife or family to occupy his mind. How many times had the corporal had to listen to the captain and been pleased not to catch each excruciating detail of the previous night's performance at the Théâtre des Variétés. If these three old duds turned out to be theatre lovers, however, the search would be delayed somewhat. If that was the case he may as well pull up a chair, save the swelling in his legs a little, maybe get himself a bowl of soup.

'Our guilty pleasure.' The bald-headed man confirmed his fears. 'We like a little pretence in this house.'

The captain gave the briefest of smiles. 'There is nothing like a little culture after a day's bloodshed,' he murmured gently. 'It calms the nerves, puts everything into perspective: planets, people, begonias, lizards.'

Two pairs of ears at least heard pagodas instead of begonias but it didn't much alter the sentiment of the captain's words. His eyes had a faraway look in them, as though he were thinking thoughts beyond the ken of ordinary men and his mouth twitched solemnly as he spoke. 'One night at the theatre and you run the gauntlet of emotion from sorrow to adulation...'

The corporal crept into the kitchen and helped himself to a bowl of soup. He spotted a hunk of bread on the sideboard and he took that too, shoving it into his pocket for later. It had been a long trek from Versailles and he was starving, not to mention his throat which felt as if it were being stabbed by hundreds of sharp bayonets. He plonked himself down on a chair by the door and ate heartily. The soup was good, warm and spicy tasting and it reminded him of his young wife in the country who always gave him tomato soup and cheese toast when he was off colour, sometimes a chocolate biscuit for dessert. He did miss her but he reminded himself that he was doing all this for her. When he shared the reward with the captain he would be able to get them all a bigger house, maybe a garden for the boy to run around in. It wasn't too bad having given up on his medical training. At least he had learned some psychological skills. He could eat and listen at the same time and he knew for a fact that very few men could do that...

'I don't know where he lives,' the old gent was crying plaintively as the captain circled him like a buzzard. 'Honestly I don't. I didn't even know he was a criminal. Did you, Modeste? Did you know he was a criminal?'

'No.' The bald-headed man was staring into the grate like Cinderella and he was obviously suffering from inner turbulence again. For the first time the corporal noticed he had stained fingers, blackened at the tip from using the *tabatière* rifle no doubt. Whatever he said about cats he was a revolutionary for sure. He must know the iceman's whereabouts. Maybe he was wondering whether to protect his own hide or that of his friend's. No wonder he was suffering from inner turbulence. If the captain noticed those fingers he'd finish him. But the captain hadn't noticed. He was focusing on the old gent by the chessboard, surprised, nay incredulous that a father should know so little about his daughter's activities and acquaintances.

'It is true.' The old gent's face suddenly crumpled and he wept so hard the old woman had to put an arm around his shoulders. 'I should have known. I should have known. I am a travesty of a father. She will end up in the Seine,' he gasped between sobs, 'green and bloated like her mother.'

The captain hadn't bargained on this genuine display of emotion. Running the gauntlet in the theatre was one thing but in real life quite another. He turned impatiently to the corporal, eyeing him unpleasantly.

'Are you enjoying your soup, Schenowitz?' he asked with a dangerous edge to his voice. 'Did you think I wouldn't hear you slurping away like a pig at the trough, you half Prussian bastard?'

The corporal stood hurriedly, placing the bowl on the table a little awkwardly with his bad hand.

'I forget which side you get the Fritz giblets from. Is it your mother's or your father's? Was your father a kraut or was it your sow? Was your sow a kraut? Was your *sauerkraut*?!'

The corporal glowered at the tired old joke, used once too often by the captain. If he were a medical man he wouldn't suffer this sort of humiliation. He would be respected, part of the establishment. People would come to him with their boils, scurvy and rickets and he would prescribe lancing, orange segments, milk for the calcium. He beckoned the captain over and whispered in his ear. 'Why don't you try old Cinderella over there. He knows more than he's letting on, just look at his hands.'

The captain turned swiftly and approached the fireplace. 'Show me your hands,' he ordered quietly and the bald-headed man turned in surprise, opening his palms out for the captain's attention.

'Oh ho, the tell-tale hands. The mouth may lie but the hands cannot. I suppose you are going to tell me you are a chimney sweep by trade.'

'No,' replied the bald-headed man, gazing steadily at the captain with his small black eyes. He was no longer suffering from inner turbulence, the corporal noted, in fact his face was a marvel of composure. He'd obviously decided to save his own skin. 'I am going to tell you where Alphonse Duchamp lives.'

There were gasps of astonishment from the two old duds in the corner and the captain suddenly started speaking unnaturally loudly; excited, perhaps, at the prospect of getting one step closer to his dream, his longing, his new box at the Odéon. 'If you are telling the truth I shall give these hands the benefit of the doubt, if you are not I shall shoot you immediately. Do you understand?'

'Perfectly.'

The captain spun on a polished heel, cracking his knuckles with satisfaction. 'Then lead the way,' he entreated the bald-headed man, almost shooing him out of the room; and the corporal opened the front door in readiness. 'Lead me to him.'

Chapter thirty

The sun burnt down on the Rue Ramponneau and Eveline stirred restlessly behind the barricade, hopping from one cramping foot to another. 'When are they coming?' she'd asked Alphonse what seemed like hours ago and he had replied 'soon'. This stretched-out time was unbearable – worse than the queue for Potin's. Ten times worse than the queue for Potin's when everyone had shouted 'Soon. Soon. Soon there will be boiled beef, greens, carrots, new potatoes, lovely grub, shrimps and watercresses,' and in the end all that had turned up was watery soup with something inedible floating around on the top. With any luck the enemy would be a let down too – watery little men with something inedible floating around on top. She hid a grin and flicked a damp tendril out of her eyes. The hardest part was always the waiting, and waiting for something bad it seemed was the same as waiting for something good. You still wanted to rush to the event – for different reasons of course. You anticipated or dreaded, got it over with and then regretted. Maybe that's what life consisted of: dreading, anticipating, getting it over with and then regretting... 'I sound like Laurie,' she muttered to herself, stretching her calf muscles one more time before settling back into her old position.

Not a breath could be felt behind the barricade though she smelt the garlic on one man's, the coffee on another's. A scent of rose crept out of an upturned wardrobe donated by someone on the Champs Élysées and Eveline wished she could take a peek at the lining in the ornate drawers, imagining the dresses that had swung and hung inside: silks and taffetas, ball gowns and evening wear... She had thought it was simply the women who waited – in queues for food, for their men to come home but now she saw that men waited too and for even worse things to come true – to fight, to kill, to test their mettle…. Some had fled already, downed weapons and fled in any direction, others prayed or perspired, crouching on their knees and bellies in the paltry shade of the barricade. She wondered if Laurie had been right after all. Was her place really here at the barricade or back home with her father and Jacques, waiting for them to come home.

She glanced nervously at Alphonse who stood stern and unyielding as always, his eyes on a thin column of smoke on the horizon which suddenly, before their very eyes, exploded into a fountain of sparks.

'There goes the Hôtel de Ville,' he muttered half triumphantly and Eveline turned on him in surprise: 'What good will that do them, blowing up the Hôtel de Ville?'

'Not them, us,' Alphonse corrected her and though his voice was harsh his frank blue eyes smiled down at her naivety. 'Fire is a legitimate weapon in war, as legitimate as any other. We've probably slowed them down by half an hour.'

'Oh, at least,' put in an oldish man who'd been praying most of the time Eveline had been at the barricade, and now seemed strangely exhilarated. He grinned across at Alphonse, raising his fist in a salute. 'Paris will be ours, *n'est ce pas*, or Paris will no longer exist! If they ever come to power they will have nowhere to sit!'

Alphonse gave a curt nod. '*Oui. Vive la Commune!*'

Vive la Commune! The cries went up into the hot, parched air and Eveline watched the flames that had taken the place of the sparks in the distance. The sparks had popped and disappeared and the flames that followed were brutal and devouring, vying with the sun itself. It was madness really, blowing up a city to stop the enemy in its tracks. Blowing up a city rather than give her up. A crazy, terrifying, foolhardy madness. Like two grown men fighting over a woman. Paris was a beautiful irresistible woman and if one man couldn't have her, nor could any other.

She pitied Paris then and her citizens, pitied herself and the men who prayed or perspired beside her, the one woman who'd lost her sons to Prussia and had nothing left to lose. How many of them were there after all in total? Including herself and Alphonse she counted nineteen. Hardly an army. Nineteen souls crouching in the paltry shade of the barricade beneath sandbags, wardrobes, a lazy Susan and mounds of earth – mounds of earth that reminded her horribly of the freshly dug graves in le Père Lachaise where her father had once stolen gravestones for statues. How ashamed she had been of him, stealing gravestones for statues… Now it seemed a very long time ago. The cemetery had been redesigned since then with paved walkways and chestnut trees so the dead could be visited in a romantic landscape. It helped apparently, for relatives to be able to visit their dead in a romantic landscape. She wondered if the Rue Ramponneau would be described as a romantic landscape with its dirty guttering and squat houses. Most of them were shuttered up, awaiting the onslaught, their owners having fled or hiding under their beds; others were hives of activity with mattresses being dragged across the windows and men taking up positions on the uneven rooftops, like cats finding a favourable spot in the sunshine. It was romantic probably, she decided, if you lived on the street, if you loved it, like all ugly familiar things were romantic if you loved them. Eveline watched an old woman negotiating a rickety ladder just to hand a glass of water to her son who sat bare-chested on the blistering tiles. They spoke, it seemed, for a while, she perched on top of the ladder, he precariously on the rooftop, then he handed back the glass, kissed her gently on the forehead, and she clambered down again, carefully removing the ladder behind her.... Maybe it wasn't madness at all but love. A crazy, terrifying, glorious love. A love beyond hope, beyond despair, beyond choice even…

She slipped her hand into Alphonse's hand and he gave it a fierce tight squeeze in return… It was the sort of love in her heart of hearts she secretly admired, for what woman didn't want a man who would die rather than give her up, kill her rather than lose her to another? It was the only love worth having after all.

'They're coming,' Alphonse whispered, his keen eyes being the first to spot the tricolour flag. And then a little louder to the rest: 'They're coming!'

In the middle of the storm with Alphonse – that's where she was. It was strangely silent in the middle of a storm, Laurie had told her that. In the middle of a storm you were relatively safe – you had the advantage of being able to go out and meet your own fate whereas at the edges, the periphery, you got dragged into things and fate met you. It was best to be in the middle of the storm. She smiled up at Alphonse one last time and he grinned back, a wide, almost impertinent grin. There was nothing to say, nothing they didn't know already. Soon the mattresses would be smoking, as the Versailles army came to reclaim the hand of Paris, the men picked off the rooftops one by one like coconuts at the coconut shy, the mounds of earth sprinkling down on the heads of the eighteen men and one woman who were crazy, foolhardy and glorious enough to fight beyond hope, beyond despair, beyond choice even…

'They're here!' Alphonse cried urgently then and his eyes reflected the flames of the Hôtel de Ville that had gone down roaring. 'They're here everybody, they're here!'

Eveline fumbled with the gun she'd been taught to use at the Rue de Turbigo, her brain forgetting everything Elizabeth and Maria had told her. 'I had better just rely on instinct,' she muttered to herself, 'and the quick reactions of youth.'

And as the bullets shrieked 'bread for a song on Marcadet' and 'fish going spare on the Rue de Rivoli' Eveline stood straight and held her nerve, just as she had done in the queue for Potin's.

Chapter thirty-one

Bernadine found the Mont de Piété easily enough though she saw at once to her dismay that it was shut. The closed sign was hanging tip-tilted on the door handle and no sound could be heard from within. She pressed her face to the pane, almost crushing Aggie in her cotton papoose, and she had to turn her round to the side to get a better look. The shop was full of heirlooms, treasured possessions, old junk and bric-a-brac. She spotted a china tea set, some good linen, hundreds and hundreds of pairs of scissors, even a mattress and an old rocking horse, its boot-black button eye staring dumbly at her out of the darkness. All waiting to be reclaimed or sold on to a new home. She'd forgotten how full the world was of possessions, possessions and obligations.

Feeling suddenly panicked, she rapped sharply on the pane. If she couldn't exchange her ring here then where could she? She needed money, cash to be able to get around with, to eat, sleep, live with. The ring was only valuable in so far as it could be exchanged for the currency of the day – whatever that was. She'd been so long in the convent she didn't have a clue what the currency of the day was – it could have been old socks for all she knew, old socks or bloomers! She didn't even know what side of the war she was meant to be on. She rapped again and waited, listening intently. Not a sound. Not a creak or a peep. The windows above were shuttered up too. There was no one home. It was something she hadn't bargained on, there being nobody home.

Come to think of it, it was deathly quiet. On her way over she'd not met a single soul and had come to the conclusion merely that people in the outside world were tardy to rise. She imagined everyone on the outside to be some sort of midnight reveller and tardy to rise in the mornings.

Not that she'd ever been out much in the mornings except to queue for food during the siege. Usually she crept out like a gnat in the twilight if she ever had to go on some errand for the convent. That was all changed now of course. She would have to brave the light of day on a regular basis now, on a daily basis in fact. But if it was always as quiet as this it wouldn't be so bad.

She decided to wait, wait for the proprietor to wake and open up. He couldn't be that much of a lie a bed. She moved away from the glass and as she did so she suddenly caught sight of a woman in the window. There was somebody there after all. She turned back with relief, gesticulating urgently and the woman waved back almost as urgently. How strange! Was she trapped in the shop somehow? Bernadine stood still, waiting for the woman to open the door but the woman just stood there staring back at her. She was holding something in her arms and even from behind the pane of glass Bernadine could sense the air of desperation about her, of loneliness, of despair. It was in the droop of the shoulders, the set of the neck, the large and haunted eyes. This woman was in trouble, needed help. Bernadine stepped forward impulsively at the same time the stranger did and only then when she was face to face with her, did Bernadine recognise the large and haunted eyes as her own. *She* was the woman trapped behind the pane of glass!

How stupid! She'd be fleeing from her own shadow next. She tore her eyes away out of habit and then a moment later allowed them to return. In her previous existence (for that was how she must describe her years in the convent now) she would have labelled that figure a woman of the night, a woman of ill repute, dressed as she was in that tight-fitting tunic, her head and ankles bare – and yet unbelievably it was herself. It was hard to look at her own reflection, hard to see herself in bodily form, having lived so long in spirit. It reminded her that from now on she would be judged as a woman, not as a nun, by men, not by God.

'Go away!' The voice came from up above, startling Bernadine out of her thoughts, and she craned her neck to see who had spoken, but the windows were still tight shut and fastened. The disembodied voice spoke again. 'Go away or I shall send for the police.'

'But I have a ring to exchange,' Bernadine protested, her heart thumping with anxiety. 'I need money to get out of Paris.' *Should she tell him the truth? Tell him she had just left the convent and was running to a new life in Rhône with a baby in tow? It sounded absurd, not possible, not credible…*

'Don't we all.' The voice was still hostile but less so and Bernadine squinted hopefully up at the shutters. 'Here, look!' With trembling fingers she brought the little pouch out of the pocket of her tunic and held the ring up to the sun where it glowed with the dull warmth of real gold. Her father had done her proud she had to admit. It was a rare and beautiful ring, even she could tell that. Surely it would tempt the proprietor out of bed…

It did. A few moments later the door of the Mont de Piété opened and a wiry-haired man stuck his head out, looked to the right and left then beckoned her in.

'I thought you were a *pétroleuse*[25],' he explained apologetically and Bernadine, not knowing what a *pétroleuse* was, shook her head in any case and gratefully entered the shop. It was cool and pleasant inside after the beating heat of the streets and she placed the horsehair basket down on the floor and checked Aggie's head for fever as she always did when it was hot. The baby was fine, peaceful and sleeping for once, her long dark eyelashes curling like spiders' legs over her cheeks.

'Let me set up my equipment,' the proprietor said then before Bernadine had had a chance to bring the ring out again, 'else I shan't be able to give you a fair valuation.' He seemed to take an inordinately long time setting his equipment up though it consisted merely of a duster, magnifying glass, pair of scales and bottle of vinegar. Then he brought out the big black book of receipts and began searching slowly and methodically for an available space. *I don't need a receipt*, Bernadine wanted to scream. *I just need to get to Rhône by nightfall.* But she stood waiting patiently, her legs aching, as his dirty thumbnail bent the pages. There was a look of suppressed excitement in his small green eyes and Bernadine wondered if he were deliberately delaying the moment when he would examine the ring in her possession just as Agnes had always delayed the moment when she could gorge herself on a chocolate pudding or citron glace.

'May I take your name.' He'd found an available space and she opened her mouth to say Sister Bernadine then closed it abruptly, blushing furiously. She must use her old name now.

'De Villiers,' she stuttered at last, her tongue twisting over the unfamiliar vowels and consonants. 'Marie-Ange de Villiers,' she added softly, almost to herself, getting herself used to it again.

The proprietor raised his head sharply, suspicion in his eyes. 'De Villiers – after the shipping line?'

Bernadine nodded. 'Distantly… my uncle…' she tailed off, not knowing what to say. In truth her father had opted out of the family business as a young man, preferring clocks to ships, leaving her uncle to amass a small fortune. Luckily for her the ring was a relic of that fortune. She brought it out then without further ado in an attempt to avoid any more embarrassing questions and placed it on the counter beside the magnifying glass.

'I will need an address.' The proprietor's voice was cold and disbelieving, almost hostile again, and Bernadine could feel the colour sweep back into her cheeks. She wondered if she oughtn't to tell him the truth, that she was a nun from St Joseph's convent on her way to a new life in Rhône but it sounded so preposterous, so absurd that she couldn't bring herself to do it. In the end she gave the address of her father's old place in town, smiling a little to herself at the thought that upon investigation it might turn out to be a boulangerie, a pâtisserie or to exist simply in memory only. The haberdasher having long gone after all... *He has a vineyard now*, her uncle had written her, *in Provence I believe*. The stupid trivial things you remembered.

'I have been visiting relatives,' she added on the spur of the moment, 'and now I intend to go home.'

'I hope you had a good visit,' was the proprietor's decidedly sardonic response but at least he was writing the address down in the big black receipt book. At least he hadn't confronted her over it.

Little Aggie let out a cry then, having woken in unfamiliar surroundings and Bernadine turned to attend to her. In actual fact the baby always cried upon waking and Bernadine found herself wishing, as she often did, that just for once she would greet the day with a smile, that just for once the transition from sleeping to waking would be a pleasant one. She took her off to look at the rocking horse, leaving the proprietor to examine the ring in peace; and the baby cooed and crowed in delight over the boot-black button eye and moth-eaten mane as the proprietor dusted, weighed, polished and stared. The way he worked reminded Bernadine a little of her father and for a moment she was back in the quaint old shop amongst grandfather clocks and grandmother clocks, jewelled, enamelled, gold, ormolu... where time itself was dusted, polished, weighed and stared at and yet still passing with every tick and tock. How fast it had gone and now here she was in the outside world with a child of her own to support and protect, not to mention a grown-up daughter somewhere in the city.... The proprietor must have noticed the tears in her eyes for he said quite kindly and out of the blue that if she wanted to tell him something then he'd be happy to listen.

'I hear more confessions in here every day, Mademoiselle de... Villiers, than a church must get in a month of Sundays.'

He clearly didn't believe her, didn't believe she was a de Villiers but then why should he, dressed as she was? Even she didn't believe she was a de Villiers any more.

'Everyone agonises over giving up some treasured possession to pay off a bad debt – a wedding ring, locket, child's baptismal gown. It is only natural. I hear the whys and wherefores of it all. The only way they can deal with the guilt is to pretend that one day they will come back to reclaim it though few of them do. Sometimes I think I should call this place the House of Perpetual Hope.'

Hope, yes. A place to dream, forget, repent. A place to find a new life in amidst good linen, silver candlesticks and pretty rocking horses, the bric-a-brac of people's lives. She'd forgotten how full the world was of things and of feelings; and it horrified her to think how full it was.

'The strangest thing anyone ever left was a parrot. A tiny old lady brought one in during the siege, her face festooned with tears. She'd been having dreams of skinning him alive – we were all so hungry then I suppose. Well, it contravened rule number 4,' the proprietor waved at the placard behind his wiry head which read, Bernadine saw mistily through her tears, *No corpses, No perishables, No edibles, No animals ('less stuffed)*, 'but I made an exception in her case. Well, what else could I do? I am not entirely without a heart. I rather lived to regret it, however. That tiny old lady must have owned the entire works of Dante Alighieri for I got *Purgatorio* from the beak of that bird from dawn till dusk! I thought it was talking double dutch until a learned gentleman came in one day selling his mattress and translated it for me.'

Bernadine smiled weakly at the anecdote, related she felt quite sure for her benefit. 'Did the old lady ever come back for the parrot?' she asked politely, scooping Aggie up in her arms and approaching the counter.

'Yes, as a matter of fact she did, luckily for the parrot. One more day of Dante's *Inferno* and I'd have skinned him alive myself.' He was smiling now and loquacious though the small green eyes, Bernadine noted, were completely inscrutable. The look of suppressed excitement had gone from them and they were shuttered and opaque as an algae-covered pond. She felt guilty now about the ring after everything the proprietor had said about people wrestling with their consciences, even though her father had given it to her for just such a purpose as this.

'Is it worth very much?' she asked quickly, wanting to get the transaction over and done with.

The proprietor scratched his wiry head. 'Less than I imagined I'm afraid,' he admitted sorrowfully, turning the ring again between finger and thumb as if contemplating it afresh. 'It is a surprisingly poor quality gold.'

Bernadine's heart sank and for a moment she railed against the memory of her father – how stupid he was preferring clocks to ships, not knowing the real value of things, no wonder her mother had left him – before coming back to her senses. He'd given her the ring in case she ever wished to escape her own life. He would have made sure at the very least that the gold was good quality. It must be the proprietor out to cheat her. She glanced quickly at the small green eyes but they were as inscrutable as ever – a stagnant, algae-covered pond – though the mouth was warm and smiling. She wondered if all men were scoundrels if they could get away with it, wondered if it would have been any different had she been in the veil, wondered if she could bring herself to haggle though she knew at the same time that she couldn't. She gave a small, nearly hysterical laugh, naive and ridiculous in her ill-fitting costume, clasping Aggie to her chest. 'As long as it gets me to Rhône,' she stammered and the proprietor nodded his head emphatically. 'Oh, it'll get you to Rhône certainly, but it might not bring you back again.'

'That is well,' She watched him place four brightly coloured coins on the counter, all of them the same size in a currency she didn't recognise but then she had expected that, 'for I shall not be coming back again.' She picked one up and stared at it curiously as the proprietor had stared at the ring, turning it over in the palm of her hand. On one side was depicted the figure of Hercules flanked by the figures of Liberty and Equality. On the other side the words: *Dieu Protège la France.* Must she be confronted by God at every turn? Must He follow her everywhere when she was trying to escape Him?

The proprietor had misunderstood her hesitation. 'If you are concerned about their validity under a new regime,' he offered up, 'I can give you a guarantee to that effect.'

'No, no, I am satisfied.' She placed them hurriedly in her pocket and gathered up the horsehair basket, wanting to be off and on with her journey; but the proprietor, having cheated her so beautifully and kindly, was suddenly solicitous of her well being.

'May I offer you a glass of water, Mademoiselle de Villiers, before you set off again? It is very hot outside.'

'Oh, no I must catch the next train that is going to Rhône – this morning hopefully.'

The proprietor gave her a look then as if he wished he'd cheated her even worse than he had done. 'There'll be no trains running today, not for a long time I should imagine. Did you not hear the rappel, mademoiselle?'

Bernadine frowned. 'No… well, yes of course.' There were always bells and rappels, guns blazing somewhere in the distance but none of it ever affected the convent, none of it ever affected her.

'We must sit tight and await liberation by the old government or go out and fight at the barricades – depending on which side you happen to be on.'

'I'm never quite sure about that,' Bernadine replied with the faintest ghost of a smile. 'I'm never quite sure which side I'm meant to be on.'

'Oh, the winning side, Mademoiselle de Villiers,' laughed the proprietor and his green eyes gleamed again as she opened the door and the sun hit them. 'The winning side of course!'

Of course. It was always best to be on the winning side. Once upon a time she'd been on the side of the Lord, but not any more. His red eye smouldered down on her from the direction of the Hôtel de Ville, all seeing, all pervading, and she put her black umbrella up to fend Him off. The heat was unbearable, suffocating and she hoped it wasn't too far to the Gare du Nord from here, hoped the trains would be running after all. She wasn't going to trust what the proprietor said on the subject, in any case, not after that grand feat of corruption! She'd forgotten how full the world was of lies and deception. How many of her own would she have to tell before she got to Rhône? How many of her own would she have to tell in order to survive, before she could start a new life…? Her fingers sought the rosary beads sewn into the lining of her pocket and instead found the four, strange, brightly coloured coins; and clasping Aggie fiercely in her cotton papoose she made her way through the burning streets.

Chapter thirty-two

Monsieur Lafayette led the two men over the blackened grass and he whistled a few bars from 'La Belle Hélène' to show that he wasn't fazed by that stick insect of a captain and his ungainly little corporal, not one iota, not one little bit. Even though he was. The air stank of corpses and pestilence and the sky had turned from a preternatural azure blue to a dingy grey in parts that rained down scraps of charred and burning paper.

'It reminds me of the ash that buried Pompeii,' he remarked in a jocular tone to show that he wasn't fazed, not one little bit, 'when Mount Etna blew her top.'

'The Ministry of Finance more like!' smiled the corporal and he went on with sudden eloquence: 'All the paperwork of Paris blowing through the air. Every law and order shrivelled to nothing! Every notary's nightmare, every debtor's delight!'

'It reminds me,' the captain's voice was a soft addendum, 'that one day the earth and planets will explode and we shall all fall through space like particles of dust.' He sniffed gently, as if he were sniffing a lady's scented handkerchief or delicate blossom. 'The dead take their revenge as we speak.'

'Yes indeed, in this heat.' The corporal gave a worried frown. He'd known a corpse to literally melt in the sunshine and it wasn't an experience he was happy to repeat.

What a pair, thought Monsieur Lafayette, trudging through the mounds of dock weed and clumps of nettle that were springing up already over the deadened grass. He almost wished he hadn't told them he knew where Alphonse Duchamp lived but his competitive side had got the better of him. The thought of the tortoise outwitting the fox in the final race had been too much for him. To dispose of his fiercest rival – it was too good an opportunity to miss. He was still in a stew over Eveline, having been taken unawares, even amazed by the strength of his own feeling for her. He had thought she was merely a distraction, an amusement, a diversion from the dreadful ennui of his existence; but he saw now there was far more to it than that. The thought of her at the barricades was like a death to him. Without her he was simply a preposterous old man, a bad joke. With her there was a glimmer of hope that he was something more than the black-hearted wretch he secretly knew himself to be. The image of Eveline kept him alive to life and all its intrigues. She was his guiding light, his star, his destination; and with his fiercest rival behind bars he had as good a chance as any... as long as she didn't die at the barricades. *Ma petite sauvage,* his heart sang and wept all at the same time and he suddenly dashed his hand against a clump of nettles in full view of the captain to steel himself for the ordeal ahead and to show he wasn't fazed by that silent creeping stick insect of a man. Even though he was.

The captain, barely noticing Monsieur Lafayette's bizarre activities, was apologising to the corporal for his previous fit of pique. That was what he did: lost his temper, was sorrowful, regretful, apologised profusely then lost it all over again.

'I have a cruel stomach ache,' he explained contritely. 'It comes in waves. It has put me in the foulest of tempers. I believe if a bird flapped its wings too hard at the wrong moment I should have to shoot it. And you know my fondness for birds.'

'Then we are both of us ailing,' the corporal responded with a sullen nod, 'for I only ate the soup because I have a sore throat. It is like hundreds of bayonets stabbing at my tongue.' He was suddenly eloquent again. 'Imagine a minute army stabbing hundreds and hundreds of bayonets at your tongue. It is not the most pleasant of evocations.'

The captain agreed calmly that it was not. They had been on the search too long, he placated, that was the trouble – but at least the end was in sight. And they walked on in an amicable silence for a while, each of them prodding the confectioner in the back when his pace slowed too much for them. The sky was a little clearer – all the paperwork of Paris having seemingly deposited itself on the face of the corporal which was speckled and blackened indeed; but he was softened enough by this time to suggest milk of magnesia for the captain's irritable stomach.

'Milk of magnesia in the first instance. Always.' He just couldn't help himself, he had so much medical knowledge at his fingertips. 'Unless it is a case of food poisoning whereupon I would prescribe purging. What did you last dine on, Captain?'

'Thank you *Herr Doktor*!' laughed the captain with a strange quiet coldness, 'I dined at Brébant's, if you must know, the night before last and have had nothing since. What do you make of that?'

The corporal gave Monsieur Lafayette a vicious dig in the ribs in the vain hope of asserting some authority over somebody, and let him have an earful.

'Get a move on you fat fool. I believe you're taking us on a wild goose chase. I don't believe you have clue where Alphonse Duchamp lives. Either that or you are in league with him and always have been.'

For an answer Monsieur Lafayette thought it best simply to pick up his pace and he hobbled as fast as he could over the treacherous wasteland. In a moment they would reach St Jacques du Haut Pas and it was an easy stretch of the legs from there. It had been the most ferocious tussle, he now decided, of his life. The most ferocious emotional tussle – whether to rescue Eveline from the barricades or try and dispose of his rival first but in the end his jealous streak had got the best of him. He only hoped he wasn't too late to save his *petite sauvage*. He would march on every barricade in Paris if he had to; descend like a god, a Roman emperor... like a hurricane, like Hercules, like Achilles on one of his immortal horses... His heart filled with pride to think that he had a worthy purpose at last. In a life filled with acts of low profiteering, blackmail, scandals and betrayals, he was surprised to find he had a worthy purpose. The fate of a soul lay in his hands. A perfect beautiful soul was in jeopardy and he must try to save it! Having destroyed so many, he must set out to save one. At the very least, he told himself, he must set out to save one.

A pigeon flapped against the stained-glass panes of St Jacques du Haut Pas and a murder of crows circled and spun above the square-topped belfry, peppering the blue sky in place of all the paperwork of Paris. Monsieur Lafayette stopped short at the sight of the largest congregation he'd ever seen in his life pouring out into the sunshine. There were boys, girls, old men, young women and they just kept coming, one after the other. Some of them bareheaded, in kerchiefs, silk dresses, National Guard uniforms... Hardly dressed for worship, he thought, and it couldn't have been the most uplifting of sermons for many of them looked a trifle subdued, their heads down, their arms at their sides. It must have been one of those hell and damnation, fire and brimstone sort of things the Catholic church always went in for. All about souls and the need for salvation... Monsieur Lafayette shuddered in the hot, bright sunshine and shaded his eyes to get a better look. They were gathering now in groups and lines in the derelict courtyard and he saw suddenly that their hands were tied – they were tied together with bits of string. At that moment a Versaillais officer cantered up on a large bay horse, confirming the confectioner's worst fears. It wasn't a collection of God-fearing folk at all but a collection of prisoners. He stepped back instinctively, as more officers emerged from the recesses of the church, and bumped into the captain who patted him on the back with one of his long spidery hands.

'You are aiding governmental enquiries and are not, as yet, a prisoner of war.'

Monsieur Lafayette didn't hear the 'as yet', it was spoken so softly, and he continued to stare with morbid fascination at the scene. The prisoners were blinking like owls in the sunlight, having been cooped up in the church for so long; and they were such a strange mix it was hard to believe that they all deserved capture. Children next to spinsters next to housewives next to arthritic old men. Most of them wearing a bemused or resigned look on their face, or gazing down at their feet to avoid attracting attention. There were different nationalities too – close by was a couple who could only have been English, the man so handsomely stiff upper-lipped, the woman quite plain and nondescript, worrying about her pet dog at a time like this!

'Don't worry about the dog,' her husband admonished her. 'You must just try to keep up, my dear, despite your poorly leg.'

'But you know how he pines so when we are gone,' wailed the woman, 'and if cook forgets about him entirely…'

'Cook won't forget Rufus.' The man's face was a miracle of stoicism. 'Cook won't forget Rufus. Are you certain your shoe laces are quite tight, my dear, for I am sure we could be freed for a moment to tie them up if they are not.'

'It is so frightfully hot for him, poor lamb, in his kennel at this time of year.'

It was indeed hot. Cries of 'water' came from all over the place and one jeering officer emptied the contents of his bottle on the courtyard just for the fun of watching lines toppling as individuals threw themselves to the ground for a lick of that rolling evaporating liquid. A young woman in a silk dress had spotted Monsieur Lafayette and his companions and was quietly edging her group over to them. Her line was smaller than most consisting merely of a small child, an old crone and a short-haired woman dressed in a National Guard uniform. The girl herself, the confectioner decided, was almost as beautiful as Eveline with her long, dark hair and bright green eyes.

'She should be on the stage,' the captain murmured admiringly as she approached them; and it was true for her bearing was proud, almost arrogant, her head held high and gracefully. She didn't look like a prisoner. She looked like a queen who'd been taken by surprise and was scathingly waiting for someone to realise.

'Do you have any water?' she asked softly, her voice hoarse and oddly accented. 'There wasn't a drop in the baptismal fonts and the wine bottles were bone dry. These filthy dogs have left us for hours without a drink. It is not so bad for I but my friends are parching.'

The corporal, who understood the devastating consequences of dehydration, uncapped his bottle and tipped a little into the small child's mouth, then the old crone's and on tiptoe into the short-haired woman's. He was on the verge of giving the girl in the silk dress a drink when an officer caught his eye and, fearing retaliation, he stepped back quickly into the role of onlooker, recapping his water bottle tightly. The short-haired woman must have had the strength and presence of mind to hold some water in her mouth for she turned immediately and pressed her lips against those of her companion who, understanding, stuck her tongue out gratefully for the few precious drops.

'Thank you, Maria,' she said quietly before bowing an acknowledgement to the corporal and leading her line back into the courtyard, her silk dress dragging over the dirt and coarse grass. She got a blow for her pains however – an officer struck her full in the face with his riding crop, cutting open her cheek. She didn't cry out or even flinch but when he moved away from her onto another victim, her eyes were brilliant green and full of loathing.

'She is just like the girl who played *Athalie!*' commented the captain; and the three men watched the herd of prisoners being whipped, bullied and shouted out of the courtyard and onto the wasteland. Threats of 'stragglers will be shot' kept the bunch moving onwards and Monsieur Lafayette saw the English gentleman smiling encouragingly at his wife who limped painfully behind him, her shoes half off her feet.

'Where are they taking them?' he asked suddenly, aghast by the whole proceedings and fearfully anxious for Eveline's safety. *What if she were to die at the barricades or worse still be taken prisoner?*

'To the Bois,' replied the captain, 'to be sifted, then on to Versailles.'

'To be sifted?' the confectioner echoed wonderingly. 'You make them sound like sacks of flour! Do you mean some are to be freed in the Bois?'

The captain gave a humourless laugh like a little scratch of air. 'No, I mean that some are to be shot – depending on how involved they have been in revolutionary warfare. You can usually tell by looking at them.'

Monsieur Lafayette shivered, despite the blazing heat, and as soon as the way was clear he set off again at a lumbering trot, over the mounds of dock weed and clumps of nettle, not bothering this time to dash his hands against them. With black and determined eyes he gestured to the two men behind to keep up with him – he dare not slacken his pace for fear of being too late to save Eveline The corns on his toes pressed painfully against his shoes and his heart drummed like thunder in his chest. He felt as if he were going to have a heart attack but he dare not slacken his pace… he had a soul to save now. A soul in jeopardy at the barricades. He almost wished he hadn't told them he knew where Alphonse Duchamp lived at all. (*The memory of it still was like a knife through the heart.*) He led the way over the last few yards and into the network of alleyways that bordered the wasteland on one side and were bordered on the other by courtyards filled with washing lines and latrines stinking putrid in the humid air. With a trembling head and trembling legs he ushered the two men out into the middle of the Rue D'Enfer. *There.* There it was, the house that had seared itself into his consciousness like a firebrand one raining moonlit winter's night.

'This isn't the sort of house I expected.' The captain eyed the dilapidated building doubtfully, craning his long stick-insect neck up at it. 'I thought the iceman would live in a much grander abode. Are you sure this is correct?'

'Don't forget,' put in the corporal, panting, with his unerring psychological ability, 'that he is a master of disguise. It would be just like him to hole up in a place like this.'

'I am sure,' said Monsieur Lafayette with a touch of bitterness for the memory of Eveline and Alphonse together was still like a knife through the heart. And he led the two men up the steps, past the empty cubicle of glass to the very door he'd had the dubious pleasure of peeping through one luminous, heartbreaking, rain-soaked dawn.

Chapter thirty-three

Stumbling out of the Gare du Nord, Bernadine almost wept with despair.
There were no trains running, not to Rhône in any case. The Commune
had commandeered the railway for its own use and she had been met with
blank stares, disapproving looks, laughter, ridicule – everything she'd been
so apprehensive of. A nun on her way to Rhône with a baby… How
stupid, how foolish, how rash she had been!

There was nowhere to go. She was lost in the wilderness. No refuge,
no shelter… She sank down on the nearest available patch of grass in
order to gather her thoughts and to let Aggie out of the papoose for she
was screaming now fit to burst, her tooth playing her up presumably or
some such trivial thing. There was a bench, a grand beech tree, the
remains of a respectable old park; and Bernadine sat wearily, with aching
limbs, fumbling over the strings of the papoose. Already she missed the
cool quiet of the convent garden, her longitude and latitude of Paradise
Lost, with its tiger lilies and ox-eyed daisies, yellow-skinned tomatoes and
orange-bellied singing toads that each struck a different note at sunset….
Dashing the tears away from her eyes, she stared up at the sky with
agitation. It could have been sunset now, though it was barely noon, the
sky grown black and heavy with regret, raining giant papery drops like
singed butterflies or a swarm of locusts. It was as if somebody had opened
a Pandora's box somewhere in the city or the fall of Babylon in the Book
of Revelations was coming to pass at this very instant.

She dug her fingers into Aggie who screamed angrily and wriggled
out of her grasp, setting off in a crab-like crawl – head down, bottom
upwards – to the grand old beech tree. Bernadine watched her
distractedly, her mind racing over and over. If she couldn't get a train,

perhaps she could get a boat. There were hundreds of them up and down the Seine, carrying the wounded – she'd seen the river red and bloody under the arches when she'd crossed by the Pont des Arts. If she couldn't get a boat, perhaps she could walk and yet, of course, it was all hopeless. She barely had enough money to get herself a sugared ice. The uniformed guard had told her the four strange coins would barely get her a sugared ice, let alone get her to Rhône. He had told her too, very roughly, to get out of the way and go home, and she had meekly obeyed. It filled her with a sudden belated rage to think how meekly she had obeyed – the habit of a lifetime was hard to break. How cheated she felt! The proprietor had cheated her. Monsieur Lafayette had cheated her. Ernest had cheated her by dying. The Mother Superior by taking her baby away – she could still hear the screams in the distance, an Almighty reprimand... even God had cheated her. And how she had cheated herself.

The fury built up in her as she sat on the park bench, the black paper butterflies falling onto her bare head and cheeks; and she watched Aggie crowing in delight over a half-rotten apple core and dirty sandwich – some outdoor repast left in a hurry. She wanted to strike the child then, that poor helpless infant, for simply existing, for forcing her to question every ounce of her being and she drummed her hands against the hard wooden bench until she drew blood from the knuckles. That quiet hymn of tenderness, the *Ave Maris Stella* evaded her heart though she searched for it. Instead she saw the Mother Superior's eyes so wholly pious, so wholly righteous, so wholly correct, as she swept the little white bundle away. Bernadine had tried to imagine her face – Ernest's grave unmistakable eyes, his tall willowy grace, her own chestnut curls for she had been proud of them once... Clad in sunlight, clothed in stars, under her feet the moon... *How could she leave her daughter to the mercy of Monsieur Lafayette? How could she shed her past like a tired old skin?*

The ground trembled – as if God had given it a good shaking. He could unmake the world, quailed Bernadine, as easily as He had made it. Let there be darkness instead of light, night instead of day. Let there be sightless, clueless, creeping creatures, great and small, fat and thin. Let there be wingless, songless birds, mute streams and waterfalls, dry and bone-filled oceans. He could end it all with a blink of an eye if He chose to... *before she had a chance to find her daughter...* She wondered now if she would even have taken a train, had they been running. If she wouldn't have turned back at some point in her journey or continued on and on into blackness and out the other side again.

She called Aggie to her firmly, then shrilly, then angrily, before finally striding over, picking her up and forcing her into the papoose. Aggie protested, kicking and screaming, but all Bernadine heard or felt were the kicks, screams and protests of her own newborn as the Mother Superior whisked her away in a tiny white and bloodstained apron. Heedless of the guns, the shells, the trembling earth, she set her face for the heart of the city – a heart of light that was being engulfed and consumed by fires of darkness and madness. Aggie, still protesting, held her dirty glorious prize aloft, the rotten apple core squashed and mashed in her fat little hand; and Bernadine set her face hard and etched as a tablet of stone. She wasn't going to shed her past like a tired old skin for only snakes did that. *Only snakes did that.*

Chapter thirty-four

The young corporal, following close at his captain's polished heels, was surprised to find the iceman at home. He'd expected there to be more waiting around or at the very least more sticking his hand into dreadful little orifices and dismal crevices. But no, there he was sitting on the floor amidst a pile of books and papers, his head in his hands – if it really was the iceman. Could this be the fellow who'd caused such embarrassment to the Versailles government, who'd single-handedly started a revolution, who'd gone on such reckless and dangerous missions? He looked too quiet, too scholarly, the corporal delving deep, might almost have said too spiritual a man with his soft, gentle eyes and nervous half smile. No wonder he'd been so hard to track down. Everyone had been looking for the wrong sort of man! They'd been searching for a bolder fellow, a daredevil, not some chap who looked as if he couldn't even say boo to a goose. That was all part of the disguise, the corporal supposed. That was all part of the clever disguise. And, moreover, still waters ran very deep.

It was a typical bachelor's pad – sparsely furnished with one or two ornaments dusted rarely. Just the right amount of cleanliness for a masculine presence, the dishes washed and stacked (apart from a rather unpleasant-looking saucepan spattered with vermicelli); the pens on the writing desk neatly arranged – betokening an ordered and rational mind; and the inevitable clock on the mantel (unusual choice, a cuckoo clock, but a good make all the same) for very few men could manage without a timepiece. Women functioned fairly well following their own natural rhythms but very few men could cope without a timepiece on their person or in their apartment or both. That, the corporal knew to be a psychological fact.

The captain, having taken the situation in at a glance, was grilling the iceman as to the materials at his feet.

'Are these revolutionary papers you were hoping to destroy?' He nudged a few printed pages with the tip of a polished toe.

'These?' The iceman, who'd jumped up when the two men entered, stared at the captain in astonishment, the nervous half smile still hovering about his lips. 'These are…' he seemed to hesitate for a moment, 'just words. Only words.'

'Just words!' hissed the captain, waving his pistol about wildly in the air, a little too wildly for the corporal's liking. It was liable to go off unexpectedly being waved about like that. 'There is no such thing as just words. They are the most inflammable things in history, in existence. They enter the heart, the brain, the imagination, reminding us of our mortality and immortality, reminding us that we are simply the spaces between the lines and cursors of the universe. They can damage a man more easily than a bullet or a fire bomb. I could kill a man as easily with a word as with a bullet.'

'Once upon a time,' replied the iceman slowly, 'I would have agreed with you but not any more.' To the corporal's ears his voice was tinged with melancholy, longing, regret… bitterness perhaps. There were too many layers even for his psychological abilities to fathom. 'Now I think it is rather our actions that make us men, not our words. What do you want of me in any case? I will not give you any names if that is what you have come for.'

'Just one,' purred the captain, his spare, angular frame bent intimidatingly at the waist, 'your own. Are you or are you not Alphonse Duchamp?'

The corporal, standing in his usual position by the door, noted the surprise and hesitation once more. He could deny it of course, but there wasn't much point. In the end the evidence would be found. It was only a question of time before the evidence was found, and he was arrested and sent to jail. The only decent thing to do was to own up to his existence, stand tall in his identity, which he did, after a few more moments hesitation, proudly and firmly, revealing himself in the eyes of the corporal at least to be that sort of man after all.

'Yes I am,' he smiled, 'Alphonse Duchamp. What of it?'

Even the captain was taken aback by the look on the iceman's face. It was a look of serenity, even joy. The sort of look you saw on the face of a corpse who'd passed an easeful death; or the rapture of a religious fanatic in communion with their god; even the transport of a swooning virgin in the arms of her lover. It wasn't the face of a man who was about to be carted off to jail, possibly for years, possibly even condemned to death. Alphonse Duchamp was a chameleon indeed! A master of disguise! And the corporal took his metaphorical hat off to him.

'You are under arrest,' stated the captain loudly, a little unnerved and waving his pistol about so wildly that it went off unexpectedly, hitting the iceman as easily as a word would have done...

The corporal watched in astonishment as Alphonse Duchamp staggered then fell, raising his fist in a final Communard salute, his fine golden hair flying about his head like a halo.

Monsieur Lafayette, reaching the bottom of the steps, heard the shot ring out through the thin rickety building and stopped abruptly in his tracks. It sounded to all intents and purposes as if his rival had been literally and unceremoniously shot! It wasn't what he'd expected, wasn't even what he'd wanted. He'd wanted his rival put behind bars, not put to death; and for the first time in his life he felt the pinpricks of guilt and remorse, worse than stinging nettles. He wished he'd never told them he knew where Alphonse Duchamp lived, wished he'd never led them here, wished he'd never let his jealous streak get the best of him. If only he'd listened to the voice of instinct and descended straightaway upon the barricades like a god, like a Roman emperor, like Achilles... But maybe he wasn't too late after all. Maybe he wasn't too late to intercede.

All that was good in him suddenly rose to the surface and his eyes glimmered softly with the faintest of lights. He charged back up the stairs two at a time, carrying with him the crazy notion of bursting into the room to confront that stick insect of a captain and his ungainly little corporal for he wasn't afraid of either of them, not one iota, not one little bit. But at the top of the stairs he changed his mind and instead crept up to the very key-hole he'd had the dubious pleasure of peeping through one rainy winter's heart-soaked dawn. There was little to see, apart from a pair of crumpled legs, presumably those of his rival, and the broad, round-shouldered back of the corporal swaying back and forth and evincing little glimpses (a leg here, a hand there) of the captain scuttling about his business – wrapping up his corpse no doubt. He had been too late after all.

The stinging nettles of guilt and remorse swept up and down his spine. To die victorious at the barricades was one thing but to be cornered like a fox, magnificent brush or otherwise, in its own dirty hole was a supremely unheroic death. Monsieur Lafayette saw ahead of him then the second most ferocious emotional tussle of his existence. How to break the news to Eveline. Whether to admit his own part in the affair or plead ignorance of the whole sordid escapade. He was doomed either way in any case for she would never forgive him for condemning Alphonse Duchamp to an untimely and unheroic death; and yet on the other hand the thought of not telling her the truth was suddenly anathema to him. Much to his own astonishment the thought of concealing the truth from another person was suddenly anathema to him. Hadn't he given up guilt many years previously, fondly remarking to people that it was a bad habit, like biting one's nails; and now here she was, a dominatrix of a mistress (worse then stinging nettles) calling him to heel, ordering him to admit to his misdemeanours, whispering in his ear that he must tell Eveline the truth though it would cost him her love. That clear shining love, not the muddied polluted furtive little loves he'd known before but that clear, good and shining one. Must he tell her the truth? He owed it to Alphonse certainly, to Eveline probably, but did he owe it to himself? To sacrifice that clear shining love for the truth? How could he bring himself to do it? Was the truth as important as all that? He struggled in the grip of the second most ferocious emotional tussle of his existence; and the floorboards creaked madly under him, summoning the spider swiftly and silently out of its web.

'Did you forget something, Monsieur... Lafayette?' the captain asked silkily, poking his long neck out of the door which he held ever so slightly ajar. 'Or did you want to join the party?'

'You should not have shot him!' Monsieur Lafayette, taken aback, blustered foolishly. 'You should not have shot him. I gather your orders were to place him under arrest, take him in for questioning, not shoot him unarmed in his own home.' He saw now that the truth was of the utmost importance. He had no time to waste. He had a soul to save at the barricades. A soul in jeopardy and he owed her the truth at the very least.

'A little mishap with the pistol.' The captain gave an apologetic smile. 'It is liable to go off at the drop of a hat.' And he demonstrated how wildly he'd been waving the firearm when it had gone off so unexpectedly, much to the consternation of the corporal who begged him to stop lest the experience be repeated.

'Oh, why is that, *Herr Doktor*,' laughed the captain callously, describing ever more eccentric circles with the temperamental object. 'Do you fear for your own Fritz giblets, is that what it is? Do you fear for your own Fritz giblets?'

Monsieur Lafayette saw the look in the captain's eyes – as large and pale as his own were small and dark – and suddenly realising the

257

precariousness of his situation, he stepped back a pace, fumblingly reaching for the banister behind him. 'Old Lafayette can keep a secret,' he almost wheedled for old habits die hard, and a leopard rarely changes its spots. 'He can be a dumb but eloquent witness. As quiet as the streets of Pompeii, of Thebes, the pyramids after centuries and centuries of...' But he never finished his sentence for something hit his ear with the oddly soft pop of a consonant, the force of which sent him tumbling down the stairs, somersaulting and catapulting over and over, two, three, four at a time, like an india rubber ball, until he lay at the bottom on the floor, spreadeagled and staring up at the ceiling. His eyes wore the astonished look of a boy for whom the lights had gone out too soon. The lights had gone out too soon. *So soon, so soon… Before he had time to…* And with the last rays of consciousness it dawned on him that the truth was always of the utmost importance and the only soul that had ever been in jeopardy was his own.

The corporal, following close at his captain's polished heels, was thinking that one mishap with a pistol could be deemed to be a fluke but two just didn't add up! He was missing something. Some hole in the knit of the captain's psychology. He had known there was a small tear certainly but now he was beginning to fear there was a gaping hole big enough to shove a fist, a head through. If so he must proceed with all caution, that's what his psychological skills were telling him now. He must proceed with all caution until he had unravelled that knit right down to the very last enigmatic stitch.

The captain was all contriteness of course, full of apologies and explanations. *He was having a bad day today and no mistake. What a dreadful mishap to happen again – the confectioner hurtling through the air like that… His cruel stomach-ache coming in waves like riding a stormy, seasick sea, making him forgetful, making him negligent… Perhaps he'd never cleaned the pistol properly, after its previous usage, he didn't know, couldn't remember… That scurrilous bunch at Brébant's feeding him snape as high as a kite. He wouldn't set foot in there again, not for all the tea in China!*

'Just looking at it reminds me of my own finitude,' he said quietly, placing the pistol on the iceman's writing desk, out of harm's way, much to the corporal's relief. 'Or should I say rather my own infinitude, for that is what we all become a part of in the end – the infinitude. Look at him over there, seeping into that infinitude as we speak.'

The corporal looked – Alphonse Duchamp lay in a small pool of blood – and he was struck again by the profound sense of peace on the man's face. Dying was usually an unsavoury, guttural affair, not this quiet self-effacing act. He only hoped his own death when it came would be as calm and dignified as this strangely heroic one.

'I hope my own passing is as easy.' He tentatively put his thoughts into words and the captain stared back in surprise. 'I am sure it will be, *Herr Doktor*,' he smiled, almost forlornly.

There was something ignoble about searching the property of a dying man but despite some misgivings the corporal helped the captain continue his hunt for evidence. All they needed was a nametag or a signed document to prove that they had the right man. In the end the body would do but some documentation or revolutionary material would be helpful. They must have spent a quarter of an hour searching the premises, uncovering nothing but books belonging to and letters addressed to a certain Laurie Marçeau.

'Who is this Laurie Marçeau?' the captain shouted angrily, suddenly losing his temper and flinging a bundle of letters on the floor. 'Who is this wretched Laurie Marçeau?'

'A friend perhaps?' the corporal replied soothingly in an effort to calm the captain down. 'Or a pseudonym. He must have used a variety of names when you think about it to have evaded capture for so long. He was a master of disguise. There are probably hundreds of rooms like this and hundreds of identities.'

'I doubt it,' retorted the captain scornfully, marching over to the door where an old woollen dressing gown and winter scarf were hanging. There was something about his demeanour that worried the corporal – he must proceed with all caution – though even he felt a flicker of doubt. What if the iceman had covered his tracks so well that no evidence could be found at all? What if, in the end, nobody could identify the body? The iceman would have literally melted into the sunshine (as he always did) and nobody none the wiser. The search would have been in vain. There would be no reward money, no garden for his son to run around in, no new house for his pretty and unassuming wife, no box at the Odéon for the captain to throw peanuts from at the ordinary, the common or garden, the prosaic… That mishap with the pistol would have cost them dear indeed. No wonder the captain was angry, angry with himself no doubt. The way he was twisting that scarf in his hands – as if he were wringing someone's neck – told the corporal that; and it made him glad that the pistol was out of harm's way.

There was only one place left to look – the body. In a moment the captain would make him stick his fingers into pockets and crevices, handle the tepid flesh of the soon-to-be departed, feel the faintly fluttering pulse like a butterfly caught in the hand. He'd done it before as a medical man, of course, but now it seemed like a sacrilege, a violation, a profanity. He didn't think he could do it, not for all the tea in China as the captain put it, not even for the reward money; and he stared defiantly up at the captain.

'I will not search the body,' he stated firmly in a pre-emptive strike and the captain who was pensively fingering the metal studs that decorated the edge of the fine woollen scarf, smiled benignly back at him. 'Of course not, *Herr Doktor*. Why ever should you?'

The corporal tried valiantly to unravel the captain's enigmatic knit, more knotted and slippery, it seemed to him, than the head of a hydra. Was he, a lowly corporal, too squeamish a fellow to ever have made it in the medical profession? Is that what the captain implied? Is that what he hinted at? The way he'd said *Herr Doktor* was deeply unpleasant. There was an army of meaning behind the way he'd said it. It would have been italicised in the pages of a book the way he'd said it. The corporal was crushed by the weight of the words *Herr Doktor* and the army of meaning behind them.

There was only one thing for it. He would have to prove him wrong. He would have to grit his teeth and prove the captain wrong. Stepping over to the iceman, he knelt down beside him and only when he stared into the soft gentle face did he realise he'd fallen for the bait, fallen headlong into the trap. His own pride had tipped him into it. His own vanity and pride.

'I'll need fifty-five per cent of the reward money for it,' he called over his shoulder in a determined voice lest the captain think he'd completely outwitted him. 'Or you can search the body yourself. Or,' he threw caution to the winds, 'fabricate some evidence.'

'What a good idea,' came the captain's mild reply. 'We can always try that if you are… unsuccessful.'

Rolling up his sleeves and gritting his teeth, the corporal set to work. If he really were a doctor it wouldn't be a sacrilege, he told himself, wouldn't be a violation or a profanity. It would be like conducting a simple post-mortem for it was far too late to save the patient. With due reverence and, making the sign of the cross in the air, he lifted the iceman's rapidly cooling wrist, feeling the small raggedy pulse like a butterfly caught between finger and thumb. He didn't hear the captain creeping softly up behind him, didn't hear a footstep or feel a thing until the noose was about his neck. And there he was suddenly staring into the hole in the knit of the captain's psychology – a void big enough to stick infinitude into, let alone a fist or a head. He didn't need to see the look in the cold pale eyes to know what the captain was thinking. He didn't need the corporal, had never needed the corporal, psychological skills or otherwise. He could fabricate the evidence, take the reward money for himself. The clues had been there all along, in the cruel curling mouth, unpredictable rages, lack of remorse, the veneer of sophistication for that was all it was, a veneer – underneath a brute, an ordinary brute to throw peanuts at… The clues had been there right under his nose but his psychological skills had failed him in the end. He had unravelled the knit a little too late and the noose was about his neck, its metal studs pressing into his poor aching throat. Never again would his wife bring him hot soup and cheese toast for his aching throat. He hoped she would be happy, hoped his son would thrive in the small backyard. He wondered what it was like to asphyxiate – running very fast perhaps and not being able to catch one's breath. He almost wished he'd never embarked on his medical training – he knew too much and yet not enough. Did life end with the brain or the breath, the lungs or the heart?

'Make it quick,' he pleaded with the last of his voice, still holding onto the iceman's rapidly cooling wrist; and the captain ever so softly obliged.

Chapter thirty-five

The Versailles army was making good progress, taking one barricade after another on the squares, boulevards, railway lines and bridges – just as Laurie had predicted. Sometimes they met with little resistance, the defendants firing a few shots then fleeing, dumping their guns and uniforms until the street resembled an arms depot. Other times the resistance was fierce, bloody, terrifying, confirming every Versailles soldier's worst fear that Parisians really were made up of half tiger, half monkey. In the red districts, particularly, defence was known to be savage and it was here the Versaillais sent their sharp shooters ahead to foil traps, winkle out rogue and maverick targets and provide a decoy if necessary. A sharp shooter by definition was a man whose eye was ninety per cent accurate one hundred per cent of the time or vice versa.

André Provost was just such a man. Having spent the last few months in a prisoner of war camp, he was itching to get his feet wet again; and he moved with a suppressed energy up the street. The prelude of shots had been fired – beating the bush it was called, to make the birds fly – and now he, André Provost, was ready. His wing man, Lapin, was keeping parallel, almost dancing up the other side of the Rue Ramponneau, so pleased was he to be back in the action at last. They'd met in the prisoner of war camp, become firm friends, swapping bootleg Belgian cigars, cadging dumb-bells and newspapers off the Prussian bear of a guard they'd nicknamed Hortense; and hotly debating what was going on in France, especially Paris, in their absence. That was how it had felt – everything going on in their absence. But now they were back on the scene again, ready to can-can. The only difference between them was that Lapin was keen to earn some stripes, if not the *légion d'honneur*, whereas he was happy simply to do his duty by God and by his country.

It was how he had been brought up – to do his duty by God and by his country. In the village he came from you grew up, found work (in the fields, the church or the army), married your childhood sweetheart, had a tribe of children, did your neighbour a good turn when you could, put aside for a rainy day... you were rooted, you belonged. You knew where you came from and where you were going – the baptismal font at St Alders and the line of Provosts under the shady chestnut trees in the churchyard had forever told him that. It wasn't a bad life if you didn't think too much about it. But in Paris it was different. Nobody knew each other, nobody spoke to their neighbour let alone did them a good turn. People worked all hours in factories then drunk their wages or debauched them! Women whored themselves mercilessly, until they were half dead from it. There was no religion, only opinions. *Morally gangrenous*, the papers had said. *Paris is the moral gangrene of France and needs to be cut off!* Even their accents offended him – clipped and emphatic sounding as if they were too busy, in a hurry and you didn't matter.

That was the worst of it. They acted as if the rest of France didn't matter. They acted as if they had sole rights to the city. They could dismantle it, exploit it, set it alight if they felt like it! Set history and tradition alight with a box of matches and bugger the rest of France! Bugger the anguish and glories of France. He wondered if all capitals were the same. Did Londoners ignore the rest of the country, poke fun and make jokes about the Irishmen, the Welshmen, rip up the lions in Trafalgar Square just for the hell of it?

Lapin was mucking about on the other side of the street, mouthing Hortense at him and he gave him the thumbs down to shut him up. After the first volley of shots it was hard to see and they needed to keep their wits about them. All it needed was a maverick target and a well-aimed firebomb and they would be set back by several lines of men, possibly a cannon, not to mention a limb of his own! The barricade was relatively formidable looking and he'd ducked a couple of singing balls already.

'Shut up!' he called across with a smile, 'and let the birds fly, you arse-hole!'

Even now he didn't really understand the revolution, didn't understand why the people of Paris had revolted. It seemed to him they had revolted simply because they'd been able to, like a pack of dogs who'd got out and, not knowing what to do with their freedom, had turned on each other, biting and snarling. Freedom rather than liberating them had sent them mad. One member of the revolutionary party, the papers related, had had himself photographed blowing his brains out, or at least pretending to! What sort of an idiot did that? If that was the kind of man running the show it explained a lot, in Provost's opinion. In fact it explained everything – the fires, the murders of two generals, the destruction of a famous war memorial... It was the fires incensed him most, he decided, gazing at the glowing horizon. How many times had he promised his brothers and sisters a trip to the city to see the sights and now it was all a roaring furnace, just dust and ashes.

He scanned the tops of the buildings, his body tense. The chimney stacks were the worst and the mattresses stuffed in the windows. He hated being fired down upon – the enemy had the advantage of the sun behind them whereas you were half blinded, squinting up into it. Sometimes their weapons flashed, giving them away, or bits of moss fell from the tiles but more often than not you had to wait patiently until they panicked and flew. Provost flattened himself as best he could against the sides of the buildings that lined the Rue Ramponneau, just as he'd done as a boy playing hide and seek in fields of corn. The sweat dripped down his neck – for even the sun was hostile here – but he dare not bring out a handkerchief yet.

'HORTENSE!' yelled Lapin and this time he wasn't mucking around – he'd spotted a flying bird and was warning his friend accordingly. Provost threw himself to the ground, keeping his rifle at shoulder height by rolling over onto his elbows, just as he'd been trained, his eyes peeled for the maverick target. He could see nothing for a moment and then there it was, a figure weaving in and out of the smoke. A civilian by the look of it, possibly a woman. She was holding something in her arms, clasping it tightly to her chest. With the flames and the smoke behind her she could have been a soul spewed from the mouth of hell. One or two warning shots came from the barricade, a few desperate shouts but the woman came on regardless. Lapin was hopping up and down on the other side of the street, practically doing the can-can, so eager was he to bring the target down; but Provost stayed him awhile with a wave of the hand. They had to ascertain her status first. You didn't get the *légion d'honneur* by bringing down a woman unless she was armed and dangerous.

This one was certainly crazy – running back and forth, spinning in circles, disorientated presumably by the smoke and the noise. Provost, keeping her in his sights, was glad of the dumb-bells he'd cadged off the Prussian guard – he could hold the position for as long as it took her to make her mind up. He hoped she'd go back, for her own sake and everybody else's. He feared she was a *pétroleuse* – one of the women they'd been warned about. Tales of the *pétroleuses* had made his hair stand on end! Half man, half monster, they had an array of tricks up their sleeves apparently from boiling kettles and deadly knitting needles to firebombs and acid tea flasks. One of their commoner ploys was to beguile the enemy by flashing their wares at him, thereby creating havoc on the battlefield. Many of them were willing to martyr themselves for the cause.

She suddenly seemed to get her bearings and Provost watched in dismay as the woman looked about her then came on with, if anything, increased urgency, still holding onto the bundle as if her life depended on it. As she came closer he could see her face quite clearly – deadly pale, her eyes huge and dark ringed from nights of debauchery, he supposed. With her tight helmet of short red curls she could have been an engraving of Joan of Arc, without the nobility of course. She was ludicrously got up in a tight bodice and short skirt (mutton dressed as lamb his mother would have called her for she must have been thirty at least); and his guts suddenly churned with anger and disgust. This was no Joan of Arc! This was the moral gangrene of Paris incarnate! The moral gangrene of Paris in the flesh! Green to the very soul she was bearing down upon him with her odd, steely determined gait and nothing-to-lose eyes, ready to spill her wares all over the place. Well, he wasn't buying today and nor was Lapin. His wing man was poised but still hopping, ready to clip her wings at any moment and he gave him the nod. There was no time to analyse, no time to think. The definition of sharp shooting was to think long enough to be able to react... hopefully the right way. Better to be too early with the wrong decision than too late with the right one. If they didn't take care of her now they could lose a few good men who, thinking the coast was clear, were bringing up the rear to pulverise the barricade. Not to mention a limb of his own. He took one last look in the deadly pale face, the dark and debauched eyes, black with determination and nothing to lose. She was on a suicide mission for sure. He touched the religious amulet on his arm and, praying he was doing his duty by God and by his country, fired immediately, at the same time Lapin did, both of the men careful to avoid the bottle of nitroglycerine in her arms, both of their firing eyes ninety per cent accurate one hundred per cent of the time; and the woman fell, still clutching onto the firebomb as if her life depended on it.

Chapter thirty-six

Laurie felt his mind slipping away bit by bit and he was almost glad to be rid of it. He lay in a small pool of blood, writing a letter to his mother in his head. He couldn't remember the beginning or the middle, only the ending, but it didn't seem to matter. Once he knew the ending he would know how to begin. It was the same with his poems – the endings were always a new beginning for him.

In his imagination he sat at his desk, a zephyr breeze billowing through the porthole window – zephyr simply because he liked the word, reminiscent it seemed to him, of warm, exotic, welcoming places. With the gentlest of sighs he dipped his pen in the ink, cast the first stroke against the clean white page, swooping and gliding like a bird trying the air, trying its wings for the very first time. Everything was in its rightful place, he realised with a profound sense of peace. Everything was as it should be: the cuckoo clock popping out its yellow beak to chime the hour; the books (books about love, courage, duty, friendship – everything a human life was made up of) very properly stacked upon the shelf; the cobweb in the corner, billowing a little in the zephyr breeze and as big as the sail of a ship but he liked that somehow, ships being reminiscent it seemed to him, of journeys ending, journeys begun; and the gilt-edged mirror reflecting nothing (his real self having been and gone already) but its own frame shining out like a galaxy of stars. Stars to guide him home by.

He wrote decisively and very, very proudly for the very last time yet strangely too the very first:

Your son, Laurie.

Swooping and gliding across the clean white page like a bird claiming the air, proclaiming its wings.

Chapter thirty-seven

Eveline saw the woman fall and her heart flew into her mouth. Alphonse had fired a warning shot but she had carried on regardless, careering blindly into the line of fire. She lay now in the dirt and the rubble of the road, still holding on to her precious bundle. They waited for the explosion but none came and after a moment Alphonse bade them reload.

'I thought she was a *pétroleuse*,' he commented, voicing everyone's thoughts; and Eveline's eyes smarted with tears and the earth that had blown up from the top of the barricade. It was all she could do to hold her rifle, take aim, fire, reload; and her breath came in great tearing pants as if she'd run a hundred miles or so. She felt embarrassed by her lack of strength, her trembling arms and hands all fingers and thumbs. This was nothing like the Rue de Turbigo! The woman who'd lost her sons to Prussia was crouching calm and dignified by the lazy Susan, her red face stern and unyielding, her calf muscles tougher than Eveline's; and the man who'd prayed incessantly while they waited was shouting now, mocking and derisive.

'Have pity on their tears oh lord!' he cried as his gun jerked into action. 'Refuse not to admit them to the mystery of the reconciliation!'

The air was thick with smoke and Eveline was glad she couldn't see the men with the tricolour flag, the faces of the men she was firing into. They looked like the wooden soldiers her father had made for Jacques, all of them with their hats pulled over their eyes as if they couldn't bear to look, all of them black moustached and gold buttoned. Jacques had thrown conkers at them and they had fallen with a plonk on the living-room floor, rolling a little to the right or the left. These ones, however, moved and fired back, had a terrible knack of gaining ground, creeping forward inch by inch. It wouldn't be long, Eveline thought, before she saw their faces clear as day, knew them as intimately as her own. She ducked down, gripped the rifle between her knees, bent the barrel back with both hands and fumbled in her cartridge belt. Her knees were already sore from gripping the rifle, her hands gashed and bloodied from loading the barrel. Alphonse had helped her once or twice but she dreaded being a burden. Not now. Not at the end like this. She glanced up at him, standing on his makeshift platform of empty wine crates, ignoring the loopholes and gaps in the barricade; and her heart pounded with fear and love for him.

The first time she heard the cry she dismissed it simply as the whine of a bullet, maybe a man in distress. The second time she wasn't so sure and listened intently. There it was again, like the cry of a baby (she knew enough about babies' cries, having looked after Jacques for so long when her mother died) and it was coming from somewhere in front of the barricade. She understood then immediately what had happened – the woman had been carrying a baby, not a firebomb. There was a baby out there, alone and terrified. Had nobody else heard it? Dropping her gun she scrambled over sandbags and crates to peer through a gap in the barricade; but to her dismay she could see nothing through the heavy wall of smoke. Alphonse, crouching down to reload, asked her what she was playing at, throwing her gun away like that but she shushed him by putting a finger to her lips. The wail came again, indignant, imperious, enraged; and she smiled through her tears, thinking of Jacques, though this, she felt quite sure, was a little baby girl. The cry was so imperious it had to be a girl!

She nodded at Alphonse's astonished expression. A baby! Yes! In the middle of a battlefield. Unbelievable but true. It wasn't a firebomb after all.

His eyes registered dim comprehension then fear and he deftly reloaded her gun as well as his own before shoving it back into her hands. He didn't say anything, didn't try to dissuade her, as she had half expected. Not that it would have made any difference if he had. She had made up her mind in any case – whatever he said, whatever he did. You didn't leave a baby alone in a battlefield for heaven's sake! But she needn't have worried. He understood entirely, understood her need to prove herself, understood about Jacques, about Laurie, understood about everything. Without words. His eyes were bluer than ever as he stared at her, as blue as the sky still was presumably above the smoke, so blue she could float across them in a balloon. She felt as if she'd stared at those eyes for an eternity though it couldn't have been more than a minute. A lifetime of possibilities crammed into a minute. Then his face broke into that wide, impetuous grin.

'You look like a little mouse,' he teased, 'but you have the heart of a lion, Miss Eveline.'

'Laurie would be pleased,' she half groaned, struggling with the strap of her gun. Laurie. That was another thing to make up for. She prayed he was safe, well, out of harm's way.

Alphonse helped her adjust the strap then covered her hands in his own. 'He's very brave too,' he said and she wondered if it was guilt that made his voice break the way it did, that made his rough, workmanlike fingers tremble against hers. 'He can admit to being afraid which takes more courage than anything else.' He suddenly delved in his pocket, brought something out and placed it in the palm of her hand, though she knew what it was even before she saw the flash of red, felt the smooth, shiny surface. It was her mother's ruby brooch, the one she'd given him for Buzenval, suddenly, on impulse, thinking later that she really should have given it to Laurie. It was warm and strangely comforting in her hand. How many times had she hidden it in the toe of her shoe lest her father find it and pawn it for drink? She'd given it to Alphonse to keep him safe. Now it was her turn. Her turn to keep safe. His fingers still trembled as he hitched the rifle over her shoulders, placed the strap carefully, gently against her neck, as gentle as a caress.

'Don't forget...' his voice faltered. 'Don't forget to keep low, stay low, and when you've got her...'

He knew too. Knew it was a little girl, like the one they might still have when it was over, afterwards when the war was over, when everything had ended they could all begin again. She, Alphonse, Laurie.

'Whatever you do don't look back. When you've got her head for home and don't look back. Remember, Evie, don't look back.'

She nodded, slipping the brooch into her pocket and scrambling over the sandbags. There was no time to waste, no time for goodbyes. The old man was on his haunches, about to reload, and the woman who'd lost her sons to Prussia, still calm and dignified, was firing with a deadly aim. There were bodies, too, already, which Eveline realised with horror she would have to crawl over to reach the end of the barricade. She shuddered, suddenly nauseous, and stared white faced up at Alphonse.

'Do your best,' he said quietly, his eyes like a hand held out to her and Eveline thought, *I shall never say goodbye to him. Whatever happens I shall never say goodbye to him.* Then he shooed her away, flapping his arms at her as if she were a small bird; and she turned, dropping to her hands and knees, and began her journey into the line of fire.

The old man was scraping about in the dirt, looking for ammunition.

'I ain't never seen an angel,' he groaned in distress. 'What d'you think they look like?'

'What?' Alphonse's eyes were unblinking as he watched Eveline's progress.

'An angel? What d'you think they look like?'

She was nearly halfway there. After a slight hesitation she had negotiated the first body, a boy not much older than Jacques with a hole in his face where an eye should have been. Alphonse let out a faint exhalation of breath and his eyes were very proud as he turned towards the old man. 'As ugly as you!' he retorted, throwing him half of his own ammunition. Then he sprang into action, dragging another crate on top of his makeshift platform and grabbing the red flag somebody had stuck in an upturned flower pot in the middle of the barricade. His eyes still followed Eveline's progress. There she was at the edge at last, about to make the turn. He slowly climbed onto the platform, holding the flag with both hands. The whole of his torso was now exposed to enemy fire. He stood for a moment, his eyes still on Eveline whose small form was just visible in front of the barricade like a shadow separating itself out from its owner. Alphonse's beautiful sculpted lips parted a little as he formed the word goodbye, then he wrenched his eyes away to face the Versaillais. He began waving the red flag wildly from side to side, his body swaying precariously with the movement.

'*JE SUIS LÀ!*' he shouted at the top of his voice. '*C'EST MOI!*'

Bernadine was hovering somewhere between life and death. She was back in her dear little garden on the warm sweet-woodruff bench with Agnes, plump and glistening, the Mother Superior fretting in her room over novels, fancy notelets, bottles of anisette... quite the theologian, he had said, her own small item of confiscated property and she had blushed, oh she had blushed deep – and time having hibernated for so long started ticking again with the snowdrops and primroses, the ancient-bellied singing toads who each struck a different note at sunset, the stained-glass panes of crocus and marigold. Only here could she praise him! The night they had lain in incense of lavender, the ha-ha overgrown with brambles, the brambles all mixed up with stars, the night the very flowers had held their breath, the moon played peek a boo with the dark and the dark closed its eyes and counted to five...

Squeezing her eyes shut tight, Eveline felt her way through the smoke. She was aware that Alphonse was risking his life for her – doing something stupid, noble, heroic – and the thought both horrified her and urged her on at the same time. She tried to blot out everything else but the thought that he was risking his life for her. Tried to blot out the noise of the guns, her feelings of terror, the stones that dug into her palms and knees, the smoke that singed at her eyeballs. She screwed them up even harder, the better, strangely, to hear (it was an advantage certainly. If you wanted to look on the bright side then that was it) and trained her mind on the wail that came intermittently through the smoke, no longer imperious sounding but terrified and alone. She wondered if the baby was injured, stuck, trapped beneath the woman's weight. The cry came again, a little to her left and she launched herself in the direction of the sound, ignoring the pain that shot through her knee. The earth seemed to tremble beneath her as if the armies were about to stampede. She was sobbing freely now, sobbing suddenly for her mother, her father, for Jacques, for her own role as little mother, for the lives that were being snuffed out as easily as candles; and the hot tears coursing down her cheeks stung almost as much as the smoke.

'Please let me be in time,' she begged, lurching forward on her side, her face scraping along the road. It was almost a relief to feel her face scraping along the road. A boot came off and she abandoned it, tore the other one off to join it. The wail came again, gouging at her heart, and she didn't even know how she felt (having always thought she resented the role) until the cry burst out of her: 'Please give me another chance to be a mother!'

'Are you the nun from St Joseph's?' someone had said and she had blushed, oh she had blushed deep red she had blushed so much for it was true. She was. She had been. Someone had penetrated her disguise!

'You're fine, the baby's fine,' someone had said and whisked her away in a bloodstained apron, out of sight, out of mind. Except she wasn't. Ever. She was alive still, now, somewhere in the city. And Monsieur Lafayette...

Bernadine frantically opened her eyes and the stonecutter's daughter stared down at her with Ernest's grave, unmistakable smile.

'The baby's trapped a little, if we could just move your arm.' The stonecutter's daughter bent over her with Ernest's tall willowy grace. Could it be he after all these years? Could it be she? His beautiful hands undoing the strap. She remembered those hands, the night they had lain in incense of lavender, the night the very stars had held their breath... Could this be paradise? Could this be death? Her own red curls brushing against her cheek as the stonecutter's daughter lifted the papoose. Curls she had been proud of once before the Sister barber got her hands on them. *All for Jesus!* They had shrieked hysterically, the lot of them – the redheads, blondes, brunettes. Free from the weight of hair, the soul a little more exposed to the air. Had she been so near for all these years? The stonecutter's daughter on her very doorstep?

'I've got her now, she's perfectly safe. You don't have to worry any more.' Was this the shining illumination she had saved herself up for. This moment. Right now. As she looked upon her daughter's face. Desolate, yes, and sweet. A place to confess, to dream, to repent. There were so many things she wanted to say: were you happy as a child, did you wear the colour pink? Do you sew and cook, pass the time with walks and books? There was so little time to choose the right words. If they could make a difference.

'Wear your very best dress,' she gasped at last, reaching out her own hands to the beautiful hands and face, her eyes suddenly fierce and alive like a light that glows brighter just before it dies, 'every day of the week. Promise me that. Tell Aggie...' But she had nothing left. Her father was peering at her over his ormolu clock as if to say where has the time gone, and her own clock set at just before midnight. There was barely enough time to escape her own life...

In the still, quiet heart of battle, Eveline laid the nun's head ever so gently down, scraping a soft surface on the rough and broken road, releasing her hand at the very last moment. She left the eyes wide open, gazing in wonderment at the world out of a strange, instinctive feeling that the nun still needed them to find her way home. She was not unlike her mother, pale and peaceful in the morgue, the life all gone out of her. She had recognised the nun immediately with that sad, beautiful, neglected face of hers – the face of a madonna – and wondered at her story. How a nun had ended up with a baby, the world all topsy-turvy. Had she been running for safety, running into the unknown? Not that it mattered any more.

The baby was sleeping now, exhausted by the ordeal, her black curls wet with sweat against her forehead, thumb stuck into the wide red mouth. Eveline stood carefully, clasping her to her chest. Should she run and risk her own life or crawl and risk Alphonse's even more than she had done already? It wasn't a difficult choice. She ran. She ran barefoot over the rough and broken road. She ran and she never felt any pain for Bernadine was running beside her, Bernadine was running too. *She would be late for Lauds if she didn't get a move on! Her Sisters were there already, lifting their hearts up altogether for the Deo Gratias. She slipped in beside them and her heart flew to join them. Their voices rose as one, raising the roof, thanking the*

Lord, and the guns baritoned in the distance an Almighty welcome. Eveline ran as if she had wings, as if wings carried her.

At a safe distance from the barricade she turned and looked back despite what Alphonse had said. She almost wished she hadn't. She could see his figure, small and vulnerable beside the woman who'd lost her sons to Prussia and the old man – they looked like a little family defending their home. She willed him to turn one last time in recognition, love, even farewell. The merest hint of a sign would do. Her mind said his name over and over and it seemed so loud in her own head that she thought he must be able to hear it, must be able to feel it. She stood straining her eyes, clasping Aggie to her chest and the wind buffeted at her face and body. It was almost a relief to feel the wind buffeting at her body, blowing dirt and dust in her face. She thought suddenly that he turned and smiled that crazy, intoxicating, impetuous smile of his but she couldn't be sure. It was perhaps a trick of the light, his smile after all a flash of light. In the end she turned away – it took all her strength and courage to force herself away – and left him there to fight alone which he did, long after the woman had been reunited with her sons and the old man beheld the face of an angel and from the look on his own found it beautiful. He fought on, the last revolutionary on the Rue Ramponneau until his ammunition had gone. Then he turned with an almost contemptuous slowness, threw down his gun and walked away. Nobody fired though Lapin was practically doing the can-can so eager was he to bring him down. Provost stayed his hand. You didn't get the *légion d'honneur* shooting a man in the back, even a revolutionary.

'And besides,' he muttered under his breath, touching the religious amulet on his forearm, 'anyone so unafraid of death deserves to live!'

Alphonse walked into the heart of the city. Nobody saw his face. Nobody knew if his bright blue eyes were brighter than ever with grief, sorrow, despair, even joy. Nobody saw his expression at all as he passed like a ghost through the heart of the city, like a god traversing the desert of his kingdom. Heavy rain began to fall with the twilight, casting a misty glow over the carved suns of the Tuileries that had burnt red hot, cooling the smouldering ruins of the Hôtel de Ville, of a city that had fought and been defeated, loved and lost. There was nothing to hear but the sound of fire meeting water with the crackle and hiss of a serpent's kiss – the flames being put out once and for all.

Alphonse walked on. The rain kept falling.

Epilogue

It was a bright clear day after some showers. New dewdrops sparkled in old cobwebs, the Seine gleamed under the bridges and the boulevards were busy and bustling again as Laurie would have wished. A small crowd had gathered beside the Préfecture de Police to gawk at the Venus de Milo as she came out of hiding. Having lain dormant, as it were, in storage for the past twelve months in an ignominious little cell used for the temporary holding of petty criminals, drunkards and rabble rousers (many of whom having unwittingly sat upon her in their darkest hour, caroused, sobered up and mended their ways upon her) she was about to face the light of day once more. She had survived so much! The wrath of the Prussians, her own cell mates, the devastating flames of the Commune. She'd come out of it all intact along with the ex Chief of Police's beloved glass paperweight and a cigarette tin belonging to a previous occupant of the ignominious little cell. A burst water pipe had saved them all. A small miracle in the middle of the night, in the middle of the flames. A jammed stopcock, a burst water pipe.

Four burly men carried her out in her coffin-like box, staggering under the weight of her – which led someone to remark dolefully that all great beauties were made of stone – and a thrill of excitement tore through the crowd.

There were oohs and aahs as the lid came off. Everyone craned their necks to peer at the statue, half naked and smiling that vague and tender smile, her lips slightly parted as if to breathe in new life, as if to breathe in the first breath of summer.

'Green!' a voice burst out from the midst of the crowd. 'Green she was and bloated when they fished her out. But they say the water saved her!' Mistigris, resplendent in a cornflower-blue jacket, his whiskers trimmed and a stonecutter's belt about his waist, was gesticulating wildly. 'In the dead of night the water saved her! A pipe sprayed all over her!'

A great cheer went up at this and Madame Larousse, blushing a little, slipped her hand into his. 'Now, now,' she warned him under her breath. 'Now, now.'

'She is risen like the phoenix from the ashes,' he went on in an awestruck voice, and his eyes shone with tears. 'She is dead and is reborn. As we all are,' he wept. 'As we all are!'

They filed past in pairs and alone, chattering excitedly or silent, reverential, getting their fill of the miracle, the phoenix, the *Venus de Milo*. There wasn't a scratch upon her. She glimmered up softly from the bottom of the box, symbol of new hope, new beginnings, like a rare and precious pearl found glowing in the mud. Everyone wanted a piece of her! Someone threw a marigold for luck, another a gold coin, one elderly gentleman even made a dive for her, cocking his leg to get in the box (much to Madame Larousse's disgust) and things might have got quite out of hand if one of the burly men hadn't quickly stepped forward. *There was to be no touching, no throwing, no kissing, only looking.*

'Always the way,' the jester crowed with a woebegone expression, 'with the great beauties. More's the pity!'

In the end they went away, back to work, to play, drifting off over the bridges into the streets and the boulevards, evaporating like droplets of rain in the sunshine. There was so much to see, to taste, to smell. Ma Gorot's liver and onion stall whiffing out the Rue des Pommes as it always had; cafés offering sodas and sorbets half price, eager to get their custom back; old boutiques dusting off their shutters and parading a new line of clothing as bright as canaries. There were jugglers, mountebanks, conjurors and acrobats. And the artists! The artists were everywhere, sticking up their easels impromptu style in any old place on the parapets, dabbling in a strange new palette of ruin and renewal and taking inspiration from the sudden haphazard impression of things, from the beauty of the ordinary, the mundane, the unique.

'Paris Herself Again!' sang the newspaper sellers from the top of the Pont des Arts to the top of Montmartre. 'Paris Herself Again!'

And the crowds bustled and dawdled through the streets where already one or two dainty flowers and vigorous plants were thrusting their way up through the fire-cracked tarmac.

Dearest Sis,

Please let it be known at the balloon factory that all letters were delivered safely as well as top-secret guvvermental desk patches despite reservacions on account of my age and inexperience. It was a perilus flight. The Professor let out too much gas all at once and passed out, so I had to fly the balloon single handed for miles and miles over seas and continenz. They look very small from the sky, like stamps. We are in Gnaw Way now, studying the Gnaw-them lights and collecting air at different elevacions to test for density. It is a cold and beautiful country. I am to enrol at the Academy pon my return under the Professor to learn about milky ways and comics. Tell Papa that a great bear is waiting to pop out at him if he stares up on a clear night.

Your brother Jacques.

PS: Neptune is bringing this message so you will have to read it under magic lanten. Also, please tell Monsieur Pagini that we let the other birds go last month so they should be coming home any day now.

PPS: Fifi has six kittens. She is an extra-ordinary harlot.

Annotations

1   Louis Napoleon III was elected President of the Second Republic in 1849. In 1852, after a bloody coup d'état, he transformed the fragile democracy into an Empire.

2   A prostitute.

3   The balloon in which the Minister of the Interior, Léon Gambetta, flew to Tours on 7th October to rally the provinces to the aid of the capital.

4   A human alarm clock. Person employed to wake up factory/market employees in the early hours.

5   General Trochu (President of the Government of National Defence) never came good with his 'plan'. Publicly he supported the attempt by Paris to withstand the Prussian siege but privately he despaired of it, calling it 'an heroic folly'. If he had any plan at all, it was known to his colleagues to be the capitulation of Paris.

6   Prototype of the machine gun – 25 barrels turned by a handle with a range of 2000 yards and a capacity to fire 150 rounds a minute.

7   Famous detective responsible for the conviction of Jean Baptiste Troppmann. Troppmann was guillotined in January 1870 for the murder of an entire family in 1869 at la Villette.

8   The correct quotation by Racine is: *malheureux l'homme qui fonde / Sur les hommes son appui.* (Unhappy is the *man* who puts his faith in men.)

9   Bourbaki commanded the Army of the North and the Second Army of the Loire, with which he operated in the East against the German communications. He was finally forced to lead his men into neutral Switzerland rather than surrender; and later attempted suicide.

10 See note 7. Troppmann came to symbolise the working man in his most negative expression. Prosecution painted a picture of a proletarian inveigling his way into a good bourgeois family and killing the lot of them for money. Some people saw the case as a portent of revolution.

11 The Prussian press and official propagandists made much of withholding bombardment until the correct 'psychological moment'. The phrase became a great joke and catchphrase of the siege.

12 The battle of Buzenval. First and only time the National Guard was used. A disastrous defeat.

13 Famous Parisian racetrack.

14 Fashionable ankle boots.

15 Breech loading rifle with sword/bayonet attachment. Accurate over a range of about 600 yards.

16 Notorious haunt of prostitutes.

17 Foreign Minister for Government of National Defence. Secretly negotiated an armistice with Bismarck before Paris was forced into unconditional surrender, despite boasting in September that France would never cede 'an inch of (her) territory, a stone of (her) fortresses'.

18 Chief Executive of newly constituted (largely conservative) assembly. Known for his hard line on urban disruption and his lack of sentimentality. Spent siege in relative comfort of Tours and lacked the imagination to appreciate the effect those months of privation might have had on the capital.

19 One of many nicknames for the diminutive Thiers.

20 On March 18th General Lecomte and General Clément Thomas were killed on the Rue des Rosiers by National Guards, army deserters and local civilians. The attempt to seize the guns in Montmartre having failed, the government retreated to Versailles, and the Paris National Guard set up a provisional authority at the Hôtel de Ville. This was the beginning of the revolutionary Commune.

21 The Commune's anti-clericalist stance (it proposed the separation of church and state, especially in education) led to many convents and churches being taken over as National Guard headquarters and looted for secret treasures.

22 *J'aimerai toujours le temps des cerises / Et le souvenir que je garde en coeur –* 'I will always love cherry blossom time and the memory that I hold in my heart.' Le Temps des Cerises was a popular song of the Commune.

23 The Commune ordered the destruction of the Vendôme column – a war memorial commemorating the expansionist campaigns of the first Napoleon – and it was eventually brought down on May 16th.

24 On May 21st the troops of Versailles entered Paris.

25 It is not certain how many *pétroleuses* (female arsonists) actually existed. They set fire to buildings that were targeted as being BPB (*Bon Pour Brûler* – good for burning); and they carried milk cans containing kerosene or nitro glycerine which they dropped down chimneys, letter boxes, cellar grates etc.

Author note

Zillah Bethell was born in Papua New Guinea. She graduated in English from Oxford University. Her first novel, *Seahorses are real*, was published by Seren in 2009. Her short stories have been published in magazines including *NewWelsh Review*. She lives in South Wales.

Also by Zillah Bethell

Seahorses are real

"Savage and tender, *Seahorses are real* is a rich, unflinching fantasy of love and abuse." – Kate Bingham

Marly's had enough of the cramped little rundown flat and wounded grey street where she lives with her fiancé, David. If they could just move away, escape to a rose-covered cottage by the sea, she's sure she would get better and everything would be alright...

Seahorses are real is a powerful debut novel of love and damage. Zillah Bethell tells the haunting tale of a relationship warped by depression, at once tender and destructive, where violence is not only perpetrated by men and love is not necessarily enough.

Available from bookshops or www.serenbooks.com